TANK

BLACK & BLUE SERIES

BY

ERIN BEVAN

COPYRIGHT

TANK

ALSO BY ERIN BEVAN

Novels
Wedding Day
Wrapped Up In You
Cupid's Angels
Love Comes In The Mourning
STEELE
(Black and Blue Series Book 2)

Novellas and Short Stories
The Party Crasher
Text Me
The Ranch Hand

DEDICATION

*To all service men and women, and to anyone who has ever
been a victim of abuse—may you find your own happy
ending.*

CHAPTER ONE

Tyler Wilde straddled the rumbling metal between his legs and stared at the envelope in his hand. The paper weighed about as much as a feather, but the weight of the words sat on his chest like a block of iron, suffocating and hard to ignore. The Wade Correctional Facility logo stared at him from the upper left corner. He shoved the letter back in his mailbox and slammed the door closed.

How did the man get his address?

He wouldn't deal with that today. He couldn't. He'd come to Black Widow to start over, not rehash the past.

His lab licked his hand, distracting him. Tyler grinned down at the black dog; his bad mood temporarily lifted as he reached down and patted his furry friend on the head.

"See you this afternoon, Alfred."

A slight whine poured from Al's throat as his sad brown eyes speared an arrow of guilt in Tyler's gut.

"I'm sorry boy, but it's only my second week. I can't be late. Be good, and don't chase the ducks."

Al wagged his tail in understanding.

"Rascal." He revved the engine on his motorcycle and eased down the dirt road leading away from his house and into town to his new job.

His new start.

————

THE SUN SEARED Tyler's back, causing sweat to pour down the length of his spine and his T-shirt to stick to his skin. Nothing like the gulf coast humidity to make a man feel as if he was frying from the inside out.

Rose bushes around the town square bloomed giant Pepto-Bismol pink petals, while a gentleman in blue overalls tended to the flowers like they were his babies. Tossing a wave to the man, he rounded the corner on Holly Drive and parked his bike in front of Sandi's, the local diner. The undercurrent scent of flowers, bacon, and fried donuts drifted in the air. Man heaven. Except for the flowery part. He'd driven by the diner everyday for two weeks but had yet to pop in. If the food tasted as good as it smelled he might have to make this place a regular hang out.

He pushed through the heavy wooden door as a bell rang overhead. Weaving around customers, all giving him a curious stare, he strolled up to the takeout cash register. Glass cases filled with donuts and the biggest kolaches he'd ever seen stared back at him. His stomach growled.

He eyed the case, his mouth watering, as he waited on a server to notice him.

"Be right there," a tall, shapely blonde called out from across the restaurant as she handed another table their check. He'd been wrong. To hell with the donuts and bacon. *She* was man heaven.

A few escaped strands from her ponytail framed her face,

and the closer she got to him the darker the black circles under her eyes appeared.

A spark of recognition fired in his brain while an equally hot spark ignited a red flag in his gut. It wasn't her slightly unkempt hair or her pure look of exhaustion that rubbed him the wrong way. Despite all of that, she was still beautiful.

But her clothes. Her clothes had his head reeling.

She wore long sleeves.

In June.

In Texas.

"What can I get you?" The beauty stared up at him.

He shook off the strange feeling. A bead of sweat dripped down her forehead, fell onto her chest, and into her shirt. Her nametag was positioned right by the tantalizing skin of her chest. Annie.

Mercy.

He glanced down at the donut case. *Stare at the food, big guy.*

"I need two dozen glazed donuts, two dozen chocolate, and a dozen sausage kolaches."

"Got a lot to feed?" Annie grabbed a box from the counter behind her and placed it on top of the glass case in front of him.

"Yeah, Donut Day, or so I was told. It's my turn to bring breakfast, and there's about a dozen mechanics over at Rakes expecting it."

"Rakes? You must be new," a redheaded waitress noted as she rounded the corner and filled a customer's coffee cup. While she was cute, she had a wet-behind-the-ears look to her. He'd stick with Beauty.

He nodded. "I am."

"I've got your table seven covered while you do this, Annie. No big deal."

"Thanks, Gina." The blonde smiled at the redhead before returning her attention back to him. "I've brought my car to Rakes a few times, and I've never seen you." Beauty grabbed a towel from the counter to wipe the sweat off her forehead, then dabbed her chest near a gold locket that hugged her collarbone.

Shit.

Her tasseled hair seemed sexier the more she dabbed. He'd never been as jealous of a towel in his whole life, the cotton fibers taunting him with their task.

He averted his gaze from the towel and her amazing chest before she labeled him a pervert. Not exactly the reputation he wanted for his new life.

"I'm sad I didn't get to work on your car."

God, what a horrible pick-up line. She probably thought he was a giant perv and a complete moron.

She flashed him a half-smile that burned his insides. The diamond on her finger nearly blinded him as she brushed a stray strand from her forehead. The fire inside of him fizzled out like baking soda to a grease fire.

He forced a grin then shot his gaze down to the pastry case.

"Though, I will say..." She tossed the towel aside and stared at him. "Something about your face looks oddly familiar."

Me? Familiar?

He glanced back up. "Yours does, too, but I don't really see how." The spark in his brain burned brighter the more he stared at her.

"Are you from here, or is your family from here?"

"I'm not, but my grandpa was. He lived in a cabin about ten miles outside of town."

"By Virginia Creek, right? Mr. Wooly." Her smile grew.

"Yeah, you used to come visit him. You guys would go fishing."

"How'd you know?" He'd never talked to anyone when he came to visit his grandpa. He'd stayed in the woods, hidden and safe. Or at least, that's how he'd felt.

He stared at her a bit longer. The blue in her eyes reignited a small light of recognition. *Could it be?*

"I remember you." She grabbed a pair of tongs off the counter top. "I used to play out by the water, and I would see you across the creek casting your line. You taught me how to skip rocks one day."

Moments of his past flashed across his mind. It *was* her.

The girl across the water.

The one who'd wave every time she saw him. She'd been the prettiest girl he had ever seen. Her shiny blonde hair had glowed against the afternoon sun, and a funny surge of excitement rolled through his stomach every time he stared at her. All he could do was wave a slight hand back and put his head down, too timid to talk to her. His limbs would itch in anticipation, trying to work up enough nerve to say hi back— until one day.

She practiced skipping rocks while her dad and Gramps talked. It took everything in him to work up enough nerve to walk over and speak to her. And like the nervous boy he was, he'd forgotten to ask for her name. That had been the last day of his trip that summer, and when he returned the next year, she was gone.

He thought he'd lost his chance.

Now, all these years later, here she was, the girl of his boyhood dreams…and she was married. Tyler glanced back at the diamond ring. No wedding band with it. Perhaps it wasn't too late. His heart rate escalated.

"You're the girl that always walked barefoot in the stream?"

Be cool, dude. Be cool. He couldn't come across too awe struck.

"That was me. Wow, you've really..." She stared him over. "Grown."

He grinned, used to the slight widening of eyes at his size when he walked into a room, just like he experienced moments before. "Yeah, I grew a few inches and took to weight lifting in high school. I enjoyed it so much I just never stopped lifting."

"Good for you." She gave him a pleasant smile. The same smile she gave him when she'd successfully skipped her rock across the water after he taught her. A smile he never forgot.

"I'm sorry about your loss."

His good mood deflated. Gramps had been gone three months already. Three months too long. "Yeah." Sighing, he glanced back at the pastry case. "Thanks." He spotted a bear claw; Gramps' favorite.

"I know what it's like to lose someone you care about," she said, her voice gentle. "My dad...he...he died in a car accident several years back, and my mom, well...I'll just say, I know how bad it sucks."

She'd always walked along the rocks holding her dad's hand—was that the reason he stopped seeing her? Because of her dad's death?

"I'm sorry to hear that. I didn't know. I used to see you guys together all the time."

"I miss him." Her eyes held a distant gaze then her sad demeanor suddenly picked up as she focused back on him. "Anyway, what about you? You staying for good?"

"Yeah. The cabin's mine now. I've decided to make this place my home."

A sense of peace had washed over him when he accepted the estate. The feeling was his Gramp's final gift. He could start over in Black Widow, and his grandfather understood his need. Tyler had business here he had to do. People to help.

"Good. I moved back to town at the end of last year. It's been...nice."

He caught her hesitation.

"I hope *you* like it here." Annie gave him a brief smile as a bell in the background chimed. Her gaze cut to the door, and her back stiffened.

Looking to the right, he spotted a group of police officers as they walked in. His palms began to sweat. He glanced back to the case, and wiped his hands down the side of his jeans, keeping the sight of the cops in his peripheral vision.

"Morning, Sandi," one of the officers called to an older lady with curly brown hair as she grabbed some menus from a wooden stand by the front door.

"Morning, boys. Right this way."

The uniforms followed the woman to a four top table in the far corner.

Sandi tossed the menus on the checkered tablecloth and stepped out of the way so the officers could take their seats. "Annie'll be with you guys in a moment."

At the mention of her name, Tyler peeked back up and watched her. She fumbled with the donut box, nearly dropping it to the floor, her movements quick and shaky.

Is she in trouble with the law?

The group pulled out their chairs, the wooden legs scraping against the floor. He observed them as each officer plopped down and flipped their coffee cup up. Even though he didn't hear the comment, all of them seemed to be laughing at something the shorter one said...all except one.

Tall with dark hair, the police officer had smiled as he

passed certain customers, but his focus kept cutting back to Annie. Now, the man's glare shot to him.

Cold.

Hard.

Rigid.

Tyler had seen eyes like that before.

He looked back at Annie as she reached into the case to grab more of the donuts. Her shirtsleeve pulled up slightly, revealing the faintest hint of blueish-green. Quickly, she pulled the cloth back down as she replaced the tongs back on the counter top.

Sporadic and fast, his heart pounded at what he thought to be true. *Abuse*. She needed help. But even though they had a brief encounter when they were kids, they were different people now; he didn't know her. Not really. He could be jumping to conclusions. For all he knew, she could just be clumsy. If he repeated the thought, maybe he would start to believe it.

She's just clumsy.

She's just clumsy.

She's just clumsy.

Annie packed his boxes in a sack, her mouth straight as she hurried and placed his to-go bag by the register. "Is there anything else I can get for you?" She didn't meet his gaze.

Damn.

His instincts warned him being clumsy wasn't her problem. She needed help. But now wasn't the time or the place.

"No, that'll do it."

Hastily, she punched some buttons on the computer screen. "Twenty-two seventy-five."

He pulled out his wallet and extracted two twenties. "Keep the change."

She stared at the generous tip. "Thanks." After tucking

the spare change in her apron, she briefly glanced up at him and offered a half-smile.

Fake.

Nervous.

Shy.

He grabbed the bag, his own clammy hands causing the plastic handle to stick to his palm. He headed for the door as Annie took a coffee carafe and rushed toward the officers. The men held their cups up for her to fill, everyone except for the *one*. The guy gave him another hard stare as Tyler left the building.

A sinking feeling sat in his gut—the same feeling he used to get as a child…just before everything went bad.

Damn, Beauty. What have you got yourself into?

He needed to find that group his grandpa mentioned, and soon. Maybe they could give him some insight on how to help her.

———

"THAT'S a lot of donuts you got there."

Tyler placed the bag down on the small linoleum table in the break room and eyed his boss, Rake. "You've got a lot of men that like to eat." He pulled the boxes out of the sack and flipped the tops up.

"You fell for the Donut Day prank, huh?"

Tyler shook his head. "Bastards."

"Man, boss." Dave, a middle-aged mechanic, entered the break room and grabbed a chocolate donut out of the box. "I think this new guy's going to work out after all."

"Yeah, well, I didn't hire him for his generosity." Rake grabbed a kolache. "I don't pay him enough to keep the likes of you boys in food."

"Donut Day, Dave?" Tyler asked. "You ass."

"Worked, didn't it?" Dave took a bite of his pastry, chocolate smearing on his bottom lip.

Tyler didn't bother to tell him.

"Hey, hey, what do we have here?" Bryce sauntered into the kitchen. The buttons on the man's shirt threatened to pop loose over his belly, and his belt strained against the last notch. "Donuts! That's what I'm talking about." He reached a meaty hand into the box.

"Bry, you better wolf that down, and quick. Customer's coming this morning to pick up his bike, and you still don't have it complete." Rake stared at the clock on the wall. "I told him it would be done by nine."

"Nine? Boss, it's like eight-thirty." Bryce took a bite of his breakfast.

"Like I said, get to work," Rake demanded.

"Damn." The guy pouted.

"Come on, man. I'll help you." Tyler motioned for Bryce to start walking.

"Good." The mechanic followed him into the shop. "I'm going to need you to do all the heavy lifting."

"Heavy lifting?" He raised an eyebrow. "Why me?"

"Dude, you're built like a Mack truck. Why do you think Rake hired you?"

"I thought it was for my skills under a hood."

Bryce shrugged and stuffed the rest of his donut in his mouth, mumbling around his food, "Maybe so."

"Morning, boys," Leona greeted from behind the front desk.

"Morning," they said in unison.

"There's donuts back there, Lee, if you want any." Tyler hooked a thumb to the break room.

"You mean if Bryce doesn't eat them all first," the buxom brunette jibed.

"You know you've got nothing but love for me, baby." His pudgy coworker petted one of his nipples and puckered at her.

Lee stifled a giggle and rolled her eyes then pointed to a man signing a receipt. "Customer's here."

The guy lifted his head to stare at them. "My bike ready? I'm thinking not since I see pieces lying on the floor." Long black hair with silver streaks trailed halfway down the guy's back. A ratty, red bandana squeezed the top of his head while a roughed up brown leather vest hugged his chest. An emblem of a blue angel sat on his left breast, and a black widow spider patch lay stitched in a way to make it appear like it crawled up his shoulder sleeve.

What were the odds? A Blue Guardian. In the shop. Now. This was his chance.

Be cool, dude.

Tyler picked up a cloth off the worktable and began cleaning a wrench. "Nice leather," he said, barely giving the guy a glance.

"Yeah, I think so, too." The man finished signing the receipt and handed it to Leona.

"These guys will have your bike ready in a minute," she said. "Want a donut while you wait?"

"Sure, sweetie. Thank you."

She pushed off her stool and sauntered to the kitchen.

Tyler shuffled closer to the Guardian. "That patch." He kept his voice low so Bryce couldn't hear him. "You're part of the Blue Guardians, right?"

"Yep, that's right."

The group of bikers helped abused children. He'd learned

all about them from his grandfather. He stood to his full height. "How do I get in?"

The man cocked an eyebrow. "We don't just let anyone in our club, kid."

Kid?

"I'm not just anyone." He gave the man a hard stare.

"I've seen a Road King parked outside lately...yours?"

"Yes, sir."

Long Hair glanced him over. "I'll tell you what, kid."

Tyler's jaw tensed at the nickname.

The man took a pen from the cup on the counter and flipped over a tire flyer. "Meet me at this address a week from tonight. Seven. Don't give anyone this address, and don't be late. When you walk in, tell JoJo I sent you."

"And what name should I tell JoJo?"

"Name's Father."

Father? God, did this guy have a complex or what?

"And you're..." The man glanced him over. "Tank."

Tank. He liked the sound of that, better than Mack Truck at least. "No offense, but I haven't had the best luck with father figures in my life."

The man popped the pen back in the cup holder, and cut him a side glance. "It's time we changed that, son."

Son. He wanted to crack his neck from the tension in his jaw. He hadn't been any man's *son* in a long time. If ever.

"One week. Show up and don't be late. If you are, don't bother showing up at all."

"I won't be."

"I didn't figure you would; that's why I gave you a name."

"Here's your donut, and a fresh cup of coffee while you wait." Leona pushed past him to get to *Father*.

"Why thank you, sweet girl. I'll just go have a seat and

wait on my bike." The customer glanced over at Bryce struggling under the weight of the motor. "Might want to get me a few more." He motioned to his plate. "It looks like I might be here a while." The leathered-clad man ambled to a seat in the waiting area.

When *Father* was out of earshot, Tyler leaned toward Leona. "You know him?"

"Not really. I do know he's the reason why the Blue Guardians are here in Black Widow. To start a group like that, protecting innocent woman and children, makes him a good guy in my book."

So this man was the person responsible for the Blue Guardians in Black Widow. He glanced at the reason he'd decided to move to the town—a leather wearing, longhaired, hippy-looking dude with scuffed up boots and eye wrinkles. Some of the tension from his jaw eased.

"Huh." He shrugged. "I guess that's why he calls himself Father."

"Makes sense," she agreed. "But I could have sworn you knew him. The way y'all were talking, and well…"

"Well, what?"

Leona glanced at the customer then back at him. "Never mind." She flipped a manicured hand. "You don't know him…then…you don't know him."

"No." He shook his head. "I don't know him."

He finished wiping the wrench with the cloth as Leona's words played over in his mind. *Protecting innocent women and children.* Innocent women—like the one at the diner.

He couldn't shake Annie's tired appearance or her quick unease when the cops walked in the door. So much different from the carefree girl he remembered splashing in the water. Perhaps the group already had plans in place to help her. He'd be sure to find out next week at that meeting. He just hoped next week wasn't too late.

"Dude, you coming or what?" Bryce yelled.

"Yeah, yeah. I'm coming." He dropped the wrench and glanced back at the man in the waiting room.

Father.

Hopefully this one would be better than his real one.

CHAPTER TWO

Tyler tied his Batman bandana around his head and cranked his motorcycle. Plugging the address into his phone, he followed the directions down the street, but made a detour to circle around the diner. He stopped at a light right outside the restaurant's window.

Annie stood there in another long sleeve sweater, waiting on a customer. For the past week, her eyes held a bit more wariness each day. No matter how much he tried, he couldn't get her out of his mind. Every morning for the past seven days, he'd gotten the same donut and cup of coffee. And each and every day she'd smiled politely, made small talk, even remembered the way he took his coffee, but he could never get past the superficial conversations of the weather to pry into her personal life. The moment anyone would stop and take notice of them, she would clam up. Go all robotic on him.

He had to keep reminding himself he barely knew her; perhaps that was just her demeanor. However, a nagging irritation in his gut warned him that wasn't true. She'd smiled too much as a kid to be so skittish now. Something wasn't right and damn if he hadn't tried to ignore it, let her take care of her own business, but he couldn't stand by and suspect someone was getting abused and not act. Not his way. But what *could* he do? He'd never helped an abuse victim before. He hoped the Guardians had answers.

He glanced at the clock. Six-fifty. Did she take a break? She'd been there all day.

A car honked its horn behind him. The light had changed to green. He caught her stare just before he zoomed down the street.

Two left turns and a right later, he parked his bike in a grass field outside of a steel barn. Several other bikes sat there. Must be in the right place.

He pushed through the metal barn door, but instead of being met with hay shavings, his feet were met with cement. Collapsible lawn chairs leaned against the wall. A giant flag sporting a blue angel with a black background hung from the rafters of the barn. Under that, an equally large Texans football flag. A table to his left stood propped against one of the horse stall doors. A plate of cookies and a pitcher of iced tea with a stack of Solo Cups sat on the tabletop, and underneath, a cooler filled with ice and beer. A horse neighed and tried to reach his head over the wooden gate to grab a cookie.

"Get back, Angus," a petite woman reprimanded the horse as she strolled up to him. "You must be the new guy." Her jet black hair lay braided to one side, and the gait of her walk told him she wasn't someone he wanted to piss off, despite her small stature.

"Yeah. You JoJo?" He held out his hand.

"Yep." She just stared at him.

Tyler pulled his hand back. "Not a hand shaker?"

"No. Fill these out." The curt woman thrust a clipboard to him.

"Okay." He took the board from her. Background check. "I suppose if someone wants to help abused children they can't be a child abuser themselves," he muttered.

"Ding. Ding. Ding. Grab a cookie if you want one." She pointed to the plate on the table. "Father's plaything made them. She thought snacks meant cookies." JoJo rolled her eyes. "Usually, we have real food."

Father really needed to get someone else in charge of the welcome committee. This woman was about as inviting as a hemorrhoid and seemed as much of a pain in the ass.

"What's up with the Batman symbol on your bandana?" A slight sneer took over her face as she pointed to his head. "A bit old for superheroes aren't we?"

Pain in the ass all right.

"Sometimes, we all need a superhero."

He shook off her comment and scribbled his information on the pad. His love of Batman was none of her business. As far as he was concerned, their business was over.

"I can see why Father agreed to let you come." The little woman stared at him from head to toe. "He doesn't just let anyone in, ya know?"

"No, I don't know."

"And I heard he's already given you a name."

Tank. Was he supposed to start calling himself that? He stopped writing. The woman wouldn't stop staring at him. "And what exactly do you think you see?"

"A big man with a hurt soul."

He glanced away. Yep, they were through. "I think I'll take my seat now." He slapped the pen on the clipboard and handed it over before he pushed past her. Her small hand gripped his upper arm.

"It's okay," she leaned in and whispered. "That's why we're all here. You'll do well."

JoJo glanced at his paperwork. He'd left the nickname portion blank. She wrote *Tank* on the line.

Little Bit had managed to insult him and compliment him all in the same conversation. What the hell was her deal? He met her stare. A flash of understanding hid beneath her tough exterior.

Hell. His stomach sunk. Perhaps him and this lady had more in common than he'd like to admit.

"Yeah, well, thanks, I guess. Like I said, I'm going to take my seat now."

"Save me one, *Tank*." A wry smile touched her lips as she walked toward the front of the room.

Great.

Shortly after he'd found a seat, Father stood in the center aisle at the front of the group. Ten other men and two women sat in the small barn area with him. Every one of them wore the Blue Guardians leather jacket, *except him.*

"Hey, Guardians," Father addressed the crowd. "I'm sure some of you have seen by now we have a visitor. Everyone meet, Tank, aka Tyler." The leader pointed in his direction. Several turned but didn't bother to speak.

Friendly bunch.

"Tank here joined us tonight to see if we're something he might want to get involved with. Now, let's get on to business."

A muscled man with dark hair leaned in. "Hey, man," he whispered and stuck out his hand. His biceps were visible under the roughed leather, and his body seeped the undercurrent of smoke. "I'm Blake Steele, everyone calls me Steele."

"Hey." He offered his hand. "Tyler Wilde...Tank."

The man nodded. "'S'up, Tank?"

At least one person seemed friendly.

JoJo cleared her throat, and they both stole a glance at her.

"What's her deal?" Tyler whispered.

"JoJo? Give her time. She hates anything male at first."

"Glad to know I'm not the only one."

"Time for our pledge. All rise," the leader of the pack instructed.

Steele and JoJo both stood beside him. He took that as his cue to follow suit. Father began as everyone else joined in.

"We pledge to protect women and children of Briar County. We follow up on all leads given with dignity, respect, and love to the person who has been harmed. We respect their wishes and do what is needed day or night. We are the Blue Guardians, Black Widow chapter."

Women and children.

Leona had been right about the Guardians, and the truth stood right there in the pledge. If Annie was in trouble, was anyone doing anything to protect her?

"Now, down to business," Father said. "Tree, you're up."

A tall, thin man with a black bandana wrapped around his head and a scar below his left eye stood with a notepad. The nickname fit. "Not many minutes to speak of," the biker said. "We discussed the success of Ray Lynn's court date. The little girl's father was put in prison for ten years, while her mother told us she was proceeding with divorce. Last month, we celebrated JoJo's birthday with cupcakes—"

Tyler glanced over at the tough chick and leaned in. "Happy late birthday," he offered with a slight smile.

She narrowed her gaze and stared at him for a few seconds before she relinquished a slight glimmer of a smile back. "Thanks."

He was wearing her down.

"Okay, anything new?" Father glanced around. "Any new leads, anything anyone wants to share?"

"Yeah." A short, heavyset man with a rounding belly stood. If the other guy was a tree, then this man would be the stump.

"What is it Stump?"

Tyler had to bite his tongue to keep from laughing out loud.

"Macy told me about a kid in her school. Nathaniel Franks. Said he showed her a bruise on his arm on the play-ground one day last week. Claimed his dad did it."

Tyler leaned in to JoJo. "Macy?"

"Stump's daughter," she whispered back.

"Does the child's teacher know?" Father asked.

"I talked to their teacher. She couldn't tell me a whole lot since the kid wasn't mine, but in not so many words gave me what I needed to know. She suspects, by his recent, odd behaviors, the kid's being knocked around. He's grown quieter, moody. I think we should go knock on the door, talk to the mother, and see if we can talk to Nathaniel. Offer some support."

"Good idea," Father said. "I'll talk to the school counselor myself. Anyone willing to go tomorrow?"

JoJo and Steele raised their hands. Tyler joined them. This was what he came here for, to help, and he was ready to get started. Annie flashed in his mind again.

"Awesome. Glad to see so many able to help."

"Can the new guy go?" Tree pointed a pen toward him.

"As long as his background check passes, Tank's good," Father agreed.

"All right." The tall biker wrote their names on the notepad.

Steele leaned in. "Father's a counselor. Abuse is his specialty."

He glanced at the leader's wardrobe. Blue jeans, red cotton shirt, and the same scuffed up boots he wore last week at the shop. The laid back look suited the old man, and he supposed the facial wrinkles gave the guy a soft edge, an appearance victims could trust. Someone they could really open up to.

"Ah." Tyler nodded. "Makes sense."

"Remember, our ride's in two weeks," Father spoke up again. "Meet here. Seven a.m. sharp. We'll pack our tents in the back of Sandi's truck. She'll follow us to the lake."

"Tents?" Tyler whispered to Steele.

"Fourth of July ride. We always go to Jasper, to the lake."

"Okay. Is it mandatory?"

"It is if you want to be a part of our club."

"Got it."

"Tank," Father called over the crowd. "We don't tell anyone about our rides. We just meet and ride, got it?"

"Yes, sir." What excuse was he going to come up with at work? Being the new guy, he doubted asking for a holiday weekend off so soon was going to be in his favor. Still, he'd figure it out. Had to if he wanted to be in the group.

"Great." Father clapped his hands. "Is there any more business?" He glanced around the room, waiting for someone to speak up.

Annie's tired face burned a hole in his mind. His stomach rolled imagining her beautiful features, her smile—the few times she had given him one. What if he never saw it again?

"Short meeting this month. Next month, we'll start talking about our Christmas project. Well if there is nothing else—"

Shit.

If his suspicions were true, he had to make sure she got the help she deserved.

"Wait." He held his hand up.

"Yeah, Tank, what is it?" Father asked.

"In the pledge you say you protect women and children. What if a woman is getting knocked around? What's the procedure?"

"We don't help women unless they come to us for help."

"What if they don't know where to go? I mean you keep this place kind of hidden." He referred to the barn.

"They see us in town. They see our jackets. While our meeting space is kept secret, our agenda and who we are isn't. Adults are a different story from children. If a woman needs help, she has to come to one of us first. We don't help those who don't want to be helped, son."

There was that father figure mentality again. "Right, okay. I understand. Can I ask one more question?"

"Yeah, what's that?"

"Are there any woman you are helping now?"

"At the present time, no."

He gritted his teeth and took his seat. "Okay, thanks."

"Well, if that concludes our meeting…"

If Annie was being abused, why hadn't she come to them for help, or went to the police? The way she stiffened when the group of officers walked into the diner didn't sit well with him. If she didn't feel she could go to the police, and she wouldn't go to the Blue Guardians for help, well then, he would just bring the Blue Guardians to her.

"Hey, JoJo." Tyler leaned closer to the welcome committee. "I feel bad for missing your birthday celebration. What do you say you head to the diner with me, and I'll buy you a slice of cake?"

"You asking me out?" JoJo snickered.

Time for the truth. "Not really. I need help with something."

"Help?" She raised an eyebrow. "You're not going to tell me what it is are you?"

"Not until we get there."

"Does this have something to do with that blonde wait-ress, Annie, and your Batman mentality?"

Tyler pulled back. "How'd you know?"

"Take it from a girl who's been knocked around. You know when it's happening to another one."

Knocked around. So *that* was JoJo's story—why she didn't warm up to men easily. Annie probably had the same trust issues as JoJo.

"Will you help me?"

"I think it's a bad idea." She crossed her arms and pushed back deeper in her chair.

"That's a no? I get it." He stood. "Thanks anyway."

"I didn't say no, I just didn't say yes."

Mercy, this girl is irritating.

"So, what exactly are you saying?" He stared down at her.

She shot up to her feet and straightened her spine. He had a feeling she wanted to stand on her chair so they were eye level, but pride kept her from it.

"I'm saying, I think it's a bad idea, but I'll go. Everyone needs a superhero from time to time, right?"

Was she mocking Batman again? He bit back his irritation only because he needed her. "Thank you."

Little Bit turned and stalked toward the exit, her boots clicking on the concrete. "And I don't want a slice of cake. I want a burger," she hollered over her shoulder.

Steele stopped and stared at him. "Taking the piranha on a little date, are you?"

"I wouldn't call it a date. More like she's my mission's accomplice."

"Dude, you must have a tough mission to recruit the help of JoJo." Steele slapped him on the back. "See you tomorrow. Oh, and about our rides. Make sure you're not late. We don't wait."

Tough bunch.

"Yeah. No problem."

"You coming or what?" JoJo called from the front of the barn.

"You better go man. She doesn't wait on anybody." Steele stared back at JoJo and rubbed the back of his head. "But wait...uh...you sure you want to take her?" The group member glanced back at him and gave him a questioning look. "I could help you."

"Thanks, man, but I think for this task, I need someone more feminine."

"Yeah, dude, that ain't me." He held his hands up in the air, palms out, and took a few steps back. "See you around, Tank."

"See ya."

Tyler headed out and hopped on his bike. "Follow me."

JoJo slapped her helmet on and revved her roadster.

He hoped this worked. That sinking feeling in his gut from last week had never went away. Beauty was in trouble. He was sure of it, and if no one else would help her, he *would*.

CHAPTER THREE

Tyler parked his bike in the same spot in front of the cafe as that first morning. He unsaddled the giant piece of steel just as JoJo pulled her black street bike beside him. The lightweight and small frame of the motorcycle suited her, but the sissy noise of her bike rang in his ears. The machine sounded like it was ready to sew something instead of take a trip. He kept his mouth shut as a slight grin tugged his lips. He couldn't imagine this biker chick sewing anyone a sweater, much less him.

She unstrapped her helmet and stuck it under her arm. "What's so funny?"

"Nothing." Turning his head to hide his smile, he asked, "You know anything about this girl?"

"Not much." She shrugged then passed him her helmet as she unsaddled her bike. "I know she waits tables most days, all day long."

"I've noticed."

"Been scoping her out?"

"I've driven by a time or two. Nothing major." He

shrugged. Make that more like ten, but admitting the fact out loud seemed...creepy. "What else do you know?"

"I assume she gets knocked around, but I've never seen any proof other than her limping a little or favoring an arm or a certain leg most days." JoJo tossed her braid off her shoulder.

"I noticed the same last week."

"So, you've been coming by a lot?" Accusation crept in her tone.

"I've been getting breakfast here, and I drove by a time or two in the evenings to get a glimpse."

"Okay, that's kinda stalkerish." JoJo took a step back.

His jaw tensed. "Look, I'm no stalker. Last week, when she reached in the donut case, her sleeve pulled up. The bruise was faint, but the coloring was definitely there. I needed to make sure my theory was correct."

"That Batman mentality." JoJo rolled her eyes. "Okay, so, we know her name is Annie, and we know she's most likely being abused or extremely clumsy. What I don't know is why *you're* so worried about this girl."

He'd been asking himself the same question for the past week. While she was still beautiful, the carefree spirit he remembered seeing in her as a child was gone. He wanted her to have that back.

"You know her or something?"

Not as well as he wanted. "A little, but not much. She used to live across the river from my Grandfather, but I have to admit, I'm surprised you're asking me why I'm worried about her. Isn't this part of your mission as a Blue Guardian —to protect the innocent?"

"My mission, not yours. You're not a Blue Guardian."

"Yet." He tossed her helmet back to her and headed for the sidewalk. "Let's go."

"Wait." She gripped his arm. "What's the plan? We can't just go in there and pepper her with questions. You know how dangerous this can be, right? Hence why Guardians don't confront abused women first."

He motioned for her to step against the building to let an elderly couple pass. They each nodded to the twosome, appearing as if everything was fine.

Once the people were out of earshot, he leaned closer. "I've got a plan, okay? Just follow my lead."

"Tank, this is not a good idea."

Of course it's not, but he couldn't stand by and watch from the outside any longer. He had hoped once he went to the meeting, he could confirm Annie got the help she needed. But if the Blue Guardians wouldn't act first then he would.

"It's the only one I've got. Are you coming or what?"

"Ugh." The woman blew out a breath. "I'm going to help you, but it's not because I like you. So don't go getting any ideas." She pushed off the side of the building.

"Wouldn't dream of it. You want to let Father know what we're doing? I gathered it's against group rules."

"Better to ask for forgiveness than permission, right?"

"Right."

He wanted to be in the pack. More than anything. Well, almost anything. His desire to see to Annie's safety began to run deeper than almost any other in his life. She was apart of the few happy memories from his childhood, whether she knew it or not. He needed to see her happy again. He shook a nervous feeling building inside of him as he stepped over the threshold. Against the rules or not, he needed to talk to her.

A man with his nose stuck in a book nursed his coffee at a table to the far left. Two other couples, one young, one old, occupied two other tables, while a family of four took another. Slow night. He expected as much for eight-thirty in a small town like Black Widow.

Annie tossed an order on the cook's reel and headed for them, her gait a little unsteady. "You're back."

She gave him a brief smile. Albeit small, it was genuine. Not the robotic ones he'd been getting most mornings.

"Just the two of you?"

"Yeah."

"Right this way."

He motioned for JoJo to walk ahead and followed the women to a table surrounded by the two couples at the front of the restaurant. He squeezed his way through the small space between the tables just as Annie tossed the menus down on the tabletop. "Here you go."

"Can we sit back there?" JoJo pointed to the back of the diner. "This guy is so big, there may be more room for him back there."

Annie looked to him then behind her. "Sure. I'm sorry. I didn't think about that." Her cheeks flushed as she gathered up the menus. "Wherever you want is fine."

Little Bit led the way to a table in the very back corner. "This one's good."

Tyler gave his cohort a nod of understanding. While it appeared JoJo was looking out for him, and his legroom, he knew the truth. If they were going to have any chance of talking to Annie, they needed to do it privately, as far away from the other customers as possible.

"Great." Beauty placed the menus down again. "I'll give you guys a minute to look over your choices. What would you like to drink?"

"Water for me," JoJo said.

"Same here."

Annie limped off behind the bar to pour their drinks.

"You ready, hot shot? You got it all figured out?" JoJo pulled out her chair and sat.

"I think so." Tyler sat, and his knee bumped the leg of the table. He turned his body sideways to give himself enough room and picked up his menu. "She's favoring her right leg. Did you notice?"

"Yep, sure did."

"She wasn't this morning when I came in, but she has been on her feet all day."

"She could just be tired."

Doubtful. He hadn't been reacquainted with Annie long, but in the short time he'd seen her pull double shifts nearly every day. A schedule like that, she'd be used to the rigors of standing on her feet all day.

"We both know that's probably not why," he whispered as Beauty walked back toward them.

"Here you go." She placed their drinks down beside them. "Are you guys ready to order?"

Now was his chance.

"Annie, I want to talk to you about something," he began, his voice low. She had to duck closer to hear him— exactly what he wanted. He kept his gaze focused on the menu.

"Okay, sure. What's up? Something on the menu you don't understand?"

"No, it's nothing about the menu." He tossed her a stare, and kept his voice down. "Just act casual, okay?"

"I don't understand." She pulled back a little.

"Smooth. Real smooth." JoJo rolled her eyes.

Beauty glanced from him to his friend and back again. "What's going on?"

"Annie." He met her gaze. Her eyes held a bit of fear in them along with the weariness he'd seen the past week. What was happening to this poor woman? He cleared his throat.

"Please, just act casual and keep your voice down. I just want to help."

"Help with what?" She took a step back.

Now that the time was here, offering her help seemed much easier in his mind than the real action. He had to be honest, dive in headfirst. No other way.

"I know you're being abused," he whispered.

Her eyes grew as her head shook from side to side. "You're crazy. Now, do you want something or not? I've got work to do."

Her voice held more passion in that one sentence than he had heard or seen all week. His instincts had been correct. The Annie he'd seen the past week, that wasn't the real her.

"Annie." JoJo's voice soft, and sweet as a pained expression passed her face. She placed her elbows on the table and leaned in. "It doesn't have to be this way."

"It's not any way. Now, if you'll excuse me." She turned on her heels.

They were losing her. He was losing her.

"The beatings won't end," JoJo said loud enough for Annie to hear.

Beauty stopped and turned around again but didn't step closer.

Tyler glanced around the restaurant and kept his voice low. "I want you to know you have options. There are people willing to help you. *I* want to help you."

She fidgeted with the locket around her neck, her gaze cast toward the floor. "How do you think you're going to help me, huh?" Annie scoffed and stepped closer, her voice small. "My fiancé is a cop, and not just any cop, but the Chief of Police. *No one* can help me." Her lower lip trembled.

Fiancé. The man with the eyes. Had to be him.

"I can give you a place to stay." The words tumbled from his lips before he gave them a second thought.

Where would I place her?

"Where?"

His thoughts exactly.

She stepped closer. "The county shelter?" Her voice escalated, and she took a deep breath and closed her eyes. Perhaps to control her temper. When she opened them, her voice faded back to a whisper. "He answers calls for domestic violence. He helps place women who are abused in that shelter, and he has access to other shelters all over the state due to his connections. He'd know where or how to find me."

Tyler couldn't see her in a shelter, nor did he want her in one. He wanted her somewhere he would know she was safe. Somewhere her fiancé wouldn't know where to look.

There was only one place.

"He doesn't know me. And he doesn't know that you know me. You'd be safe if you came to stay with me."

"You?" She laughed.

His ego took a plunge at the sound.

"I don't know you. Not really. All I know is you were once a boy who fished with his grandfather and taught me to toss a rock. Now, you're a man, just like my fiancé. Only difference between the two of you is you like chocolate donuts and drink your coffee black. *Why* do you think I'd stay with you?"

Her words struck a nerve, the reference he was anything like her fiancé caused his blood to rage. He would never be *that* kind of guy. He reined in his anger. She had no idea what kind of guy he was. He'd have to show her.

"Because I'm *nothing* like your fiancé," he whispered. "I would *never* beat you, nor would I let anyone else."

She blinked several times as a tear threatened to fall down her cheek.

"Yeah?" She sniffled. "Well, thanks, Romeo, but I've had my fair share of living with men."

"Listen to him, Annie," JoJo cut in. "He just wants to help you."

For a second, he'd forgotten his sidekick was there, and for the first time that evening, he was glad he'd ran into JoJo, even if she came across a bit surly. At least the chick seemed to have a clear head on her shoulders.

"Annie, what's taking so long with that order?" a big man from the back hollered. "I'm ready to close up back here."

"Sorry, Mo. Customer just had some questions about the menu."

"It's a cheeseburger or a patty melt," the big man grumbled. "What's so complicated?"

A bell chimed at the front door. The short cop he saw at breakfast last week headed to the pick-up register. Tyler's hands clammed.

The man waved at Annie.

"Hey, Brayden." She waved back, her voice a bit shaky.

The robotic smiles, the small talk for the past week, it all started to make sense. Small towns had eyes and ears everywhere.

Tyler reached for JoJo's hand and gave her a hard stare. Reluctantly, she reached across the table to hold his as if they were a couple, and turned up her nose at the obvious dankness of his palm.

Sweat or no sweat, if short cop reported back to the Chief of Police, he wanted to make sure the man had absolutely nothing suspicious to report of Annie's behavior. The last thing he wanted to do was cause her more harm than she'd already encountered, and if that meant pretending to be JoJo's sweaty lover, well, so be it.

"Just look down at the menu and pretend like you're focusing on what I'm pointing to," he said to Annie.

He pointed to the cheeseburger. "You know where I live. You can come day or night. I'll give you a place to stay."

She backed up from him and scribbled on her notepad. "I'll have your burgers right out," she said in a tone loud enough for everyone to hear, but not too loud to appear like she was trying. Good acting; then again, she'd probably had a lot of experience with the art while hiding her abuse from everyone.

She whispered, "What's your name?"

In their entire week of morning donuts and coffee, not once had she asked him his name.

He glanced at JoJo then stared at Annie. If he was going to help her, and represent the group, then he needed to accept everything about the club...including his name. "Name's Tank."

Annie moved her gaze from his eyes to his shoulders, chest, then down to his one leg propped out from under the table. "Fitting." She turned on her heels and stuck their order on the cook's reel.

"Well, that went well." JoJo pulled her hand back and wiped it on her napkin. "What's up with the dishwater hands?"

"Uniforms make me nervous."

"You got a thing against cops?"

"Not really."

She gave him a puzzled look.

He rubbed his hands down his glass and changed the subject. "You think she'll take my offer?" Despite the fact Annie thought so low of him, he couldn't help but steal a glimpse at her as she did her job. Whether she cared for him or not, his pull for her only grew stronger with her resistance.

"Don't know." JoJo took a sip through her straw then leaned back. "Depends on how desperate she gets."

Gets?

In his mind, she was already desperate. He might not have known her father, but he knew a loving father wouldn't want this kind of life for a daughter.

Hell, *he* didn't want this life for her.

He wasn't a frightened kid anymore. Knowing an innocent, defenseless woman like her was being abused... He wrung his hands; his gut twisted as he waited for the nausea to pass. He might not know her well, and she sure as hell didn't know him, but she was his first crush. And if she didn't listen, she could wind up dead.

She had to listen and know she deserved more. He would make it his mission to get through to her and help her understand. *Somehow. Someway.*

CHAPTER FOUR

Annie pulled her car into the carport she shared with Duke. His truck sat parked in its usual spot, while his police cruiser resided on the street. He liked to park his patrol car on the curb to scare people as they drove by. Vehicles would slow down the minute they thought a cop watched. Authority gave him a thrill.

She grabbed her purse off the passenger seat and took a deep breath. *God. What the hell had happened tonight?*

That big, burly blond guy—Tank. And his little dark-headed friend—his girlfriend? For his sake, she hoped not. They appeared about as good for each other as a drug to an addict, not to mention the thought made her slightly jealous.

How stupid.

When she was a little girl, she'd begged her dad to walk to the water with her so she could play. While she loved spending time with him, what she really enjoyed was staring at the shy boy across the stream. For seven summers, she'd waved, hoping to get a chance to talk to him, and every time she waved, he would keep his head down, and barely raise his hand.

When she began to take it personally, her dad would excuse the boy's behavior as him being shy. Until finally, on one hot day, he'd worked up the nerve to talk to her. That summer, when he left to return home before she could get any contact information from him, a bit of her heart sunk. Too embarrassed to ask his grandfather for the information, she resorted to counting down the days until he would come back again the next summer. But, right before he did, everything in her life changed.

For the worse.

And now, that boy was back in her life. Except he was no boy. He'd been in the diner every day for the past week, and every day she'd had to concentrate on not staring at him. Problem was, he was so big she couldn't help but see him. And if the small tingles of fascination she experienced for him weren't bad enough, he'd always make the sensation worse by coming in and talking to her. Only *her*. Never the other girls. And his shyness...he must have outgrown it.

Anytime one of Duke's friends would stop in and notice, she'd cut the conversation off, and a balloon of panic would swell in her gut. She often feared Duke could read her mind.

If only Tank had spoken to her more when they were children, maybe things would be different for her now.

Who was she kidding? Young love didn't last. Not that she'd ever been in love with the big burly man anyway.

She pushed the childish notion aside and reached for her locket, kissing the gold. "Give me strength, Daddy," she whispered as she stepped out of her car.

She cringed at the pain in her joints, but the dull ache was quickly replaced with dread of what she would walk inside to. Duke's moods were always a surprise. Some days elation, some days anger. Maybe he was passed out on the sofa. She could only wish.

Discomfort ricocheted up her leg with every step as the noise from the television greeted her entrance. She crossed the threshold, checking the house alarm. Off.

Her fiancé's brooding expression made her wish the diner stayed open twenty-four seven. She'd work triple shifts if she could. "Hey, honey. How was your day?"

"Fantastic, *honey*. How was yours, *honey*?" He chugged his beer and crushed the can in his hand.

"What's wrong?" She dreaded asking.

"Turns out, Murphy's re-running for Sheriff after all."

His campaign. Of course.

"Floyd Murphy? I thought he decided not to run for a second term."

"He did. At least, that's what he told my father. Turns out the bastard changed his mind."

Gently, she placed her purse on the kitchen counter. His prescription bottle still sat full near the sink. He hadn't taken his medicine in months.

Tread carefully.

Keeping her voice soft, she said, "That's okay. I'm sure you'll still win."

"Of course, I'll win. This just means I'll have to work harder, but I can't campaign full time while working as Chief of Police. I need to start a committee, immediately." He stood and paced in front of the couch. "And as my future wife, you'll lead it. You'll stop working at the diner so much. I don't like you there all the time anyway. There are too many men that come in and out of there."

Men. *No.* Had someone said something?

Before she could comment, he blurted, "How much money did you make today?"

"Seventy-five dollars."

He stopped and stared at her. "That's twenty dollars more than yesterday. You flirted with someone, didn't you?"

Please not this. Not the accusations.

Keeping the tiger at bay wasn't something she had the energy for tonight. Her heart raced as she shook her head and took in a deep breath. "No. Of course not." She didn't have a death wish.

If Brayden talked to him about waiting on Tank, no matter what she said, Duke wouldn't believe her, especially if anyone else mentioned seeing the big biker in the diner throughout the week. Duke would instantly think the guy was flirting. Though, she wasn't sure if the man offering her a place to stay would be considered flirting or downright crazy.

Duke stomped toward her, and his eyes changed from stormy to wild.

Her heart sped at the animalistic gaze. She braced herself for a blow, but instead, he yanked her arm, pulling her beside him on the couch. Pain seared up her week-old bruises and to her shoulder. If he didn't stop pulling her arm so hard, she would have to quit the diner altogether from injury instead of just cutting back her hours.

"Duke, baby, you're hurting me." She did her best to keep the panic out of her voice. If she remained calm, he might back off.

Just stay calm.

He eased his grip and gently placed the backside of his hand to her cheek. "Oh, Annie, I just love you so much." His voice was nearly a whisper. "You're *so* beautiful. It's no wonder you made more money in tips today. All those men, they *are* flirting with you, and I can't stand the thought." He reached behind her head and pulled the band, releasing her ponytail. "I love it when you wear your hair down. You should do it more often."

"Okay," she said, scared of the look in his eyes. If she did whatever he said, kept him happy, they might still have a good night. She could get some sleep.

He played with a lock of her hair. "You need me, you know that? Before me, you were barely surviving. I've given you a house, clothes, and food. Soon, you will have my name. Do you know how lucky you are?"

Yeah, lucky.

Keep him happy.

"I do." At one time, she believed herself lucky landing a guy like Duke. He'd charmed his way in her heart and her bed. But now, times like this, when the medicine was no longer in his system, she feared the worst from him.

"I'm so lucky I found you, and I need you, too, Annie. God, you're my everything. But..."

The grip on her hair tightened, straining the roots at her scalp. She gasped more from fear than agony.

"If I were to find out you've been flirting with someone, I don't know what I'd do."

He snaked his other hand to her face, cupping her chin. The pressure from his fingers pressed into her cheeks, causing her lips to pucker. She turned her head, tried to wiggle free. No use.

The pounding in her chest increased as he leaned closer, his mouth an inch from her ear. An uncontrollable shake took over her body.

"You're mine," he whispered, his breath touching her cheek. "Do you understand that?"

Unable to speak from his hand clenching her mouth shut, she nodded.

He released his hold. "I knew you would, baby. And that's one of the reasons I love you so much. You're so understanding." Placing a quick kiss on her forehead, he sat back as if nothing had happened. "Now, how much closer are we to paying for the wedding? We've got to set a date, and soon. Mother is getting anxious, and she's annoying the hell out of me."

He popped the top of another beer can, which did nothing to help her racing heart.

"And my father...pressuring me to 'have a wife on the campaign trail.'" His last words were emphasized with air quotes. "Jesus Christ, they get on my nerves." He took a swig. "So, how much closer?"

She rubbed her jaw and glanced at the crushed beer cans on the end table. Six. Working on seven. She had to choose her words wisely. The added stress of his campaign, his family, and the wedding were enough to set him over the edge. Without his anti-anxiety medication to keep him on an even level, he was a ticking time bomb.

"We're getting much closer."

"*How* much closer."

"Well, the guest list is pretty long. We still need about six thousand more dollars to reserve the services your mother wants."

"Six thousand? Just to reserve. Jeez, Annie." He slammed his beer can against the wall. Gold fizz sprayed in the air, covering the living room curtains and the floor.

She jumped and pushed back in her seat, her back rigid against the sofa. He stood and began to pace, his hands balled into fists at his sides.

Running wasn't an option—he stood between her and the door. She had to calm him down. Her body couldn't handle another strike. Not today.

"Why the hell is *your* mother such a bum, huh?" He slicked his fingers through the sides of his hair. "Why can't *she* help?"

There he went again. "I'm sorry. She's disabled, you know that."

He paced in front of her some more. "Disabled. Is that what you call crazy? *Disabled.*"

His words set an inferno ablaze inside of her. Her mother was no crazier than he was sane at this moment. "My mother is *not* crazy. Don't call her that."

He stopped and stared. "Did you just command *me* not to do something?"

She glanced up at him with hooded eyes. "Duke, baby, we could have a wedding tomorrow if *your* mother didn't want to invite the entire county. Five hundred people is a lot to feed."

"So, not only are you talking back to me, but now you're blaming my mother for *your* shitty pedigree."

She should have kept her mouth shut. Maybe she did have a death wish.

"Duke, I'm...I'm sorry."

He stormed toward her, his hands balled in tight fists at his sides, and his teeth clenched. "You're damn right you're sorry."

Holding her palms up in a stopping motion, she stammered, "I didn't mean to upset you, but I think you need to take your medicine, baby. You think better when you take your pills." She glanced from his angered eyes to the door. If she ducked quickly enough, could she get past him?

"I don't need my medicine."

A searing pain blasted through her skull as flashes of light popped before her eyes. In her haste to search for an exit, she hadn't even seen his hand rise. She held her cheek and blinked several times, willing the haze in her vision to go away, and the sting from his blow to subside. In all his hatred, he'd never hit her in the face before.

"That was for your own good. *Never* talk to me like that again. A good wife never back talks her husband."

As she regained her focus, the throbbing in her cheek caused tears to well in her eyes, starting the blurriness all over again. Warm blood trickled down her face and into her palm as more blood whooshed in her ears. The pounding in her head matched that of her racing heart.

"Now look what you've made me do. You call in sick tomorrow and every day after until that cut goes away, do you hear me?"

The bright red tinge staining her palm held her focus. Something inside of her snapped as she glanced from her hand then back to the angry man before her.

Her life would never get better. Not with Duke.

The shaking in her limbs intensified as a rush of adrenaline took over. "Why?" She gripped the arm of the sofa for balance and pushed to stand. "Because that's what a *good wife* would do, or because someone would realize their dearly beloved Chief of Police is nothing more than an abuser. No better than the scum he picks up every day off the streets."

As soon as the hasty words flew out, she regretted them.

He grabbed her by her shirt, her locket getting caught in his grasp as he pulled her head toward him. She just knew the chain would snap as it dug into her neck.

A traitorous whimper escaped her. "Duke, please..." she pleaded, more for her locket than for herself. One of the few possessions she had to remind her of her father. Why didn't she keep her damn mouth shut? She'd never spoke to him like that before.

He leaned his face over hers; his hot beer breath hit her nose, and the pungent smell insulted her senses.

"You will *never* talk to me like that again. Do you understand?"

She understood.

Finally.

After months of abuse, everything began to click. What the biker woman had told her was true. No matter how good she was, how much she tried, Duke would never stop beating her. Her spine stiffened. So what if she continued to talk back? What did she have to lose? Her life?

How wonderful that's turned out to be.

At least she'd get to be with her dad again.

"Why can't I talk to you like that? It's the way you talk to me. Afraid you might hit me again, or worse?" she strained to ask against the pain pulling in her neck as she stared into his crazed eyes. Eyes somehow, someway, she had to get away from.

Fire flashed in his pupils.

He reached to his side, pulled out his pistol, and pointed the barrel straight to her head. The cold steel grazed her hairline. She stood there helpless as the man who claimed to love her threatened to kill her.

Fear rolled through her stomach, and her breaths came out quick and shallow.

"*Don't* push me, Annie." He thrust the barrel deeper into her skin. "There are other pretty women out there. Others who will keep their mouths shut and look better than *you* standing beside me when I become Sherriff."

His hand shook. The pistol wavered slightly against her head, as his finger hovered over the trigger. All it would take was one pull. One pull, and she would be dead. She heard the safety click and prayed for the bullet to do the job quickly. The thought of dying scared her, but the thought of living a life with Duke, this life forever, terrified her even more. Some things were worse than death.

"Well, go find one." She closed her eyes and began to recite the Lord's Prayer in her mind.

To her surprise, instead of hearing the blow of the bullet, the tension holding her neck released. She opened her eyes; the butt of the gun came into her peripheral vision before a loud crack against her temple pounded in her ears. Shades of blurriness engulfed her vision, the light and dark coming in and out like a kaleidoscope. As if weightless and in slow motion, she tumbled downward. Her side hit something hard, causing her breath to rush from her lungs, and she suffocated the cry that tried to escape. Her body made contact with the carpet, the world around her a medley of haze and light.

She would be still. So still. If he thought she'd passed out, perhaps he would leave her alone.

God, how she prayed this could all end.

CHAPTER FIVE

T ank pushed the barbell back on the rack and turned his music down. The thumping of the bass distracted him. He needed silence and sweat to clear his muddled mind.

Thunder from outside boomed around his cabin as lightning lit up the night sky. The noise of the rain soothed him, but nothing helped his brain.

Usually, physical activity did the trick. Made things he didn't understand clear. Tonight, not so much. With every chest press, his body grew weary, his mind heavier. He had to get Annie to listen to him, and see the truth—her soon-to-be husband would never stop abusing her.

"Why won't the woman listen, huh?" he asked Alfred. The dog cocked his head to the side and gave him a blank stare. "I know, buddy. I can't figure it out either."

A loud banging thrashed against his front door, followed by another roll of thunder. The banging grew louder and faster. Al ran down the hall, barking and wagging his tail.

What the hell?

He raced through the house and peeked out the living

room window. A car sat in the grass. Al clawed the front door, anxious to greet the person on the other side.

"Down, boy." Tank pulled the door open.

Annie stood just outside the threshold, her hair slick against her face, her cheek colored a deep shade of blue, and her left eye nearly swollen shut.

"Annie?"

Seeing her standing there on the other side of the door freshly battered and bruised, looking like a lost puppy, sent a tremor down his spine and gave him an immediate knot in his stomach.

The bastard had done it again.

"Can I c-come in?" Her lower lip trembled. From pain or the cool of the rain, he didn't know which.

He pushed the door open wider. "Of course." Alfred jumped on his back legs, front paws in the air. "Down, boy," he commanded and shooed his dog out of the way as she walked inside. "Were you followed?" The thickness of the storm made it hard to see as he glanced out the door.

"I don't think so. I took extra turns just in case." She stood on the floor mat in his living room, shivering. Her hair dripped water down her back and onto the floor. Blood droplets covered the left shoulder sleeve of her diner shirt, and a cut grazed her cheek, dried blood keeping the wound closed. A red line covered the side of her neck.

"Your neck?" He pointed as he shut and locked the front door.

She reached for the back of her neck. "My locket." Her eyes widened as she moved her hand to her throat. "The chain must have broken."

"Do you think it fell off outside?" He hooked a thumb toward the door.

"No." She shook her head. "I don't." Fresh tears began to well in her good eye.

He fought the urge to wipe them away. "Let me get you a towel. Do you need to go to the hospital?" He rushed toward his bathroom.

"No, I'll be fine," she called from the living room.

Fine? She was anything but fine. This situation was anything but fine.

Rummaging through his cabinet, he grabbed the biggest towel and headed back to her. "Here." Unfolding the cloth, he placed it over her shoulders. "Did you bring anything else with you?"

"Just my purse. I got out of there as quick as I could, and I guess I didn't notice my locket had fallen off." She reached for her bare collarbone then dropped her hand. "Duke is on the night shift tonight. When I woke up, he was gone." Her eyes gazed to the floor as if in a trance. Another rumble of thunder shook outside, and she gave a jerk. "I... I noticed the time when I got up." She focused back on him, her words tumbling from her mouth. "His shift had just begun, so he should have been at the station clocking in and getting a detailed report of anything that happened earlier today. Oh, God, what if...what if he was already done at the station? What if he followed me here?"

"Annie." He held a hand up. "Calm down. I just looked outside. Remember? No one is out there."

"Right." She nodded, her hands clearly shaking as she gripped the towel on her shoulders.

"You said you woke up. Did you fall asleep?"

"No. Well, yes, I guess I did, after..." Annie pointed to her face.

He gazed over her bruises again, his stomach churning at

the agony she had to be in. "What the hell did he do to you? Did he knock you out?"

"No. He just knocked me down. I faked the blackout part, but then I actually fell asleep. I guess my body needed to recover from all the pain."

"Damn it." *That son of a bitch.* A tense yearning to pound his fist into the door tried to take over, but he controlled his temper. If he acted too harshly, she would think he wasn't any better than the man she ran from. He didn't want her running.

He just wished he'd been there to prevent it.

The weight of his stare must have made her uncomfortable, because she turned her face away to glance down at Alfred.

The dog licked her hand.

"He likes you," he said to lighten the mood, if such a mood could be lightened.

"He seems to." She knelt down, placed her bag on the floor, and rubbed his ears. Almost as quick as she bent down, she shot up, her face contorting from the hasty movement.

"Are you okay?"

"Yes. God." She sucked in a breath. "I'm sorry. What am I doing?" The towel fell to the ground as she grabbed her bag, and slowly lifted the strap back over her shoulder. "I shouldn't have come here. When Duke gets home, he's going to be so angry I left. You're not safe with me here. I-I'm sorry." She turned and grabbed the door handle.

Tank placed his palm flat on the door and pushed the wood closed, blocking her with his body. She tensed her shoulders and jerked her hand back to her side. Fight or flight ready to take over.

"Listen, Annie." He kept his voice controlled, low. "I'm not going to tell you what to do. You're a grown woman, but if you go back there, if you go back to him, what will happen

next time? Will he break something? Will you be hospital-
ized? Worse?" He didn't want to say what that worse
would be.

Her eyes flashed a pain he, too, had long ago experienced,
and he fought for control not to raise his voice, scare her even
more in his desperation to make her understand. He would
never gain her trust by frightening her. Her fiancé proved
that.

He lowered his hand on the door and stepped slightly to
the side. Her escape route clear. "Annie, please stay. Your
face."

She held a hand to her cheek.

That cop should be in prison for what he'd done, and
Tank urged to bring retaliation on the man. Instead, gently, he
raised his hands and rested them on her shoulders. Her face
contorted in agony as she winced. He eased his grip even
lighter and stared her straight in her eyes. Green irises
glanced back at him, surrounded by little red veins, her left
eyelid daring more and more to close shut. The beautiful,
smiling waitress he met last week seemed a distant memory
to the one he saw now.

"You have a place to stay if you want. You can stay here
as long as you'd like."

"You don't even know me. Why are you doing this?"

The million-dollar question. The pull he felt toward her
didn't make sense, but no matter how hard he tried, he
couldn't ignore it. He had to protect her.

"Because I hate seeing innocent people abused, and I
promise you, if you stay here, you'll never be a victim again."

Her body tensed under his gentle hold, and her gaze
danced around the room.

"Besides," he added, nodding to Alfred, "we have the best
guard dog in the woods."

She let out a small chuckle. The sound of her slight happiness echoed through his walls, affecting him more than it should. The smile wasn't much, but regardless, laughing was good.

"Okay." She eased under his grip, pushed back a tear, and glanced down at his dog. "But on one condition."

"Yeah? What's that?" He placed a finger under her chin, easing her head up. Scared she might pull back, he made sure his touch was feather light. He wanted her to look at him. Trust him. She needed to see he wasn't going to hurt her, ever.

To his surprise, she didn't pull back but glanced up and stared.

"You tell me your real name."

A smile touched his lips. Even in turmoil, she still had her spirit.

"Tyler. Tyler Wilde."

She slowly extended her hand. "Tyler Wilde, I'm Annie Carter. It's a pleasure to officially meet you."

He took her small hand in his. "Pleasure's all mine, Annie."

Her lip raised, and the smile met her good eye. His heart pulsed as an even stronger and overwhelming urge to guard her took over.

"Get comfortable." He took her bag from her, placed it on the coffee table, then picked up the towel off the floor and set it back on her shoulders. "Take a seat on the couch. I'll be right back. I'm going to get you some dry clothes." He turned down the hall and into his room.

Nearing his dresser, he stopped and stared at the pile of letters on top. Every single one of them left unopened, all from his dad. A heavy reminder of why he was in Black

Widow stared back at him with the untouched letters. No one deserved to live in fear.

Especially not Annie.

He grabbed a fresh pair of pants and a shirt from a drawer then took the pile of letters and shoved them in the empty spot the clothes had been.

When he entered the living room, Alfred jumped on the couch and rested his head on her lap. "Al, leave her alone."

Annie smiled. "He's fine. I've never had a pet before."

"Really? Never?"

"No. My mom was allergic, and I didn't want to bring an animal into my home with Duke because I was afraid of... well." She pointed to her face. "Ya know."

"You were afraid he would abuse the animal."

"Yeah." She glanced down at his lab and lazily scratched his black ears.

"That's how I got this rascal here." He sat on the other side of Alfred. "I was out for a ride one day and just happened to see the owner mistreating him. I pulled over, asked the man to stop."

"What happened?"

"The man wanted to make something of it. I didn't. I saw he had an empty box of beer by his lawn chair, so I told him I'd give him two hundred dollars for the dog. He could have a pretty good weekend on two hundred dollars' worth of beer."

Annie rubbed down Al's back and glanced at him. "You paid two hundred dollars for him?"

"Yep. Best two hundred I've ever spent." He looked her in the eyes. "No one deserves to be abused, Annie. Not even a dog."

She turned her head down to face her lap. "I know," she replied, her voice low.

The moment was tense. Too tense. He wanted her to feel

safe, not uncomfortable. "Here. I brought you some clothes." Handing her the pile, he suggested, "Why don't you go take a bath? I can give you some frozen peas for your eye, and you can relax for a little bit."

"Oh, no. I don't want to intrude. You've done more than enough. I'll try to figure something out tomorrow."

Tomorrow? She couldn't leave. Not until they had a proper plan in place. "Annie, no one will hurt you here. I promise. You can relax." Gently, he reached for her hand, and squeezed. Was he touching her too much? Last thing he wanted her to think was that he was looking to get something from this situation.

He pulled his hand back. "There is a lock on the door, and you can even take Alfred with you as a guard if you'd like."

She nodded. "A bath does sound good. Are you sure?"

"One thing you'll learn about me, Annie, I don't say things I don't mean."

"Okay, I think I will then, but you can keep Alfred."

"Probably for the best. He has a bad habit of sniffing butts."

She let out another giggle, the pleasant sound unusual in his small home. Something he could definitely get used to.

"I'll get your peas."

He placed a fresh towel, washcloth, and a package of frozen vegetables by the bathtub then stepped out into the hall to give her some space. "Soap, shampoo, everything's in there. You think you'll need anything else?"

She stood in the middle of the bathroom; her arms wrapped around her torso, and stared at the tub. "No, I think I'm fine. I must say your tub is huge."

"Yeah, well, I'm a big guy. Gramps was, too."

"Yeah, I remember." She gave him a soft smile.

He stared down at the ground and nodded. "Yeah. I'll... uh...I'll be in the living room when you're done."

"Yeah, okay."

"Come on, boy." Alfred stood beside her in the bathroom, not moving. "Al, let's go." The lab stared up at Annie, wagging his tail.

"Go on, boy. I'll be out in a minute."

Reluctantly, his dog trudged out of the bathroom.

"I don't know what's gotten into him," he said, trying to play off Alfred's disloyal behavior before he closed the door. Standing on the other side of the threshold, he heard the sound of water slapping the porcelain tub. Al followed him into the living room and jumped on the sofa.

He knew what had gotten into Alfred. There was a good-looking woman getting naked just on the other side of the door. "You hound dog." He scratched the pup's ears.

Mercy.

What had he gotten himself into?

———

ANNIE SLIPPED OFF her rain soaked clothes and winced as she eased into the tub. Bruises peppered her arms and legs, some old, some new. Her head pounded, the back of her neck burned from the chain digging into her skin, and the vision in her left eye blurred. Yet, none of those things were her biggest concern.

Her most sizeable concern was the man sitting in the living room, watching television. Big didn't even describe him. Large, giant, massive...she wasn't sure which adjective fit him best.

Looking at him would have even the bravest of men turning to run. Yet, under all that muscle, he seemed kind, and the lightness with which he touched her, she could even dare to say gentle.

You sound like a Disney princess. Might as well break out in song.

Major difference, though, Tyler was no beast.

Still, kind and gentle didn't justify the fact she sat in his bathtub. She was naked in another man's house that wasn't her fiancé's, and she hadn't even known the man's real name until ten minutes ago. What was wrong with her?

She reached for the shampoo; a sharp pierce ricocheted through her ribs making her want to cry out in pain. The gold of her ring clanged against the porcelain tub as she gripped the edge and willed the pain to go away, praying nothing was cracked or broken. An intense pain coursed through her when she'd bent to pick up her purse, and a slight twinge had pinched her side when she laughed and shook Tyler's hand, but *this* pain from her twisting was almost unbearable. She must have hit the coffee table harder than she remembered.

After a couple of minutes, when the pain finally subsided, she decided against washing her hair. The sharp, severe discomfort gave her the answer she'd been seeking. She stared at her hand, the giant diamond sparkling back at her. Nothing like the grim life she lived now. Loving Duke had come easy, and so had accepting his proposal. But unlike the glimmer in her ring, their love faded. Taking shelter with Tyler meant living, and facing Duke would be her death.

And despite the nightmare she'd been living for the past six months, something in the big man's eyes gave her hope. Hope for a better life than the one she currently had. There had to be more.

Sinking lower in the water, she slipped off her ring and laid it on the tub, praying Tyler's behavior wasn't a facade like Duke's had been when they first started dating.

CHAPTER SIX

T ank sipped from his water bottle as he sank deeper on the couch, staring at the television. The show he watched flicked on and off as the storm picked up strength.

"Shoot." He clicked the power button on his remote and tossed it on the cushion next to him.

One contingency with living in the middle of nowhere, he had to get used to losing connection to the outside world. Normally, such nuisances didn't bother him, but tonight proved different. He needed something to get his mind off the naked woman in his house. The incredibly attractive and *vulnerable* naked woman.

He rubbed his hands over his face. Who the hell was he kidding? Even if she were in a position to date him, she shouldn't; he was damaged goods.

The bathroom door creaked open and steam billowed into the hall. Annie walked out in his clothes, her curves swallowed by the extra material. She held a rag to her cheek and the bag of mushy peas in her hand.

The fat rock from her finger was gone.

Stepping all over the bottom of his pants, she shuffled closer. The closer she got, the harder he found it to breathe. Gorgeous. Even with all of her bruises.

He placed the bottle on the table and stood. "Sorry those are too big. That's all I had."

"It's okay." She handed him the peas. "I couldn't roll them up. It hurts too much to bend."

The bag suffered from his grip, the pressure threatening to pop the top of the plastic open. "You probably had a surge of adrenaline getting you through, and now it's starting to wear off. Where are you hurting?"

"My side. I fell on the coffee table on the way down." She glanced to the floor.

He motioned to the rag she used to cover her cheek. "Is your face bleeding again?"

"Yeah."

"Here." He led her to the couch. "Sit down. I'll get some supplies."

Slowly, she placed a hand on the armrest and sat. Alfred scooted next to her, licking her palm.

"You want me to push him off you?"

"No." She smiled at the furry suck up. "He's fine."

Tank took the pea mush, stomped toward the kitchen, and tossed the melting bag in the trash. He reached in the freezer for an ice pack then gathered a first aid kit from the upper cabinet, along with a fresh towel from the drawer. Before he walked back into the living room, he took a deep breath and regained his composure.

She deserved more. Better than him, and a hell of a lot better than what she got from that bastard Duke, for damn sure.

Sitting the supplies on the couch, he bent down in front of her.

"What are you doing?"

"I'm going to roll up these pants first. Okay?" He glanced at her for approval.

She simply nodded. Placing her foot on his knee, he rolled the cotton fabric of his sweat pants up. Red toes stared back at him. A small tattoo of a crescent moon and three stars graced her ankle. An urge to keep rolling, explore the rest of her leg, burned inside of him. Instead, he removed his hands and rolled up the other side.

"That's a nice tattoo." He placed her foot on the ground and busied himself with the supplies.

"Thanks."

"What does it mean?" He ripped open a few gauze strips and doused them in peroxide.

"The stars represent my dad, my mom, and me. And for the moon, my dad and I, we used to star gaze at night. The tattoo reminds me of a time when things were different, better."

"You said your dad died, right?"

"Yeah. A few years ago." She wrung the fabric of his too big shirt in her free hand.

"I'm sorry."

"Me, too." She gave him a sad smile. "What about your parents? Where are they?"

"My mom lives just outside of Shreveport, and my dad, well…he's…he's dead, too."

At least in all ways that mattered.

"Oh," her voice wavered. "I'm sorry."

"Yeah, well, things happen." He didn't want to talk about his father. Not yet. Not ever if he could help it.

"May I?" On his knees, he held up his hand and reached for the rag on her face.

She let him take the cloth. The cut began at the top of her

cheekbone and stopped near her nose. Blood oozed out of the slit. He applied the gauze, careful not to apply too much pressure. "I'll do my best, but you may need stitches."

"I can't go to a hospital. He'll know." She squeezed his wrist and stopped him. "Please," she pleaded. "Please, do your best."

Her fear gripped him. Annie reached him in a way no one else ever had. But he knew that the first day he saw her little toes dip into the water. Beauty was special. Always had been.

"Of course." He looked down at his kit, the emotion in her eyes too frightening to face. Terrified, nervous, two feelings he promised himself he would never feel again, and he'd see to it she didn't either. He placed a butterfly bandage against her cheek, and grabbed the icepack. "I'd like to put this around your side if that's okay with you."

"Yeah, I think that's a good idea."

He grabbed the clean washcloth and unfolded it. "I'll put this against your skin, then the ice pack and wrap it up, okay?"

She nodded.

"Where exactly is your side hurting?"

"Right here, on my ribs." Slowly, she raised the shirt and winced, stopping just under her breast. A small freckle dotted her smooth skin, right below where her womanly curves began.

Mercy.

His hands shook. "Okay." He placed the cloth on her skin then dropped it. "Shoot." Bending down, he reached for the rag at the same time she did, their hands grazing again. A tingle seared through his shaky fingers as they each let out a nervous giggle.

She pulled her hand away and sat back upright. Her face contorted in agony. "Oh, man, that hurt."

"Are you okay?" He scanned over her. "You shouldn't bend. Let me take care of you."

She bit her no longer trembling bottom lip and nodded. He'd like to think her trembles subsided because she felt safe. In reality, it was probably because she wasn't wet and cold anymore.

"I'll try again." He straightened the cloth back out, held the rag against her skin, then the pack. "Can you hold this here while I wrap you up? Does it hurt too much?"

"No, it's fine."

She held the pack while he took the bandage and circled her ribs a few times, careful not to let his hands graze her breasts, before securing it to her body.

"There, now." He rubbed his hands against his jeans to try and secure his shake. His traitorous body acted as if it had never touched a woman before. Although he never had touched one quite like her.

"Here." He shook his head to clear his thoughts and reached for the water bottle. "Take this."

"Why?"

Fishing a few pain relievers from his medical supplies, he handed her a couple of pills. "They'll help the pounding your head is sure to be experiencing."

"What is this?" Holding the tablets in her hand palm up, her eyes narrowed as she gazed at the medicine.

"Just a pain reliever. Here's the bottle." He handed her the plastic so she could check the capsules out for herself. Her skepticism of his behavior came as no surprise. Knowing how abusers worked, it was a shock she had trusted him this far. In the beginning, abusers were charming, nice, doing everything they could to hide their true colors. But he was no abuser, and hopefully she could sense that.

"I can go out and get a new bottle if you'd like. I'll leave everything in the packaging and you can open it for yourself."

A crack of lightning lit up the night sky followed by a rumble of thunder. She glanced out the window. "You'd... you'd go out in this storm, all the way to town for a new bottle of medicine?"

"Yeah." He nodded. "I would. For you."

Her chest rose. "I don't...I don't know what to say."

"No need to say anything." He shot to his feet. "I'll get my keys."

"No." Annie grabbed his wrist.

Electricity, as intense as the lightning dancing around his house, ignited his arm. She had to stop touching him or he might burn up. He wanted to pull away, but the feeling was too good, preventing him from doing so. Besides, his personal reasons why he didn't want her touching him had more to do with his shame. It had nothing to do with her. That itself was the problem. He'd begun to want her too much in the short span of what? A week? If he didn't watch himself, she would think that was all he was after. She would label him no better than the scum she left.

"I'll take these. Thank you." Annie tossed the medicine in her mouth and washed them down with water.

By her taking the pills, they were breaking barriers. He swallowed his relief. "Okay, well, it's late, and you're probably tired. You can take my room, and I'll sleep here on the couch. I would offer to change the sheets for you, but I don't have any extras. If you want to stay up another hour or two, I could wash them real quick."

"You don't have a spare bedroom?"

"Yeah, I do, but that's my weight room. No bed in there."

"Then, I'll take the couch. You can have your room."

"Not happening. Besides, I want to be by the front door."

Sure she understood his reasoning, he didn't need to elaborate. "Alfred can sleep with you if you'd like."

"Yeah, I think I would like that."

"Okay, so want to stay up, watch a movie? The cable went out, but I have a large movie collection. You can pick while I start the sheets."

"No, don't do that. I'm sure the sheets are fine, and I'm pretty tired. Rain check?"

His heart shrank, and he lowered his head. "Yeah, sure." He shrugged and glanced back at her. "But before you go to bed, I think we need to move your car to the shed. I'll park my truck in the grass, and I'll lock the garage door so no one can get in."

If she was skeptical about taking his pills, there was a slim chance she would let him lock up her way of escape. But if someone came to his house, they would have no way of knowing she was inside if her car was hidden and secure. Concealing her vehicle was his best option in helping to keep her safe.

"I'll even leave the key to the garage on the counter top in the kitchen. You can get your car out anytime you want, okay?"

The same concerning look from moments ago spread across her face again.

"Or we don't have to lock the garage at all. I just thought—"

"No, you're right. You should lock it up. I'll fetch my keys." She glanced around. "Where's my bag?"

"I put it on the bed in my room." He pointed to the hallway. "Right past the bathroom."

He left her in peace as she walked into his room to get her keys. Her mind had to be spinning right now. His size alone intimated most people. He waited by the front door, giving her plenty of space.

"Here you go." She handed him her keys.

"Thanks." He couldn't fight the small smile that tilted his lips. She'd taken another small step toward trusting him. "I'll be right back."

Rain pelted his back as he ran from his house to the shed. He threw the creaky door open and hopped in his grandpa's old truck. Shoving the key in the ignition, he turned, and the motor rumbled to life. Backing out onto the grass, he quickly parked and switched to her car. The rain poured down faster as lighting flashed all around. He glanced around, but didn't see evidence of anyone. The only thing he could see: trees. Lots and lots of trees.

And about a million places for someone to hide.

He put one leg inside her car; his knee knocked the steering wheel. Reaching for the lever, he pushed the seat back as far as he could in order to fit behind the wheel. Even still, the space was tight.

He cranked the ignition and glanced around her car. Though the interior appeared clean, a slight aura of sausage and grease lingered. How many hours a week did she work at that diner?

Tyler whipped her small car into the shed next to his bike, locked up, and then ran back inside. Alfred howled like mad when he crossed the threshold.

"Calm down, buddy. It's just me." The dog thumped his tail and bumped his booty against the floor as he scooted closer to their guest. "He's already taking his job of protecting you seriously." He handed her the keys to her car.

"I can see that. I'm glad I came." She ran a palm down Al's slick fur.

"We are, too, Annie."

She stopped and stared. The green iris of her good eye penetrated him deep and long. Instinctively, he took a step closer. "You're going to be safe. I promise."

"I know," she whispered. "I trust you." Her eye glazed over before she shifted her gaze downward. "I think I'll go to bed now." Gripping the armrest of the couch, she stood and glanced at him again. A drop of moisture hit her cheek, and he fought the desire to wipe it away. "Thank you, for everything. Really." She reached for his hand and squeezed.

He glanced down at their embrace. His chest tightened like her grip on his hand as he squeezed back. "Good night, Annie."

"Good night, Tyler." She let go and eased down the hall, Alfred following close behind.

With every step she took, the constriction in his chest eased. Annie turned and flashed him a smile before she shut herself and Alfred in his room. He heard the click of his bedroom door then plopped on the couch.

Mercy.

A pounding in his heart and head replaced the clenching in his chest. Even with her bruises, and the ice pack protruding from her side, and all the anger and hurt she'd been through that evening, she trusted him. Pride swam through him, honored she'd put her faith in him with her safety. Problem was, he wasn't sure he trusted his self-control.

She'd always been beautiful to him. A few bruises couldn't change that.

He punched a pillow on the couch a few times, giving it a fluff, dreading the night ahead. His legs hung off the side of the sofa. Bending his knees, he curled up, and grabbed a throw blanket off the back of the couch to toss over himself. While he lay curled in a tight ball, or tight for him, all he could think about was how she lay wrapped up in *his* bed, in *his* sheets, without *him*. He wasn't going to get a lick of sleep. Not. One. Damn. Bit.

And if he were lucky enough to fall asleep, he prayed he didn't wake her with one of his nightmares.

Please, Lord, not tonight.

———

TANK TOSSED and turned all night, dreaming of crescent moons, red toes, and freckles. Thankfully, his regular nightmares stayed at bay. However, dreaming of Annie turned out to be more pleasurable than he would've like. The bulge in his boxers proved as much.

His urge to be with a woman had never been so intense, and he desired the absolute one woman on earth he couldn't have. He promised to protect her. Mixing his desire with his duty was a bad idea. Besides, there was no way she was ready for anything with anyone else right now.

I'm such a dumbass.

The creaking of his bedroom door alerted him Annie was coming. He tossed the blanket over his lap and placed his hands in front of him.

Her hair framed wild around her face, as she wiped sleep from her one good eye. His shirt she wore pulled a little to the right, exposing her shoulder, and her toes peeked out from the bottom of his pants.

Holy shit. He was in trouble.

"Good morning," he squeaked like a pubescent teen. Trying again, he cleared his throat first. "I mean, good morning. Did you sleep okay?" He leaned his torso over his lap to cover up the bulge.

"Yeah," she said through a yawn. "But Alfred snores."

Think about Alfred. Think about Alfred.

His not so little problem started to control itself.

"Sorry about that. Did he disturb you too much?"

"No. Actually, it was the best sleep I've had in months. Even with his little paws kicking me in my arm."

If her having the best sleep in months included a snoring dog kicking her, there was more wrong with the picture than he had imagined. What all had this Duke guy done to her?

"You want some breakfast? I can make bacon and eggs."

"I don't eat pork, but eggs would be great."

"You don't eat pork?"

"No, it tastes weird to me."

"Tastes weird? But you work in a diner, where almost every dish comes with a slab of bacon."

"Yeah, I know. Sandi's been working on me since I started, but I just don't like it." A look of frustration crossed her features.

Shit. Did she see his problem? He glanced down. Little Tank was finally under control.

"What's wrong? Did I pry too much about the bacon?"

"No, no." She shook her head. "It's not that. It's just, I'm supposed to go in to work this morning, and there is no way I can. Not looking like this, and if I do, Duke will be sure to know. I won't be able to escape him."

"Yeah, I thought about some of that last night." One of the ways he tried to get his mind off her crescent moon. Needless to say, it didn't work—completely.

"And?"

"And what?" What had he said? His mind was back on her stars.

"You said you were thinking about me going to work. What did you come up with?"

"Oh, that." *Come on, man. Get it together.* "I agree. Safe

to say you shouldn't be going in to work for a while. You need to heal, Annie, and we need to figure out a game plan before you make any moves."

"You're right." Wrapping her arms around herself, she crossed the room and gently sat on the couch. Al followed and sat on the floor beside her. "I honestly hadn't given much thought to any of this last night. I just ran. I was so scared." Her gaze tilted to the clock on the wall. "Duke should be home from work any minute, and he'll notice I'm not there. Once he realizes I'm not at the diner, either, he'll be so angry." She squeezed herself tighter.

"Your phone." He shot up, his veins pulsing with adrenaline. Little Tank was no longer his concern, but the Big Bad Wolf was. "Annie, where is it?"

"In your room, why?"

"If Duke is as horrible as I think, I'm sure he's got you tracked." Damn it, why didn't he think about this before?

"Oh my. I didn't even think of that."

Heart pounding, he ran into his room. The scent of her perfume had invaded his personal space, and damn if he didn't like it. He pretended like the floral smell of Beauty didn't excite him as he grabbed her cell from his nightstand and rushed back to her.

"You're going to have to turn it off." Another look of concern crossed her features. This was harder than he thought. Everything he did and said seemed to push her boundaries. "Here." He took his own phone off the counter. "You can have mine if it'll make you feel better. At least until we can get you a new one, or figure everything out.

"But you won't have one."

"It's okay. I won't need it. Take it. Really. Besides, most of the time cell service doesn't work all that great out here."

"Well, why do I have to turn mine off then?" She accepted his phone.

"Because, if the satellites or the towers *are* having a good day out here today, we don't want to take the chance of Duke tracking you."

"Okay, you're right." She powered hers down. "I'll need the code for yours."

"One-nine-eight-nine." He turned toward the kitchen, and reached in the refrigerator for the eggs.

"Your birth year?"

"No, the year the best ever Batman movie came out."

"I wouldn't figure you for one of those superhero kind of guys." She placed his phone on the coffee table.

"I'm not." Something else he wasn't ready to talk about— his appreciation for Batman. Not yet.

He set the eggs on the counter and stared at his pup on the floor. Annie's own vigilante standing guard. Alfred's allegiance to him had been totally abandoned the minute the hot blonde walked in the door. Hell, he couldn't blame his four-legged friend, but even vigilante's had to pee. "Come on, Alfred. Go outside." He opened the back sliding glass doors. Al cocked his head sideways then looked back at Annie.

"Go on, boy." She nudged him with her foot. He gave them each a passing glance, then trotted outside, and ran for the water.

"Disloyal dog," he mumbled, then shut the door. "How many eggs do you want?" He stepped back into the kitchen and grabbed a bowl.

"Two." She walked around the counter and took the bowl from him. "I can do that."

"You don't have to."

"I know, but you didn't have to take me in and you did."

She gave him another sultry smile and his pulse quickened. He took a few steps back.

"Okay, well, then, I'm going to go and get dressed. I'll be out in a few minutes."

"Is scrambled fine?"

"Scrambled?"

"Eggs." She pointed to the carton. "Will you eat your eggs scrambled?"

"Oh, yeah. Sure." He scratched his head and turned down the hall. His brain was scrambled standing next to her. Good God, what had he gotten himself into? He needed a cold shower. Quick.

He glanced at her again. His shirt fell lower down her shoulder as she cracked the eggs.

Little Tank throbbed under his boxers.

Damn.

This was going to be a long, cold shower.

CHAPTER SEVEN

Tank towel dried his hair as he entered the living room. Alfred wagged his tail in greeting.

"You didn't stay out long," he said to his dog.

"He was waiting by the back door," Annie explained. "So I let him in. That's okay, isn't it?"

"Of course. Usually he stays out for hours. He's taking his guard dog duties seriously." He glanced at the table. She had set their plates and poured each of them a cup of coffee. "Wow, this looks great."

"Black, just like you like it." She pointed to the coffee cup and stood beside the table. "I just didn't know where you sat, so I decided I'd wait until you came out. I cleaned the table off and moved the sales papers over to the counter top. I hope that's okay. And I can move the plates if mine is in the wrong spot."

Wrong spot? He glanced at the table and into his kitchen. Tidy. Clean. He could get used to this—but not for the reason she obviously believed. He never wanted her to think she had to cook and clean for him.

"No, it's fine." He motioned to the plates. "I don't have a

spot. You can sit wherever you want." He walked up to the table. "Thank you for making breakfast, but you should be taking it easy. Not cleaning my kitchen."

"It's nothing." She blushed. He gathered she wasn't used to getting many compliments.

"Are you sure I can sit here?" She pointed to the chair.

He pulled it out for her. "I don't say things I don't mean, remember." He gave her a slight smile and motioned for her to take her seat.

"Yeah." She turned her head down. "I remember." Her blush grew.

He'd embarrassed her. *Good job, jackass.*

He pushed her chair in and took the seat opposite of her. Alfred lay on the floor beside him. "Annie, I've thought about your situation more and what the best plan for you is."

"Please." She held up her hand. "Don't say anymore. I know I've overstayed my welcome already. I'll leave after breakfast."

Leave?

That's not at all what he was getting at.

"No, that's not what I mean. Staying here is no problem. I meant plan for your safety for the long term. We need to get the police involved."

She stopped her coffee cup short of her mouth as her shoulders tensed. "No." With trembling hands, she placed her mug back down. Coffee sloshed over the rim. "Absolutely not. I know Duke. He'll charm his way out of trouble, and if he can't talk his way out of it, his dad will for him, or pay his way out of trouble. Telling on him won't do me any good." Her voice grew louder. "Why do you think I didn't go to the police before I came here?"

There was her passion again, but for the wrong reasons.

"Okay. I'm sorry. I didn't mean to upset you. We'll do

this your way, but at least, *please*, let's get the Blue Guardians involved."

"The Blue Guardians?" Wariness grew in her voice.

"You've seen biker guys around town wearing their leathers with a patch of an angel, right?"

"Yeah. Sandi even mentioned she'd started dating one. I've waited on a few of them, but I tried to steer clear of them as much as possible. Duke always got upset when I tended their tables. Said they were thugs, and he always accused me of flirting. To avoid his wrath, I would avoid the Guardians."

Of course. Duke *would* scare her away of the one group that could help her.

"They're not thugs, but bikers, who help protect women and children from abuse. JoJo, the girl with me last night, she's a Guardian."

Funny. His first impression of JoJo seemed far more devil than guardian angel, but the little woman pulled through when he needed help.

"She's a Guardian? Not your girlfriend?"

His girlfriend?

"No. Lord no. JoJo is a friend, an acquaintance really. Nothing more."

"Oh." She sat up a bit straighter.

"They can help you, Annie. We should get them involved."

"No." She pushed her chair away from the table and stood. Her face grimaced at the movement. "I'll figure this out on my own. The more people I tell, the more of a chance it'll get back to Duke."

"Annie." He reached for her shaky hand and gave it a gentle caress. This wasn't exactly the way he wanted to touch her, but he would take what he could get. "Please." He stood next to her. "I know I've just met this group, but I don't think you have anything to worry about. Their job, their mission, is to protect abused woman and children. If you can trust anyone in this town, it would be them. All you have to do is ask."

She glanced up at him, her eyes pleading for some sort of truth, safety in his words. "You really think it's a good idea?" she whispered.

"I do."

The group could give her some guidance on how to handle her situation. Better than he could. The more she looked at him with those frightened green eyes, and the lower his shirt inched on her shoulder, the more he found it hard to concentrate.

Shit. This really was a bad idea after all.

"Okay," she said, her voice still low, and her gaze never left his.

His body moved closer to hers as her stare passed between his eyes and his lips. She lifted her head faintly, her lips opening in the slightest part, still and ready to be kissed.

Was he going to do this?

He felt his body leaning closer.

He was going to do this.

The tease of her red toenails and that freckle near her breast had him dreaming of X-rated things all night. The caress of her tongue, the softness of her lips, he'd wanted to taste it all. Had since he was a child. He leaned in, and eased her good cheek in his hand, her hair prickling his fingertips. His lips ready to caress hers, she let out a slight moan, and reached closer. He took his hands and gently guided her body closer, flush with his.

Boom. Boom. Boom.

The pounding rocked through his chest, just as it did the front door. Annie pulled back and threw her hands to her mouth as she let out a gasp. Her eyes refilled with fear as Alfred let out a wail of barks.

Damn it.

He placed one finger over his lips in a silent motion to tell her to be quiet and glanced around for a weapon, anything. Only thing of any use would be a lamp. His fist would work better. Inching over to the living room window, he placed his back against the wall and peeked out of the curtain.

Father, JoJo, and Steele stood on his front porch. *The kid.* They were supposed to go see a child today. Exhaling, he let go of the window covering, and stared back at Annie. Tears filled her eyes, her hand still to her mouth.

"You don't have anything to worry about," he assured her, and reached for the door handle. "Help has arrived."

ANNIE MOVED her hands from her mouth to her chest and stared at the three people standing on the other side of the threshold. Her fear of who stood outside nearly paralyzed her, while her heart tried to pulverize her chest cavity with its breakneck beating. Wiping the tears from her eyes, she sucked in a sniffle and let out a deep breath. There had to be a better way to live.

She stared back at Tyler, and a look of care filled his eyes. Too much care. She had to be more cautious. She'd almost kissed the big delicious muscle right there in his kitchen. So what, she'd had a crush on him when she was a girl or even now for that matter? Her situation wasn't child's play, and the way he stared at her said he wasn't playing either. Her bruises were in full pain, and her body ached from the gentle movements of trying to reach up to Tyler. She wanted to end a relationship, not start one.

Thank God the Guardians came when they had despite the fact she didn't want them there. Now not only did she have to worry about these emotions surging, more like raging through her, she had to worry about three new people knowing where she hid out.

Alfred stepped back from the doorframe and barked another round.

"Hush, Al. Go outside," Tyler demanded.

The dog stopped his barking, and the crew parted to the side to let Alfred pass.

"Holy shit, what the hell happened to you?" JoJo asked as she crossed the threshold.

Her hair popped out of a red bandana and fell in a dark braid down the side of her neck. Big hoop earrings adorned her ears, and her composure looked as stiff as her leather jacket. A blue angel hugged her arm sleeve. The other two men must be Guardians, too.

"Annie, you remember JoJo?"

"Yeah." Annie held a hand to her eye.

JoJo's stare was a little too intense and too personal for their second time meeting. Then again, Annie had almost gotten *real* personal with a man she barely knew a few minutes ago.

She moved her hand and decided to let them stare. If their job was to protect women and children from abuse, then her bruises were nothing they hadn't already seen.

"Wow, that's horrible," the older man she recognized as her boss' boyfriend said, while the younger guy just stood there, doing his best *not* to stare.

"Annie this is Father and that's Steele." Tyler pointed to the two men.

"Nice to meet you." Steele said, still trying not to stare at her eye.

Uncomfortable with everyone being uncomfortable, she decided to do what she did best. Disappear.

"Why don't you all sit down, and I'll make you some breakfast." She pointed to the kitchen table.

"No way." Steele shook his head. "Not happening. No way are you cooking for us." He led her to a chair at the table and helped her ease into it. "You sit. I'll cook." The Guardian gave her a subtle wink.

Her stomach gave a little flip at the man's attention.

Tyler nudged in next to Steele, his broad shoulders pushing the man two steps to the left. Tyler reached for his breakfast plate and moved it and himself. Right next to her.

The flips in her stomach had turned into full-blown somersaults.

"You cook, man?" Tyler asked.

Steele slapped him on the shoulder then eased into the kitchen. "I've been known to make a mean omelet every once in a while at the firehouse."

A firefighter. This man held the looks and the occupation *most* girls would swoon over. Yet, she still sat upright, and, instead, stared at the beefcake beside her.

"Firehouse?" Tyler asked. "That explains the smoke smell from last night. I thought you were a perpetual chain smoker."

"No, man." Steele's back stiffened. "I *never* touch the stuff." His tone didn't leave room for question. He avoided everyone's gaze as he began opening drawers.

Weird.

And now that Tyler mentioned it, Steele did have a subtle hint of smoke to his skin.

"Need me to show you where things are?" Tyler broke the tension in the room.

"Nope. I got it. You and the lady sit and eat before your

breakfast gets cold. I'll get Father, JoJo, and myself something whipped up in no time."

"I'm going to grab a cup of coffee. I haven't had enough caffeine for what I've just walked into." Father grabbed a clean coffee mug out of the dish drainer.

"I was just about to call you." Tyler glanced at JoJo. "How did you find me?"

"Your background check had your address on it," she said in an everyone-in-the-world-is-a-moron cadence.

The woman was turning out to be a little ball of delightfulness.

"Oh, yeah. That's right," he said as if JoJo's tone didn't faze him.

"You mentioned wanting to meet Nathaniel, the boy we discussed at our meeting last night." Father poured coffee into the mug. "JoJo tried to call the number you gave us, but it wouldn't go through. She remembered you mentioning you lived out this way, figured you might not have good cell service, so we all decided we would enjoy the morning breeze on our bikes and see if we could find you. I must say, without the address, it would have been easy to get lost out here."

Annie sat back and listened. Tyler had just discussed needing to call the Guardians. For a moment, she'd thought he'd done so behind her back before he okayed it with her, but listening in, that wasn't the case. He hadn't done anything so far she hadn't agreed to. The tension in her shoulders eased.

"Well, you found me." Tyler picked up a piece of bacon, and his arm grazed hers with his movement.

Annie found the closeness to him comforting, a feeling she hadn't felt in a long time. She should scoot over. Give him some space, but that would put her closer to JoJo. She stayed put.

"I'd love to go meet Nathaniel with you," he continued, "but I don't think it's a good idea to leave Annie here by herself."

A metallic clang, then the crunch of shells cracking sounded behind her. She swiveled her head.

Steele whisked the yolks with a fork then slid the eggs into a frying pan. "I agree, man. Annie, until you can file a restraining order, you shouldn't be alone."

"No!" She whipped her gaze to Tyler. He and his friends needed to understand she was serious. "No cops, okay? My fiancé, Duke, is the Chief."

"Yeah, well, some Chief of Police we've got then." Father sat. "Annie, you need help. You need protection."

"I know, but what good is a restraining order going to do me? Duke is the police. And when he gets in one of his rages, nothing will stop him. Not the police, and certainly not a useless piece of paper."

"She's right," JoJo piped in.

Finally, someone began to take her seriously, and it was the moody female of all people. Annie flipped her gaze to the woman. JoJo's hard stare screamed no nonsense. A quality Annie could appreciate right now.

"I hate to say this, sweetheart, but you only have yourself to rely on."

Anxiety, as heavy as a brick, sank in her gut. The words were true, and the exact reason why she hadn't done anything in the past. She wasn't strong enough.

"No, she doesn't." Tyler leaned back and snaked his arm around the back of her chair.

He stared at her. His gaze held the same intensity it had by the front door, and the brick in her stomach wanted to leap up into her throat. Or maybe that was her heart, with its erratic beating again. Her knees knocked and her hands trembled, for entirely different reasons than minutes before.

In a voice loud enough for everyone in the room to hear, he said, "She's got me."

Oh, snap. Her heart pounded faster, while her head grew lighter.

"And me."

Thankful for the distraction, she broke their intense stare and watched as Steele waved a spatula in the air from behind the stovetop.

"And the rest of the Guardians." Father's voice had her turn her head toward him. "But Annie, you need a plan."

A plan. The same thing Tyler mentioned earlier, and it was the absolute one thing she did not have. Along with anywhere else to go or much money.

Shit, my job.

And if she didn't talk to her boss, she wouldn't even have that.

"Oh, no. What time is it?" She darted her gaze around the room for a clock.

"It's a little after eight, why?" Tyler asked.

"I'm supposed to be at work in fifteen minutes. I forgot to call Sandi to tell her I can't come in."

"Don't worry about Sandi." Father leaned back in his chair. "I'll talk to her."

"Talk to her?" She turned to the man. "What do you mean talk to her? Nobody can know what's going on. If they do, and it gets back to Duke, he'll be so angry and embarrassed. He might…well I don't know what he might do."

The fear she tried to bottle all morning surged through her. If she publically embarrassed Duke, she might not just have a gun barrel pointed to her head—he could actually pull the trigger next time.

"Relax, sweetheart." Father reached across the table for her hand. "Sandi already knew what was going on."

"She did?" She and Tyler asked at the same time.

"How long has she known?" she asked.

"A while. Sandi didn't know what to say, that's why she dropped the hint that she was dating *me*. She'd hoped you would come and seek help."

It all made sense now. Duke keeping her away from the Guardians, and Sandi talking about Father. Only, anytime the Guardians were mentioned, she'd turn away from the conversation or purposely change the subject. All because she was afraid of what Duke would do or say if he found out she even entertained a conversation about the motorcycle *thugs*.

The bastard.

"Why do you think she agreed to you working all those hours?" Father asked. "She's been worried about you since you started dating Duke, but she didn't want to do anything or say anything that might put you in harm's way more than you already were. The woman's been begging me to talk to you, but every time I came around the diner, Duke was there. Also, it's a Guardian rule. Abused adults have to come to us and ask for help. Still, I didn't realize it was this bad. I'm sorry, Annie. I truly am." Father squeezed her hand. "But you have the Guardians help if you want it."

She glanced around the table and into the kitchen. Steele had placed three perfect omelets on three plates, and offered her a smile. JoJo sat back in her chair and crossed her arms. A fierce look of determination thwarted her features, and the little lady looked like she was ready to start kicking ass and taking names.

When Annie glanced back at Tyler, her body tingled. He was big and strong, and sitting next to him made her feel safe. For the first time in months, she didn't feel scared. With his

arm still wrapped around the back of her chair, he stared at
her with such a fierce loyalty. She felt an odd connection,
almost as if he spoke to her soul through his eyes. With him
by her side, she was strong enough. Strong enough to leave
Duke.

Fight for a better life.

"What do you say, Miss Annie?" Steele asked. "You want
us to help you?"

She cocked a glance to the chef and his friends before
staring back at the blue irises that made a strange warmth
flow through her. A warmth she could get used to, and a
feeling worth fighting for.

"Yeah." She nodded. "I do."

CHAPTER EIGHT

D uke parked his cruiser on the street and grabbed the flower arrangement sitting on the passenger seat. He'd wanted to come home in the middle of the night, check on Annie, but some damn mom called about her son being abused. So what if the father knocked the kid around a bit? Hell, the little shit probably deserved it. Kids these days lacked respect and needed a firm hand.

Still, in order to be considered for Sherriff, he had to dot all of his I's and cross his T's when people were watching. And because of the event, he'd been stuck trying to catch up on paperwork all night long.

Damn campaign.

Damn dad.

He rolled his shoulders and marched to the door.

The space from Annie actually did him some good. Made him realize he may have been a little harsh with her. She wasn't used to being submissive, but she would learn. He would just have to teach her how a good wife should act before they got married.

He keyed in through the front door and punched in the

alarm. The usual aroma of morning coffee didn't hang in the air. "Annie? I'm home, babe."

Silence echoed through the house.

"Where are you, honey?" He walked into the bedroom. The bed lay perfectly made. "Damn it." Racing to the window, he looked for her car in the carport. Missing.

"Bitch."

She'd gone into work after he had told her not to. How was she going to hide the cut on her face? Say she fell? No one would believe her. Her lapse of judgment would ruin his image.

He pulled out his cellphone. His heart pounded as her phone went straight to voicemail. She never turned her cell off. Thumbing through his contacts, he clicked on the diner's number.

"Sandi's," the owner's voice greeted over the receiver.

"Hey, Sandi, this is Chief Fields." He kept his voice smooth and low. The same voice he wooed Annie with to get her into bed. "I'm trying to get a hold of Annie. Is she there yet?"

"Just got off the phone with her. She called in sick today, Chief. *Surely*, you would know that." The older woman's voice oozed with condemnation.

What the hell did she know? Annie might be stupid at times, but she wouldn't tell anyone about their relationship. She would destroy everything he'd worked so hard for if she opened her fat mouth.

Taking in a deep breath, he warned himself to play it cool. "Oh, I hate to hear that. I haven't made it home from work yet, so when I get there, I'll be sure to take extra care of her."

"Yeah, I'm sure you will." The woman hung up.

He clicked his phone off and glanced around the room. Nothing looked out of place. Stomping into the closet, he checked her clothes. Her overnight bag still hung on the hook. From the evidence, it looked like Annie had just went somewhere and forgot to charge her phone, but a nagging feeling sat in the pit of his stomach.

He stomped back through the living room. Her locket lay on the floor where she had fallen. She never left without her locket. He raced into the kitchen, the hook on the wall sat empty. Her purse—missing. He pulled the pig head off the cookie jar. Her tip money—gone.

"Fuck!" he screamed as he tossed the top of the jar. Glass shards scattered over the floor.

Not able to track her because she had her phone off, he pushed some buttons on his own phone to alert him when she came back on radar. She could run, but she couldn't hide. He would find her, and when he did, he would be sure to teach her how a wife of his was supposed to behave.

First things first, he had to get to the bank and get all of her money. Assuming she hadn't done that already. A few hundred dollars in tips wouldn't take her far, and with no family and nowhere to go, she would come back. She'd have to.

And when she did, he would be waiting.

CHAPTER NINE

Tank straddled his bike and grabbed his bandana out of the saddlebag. As much as he didn't want to leave Annie, helping an abused child was important, too. This was what he moved to Black Widow to do.

"Are you sure you're going to be okay?" He tied the Batman symbol around his head. "I know JoJo doesn't come off as the friendliest, but deep down, she seems good."

"Yeah, of course. I'll be fine." Annie offered him a small smile and shrugged her shoulder—the bare shoulder that he so desperately wanted to kiss—as she stood beside him.

Mercy. He placed his hands on his handles and squeezed. Hard.

"Besides, I've got my guard dog right here." She patted Al on the top of his head.

His dog had his tongue sticking out and his eyes rolling to the back of his head from her affection. Tank couldn't blame the pup. His eyes would probably roll to the back of his head from her affection, too.

"I think JoJo is a good person to have on my side," she added, breaking his thoughts.

While his Guardian friend was doing him a favor sitting with Annie, he still wanted to be the man for the job. The tension in his hands shot through his body. "Listen, Annie, I won't be long, okay? I'll bring us back some lunch, and we can talk some more."

She nodded. "Yeah, okay."

"Your keys are on the counter top if you decide you want to leave. I don't want to make you feel trapped or stranded, but please, Annie…" He stared at the mouth he longed to kiss and brought his voice to a whisper. "Please, don't leave. At least until we can make sure you are safe."

He saw the rise of her chest and the twinkle in her eye.

"I won't."

He breathed a small sigh of relief. She would stay, at least until he got back.

The rumble of motorcycles broke the moment. She shifted her gaze toward the other two men and took a step back.

"You ready, son?" Father yelled over the noise.

Boy, does this man have shitty timing.

"Yeah," he yelled back and cranked his ignition. "I'm ready."

"Let's go." The leader pointed toward the road and zoomed ahead, Steele following close behind.

Tank glanced back at the house where JoJo waited inside.

"You should go," Annie said. "They're leaving you."

"Yeah, you're right. I should." Turning his head, he spotted the two men waiting at the end of his drive. Something, according to Steele, they didn't do.

He glanced back at Beauty and held out his hand. "Do you trust me?"

She watched him, hesitant. The frightened woman from last night showed herself again. Of course she didn't trust him. He began to pull his hand back, when she reached out and grasped it. The tingling flew through his arm.

"I do." She squeezed his fingers, and the movement shot to his heart.

"Good." Gently, he embraced her hand, and dropped it before he pulled her closer. He wanted to kiss her, show her what a real man felt like, but not now. Not yet. It was too soon, for both of them. The moment in the kitchen they shared…poor judgment on his part. She needed time.

He reached for his helmet, tossed it on, and sped down his drive, putting space between them before he changed his mind about kissing her. The faster he did his duty for the day, the faster he could get back to her.

———

TANK FOLLOWED Father and Steele up a cracked sidewalk. A pot of red flowers hung by a rafter from the top of the porch. The screen door had a hole in the mesh the size of a baseball.

Kid probably got a beating for that.

Father put a hand out to stop him at the top of the steps. "We always give plenty of space between the door and us. If we stand too close, people, especially women, get turned off. They are less likely to answer if they feel threatened or pressured."

"Makes sense."

Tyler took another step down so he and Father were eye level. If he appeared shorter, maybe he wouldn't look so menacing.

"And take off your bandana. We try to look as gentlemanly as possible when we handle a situation like this."

Tank did as he was told, and slid the cloth in his front pocket.

Steele opened the screen and racked his knuckles across the wooden door. "I'll take it," he said as he stepped back by the stairs.

"Sure." Father nodded. The man leaned his head closer to Tank and whispered, "Just follow our lead, okay?"

"Got it."

"And smile for Christ's sake."

He flashed Father his teeth, and the man backed up.

"Not a grimace," he whispered. "I said a smile, damn it."

He softened his features as a sinking feeling settled in his gut. He could do this. He would help this kid. From the looks of the neighborhood—nice cars in the driveway, middle class homes—it wasn't a place someone would suspect child abuse. Then again, abuse didn't discriminate amongst class.

A brunette woman opened the door. She wore a light pink tank top and jeans. The lady was close to the same size and stature as Annie, but the resemblance stopped there. From the woman's face, she appeared to be in her late twenties or early thirties. A fresh, purple bruise covered her bicep. Imprint of a thumb. The coloring reminded him of Annie's swollen eye.

He tightened his fists then immediately loosened them. If the lady would of noticed, he might have frightened her. Instead, he concentrated on smiling.

Don't grimace. Don't grimace.

She glanced over the three of them, and straightened her shoulders. "Can I help you, gentleman?"

"Umm…hello, ma'am." Steele rubbed the back of his neck, his cool demeanor slipping for a second. "My name is Blake Steele." He held a hand to his chest then pointed to each of them. "And this is Jack Grimes and Tyler Wilde."

Jack? The fact Father had a real name never occurred to him. He glanced back at the long-haired man. He did kind of look like a Jack. Kind of.

"And you're Ma..." The fireman cleared his throat. "Mary Franks, right?"

What the hell was wrong with him? Did all women make him stutter?

"Yeah?" She gave him a questioning look.

"We're with a group called The Blue Guardians. Have you ever heard of us or seen us around town?"

Mary glanced over Steele and Father's vests. "Yeah, I've seen a few of you guys around, but a nurse at the hospital this morning told me about you. Said you guys could be trusted, and I could go to you for help. She also mentioned you guys even visit kids in the hospital sometimes."

"Yes, ma'am. If we get enough notice and have permission, we do." Steele seemed to have found his regular voice again. "Our group's mission is to help protect women and children who've been abused. We got word from one of our members yesterday that your son has been hurt, and someone from the hospital called Jack this morning stating the same thing. We just came to see if we could offer any help."

"Yeah?" Mary let out a sigh. "Well, we sure could have used your help last night." She pushed the screen door open wider. "Would you men like a glass of sun tea?"

"That'd be nice, ma'am. Thank you." Steele gave her a side smile.

Tank imagined that smile came in handy for the firefighter every once in a while.

He followed the Guardians into the living room. A little boy, about seven or eight, sat on the couch, hugging his teddy bear, his stare glued to some animated cartoon on television. The child didn't bother giving them a glance.

Nathaniel.

For a moment, Tank saw himself sitting there.

Yes, he *could* help this little boy.

"You men can have a seat at the table." Mary pointed into the small kitchen area to her right. She walked ahead of them and grabbed three glasses out of the cupboard.

Tank followed the guys, all the while trying to catch another glance at the boy.

"He won't talk to you," the mother said. "He's scared."

"Where is the father now?" he asked.

"Jail." Mary dumped ice into the three glasses. "We had another altercation last night. I didn't know he was abusing Nathaniel. I swear I didn't." She stopped putting ice into the glass and gripped the counter tops. Her knuckles matched his moments before.

He ached for Mary, and a part of him wished his mother were here to console her. No one could offer advice to a mother better than another mother.

Steele rushed to the woman's side and placed a hand on her shoulder. "It's okay. You're safe now. We're here to protect you. Both of you."

She glanced at Steele, then him and Father, and nodded her head. She wiped a tear away, and took in a deep breath. When she went to reach for the pitcher on the windowsill, her hands shook so much she nearly dropped the jug.

"Let me do that." Steele reached for the tea and poured the three glasses.

"Thanks." The nervous woman leaned back against the counter. "Craig, he's hit me some, but I swear I had no idea he did it to Nathaniel until this past week," her voice wavered, and she glanced into the living room to see if her son could hear their conversation. "Sure, Nate would have a bruise here and there, but he's a boy. I just thought he was doing what boys do, ya know? Being a kid, getting dirty, that sort of thing. It wasn't until he tossed the baseball through the screen door that

I realized Craig's anger didn't stop or even start with me."

"Start?" Father asked before he sat.

Tyler followed the man's lead.

Mary glanced back into the living room. "Nathaniel is my stepson. His mother died during childbirth. I've raised him since he was four."

Perhaps that's why she didn't know he was being abused. She wasn't the child's real mother, but the notion didn't set well with him. Even the best actress in the world couldn't fake the care and concern this woman seemed to show for her son.

"When was the baseball accident?" he asked.

"Last week." Mary turned to look out the window. "Nathaniel's a good kid. He didn't deserve to be hit like that."

"No one deserves to be abused, Mary," Father said in a low voice.

Her shoulders relaxed at his tone. No wonder the man was the leader; he probably learned to talk like that in school.

"Maybe so, but especially not Nathaniel. He's not my blood child, but he's my boy, and that's all he was doing. Being a boy. He and a neighborhood kid were playing catch. The other kid didn't catch the ball, and off it sailed through the screen and into the living room." Her grip remained firm on the countertop's edge.

"Craig popped Nathaniel so hard across the face, it's no wonder he didn't pass out. I picked up the phone to call the police, but Craig knocked the phone out of my hand and stormed out. He disappeared for a few nights. He'd never been gone so long before. I thought maybe something happened to him."

"Did you ever call the police about him missing?" Tank took the tea glass Steele offered.

"No." Mary glanced at him and shook her head. "Is it mean to say I hoped something bad had happened to him? If the police looked for him and found him, well then, they would send him right back home. I didn't want him here."

"But since something happened again last night, I'm guessing he came back, right?" Father asked.

"Yeah. Things got pretty bad." The mother stopped and took in another breath.

"Take your time," Steele suggested. "You don't have to talk about this if you don't want to."

She shook her head. "No, I want to."

"Here, have a seat." The firefighter crossed the kitchen and pulled out a chair for her. She followed and sat down.

"While Craig was away, I had some time to talk to Nathaniel. He'd been extra quiet lately. He's seven. I thought maybe it was just a difficult time for him, being between the little boy stage and big boy. He's starting to get homework from school, so I thought maybe he was just tired. But after asking him a few questions, I realized all the times Nathaniel would clam up and not talk were times after Craig had hit him. I was always at work or out grocery shopping whenever it happened."

Typical abuser. They hurt someone a fraction of their size to make them feel in control, dominant, important. He gripped his tea glass tighter. If this Craig man had been home, he would have chunked it at the man's head. Then again, that wouldn't make him any better than Craig. And he would *never* be an abuser.

Mary continued, "I asked Nate why he never told me, and he said it was because he was scared if he told, Craig would hit him or me more. I didn't know he knew Craig hit me. He always did it in private, and I tried to hide the bruises. I didn't want Nathaniel to know." Her pained gaze turned to her arm.

"Turns out, I wasn't doing a very good job of disguising my problems. Today, I guess I didn't see much of a point." She sighed and fought back another tear. "Can you imagine? Your seven-year-old not coming to you because he was worried of being hit more? No child should have to go through that. I know he's not mine, but I would give anything for him. I suppose that's why I didn't know Craig abused Nathaniel. I'm not his real mother. I don't have that mother's intuition everyone always talks about."

Steele grabbed a paper towel off the counter and handed it to her. "I'm sure that's not true, Mary. I'm sure you're a great mother."

"I agree," Tank said, echoing Steele. His thoughts had been accurate. This woman was no fake. She loved the little boy sitting on the sofa.

"Thanks. A month ago, I might have agreed with you. Now, I'm not so sure." She dabbed her eyes.

His heart broke more for her. He imagined at one time his own mother had some of the same mixed emotions this woman faced now.

When Mary stopped crying, he pried more. "What happened last night?"

"Craig came back all apologetic. Said he would never do it again. Even tried to apologize to Nathaniel, but Nate didn't care. That little boy in there"—she pointed into the living room—"that boy who's always been so full of love, looked at his father with sheer hate. I can't blame him. I hate Craig, too, but he's not my father. No boy should hate his father."

He glanced back at the kid, the bear still tight to his chest. At least this little man would never have to suffer again.

"Anyway, I told Craig I had talked to a lawyer, and I was in the process of filing for a divorce, as well as seeking custody of Nathaniel. He went ballistic. Started throwing things, threatening to kill me. Nathaniel got scared and ran to our neighbors'. They called the cops. Craig's in jail today. My only hope is he stays there, and Nate stays with me. Forever."

"Since your husband is in jail, and the counselor from the hospital called, then I can assume you had to talk to the police. It's how protocol goes," Father explained.

"Yes, so did Nathaniel. Well, as much as the counselor could coax out of him to tell the police at least. We just got home not too long ago from the hospital. Craig's going to trial. I hope the bastard gets a long time in prison, and loses his rights to Nathaniel."

"So do I, Mary," Tank said. Blood or not, love couldn't be hidden. And just because Craig was Nathaniel's biological father didn't mean he was a real father. There had to be someone better out there for this little boy.

"Mary, we'll help you as much as we can. We want you to know that." Steele sat next to her at the dining table.

"We can position men outside your door twenty-four seven," Father informed her. "But seeing as how Craig still has full custody of Nathaniel, we can't relocate you guys. That would be considered kidnapping. Another downside is if Craig gets out of jail on bond, then we wouldn't be able to stand guard either. Since this is his house, he would say we were trespassing."

"I appreciate your help." Mary reached out and patted Father's hand. "But there is no need to worry. The judge took away any chance of bail. Something about him being a threat to possible witnesses. Which is true, and the only person harming us was Craig. As long as he is locked away, then we're okay."

"If there is anything we can do, let us know, okay?" Father asked.

"Sure. My parents are wiring me the money for a divorce.

If all goes as planned, I'll be moving to a place a little smaller, a little cheaper. If you guys want to lift some boxes, well, I suppose when I do move, I could use your help."

"That's a promise," Father said.

"Ma'am." Tank glanced back at the boy. "I know you said Nathaniel doesn't talk much after the incidents, but if it's okay with you, I'd like to try."

The woman gave him a dubious look. "By all means, but don't be too disappointed if you can't get through to him. The counselor barely got ten words out of him all morning."

He stood. "Thank you."

Father placed a hand on his arm and raised an eyebrow. "You sure about this?"

"Trust me, Counselor." Tank slapped the man on the arm.

"I'll introduce you." Mary stood and escorted him to the living room. She sat next to her son and rubbed a hand through his hair. "Hey, Nate, baby, these men are here to talk to you. This is Tyler. He's nice."

"I don't want to talk." Nathaniel sulked and sunk lower into the sofa.

"I know, baby. Why don't you just listen, okay?"

The kid looked up at his stepmom and nodded. A bruise covered his cheek and grazed his hairline. Tank's chest tightened.

"Thanks, sweetie." Mary kissed her son on the head and stood. "I'll go back to the kitchen with the other two men. I'll just be right there, honey." The mom pointed to the kitchen table. She gave Tank a side-glance and ambled back toward Steele and Father.

When she was out of earshot, Tank took a slow step closer. "Hey, Nathaniel," he said, keeping his voice gentle and low. He didn't want to scare the kid before he really began. "May I sit here?" He pointed to the recliner next to the couch.

Nathaniel kept his head low, but gave the chair a side-glance and yielded the briefest head nod. Carefully, Tank sat.

A picture of the boy and a man sat on the sofa table.

"Is this your dad?" He pointed to the picture.

The kid glanced over and pouted his lower lip. "I don't have a dad anymore."

The pain of losing a father ran deep inside of him. He swallowed the anger and sadness and focused on the kid.

"I hear you like to play baseball. Is that true?" Tank asked, changing the subject.

The boy stared at the floor and gave a shoulder shrug.

"Yeah, I like baseball okay, but my favorite sport is football." He leaned in and whispered, "Can I tell you a secret, Nathaniel?"

The boy cut his glare back to him.

Tank took that as his cue to continue. "See, I'm from Louisiana, so I'm a Saints fan myself. I've only lived in Black Widow a couple of weeks, but since we are so close to Houston, I see lots of Texans gear. I like it here in Black Widow, but if I tell those guys in the kitchen I'm a Saints fan, they may not let me stay in their group. Don't tell them, okay?" He pointed to the men in the kitchen.

The boy looked him straight in the eye. "Okay."

"You promise?"

The kid nodded.

"Whew." He grabbed his bandana out of his pocket and swooped the rag over his forehead. "Good. Glad to get that off my chest."

Nathaniel stared at the cloth. "What's that?"

"This?" He unfolded his bandana and held it up so

Nathaniel could see. "It's my Batman. I take him everywhere I go."

"Why?"

"He helps remind me of what I've gone through." He stared at the logo. "And it helps me not be so scared anymore. When I was a boy, I had a bad father, too."

"You did?"

"Yeah, I did. He used to give me some bruises, kinda like that one on your cheek."

Nathaniel ducked his head and whispered, "How did you fight him?"

"I didn't. I was too scared. My mom tried to protect me just like yours did."

"Mary's not my real mom. I don't have a real mom or a dad anymore." Nate glanced down at his bear.

Nathaniel felt orphaned...at seven. Another experience no child should go through.

"Mary loves you. She wants to be your real mom, and she wants to make sure you never get hurt again."

"Is that what your mom did? Make sure you never got hurt again?"

"Yeah." He nodded. "She did, or at least she tried real hard to make sure I never did, and my dad went away to a place where he couldn't hurt me anymore."

"Prison?"

How does a seven year-old know about prison? As much as it pained him that the kid had a rough start, he wouldn't lie to him. "Yeah, my dad went to prison."

"I hope my dad goes there."

"Me, too, son." He wrung his bandana in his hands. "My dad, he made me feel real bad about myself for a long time. Then, one day, I decided I never wanted to feel like that again, and I wouldn't allow him to have that control over me."

"What did you do?"

"I began to lift weights. I grew big and strong, and I swore to myself I'd never be hurt again." Tank wrapped his bandana around his head.

"Why do you wear it on your head like that?

"Not only is this a reminder." He pointed to the kerchief. "But it's also my head gear. When I ride my motorcycle, I like to have something to hold my hair in place." He tapped the top of his head. "I don't want it to get messed up. You know, I gotta impress the ladies." Not like his short hair could really get mussed, but Nate seemed to like his reasoning.

"You have a bike?" The kid's eyes widened innocent and pure.

God, he prayed there was still some innocence left in this child.

"Yep. Sure do. In fact, we all do. You want to go see them?"

Nathaniel nodded as a slight smile touched his lips.

Tank's stomach flipped. As anxious as he had felt to get back to Annie, being here, doing this with Nathaniel had been the right choice. He'd helped this kid smile.

"Okay." He clapped his hands and stood. "Great. Let's go. Hey, guys," he called to the team in the kitchen. "Nate, here, wants to go see our bikes."

"Hot dog," Father said. "Let's go. I've got the best one out there."

"Yeah, for an old man," Steele joked.

He heard Nathaniel let out a small giggle. The guys must have, too, because their bantering continued.

"Hey, don't knock Harley. She's my baby." The leader poked a finger into the firefighter's shoulder.

Swatting the old man's hand away, Steele said, "Harley? That's what you named your bike? How original."

"Hey, I have my reasons." Father placed his hands in his back pockets.

"Sure you do." Steele nodded.

Tank leaned down and whispered to Nathaniel. "These guys are crazy." He was rewarded with a huge smile.

Steele bent down on one knee in front of the boy. "Nate, you want to see a real bike, you've got to see mine." The man pointed to his own chest.

"Dude, that granny ride? No way. I've got the real, deal," Tank said.

"That little baby machine. Please," Father ribbed.

Nathaniel let out another round of giggles. "I have an idea," Tank interjected. "Let's let Nathaniel decide. What do you say, Mary?"

"I think that sounds like a winner." The mother smiled at her son then pulled him tight to her body. Nathaniel squeezed his stepmother back then shot out the front door. Mary glanced up at him. "Thank you."

He nodded. "No problem, ma'am. Just doing my job."

"Well, you're wonderful at it." She wiped a fresh tear from her eye.

His chest swelled more as he followed everyone out the door. He really *could* do this.

All three of the bikes stood on the curb in front of the house. He trotted down the steps and opened his arms like a game show host. "Okay, Nathaniel, which ride do you like the best?"

The boy's eyes grew wide as he took slow steps and walked around the three bikes, examining them each carefully. He held his hand out then pulled it back quickly, like the flames on Steele's chopper might actually burn him.

"It's okay," Father said. "You can touch them."

Nate lifted his hand and rubbed an open palm down the body of Steele's bike, then he lifted one arm to reach for the ape hanger.

"You like it, man?" Steele stepped beside the kid. "This one's mine. Fire engine red just like a fire truck."

"You like fire trucks?"

Tank saw the glint in Steele's eyes change for a brief second at Nathaniel's question, then his eyes turned back up to match his smile. If Tank hadn't of been looking at the firefighter, he would have missed the changing facial expression.

"I sure do, son. I'm a firefighter."

"Cool!"

Tank reverted his gaze back to Nathaniel. The boy's eyes got big again, and his heart split a little. The kid found a new hero.

"Whose is this one?" The boy pointed to his bike, and his heart gave another little jolt.

"That's mine." Tank straddled the metal frame.

"It's gray, like his hair." Nathaniel pointed to Father's head.

The leader let out a bark of laughter. "Kid, you're funny."

"My bike is not gray," he corrected. "It's gunmetal, but you're right." Tank tapped the kid on the arm and smiled. "Jack's hair is gray."

"Can I go for a ride?" Nathaniel hugged his bear tighter.

"Nate, baby." Mary scooted closer. "I don't think these gentlemen have time—"

"No, it's okay." Father reached into his saddlebag. "We brought a helmet just for him."

"Oh, can I go, Mom. Please?" The kid bounced on his toes, a full-blown smile showing on his face.

"I don't know, Nate, honey. You've never been on a motorcycle and—"

"I've only wrecked twice, ma'am." Tank mocked seriousness.

Steele sucked back a snicker.

"In all honesty, we did a background check on this one." Father slapped his shoulder. "His driving record is clean, and so is Blake's and my own. We'll be very cautious."

"Oh, okay, but just for a little bit and just around the block." Mary pointed a finger at the men.

"Yeah!" Nathaniel tossed his teddy to his mom and grabbed the helmet. Father strapped it on for him.

"I like your enthusiasm kid, but first things first. You have to have a biker name. Mine's Father." Jack pointed to himself then hooked a finger at him. "This is Tank, and that's Steele, and you're…" He glanced the child over then stared back at the kid's teddy bear. "You're Bear. Now, Bear, who do you want to ride with? Steele doesn't have an extra seat, so it's either me or Tank."

Nathaniel shot a quick finger toward him, and another ounce of pride filled Tank's chest.

"Tank it is. Hop on kid. Let's go."

"I'll stay back with Mary, if that's okay with you?" Steele asked the mom.

"Sure," the woman said all too quickly.

"Well, then, let's ride, boys." Father saddled his bike and revved his engine.

"This is so cool," Bear squealed.

"Yep." Tank placed the kid on the bike's seat in front of him and barricaded the boy with his arms. "Hold on, Bear. This'll be fun."

The boy giggled all the way down the street.

CHAPTER TEN

Tank entered his home with three take out bags. "Hey," he called to JoJo. She sat on the sofa with the remote in her hand watching some trashy woman's show. "What's that garbage on my television?"

"Real Housewives of Houston."

"Wouldn't figure you for a girl to watch something like that."

"I've got to get my smut from somewhere." She placed the remote on the coffee table. "What's in the bags?"

"Food. You hungry?"

"No, I'm still good from Steele's omelet."

He glanced around the kitchen and down the hall. No sign of Annie. His heart raced until he glanced on the counter where her keys lay earlier. Still there.

"Where's Annie?"

JoJo pointed to the sliding glass door that sat partially open. Beauty sat on the dock down by the water, her toes lazily stroking the stream, her guard dog steady by her side.

"I've had one eye on her the whole time, but I figured I'd give her some privacy. She's got a lot on her mind, not to mention, she's in pain. Her bruises are starting to settle in, and extra strength pain reliever isn't cutting it."

"Should I take her to a hospital?"

"I'd let her decide that, but I doubt she'll go. If she wouldn't go last night, she's not going to go today. She's too afraid, and for good reason."

He crossed the room in a few quick strides and stared through the glass. "What's she wearing?" Her shirt and shorts fitted snuggly against her skin, much more attractive than the too big clothes he'd given her last night.

"She found an extra pair of clothes in the back of her car, but she's going to need more." JoJo shoved her hands in the pockets of her jacket. "I can bring her a couple of things, but I'm gathering if she is here with you she doesn't have much money."

Tank strolled back to the kitchen. "Yeah? Why you figure that?" He pulled Chinese takeout containers from the sacks.

"Because, if she had the funds to flee, I imagine she would have gone farther than ten miles from her fiancé."

His self-esteem took a hit, but JoJo was right.

"Good point. We haven't discussed funds yet, but if Duke controlled her like I think, then you're right. She probably doesn't have much."

"I know you're new to town, but let me clue you in on her fiancé, Duke Fields. He's from money. Annie's right—going to the cops about this, asking for help isn't the best idea. His family has had their influence in the politics of this town for a long time. Besides." She shrugged. "I only know one good cop, and he doesn't live in this jurisdiction."

Just picturing an image of a police officer in his mind made him want to break out in a sweat. He kept his head down and continued his task with the food to distract him.

"I can break in to Duke's place. Get her some stuff."

He stilled his hands. Breaking and entering. This woman was a little...nuts. "I don't know. That doesn't sound safe."

"Well, it's either that, or spend money and buy her some clothes. I don't know about your income, but mine is enough for me and me only. The tattoo parlor doesn't pay a whole lot. Speaking of which, I haven't seen any tats on you."

"That's because I don't have any, and I could say the same for you."

"I like to ink on others, not myself." She shrugged.

Turning, he pressed his back against the counter. "I hear you about the money, though. I have a little, but not a lot. My first paycheck hasn't come in yet. If we could get her some of her things that would be good, but still...the idea. It's risky."

The glass door whooshed open a little more. Al barreled into the kitchen and plopped his belly on the cool tile. Annie stood just inside the house. "What are you guys talking about? My stuff? Risky?"

"Annie." His heart raced and he longed to gaze down her legs. Another time. Another place. He flipped a thumb to the daredevil. "JoJo thought we could sneak into your house, and get some of your things."

"My locket." Her hand flew to her chest, and her eyes widened. Hope spread across her face for a brief second before her shoulders slumped.

If his instincts were right, that locket was a special gift from someone she loved.

"Your locket?" JoJo asked.

"Yeah, it was from my dad."

Bingo.

"But, I don't know if breaking in is such a good idea. I do have a little money. I could buy some things." Annie bit her bottom lip.

Undoubtedly, her concerns were the same as his. Why risk going near danger when you don't have to?

"I don't mean to pry, but how much is a little?" JoJo asked.

"About five hundred. It was my tip money for the past two weeks. Our wedding money. I like to build up a larger amount before I deposit it in the bank, so I put it in the cookie jar until then." She shook her head and crossed her arms.

"I can't believe I remembered to grab the cash out of the jar, but none of my clothes. My purse was by the stupid smiling pig. I grabbed the money and ran without giving anything else another thought. Deep down, I guess a part of me thought I wouldn't ever go through with actually leaving him. That I would be back, so there was no need to grab anything else."

Tank took a step closer. "You don't have to go back. Ever."

Glancing from him to JoJo and back to him again, she nodded. "I know. Thanks to you guys."

Glad she wouldn't return to Duke, the reality of her situation began to settle in. Five hundred wouldn't get her far if she decided to leave and start over somewhere. And five hundred was about all he had to spare, too. Even combining their funds wouldn't get her far. And her necklace. He could see how important the jewelry was to her by looking in her eyes.

But her story wasn't adding up to what JoJo had just told him.

"Wait," he began. "If Duke is from means, then why is your wedding money in a cookie jar? And only five hundred? I get it's your tip money, but—"

"Duke's parents are born and bred southern tradition. The bride is to pay for the wedding, and they've made sure not to lend a penny. That means the wedding is on me, and his parents have a guest list of over five hundred. Being a wait-ress, that kind of money can take a while to build up."

Who the hell are these people?

"What about his money? Do you have access to it?" he asked.

"No." She shook her head. "None of it. We share a joint account, but there's not much in it. Last I looked, we had two thousand in there—all the money I've been saving up. So, combined total, I have twenty-five hundred."

"Sweetheart, I'm going to be real with you. If Duke is as controlling as we all think, he's already swiped your money out of that account. All you can count on is that little bit of cash you're holding on to." JoJo glanced at Tank. "What if we asked the Guardians for help? See if the guys would pull together and take up a collection?"

"No." Annie shook her head. "I've already been enough of a burden. I won't allow them to give me money."

"Well, then it looks like we don't have much of a choice but to go back and get your belongings," JoJo said.

"Duke's not just going to sit back and let me get my things. No matter how many of your guys you have standing guard. He won't allow being publicly humiliated. He's dangerous. I don't know how far he would go to save face."

If he's so monstrous, why did a woman like her stay with a guy like him?

"I figured as much. That's why I'm going in," JoJo ordered.

This woman barely grazed five feet. She reminded him of one of those yippy small dogs that thought it was a mastiff. Too big for her own boots. "JoJo, I really think we should stop and think about this some more."

"What's there to think about? She needs clothes and I

know how to get them." JoJo gave him another one of her *you're a moron* looks.

"I can't let you do that," Annie interjected. "As much as I would like my things, especially my locket, I can't let you risk your life."

"I agree with Annie. This sounds too dangerous." Despite the little gal's hard edge, this plan sounded precarious, not to mention idiotic. He didn't dislike her enough to put her in such a bad situation.

"I've had experience with stealth, guys. It wouldn't be my first time going in and retrieving some items."

Not her first time?

"Annie, do you know his work schedule?" JoJo asked.

"Yeah, he worked last night, and he's scheduled to work tonight."

"And with you gone, do you think he'll stick to his schedule?" he asked.

Annie turned and looked out the glass door again. "Yeah, I do. He may be mad, but right now, he can get away with lying. He can tell people I'm sick or I've gone to visit my mother. He'll try to act like everything is normal. After all, he's got his campaign in mind right now."

"Okay then." JoJo clapped her hands. "We go in tonight. What time does his shift start?"

"Seven."

"Tonight? Wait. No." Tank shook his head. "JoJo, you should sleep on this. Think it over."

He wanted Annie to have her things back, too, but something this dangerous should be well planned, thought through. Not rushed.

"Tonight." The little woman commanded. "I'll come back about six. We'll figure out our plan. If I go in right when he's getting to work, there is less of a chance of getting caught."

Getting caught. Shit.

"In the meantime, draw a layout of the house. I'll need to make sure I have it down before I go in." JoJo reached in a box and pulled out an eggroll. "Later." She held the roll in the air as a salute.

"Be right back," he said to Annie and followed the Guardian out the door. Once they were both on the front porch, he held a hand out to stop her. "I don't like this."

"You don't have to."

"Damn it, JoJo, I'm serious. This is dangerous."

"What's life without a little danger?"

"I don't want you to get into trouble or get yourself hurt. I can just buy her a few things in the meantime, and try to work a couple of extra shifts or something."

"Aw." JoJo gave him a pat on the cheek. "Nice to know you care."

He turned his face away from her touch and crossed his arms. "Yeah, well, don't let it go to your head."

"Noted. Besides, extra shifts won't give her back her dad's locket." She slapped him on the shoulder. "See ya tonight."

Insufferable. That's what she was, but damn if she wasn't right. He gathered that little string of gold held more sentimental value to Annie than anything else in this world. But JoJo had to know this was a really bad, terrible, horrible idea.

"Please—"

"Tank, no one deserves to have their life and their belongings taken away from them because of abuse. I'm going in." She swiveled and marched down the steps, her riding boots clomping on the wood. "Besides..." She stopped and turned back to him. "This is the most fun I've had in a while. Don't take that away from me, and don't you dare say a word to the group. Got it, greenhorn?"

"You're going to do this whether we help or not, aren't you?" A bad feeling settled in his gut. This woman had a death wish.

"Yep. See you at six." She pivoted on her boots and strolled down the driveway, her gait as cocky as her words.

Damn woman. She was doing that like/hate thing to him again. He hated her one-minute, then liked her the next.

"You're a good person, JoJo," he called behind her.

"I know, but don't tell anyone." She stuck the eggroll between her teeth and straddled her bike, not bothering to give him another glance.

Out of all the people in the group, he had to befriend *that* one. He watched dust fly behind her bike then turned and strolled back inside. Annie sat on the couch, fumbling through her purse. She pulled out a checkbook ledger and flipped through the pages.

"Everything all right?"

"I really need to see if there is any money in this account. I want to get it out before Duke does."

"If you're worried about money, or food, or anything, don't. We'll figure it out."

"No offense, Tyler, but that's one way Duke charmed me. By telling me he would take care of me." She stood and reached for her keys on the counter. "I need to start taking care of myself."

"Annie? What are you doing? If you take your car, someone will spot you."

"Have a better idea?"

"We'll go in my truck. Once we get close to town, you can scrunch down in the seat."

"I hate that I have to hide."

"I know, but just until we get this figured out. Please, either don't go, or go with me."

"Fine." She blew out a breath, dug in her purse, and thrust her ATM card his way. "Here. Zero-zero-zero-zero is the pin. Not very hard to remember."

"Zero's. Got it. Let's go." He grabbed his truck keys off a hook by the front door. "Al, outside." His dog took his time getting up to stretch, his legs so far apart from each other he was nearly in a horizontal position again. Coming back to all fours, he trotted to the front door. Once outside, the dog plopped on the shaded porch.

Hard life.

"Be back soon, buddy," Annie spoke to her new friend as Tank marched toward his grandfather's truck.

He opened the passenger side door for her. "I'm sorry it has to be this way right now, Annie."

"Yeah. Me, too." She slid onto the seat, avoiding the tarp and giant, rusted rim that sat on the floorboard.

"I've been meaning to take that out. Gramps left it there. I just hadn't had the heart to remove it yet. He was always tinkering with something." He reached for the dirty covering.

"No, it's okay. Don't move it, and besides, we aren't going very far."

"Sure?"

"Yeah."

She smiled a smile so genuine, it threw his thoughts totally off kilter.

"Okay. Well… Here." He gripped the seatbelt and pulled it toward her. "Buckle up."

"Thanks." She took the belt and clicked it in place.

Using his palm, he gave the door a good shut, ran around the truck, and got in. He cranked the ignition, and rolled his window down using the hand turn. "The AC doesn't work."

"Oh, okay." She moved to roll her window down, wincing.

The muscles in his chest tightened.

Dumb ass. I should have done that for her.

"Here, let me get that." He leaned over her and reached for the window, his arm grazing her leg. The realization he'd inadvertently touched her thigh hit. "Sorry." He pulled back quickly. "But that should help with the heat." He motioned to the window and avoided eye contact.

Deep down, a part of him still felt like that shy kid on the dock, too scared to talk to her. But he wasn't a child anymore. He was all adult male and while the wind might help her, nothing seemed to help with the temperature rise he experienced from the small contact with her body. Not the hot, muggy wind, and certainly not being in such a confined space with her.

"Thank you. And I understand."

He dared to look her way.

She kept her gaze on him. She understood she excited him? *Great.*

"About the floorboard, I mean." She pointed down toward the junk. "My dad, he had this coffee cup he always used. Drove my mom crazy the way he would leave it on the counter instead of putting it in the sink when he was finished." She giggled slightly, reminiscing about her parents.

"Yeah?"

"Yeah." Her smile faded. "On the day of their accident, he drank a cup of coffee before they went out for their date. He kept saying he didn't sleep very well the night before, and even though it was five in the afternoon, he claimed he needed a little pick me up before their evening." She fumbled with the clasp on her purse. "He drank about half the cup and placed it on the counter, right where he always did. My parents went out on their date, and I had planned to pick up the house and wash the dishes before they got back. That never happened."

"Why not? Have your own hot date?"

A different smile covered her face. Pleasant but forced. "I wish that were the reason."

He had an idea where the conversation was going. Her father was dead, that much he knew, but he wanted to know how, why. He wanted to know as much about her as she would tell him. To open up. Trust him. "What happened, Annie?"

"An officer had come to the door before I got around to cleaning the house. The man informed me my mom was in the hospital, and my dad was dead." Her lazy smile disappeared only to be replaced with a frown as she wiped a tear from her good eye.

A deep yearning to reach out and touch her burned inside of him. He tightened his hands on the wheel instead.

"You know, they say driving while you're tired is just as bad as driving drunk. My dad didn't notice the car in front of him had stopped. It was a sunny June day, so I suppose the brake lights may have been hard to see. He hit the car going sixty miles an hour. My mom..." She stopped and took in a breath and stared into her hands.

He kept his focus straight ahead. Gave her the time she needed to go on.

"My mom suffered severe brain injuries, while my dad died on impact. The person in the other car miraculously survived, but not without suing my mother for everything she had left. I didn't get to stay in our house long after the accident. But while I was there, the coffee cup stayed on the counter. It was the last thing I packed. As long as it was on the counter, right where my dad had left it, it made me feel like his presence was still there. If that makes any sense."

"It does." He reached in the glove box and pulled out a tissue.

She took it and sniffled, offering him a sheepish grin. "Thanks." She wiped her eyes.

"I'm sorry." He fidgeted his fingers on the wheel, while he concentrated on *not* reaching across the truck to touch her.

"Thank you."

"You said June. How long ago was this?"

"Nine years ago yesterday."

Yesterday? The anniversary of her father's death, and the same day her own world fell apart again. He would change her Junes. Somehow, someway, he would see to it she could be happy again.

Screw not touching her. He placed a hand on her shoulder. "I'm very sorry, Annie."

She covered his hand with hers. "Thanks."

As much as he enjoyed her caress, and wanted it to linger, he didn't want to see her tears. The conversation needed to be changed.

"And your locket?"

"My fourteenth birthday present. I wanted a real piece of jewelry, and that's what I got. My parents' pictures are in it, like I remember them growing up."

Memories. JoJo was right. No amount of money could bring that back. She deserved to have her first piece of jewelry, her only connection left to her dad, returned.

"Where is your mother now?"

She released her hold on him. "She lives in an assisted living center in Austin."

That explained why she couldn't go to her mother for help.

"And what about the mug? Where's it now?"

"Wrapped up tight in the back of my car." She crumpled

the wet tissue in her hand. "Besides my personal items, Duke wasn't crazy about me moving anything of my own in his house. That wasn't much of a problem since I didn't have much. I bounced around from foster home to foster home for a year after the accident before I was able to go out on my own, but I'd managed to keep my dad's moose mug through all of it. I couldn't bear to throw it out, or let anything happen to it, so I hid it from Duke."

"You can use it at my house." He glanced at her "I won't ask that you throw it out. I won't even touch it. I would hate to accidently break it."

She smiled again, even brighter. "Thank you."

He had an even more difficult time breathing. Had to be the thick, muggy air. Had to be, but the more she talked, and the more she smiled, the more he cared for her.

Damn, that wasn't in his plans.

A sign for Black Widow came into view. "We're entering the town, so you might want to duck."

"Yeah, sure." She unbuckled her seat belt and crouched down in the seat. A slight gasp parted from her lips.

"Are you okay?"

"I'm fine. Just hurts a little."

"I'll be quick. Which bank is it?" Black Widow's main drag housed the only two banks in the whole town.

"Livingston's."

He turned into the parking lot of the bank and headed toward the drive-through ATM. A police car sat in a parking spot. His hands began to clam as he grabbed her ATM card out of his cup holder.

"Stay down. There's a cop car in the parking lot. I can't see if anyone is inside or not."

He rolled his window down farther, and slid the card into the machine. Once he punched in Annie's code, the machine flashed the account had been closed. No surprise there. He retrieved the card, and rolled up his window part of the way.

"Your account's been closed."

"That son of a bitch," she mumbled.

"I'm sorry."

Rubbing her forehead, she said, "Not your fault."

He eased out of the parking lot and made it twenty feet down the street before he had to stop at a red light. The sound of a siren whirled behind him.

"Shit."

Tingles shot through his clammy hands.

"Oh my God, Tyler, what do I do?" Annie whispered.

The floorboard still covered in his grandpa's old junk, there wasn't anywhere for her to go.

The tarp.

"Hide under the tarp. I'll put the rim in front of you to make it look like it's a floorboard of junk. Hurry, and be very still."

Annie lifted the dank covering over her head, pulling her purse with her, while he signaled to turn into a parking lot. Perspiration beaded on his forehead. He placed his truck in park, sat the rim in place, then rolled his window down all the way and reached for his wallet.

The same cop with the hard stare from the diner ambled to his truck. His name badge read Chief Fields.

Annie's abuser stared back at him.

Tank gripped his steering wheel, his knuckles tight on the rim.

Stay calm. Play this cool.

He cut his gaze to Annie. The tarp didn't move.

Duke peered in his window, and removed his shades. The man's bloodshot eyes narrowed in concentration.

"What seems to be the problem, officer?"

"You've got a taillight out."

"Oh, I didn't know that. I'll be sure to get that fixed."

"I need to see your license and insurance."

Tank handed him his license then reached for the insurance card out of his glove box. The lid of the box slipped from his sweaty hand and landed on what he thought was Annie's head. The tarp shifted slightly. He grabbed the information, flipped the lid closed, and sat back up, shifting his body to block the floorboard. A silent prayer played over in his mind, pleading the bastard didn't see the movement.

"The registration's not in your name."

"No, sir." A bead of sweat dripped down his cheek. "This was my grandfather's truck. He left it to me."

"I see." Duke gave him a hard stare. "Why are you sweating so much?"

"You know these old trucks. The air went out about a year ago, and gramps never got it fixed. Now, I guess it's my problem." Tank wiped his brow; thankful he could blame his sweating on the busted AC.

"What's all that in the floorboard?" Duke pointed to the tarp. "I saw you bending over."

"Oh that. Just more stuff my grandpa left me. Old car parts and such." He patted the rim. "And I bent over because my wallet slid off the seat and fell to the floorboard. I don't like sitting on it. It's uncomfortable."

"Yeah?" Duke raised an eyebrow. "I understand that. Did your gramps… He like to tinker?"

Small talk.

Something he never thought he'd be having with Annie's abuser. As long as it kept the maniac away from her and off their trail, he'd oblige the man.

"Yeah, you could say that."

"Mmm…well…" Duke glanced back at his license. "Tyler, I'm just going to run this. I'll be right back."

"Sure."

He waited the agonizing five minutes for the no-good chief to finish. "I'm sorry, Annie. Just a little longer," he whispered as he checked his rearview mirror. "Here he comes."

"Get that light fixed, Wilde, or next time I won't be so nice." Duke slapped him with a warning.

"Yes, sir." He scribbled his name on the form and thrust the pad back to the man.

The cop gave him his copy and smacked the side of his truck before he strolled back to his patrol unit.

Slowly, Tank put the truck back in drive and pulled out of the parking lot. He watched out of his mirrors as the cop turned and headed in the opposite direction.

Relieved the man was gone, he loosened his tense grip on the steering wheel. "Okay, Annie, it's safe now."

She pulled the tarp down, a fresh batch of tears in her eyes. "That was him."

"I know. Are you okay?"

"Yeah." Her voice shook. "Do you think he realized I was down here?"

"No, I think you're okay." He turned off the main street and took a side road. "In a couple of more blocks, you can get up."

"Okay." She wiped a tear. "But you may have to help me. My ribs are hurting."

"That's it." He put on his signal. "I'm taking you to a hospital."

"No." She reached out to touch his leg. "Tyler, please. No."

He glanced down at her. Her eye was still nearly swollen

shut, and the bruise across her cheek screamed a blood red, her pain almost palpable. He grit his teeth. "Okay. But I'm taking you home, and you're resting until you're healed."

"Okay. Thank you."

A few minutes later, he turned down the back road toward his home. "You can get up now. We're out of the city." He pulled over to the side of the street and reached a hand down to help her up. Slowly, she raised her body, cringing at the pain.

"Are you sure you're going to be okay?"

"Yeah." She squinted her good eye and took in a deep breath. Once she got settled onto the seat, she let out the heavy breath. "But maybe you're right. No more trips to town in broad daylight until I'm healed."

"I think that's a good idea." He pulled the truck back on the road. Watching her gaze out the window as the trees passed by, he asked, "Annie, if Duke is scheduled to work tonight, why was he working today? Especially, if he worked last night too?"

"I should have seen it coming."

"What?"

"He wasn't working. Not technically, anyway."

"What do you mean?"

"He was waiting. Waiting to see if I would make an appearance at the bank."

"I see."

A lump formed in his throat. He had underestimated Duke.

If he was going to help protect Annie, he needed to make sure he never did that again.

CHAPTER ELEVEN

Duke glanced at his dashboard. The clock on his patrol unit read twelve-thirty. If he went home now, he could get about five hours of sleep before his shift started again. He took a swig from his cola bottle and swallowed his medicine. The rum burned his throat on the way down.

Annie's words echoed in his mind.

Why don't you take your medicine?

Because he wasn't crazy. He didn't *need* his medicine, despite what she or his dad said, and he wasn't the black sheep in the family. He'd show his parents when he became Sherriff. Hell, he'd show them all.

"Damn you, Annie." He slapped his steering wheel and screamed. "Where the hell are you, huh?"

The minute his dad got wind she'd run off, he'd blame *him*. Give him the whole, *can't win a campaign without a wife* bullshit. Like he didn't already know that.

He'd waited near the ATM for four hours. *Four fucking hours*.

She hadn't made it to the bank before him because their

account still had all their money in it when he closed it out that morning. A measly two thousand dollars.

So, where was she? And how could she get anywhere without proper funds? Not that two thousand was something he would consider proper funds.

Gripping the steering wheel tighter, his forearms burned from the tension. When he did find her, he would drag her ass to the Justice of the Peace and make her his wife. Being *his* was best for her. Everything he wanted for her was for her own good. She would see.

And once they were hitched, he'd be damn sure she never pulled a stunt like this again. She would also quit that stupid job of hers and focus her attention on being his dutiful wife and campaign manager. They'd still have the big, fancy wedding for show. He'd just have to pay for the fucking thing. No better way to acquire votes from Black Widow's elite than by boozing them on his dime.

He pulled his cruiser to the side of the street in front of his house.

Damn, he was tired. If he weren't so worried about becoming Sherriff, putting on a good face, he would call in sick for his evening shift. Use the day to catch up on some sleep, and then spend the evening figuring out a way to find her. His medicine would kick in by then. And while he didn't need it, he'd admit he focused better with it.

He glanced at his clock again. She'd been gone for at least five hours…maybe. Problem was, he had no real idea of when she left the house, or where exactly she could be by now.

If she fled to her mom's, she would have arrived an hour ago, if not more. He'd be sure to call the home later tonight when Nurse Maddy was on shift. He'd pleased her enough times in the supply closet the last time they drove down to visit Annie's crazy mom. His nurse would give him all the information he wanted.

He tapped his fingers on his leg and took in a deep breath. Everything would work out.

Disobedient woman better have put some makeup on to hide the bruises she made me give her. Fleeing bitch.

Duke went to turn off the ignition of his unit. Tyler Wilde's name stared at him from the computer monitor. Something about the guy didn't sit right with him. If he'd had a warrant, he would have asked to see what was under the tarp. He'd watched as the guy put his card in the machine, yet he didn't withdraw any money. Perhaps the man was getting a bank balance?

He reached for his phone and dialed the bank.

"Livingston's Bank, Peggy speaking."

He cleared his throat and lowered the tone of his voice to panty-dropping level. "Peggy, good morning, it's Chief Fields."

"Oh, Chief!"

The shrillness of her voice made him cringe.

"What can I do for you?"

"I've got a check here from someone, and I want to make sure the funds are available before I cash it."

"Well, sure, what's the account number?"

"The account number?" He hadn't planned for that. "I umm…I don't have my contacts in, Peggy, darling, so I can't make out the numbers, but I can give you the man's name."

"Contacts? I didn't know you wear contacts."

He didn't.

"I *cannot* wear those things. They kill my eyes," she squeaked into the phone.

He held the phone away from his ear. Her coke bottle

glasses and too-tight-around-the-midsection dresses killed his eyes, but she didn't seem to care.

He took a deep breath and pulled the microphone back to his mouth. "Yeah, they aren't for everyone. So, can you look up the man's account by his name?"

"Well, I'm really not supposed to. If you had an account number I could, but I'm not supposed to by name."

Damn. He was going to have to do something he didn't want to. Flirt. "Oh, Peggy, honey, I guess I understand that. And you're such a good employee. I wouldn't want you to do anything to get yourself in trouble. As an officer of the law, I can appreciate your honesty. I guess I'll just have to take the chance of this check bouncing on my account."

"Oh, well." She let out a slight giggle. "I don't want that to happen. Listen," she whispered into the receiver, "I'll do it this one time just for you. Go ahead. Tell me the man's name."

"You're a doll," he rolled the words off his tongue in a southern drawl. "Last name's Wilde, with an E on the end. First name's, Tyler."

"Okay, let me see here."

The sound of computer keys clicked in the background. "Well, Chief Fields, I do believe someone has given you a false check. We don't have anyone by that name at our bank. Did they know you are a police officer? Lordy, that man could get arrested. I'll need to send an email alert to our branch manager and let him know Tyler Wilde is writing false checks on our bank. But, oh Lord, how am I going to tell him? I'm not even supposed to be looking up his name."

He had to diffuse the situation before the pitiful teller had a heart attack. "Oh, wait Peggy, that's not necessary. I looked at the check wrong. It wasn't written off Livingston's bank after all. I'm sorry to bother you. Thanks for your time, darling."

"Oh, thank goodness. No problem, Chi—"

He hung up and glanced at his computer monitor again. Wilde's picture stared back at him. "If you don't have an account then why were you really there?"

He shut off his car and walked to his back door. The house alarm beeped when he opened the door, and mindlessly, he punched in his code. Drowsiness overtaking him, he shuffled toward their bedroom and stopped midway, Annie's locket still on the ground. He reached to pick it up. If Annie showed up while he was at work, he might not realize until much later. *Unless…* His medicine must be working. He walked back to the keypad and created a new code.

CHAPTER TWELVE

Annie had a pen and paper in hand, writing numbers at the top of the page. Her long, bare legs were curled under her on the couch, while her feet sat nestled under her voluptuous backside, and her red toenails dared to play peek-a-boo under her butt cheek.

Mercy.

"What are you doing?" Tank sat on the end of the couch and grabbed the television remote, his grip way too tight.

Alfred stood in front of her, begging to be petted. She lifted a lazy hand and slowly rubbed the dog's ears. His pup gave him a side-glance, almost mocking him because Al got her affections and he didn't.

Damn dog.

"Making the house layout for JoJo. There's an alarm she's going to have to bypass. She'll need the code."

She set the pen down and reached for her father's moose mug sitting next to her on the end table. Having something so personal of hers sitting on his table inflated his chest a little. She's getting comfortable. *Here. With me.* He dared a peek at her toenails again.

Get a grip, Wilde. Even though he'd been reunited with the girl a week, she'd only been his houseguest for a day. One day, and he had a hard time keeping it in his pants.

"Yeah?" He turned and glared at the picture-less television. "That's a good idea. She'll be here in about an hour."

"About that. I know Duke goes in to work at seven, but it'll still be light outside. You think she wouldn't mind waiting until about nine or so?"

"Why?" His fingers finally decided to work. He hit the power button and mindlessly flipped through channels. He needed something manly to watch. Something very *unattractive* to look at, like sumo-wrestlers in giant diapers unattractive.

Placing her lips to the mug, she took a sip and set it back down. "Because I want to go, too, but I can't bear to face another close call like earlier. My side is killing me from being so scrunched on your floorboard."

"You can't possibly go in that house."

"I know, but I was thinking we could park on the street, and stay connected to her through your cell as she's going in."

"Annie, No. I don't—"

"Tyler." She held up a hand to stop him. "I'm going. JoJo is doing this for me. Either go with me or not, but I'm going with her. If something should happen, I'm not going to let her take the rap."

Stubborn woman.

"Fine." He couldn't tell her what to do, but he *would* voice his opinion. "However, I think it's a bad idea."

"I know, but I'm going anyway."

"You're stubborn, you know that?" Tension coursed through his body, and he did his best not to show it.

Suppressing a grin, she asked, "Does that mean you're going with me?"

His body relaxed at her smile, and his gut sank at her question. He still had work to do to prove to her he was there to help. A lot of work. "Of course it does, Annie. You're not in this alone. Never in this alone."

Her chest rose and a glimmer shone out of her good eye. Beauty glanced back down at the paper and placed it on the coffee table. "Thank you," she whispered. "I think I'm going to take a bath."

"Okay. Take your time."

Taking her coffee mug with her, she stood and went toward the bathroom. Al followed.

"You can't come, buddy." She closed the bathroom door gently in his dog's face.

Alfred gave him a sad look.

"I know, man. Come here." He ushered his dog on the couch beside him.

How long had it been since anyone bothered to show her they cared? He gripped his remote tighter, the plastic making a cracking sound in his hand. He eased his grip, and ran a hand through Alfred's soft fur.

Water rushed through the bathroom pipes. Frantically, he flipped the channels for something very ugly to stare at, landing on an old wrestling match. Chubby dudes in spandex speedos were about as bad as sumo-wrestlers. Still, even with all the long hair, man boob glory flashing bright and bold on his screen, he couldn't help but wish he was the bar of soap sitting by his bathtub faucet right now.

————

AL BARKED at the sound of a slight knock from his front door. Tank glanced over at his microwave clock. Six on the dot. He peeked out of the peephole to be sure before opening the door. JoJo had her right arm propped against the doorframe, her feet crossed at the ankles, and a duffel bag hanging off her left shoulder. Shades as black as her hair covered her eyes.

"Evening, big guy and hairy thing." She took her glasses off and crossed the threshold.

"What's in the bag?"

"A few things for Annie. Just in case our B and E doesn't go as well as we planned."

He took the bag from her and slung it over his own shoulder. "Listen, JoJo, you don't have to do this." His gut rolled. The whole thing felt extremely wrong. Not just the breaking and entering part, but also the idea of stepping into Duke's territory wasn't giving him any warm fuzzies either. Bringing Annie close to the monster on purpose seemed stupid.

"I know." The biker gave him a hard stare. "I'm aware of what I'm doing. Where is she, anyway?"

"I'm here." Annie came out from the bedroom.

"I brought you some things." JoJo pointed to the bag, and he handed it to Annie. "I knew my jeans wouldn't be long enough for you, so it's just a few pairs of sweat pants and a couple of T-shirts."

"Thanks, lady. This means a lot." Beauty unzipped the bag and pulled the canvas apart.

"No big deal. I'd like to be able to say I'll get most of your stuff tonight and you won't need mine, but just in case." She nodded toward the supplies.

Annie pulled a shirt out of the bag. "Everything is black."

"Sorry." JoJo shrugged. "I don't do pink."

This biker chick in pink? The idea seemed about as foreign as the woman sewing a sweater.

"I'm not complaining," Annie reassured. "This will be great for tonight. I'll have something dark to wear to hide better in."

Oh, man.

Inwardly, he cringed. Not exactly the best opening in telling this Guardian how the plans had changed. He hadn't known JoJo long, but he gathered she was more of a solo act. And she sure didn't seem like the kind of person who liked being *told* how things were going to go down.

"Tonight? Hide? What are you talking about?" she asked.

"Here, let's sit at the table and talk. Go sit, Alfred." He pointed the ladies and his dog in the direction of the kitchen table, stalling for time, trying to figure out the correct way to inform JoJo they were tagging along. Annie's drawing of the house sat on the coffee table. He grabbed it before he joined them.

"I'm going with you tonight," Beauty said before he could sit down.

He cringed again. This wasn't going like he planned at all. Not that he really had a plan.

"No, I do this alone."

"Now, wait a minute." Tank pulled up a chair between the ladies. His broad frame crowded the space. The Guardian scooted away from him, giving them more room. Beauty stayed close. His heart jumped. "Annie feels strongly about standing watch for you, you know, in case anything bad happens. We'll be on my cellphone. If we see something suspicious, we can warn you to get out while you're inside."

"The point of me going in is to go in alone, *without* you guys. No offense, Annie, I appreciate your help, but you guys being there isn't safe."

"But I want to help," Beauty protested.

Tank held up his hands and slunk back in his chair.

"Ladies, the whole situation isn't safe. You both want to help each other, and I think that's wonderful. JoJo, you're used to doing things on your own I've gathered, and Annie, I've also gathered you aren't used to people doing nice things for you. Let's work together as a team. Okay? JoJo goes in alone. Annie and I will be in the truck a safe distance away to watch for anything suspicious. Okay?"

"Fine with me," Annie said.

JoJo sighed. "Sure. Fine. Whatever. But things have a way of getting sloppy when more people get involved."

"That won't happen," Annie said. Her determined stare met his and JoJo's.

"There's a side street, Dixie," JoJo said. "You can park the truck on the corner. You can see three fourths of the house from that view, but there is a nice big tree you can park under to give you some cover. It's the best place for you to look out for me without being blatantly obvious." She leaned back in her chair. "Not that I need it," she mumbled under her breath.

So, the cocky woman hadn't lied. This wasn't her first rodeo. Knowing the trees, and areas to hide meant she'd cased Duke's house before she came. The uneasy feeling in his stomach lifted. *Slightly*.

"Glad you've done your homework."

JoJo gave him another *dumb ass* stare.

He ignored the broody biker and turned back to the beauty sitting close to him. "Duke's already seen my truck, and there's no way we can take your car. That would be way too obvious. JoJo's right. We *should* hide under the tree." He stared at Annie's swollen eye. He wanted to give this to her, take her where she wanted to go, but looking at her face had his insides turning.

Please, don't let this be a horrible mistake.

"You're right," Annie agreed. "But wait." She turned back to JoJo. "How do you know where I lived?"

"I see him drive around town enough. Number 357 is always parked on the curb. I associated the cruiser number with the guy and the guy with the house. The shade from the giant pear tree in your yard makes his patrol car hard to see at night. I always see it, sitting there, like it's waiting," JoJo said matter-of-fact. "You've got a lot of trees in your neighborhood"

"*Old* neighborhood," Beauty corrected.

A flutter replaced the churn in his gut. She talked like a woman who had no intentions of returning to her past.

"And yeah," Annie continued. "You're right. Duke likes to intimidate people."

"So I've noticed." JoJo glanced at the paper he held in his hand. "What's that? The layout of the house?"

He pushed the flutters aside and passed the paper to JoJo. "Annie put the alarm code numbers at the top."

"You think these are still good? You think he's changed the code?"

"Maybe." Annie shrugged. "I don't put anything past him."

"You got any idea of another set of numbers?"

"His birthday. Seven-one-three-eight-five."

Tank rose to grab a pen. "Evil bastard was probably born on a Friday." He took one from the junk drawer and handed it to JoJo.

She scribbled the numbers at the top. "And there are only two doors. Right? No side doors?"

"Nope." Annie shook her head. "Front and back, that's it."

"What all do you want me to grab?" JoJo placed the pen back on the table.

"There's a bag in the closet, hanging on a hook. Grab that. The right side of the closet is mine. I'll need some jeans, some shirts, and shoes. My makeup bag is in a drawer in the bathroom, and my..." She glanced up at him; her cheeks reddened. "My underwear are in the third drawer of the dresser. And my locket. Please grab that if you can find it. It might be on my dresser, maybe? I'm not sure where Duke would have put it."

"Okay." JoJo tapped her fingers on the table. "Anything else?"

"Umm...yeah. I have a book on the nightstand. That, too, if you can."

"Jeans, shirts, shoes, makeup, undies, necklace, and book. Got it." The Guardian scooted her chair back. "You guys about ready to get this party started?"

"About that." Tank stepped from behind the kitchen counter. "We went into town today, and nearly got caught. Because of that, Annie had to scrunch on the floorboard of my truck. She bruised her ribs more. It's best if we wait until it gets dark outside. That way she's not as easily seen."

JoJo swiveled her head in his direction. "You mean when Duke's no longer busy with signing into his shift and is out on patrol, dark? Right?" Irritation marred her face as she glanced back at Annie.

"Umm...yeah. Are you okay with that?" Annie asked.

"Sure." JoJo blew out a breath and sat back in her chair. "I'm up for a little challenge." She pulled out her cellphone and glanced at the screen. "So, what time are you thinking?"

"Maybe nine or ten," he suggested.

"That's four hours from now." Her tone direct, JoJo placed her phone back in her jacket pocket.

"Yeah." He glanced at his microwave clock again. "It is."

All three of them stared at each other for a few seconds.

The Guardian didn't make any motion to leave, and he didn't feel right asking her. After all, she was kind of doing him a favor. Really, JoJo was doing Annie a favor, but it felt like the tough chic was helping him, too. A deck of cards had sat in the junk drawer beside the pen he'd retrieved. Time to break the silence.

"You ladies up for a little left over Chinese and a game of poker?" He pulled the drawer open and held up the cards.

"As long as it's not strip." JoJo smirked. "You two couldn't handle seeing any of this."

Beauty let out a snort of laughter. "Why do I believe you?"

JoJo smiled back at her. "Because you know it's true."

He slapped the cards on the table and sat cursing the biker in his mind. Why did she have to bring up the word strip?

"I hope you brought your poker face, Tyler." Annie reached for the cards. "Because it's on."

His fingers trembled, and he shoved his hands under the table. *Damn.* All he could think about was how he wanted it to be *off.* Why couldn't it really be strip poker?

Another time, another place, Wilde.

"Woo." JoJo reared back like she'd been burned. "Little Miss can talk the talk."

"But can she play the cards?" He glared at Beauty and grinned, focusing on keeping his gaze on her face.

She gave the cards a good shuffle, while her lip tipped up in a sly smile. "I don't know."

She shrugged, and he wished she had on his too big T-shirt again. Talks of stripping, her shrugging, and those lips.

Mercy.

Fat ugly wrestlers danced in his mind as the trembling worked its way to his palms. In four hours, they all would be involved in something stupid and dangerous for some clothes and a sentimental string of gold. While he understood Beauty needed some form of her life back, what he couldn't understand was the strong pull of emotions taking over him. Her safety was his main concern, and he would see to it Duke wouldn't get close to her.

Not tonight.

Not ever again.

CHAPTER THIRTEEN

"What the hell was that back there?" Tank eased his truck to the corner of Dixie Street and cut off his lights. Annie's old house looked dark and deserted.

"What? The cards?"

"If I knew I was going to so easily lose my five bucks, I may have been a bit slower to suggest we all put a little money in the pot."

"I told you to bring your poker face." She poked him in the arm with her finger and then placed her hand flush with the truck seat.

"What you failed to mention was how well you've developed a poker face."

"Yeah." Her voice grew softer. "Sometimes you have to learn to hide things, ya know?"

His gut sank. He did know. He'd hid his own secrets for months.

The end of her fingertips sat oh-so-close to his leg. Eager to touch her, he reached for her hand as she began to pull it back toward herself. To his astonishment, she stopped and let him hold her. They'd only been living together a day but it felt like longer. He wanted her for longer.

"I'm sorry," he whispered as he leaned in closer. The moon cast a perfect silhouette against her jawline and right to her lips.

"It's not your fault," she whispered, as she inched closer.

Just a little closer, and he could taste her. These past two days of watching her, wanting her...he touched his forehead to hers. He could smell the undercurrent of his shampoo in her hair, warm and spicy, mixed with a smell that he had learned to be her. Sweet. So sweet. He closed his eyes and prepared for the ecstasy of her subtle kiss just as ZZ Top's "Sharp Dressed Man" ringtone blared from his phone.

She jumped and scooted closer to the window. "Lord, that scared me."

Damn. These Guardians sure had sucky timing.

"It must be JoJo." He pulled his phone out of his pocket and clicked it on speaker. "Hello."

"I parked around the corner, and I'm sneaking up the back right now."

"Okay. We're here. Be safe."

"I know. I see you."

Leaning left then right, he peered through his windshield for any sign of her. "How? I don't see you."

"That's the point," she said pointedly through the receiver. There was the *dumb ass* tone again.

Annie sucked in a snicker. "Well, you're doing your job well. Be careful."

"Thanks." The biker sounded a little winded. Something rustled through the receiver. Leaves?

"What is she doing? Climbing a tree?" Beauty asked him.

"A fence to be exact," JoJo answered. "I'm putting you in

my back pocket. You're on speaker. I'll pull you back out when I need you."

"Roger that." Tank placed his cellphone down on the seat between them.

Annie tapped her leg and played with her nails.

"You nervous?"

"Is it that obvious?" She glanced over at him. "It's just sneaking around like this, breaking into Duke's house. If we get caught—"

"Hey, hey." Reaching out to still her twitching hands, he said, "We aren't going to get caught. We'll be fine. I have faith in JoJo."

"Yeah?" She gave him a side smile and gripped his hand. "Me, too."

He started to pull back, but she firmed her grip. "Tyler, I just wanted to say thank you. For everything."

This sounded almost like a goodbye thank you. Not yet. It wasn't time. He had to explore this unexplainable pull toward her. He thought he'd lost his chance as a kid. He didn't want to lose another one.

"Of course. It's my pleasure." He squeezed her hand back. "And just so it's clear, you're welcome to stay as long as you like. I need you to know that."

She glanced down at their hands. He could see the rise and fall of her chest by the moonlight.

"About that, I know you're part of the Blue Guardians and all—"

"Not yet. I have to hang around for a year before they'll let me in, but I'd like to be a part of them eventually."

"Why? Why do you care so much? Why the Blue Guardians?"

"Because of the group's mission, to protect women and children."

"I know what the group does, and it's becoming obvious why JoJo is so involved and cares so much. I imagine she was abused before, too. Why are *you* so interested in my well-being? In the kid you went to see today?"

He eased his hand out of hers and gripped the steering wheel. She wanted his past, and he didn't know if he could give it to her. If he did, she would realize how damaged he was. While he'd been irritated at JoJo's timing ruining their kiss, it was for the best. He couldn't get involved with her. She needed someone whole, not someone broken like him.

"I just...I just do."

"Why Tyler?" Annie reached for his hand on the steering wheel. "You can tell me."

Her hand, soft and clean, looked foreign in his large and grease-stained one. Yet, the warming sensation that shot up his arm and through his stomach at her touch seemed right.

"You know I told you my dad was dead, right?"

"Right."

God, was he really going to do this? Was he really going to tell her? He'd only told a handful of people in his life what happened to him, and only because he had to, not by choice. Memories of the pain and the fear flooded back. His hands grew clammy against the steering wheel. His past needed to die just like his father was dead to him.

A wailing noise from his phone distracted him.

Shit. For a brief second, he'd forgotten about JoJo, and what he was here to do. He glanced down at the receiver sitting on his seat and reached for it.

"JoJo? What's going on?"

"The alarm code isn't working. None of them. Do you have another?"

He glanced at Annie. Her eyes growing wider with fear, she shook her head. "No, no I'm sorry."

"JoJo, get out of there. Now," he demanded. "Abort."

"Not on your life. I've got a couple of minutes."

"Oh my God. I have a bad feeling about this." Annie tapped her feet faster against the floorboard, scanning the darkened outside area.

His heartbeat quickened, and his blood pounded in his temples. If they got caught, he could forget getting into the Blue Guardians. Jail's the only place he would be going. And Annie, she would be back in that bastard's arms. Then there was JoJo. While she was tough, she was small. Lockup was no place for her.

The sound of a siren wailed in the distance. "JoJo, get out. Duke's coming. Get out *now*."

"I'm almost done. You guys go. Go before you're seen. I'll meet back at your place."

"JoJo, no. We're not—" The dial tone sounded.

"Damn it." He threw his phone on the seat.

Annie placed her palm flat against his bicep. "Tyler, please. Let's leave. I don't want to be anywhere near here when he comes. Please."

Her hand trembled against his arm. Staying seemed like a bad idea, but so did leaving. Jeez, what the hell had he been thinking getting involved in this?

The sounds of the sirens grew louder. A small whine exited her lips. He'd be damned if he let that bastard have the power to scare her again.

"Okay. We'll go." He cranked the ignition and slowly backed the truck down Dixie then turned around in someone's driveway. He stared in his rearview mirror, hoping JoJo made her great escape.

———

FINALLY, Duke thought when he received the call from the alarm company. She'd finally made her move. Changing the alarm code had been genius on his part. Pure genius. He changed the numbers to the date he had first laid eyes on her. A date she wouldn't know because she hadn't been aware of him watching. She'd been wearing a little Santa's hat at the diner, and his mind envisioned her as his wife wearing costumes like that for him in bed. He'd also noticed several other men had that same look in their eyes when they stared at her. The idea sent his blood boiling, and he knew right then, staring at her from the back of the restaurant, she had to be his.

Now, six months later, she had the nerve to try to leave him. Only because he tried to set her wayward habits straight. She had to learn.

He punched in the code to silence the blaring alarm and pulled his gun, motioning for his partner to follow his lead. Entering each room, nothing appeared out of place until he reached the bedroom. He was met with a gust of hot, humid air.

"Secure the rest of the room." He moved his gaze toward the bathroom and bedroom.

"All clear," Brayden said. "Boss, they went out through the window." The little cop stomped his way toward the opening.

No shit, Sherlock.

The rookie had been the only cop on call tonight without his usual partner. Unlucky for him, Brayden had to tag along. Duke wanted to be alone whenever Annie came home. He needed to have a talk with her, and he wasn't sure how many laws would need to be broken. On the flip side, lucky for him, the kid was impressionable. He planned to use the rookie's eagerness to his advantage.

Scanning the room, he noted the book on Annie's nightstand was gone. Her locket he'd placed beside the book—also gone. In the bathroom, drawers were left open, but there was only one thing missing. Her makeup bag. He glanced in the closet. The handbag on the hook no longer there while a few of Annie's hangers sat empty, but all of his things had been left untouched.

"Boss, I'm calling for backup. We can still catch this person."

"No," he demanded, his voice a little too loud.

Brayden took a startled step back.

Duke walked closer to his partner. If the unit got involved, there was a possibility of more people catching on to what was *really* going on in his life. Right now, Annie's sudden disappearance was under wraps. He had to keep it that way.

"Let's just ah....let's just keep this between us, okay?" He gave the boy a tight smile. "This isn't anything I can't handle. There's no sense in getting the force and all the paperwork involved, okay, son. Besides, nothing seems to be missing."

"Yeah, yeah. Sure, boss."

"You do that for me, and I'll be sure you get that promotion you've been gunning for. Would you like that?"

"I would *love* that." The guy's chest puffed as his eyes took on a sudden glow. "But don't you want to dust for fingerprints or anything?"

"No, there's no need for that."

"You sure boss?"

"Yeah. It's probably just the young punk neighbor kid. I'll have a talk with him."

"Okay, well then, I'll at least go close this window for you." Brayden stomped back toward the glass and began to push down. "Hey, what's this?"

"What's what?" Duke glanced toward the rookie.

Brayden held up something small and black. "It feels like leather."

"Leather?" He charged toward the cop and took the cloth. His chest tightened as he rubbed the fabric between his fingers. Annie didn't wear leather.

"Who wears leather in June?"

Only one source came to mind. The Blue Guardians. He'd seen them enough times around domestic violence scenes. They all wore their leathers anytime they went to visit a victim. Winter or summer, it didn't matter.

Annie had taken refuge with the biker club. If he found who had a hole in their leather, he found Annie.

"It's that neighbor kid's," Duke lied and pocketed the material. "Remember, this stays between us, Brayden. Got it? I can handle the kid on my own. No sense in giving him a juvie record. If I've heard you've talked, I'll make sure you go back to paper pushing."

The boy stiffened. "Yes, sir. Besides, I think it's good what you're doing for this kid. Helping him out and all."

"I try." He slapped the guy on the shoulder. "Let's go. We've got real crimes out there."

He led the rookie out of his house and back to his patrol unit.

Annie. Annie. I'm going to find you.

CHAPTER FOURTEEN

Tank tossed his bike helmet on the coffee table and plopped a safe distance beside Annie on the couch. For a week, he'd been skirting around her. Trying not to stare at her painted toes or tight little yoga pants. He'd never been so uncomfortable in his grandpa's cottage in his whole life. And there, Al sat right by her feet as he had for the entire week. His companion no longer *his* companion.

"Hey, how was your day at work?" She glanced up from her book and eyed the sofa cushion in between them.

The distance he sat from her seemed a world apart from the close proximity they shared in his truck. Still, distance was better.

"Long. How was your day?"

"Long," she echoed his answer. "Tree didn't talk much."

He'd only met the biker on a few occasions, but he gathered the tall man wasn't much for small talk. If he hadn't heard the man recite the minutes at the meeting, he'd question if the guy could talk at all. Still, talker or not, Tree volunteered to help, and Tank wasn't leaving Annie alone while he was at work.

"I'm sorry your day wasn't very exciting." Offering his apologies, he glanced at her book. Best to change the subject. "What are you reading?" He leaned his head down to read the front of the cover. "*As the Liquor Flows.* Never heard of it. What's it about?"

"A damsel in distress who finds salvation from an unexpected source." She closed the paperback and set it on the coffee table. "This story is set in the '30s, but I feel in some ways I can relate."

"Yeah? I guess the Guardians are your unexpected source, huh?"

"No." She shook her head. "I think it's safe to call *you* my unexpected source. My knight in bandana-clad armor."

She stared at the batman symbol on his head. Her eye was finally healing. Except for the slight tinge of the yellowish bruising left, she was perfect again. Hell, she'd always been perfect, and he'd be her knight. Gladly.

Annie's gaze raked lower to his eyes, and a sparkle shown in her stare as he tossed her a hint of a smile.

"But." She uncurled her feet from under her behind and sat them flat on the floor.

This doesn't sound good. His smile faded at the erectness of her posture.

"As much as I appreciate everything you've done, I'm going stir crazy, and I'm tired of babysitters. It's not fair for everyone in the group to take turns sitting with me on their days off."

He shook his head. "It's what they signed up for," he assured her. "These guys wouldn't do it if they didn't want to."

"Maybe so, but I don't want them to. I feel better. My ribs don't hurt nearly as much anymore, and I can cover what's left of my bruises with makeup." Annie stood and walked toward the sliding glass doors that led out to the patio. She reached a hand to her locket. JoJo's retrieval had brought a fresh batch of happy tears to her eyes a week ago. Now, those same eyes appeared wary, stressed. "I'm tired of hiding, Tyler," she said, her voice deflated. "I want to live again."

He slid his bandana off and ran his hands through his hair. How could he make her understand everything the group did was to keep her safe? "I know, Annie, but please." He stood. "Please, just wait a little while longer. I don't want us to do anything else too rash. We had a couple of close calls last week with Duke, then with JoJo nearly getting caught. At least, let's get you some safety before you go back into town. I'm sure someone in the group knows a range somewhere where we can at least teach you gun safety—"

"No." She whipped around fast on her heels. "No guns, Tyler. I had one pointed at my head a week ago, and I thought —no, I *knew*—it was going to be what killed me. No guns."

His jaw clenched. "He *pointed one* at your head?" Not only did that bastard abuse her physically and emotionally, but also threatened to kill her with the means to follow through. Son of a bitch needed to pay.

He took a few slow steps closer, reeling in his anger. "I'm …" He forced himself to stay calm. "I'm sorry. I didn't know."

She turned back toward the doors. Her shoulders slumped. "I know. I'm sorry for getting so upset. What Duke did wasn't your fault."

The last thing he wanted was for her to be sorry. For anything.

"No, it's okay. You have a right to your feelings, and I'm glad you expressed them." He tried to relax the tension in his face and took a few steps closer until he stood beside her. "No guns, I agree, but at least let me teach you some self-defense moves. I'll be around you when I can to protect you, but in the event I'm not, I'd like to know you can handle yourself."

"Self-defense." She said the words like she was rolling the idea around in her mind. "Okay." Nodding, she said, "That's reasonable."

"Great. Well then, I'll just wash up, and we can get started."

"Right now?"

"You're tired of being inside aren't you?"

"Extremely."

"Then, let's do it."

———

THE GRASS CRUNCHED under Annie's sneakers. A sound she'd almost forgotten. She'd hardly seen outside all week. Every once in a while, she would walk out to the dock, let Al splash in the water, but being outside—alone—scared her. Even with her furry protector. The likelihood anyone stood by peeking through the trees spying on her was slim, but with Duke, she never knew.

"Okay, are you ready?" Tyler walked up next to her.

The vast green openness around her, the creek, the forest, the embankment, she took it all in and inhaled its beauty as a small, nagging feeling pricked the back of her mind. "Do you think we're safe out here?"

He glanced around the horizon, scanning the trees. "I think we're as safe as can be. And that's why we're out here. To make sure you stay that way. Besides, Al will alert us if he hears something."

She glanced at the dog. He had his belly up in the air, basking in the sun. "I don't think he's worried about us." She pointed.

He followed her finger. "Ha. Maybe not. Rascal." Turning his body back again, he faced her. "Now, there are a few basic moves every woman should know when it comes to self-defense. May I?" He held up his hands ready to grab her shoulders.

She nodded. "Of course."

Tyler squared her body to his. His broad shoulders and chest had her brain buzzing as a pleasurable numb took over. He really *was* handsome.

"Neck, middle, groin. Repeat that."

She moved her eyes back to his. "What?"

"Neck, middle, groin. Say it."

Groin. Why was he talking about groins? "Why?"

"Just do it."

"Neck, middle, gr…groin," she stuttered the word. *Smooth, Annie, real smooth.*

"Those are the areas you want to target. Okay?"

"Okay. Sure." Self-defense. He's teaching you self-defense. Stay focused.

"Now, first things first. If someone is coming at you head on, I want you to take this part of your arm." He raised her arm and placed two fingers on her forearm.

His touch was feather soft and electrifying at the same time. How was that possible?

Stay focused.

"And strike for the neck. Don't use your wrist or your hand, only this part." Tapping her forearm again, he asked, "Got it?"

"Yes. I think."

"You sure?" He raised an eyebrow.

Great job of staying focused, Annie.

"Yes. I've got it."

"Okay. When you do this, move your whole body into it.

It's going to look like this." He took her forearm and aimed straight for his neck, his grip firm, and confident. When her arm made contact with his neck, he did a pretend shove back like her blow had some power to it.

Cute.

"Now what you've got is someone who instinctively goes to grip their neck." He released his hold on her and reached for his neck with both hands. "At that point, you want to hit them directly in the torso with an elbow. And put all your weight behind it." Gripping her arm again, he held her elbow at shoulder height then helped her swing her arm to his torso. "And once that happens, the person will go to grip their stomach, and their stance will widen like this." He opened his legs a little. "And that gives you direct target to kick the jewels. Got it?"

Could she really remember all of this in real life? Hopefully, she would never have to.

"Yeah, I think so."

"Okay, let's practice."

Practice?

"You want me to really hit you? Like, really hit you, hit you?" She dropped one arm lax by her side while pointing the other in his general groin area, trying not to make eye contact with it. Pointing was bad enough. Coming in contact with his "jewels" sent a little shiver down her spine.

His gaze followed the line of her finger, and he closed his stance a little, clasping his hands together in front of him. "Well, no, not really."

She bit her bottom lip to fight a giggle. Still, the sides of her mouth rose in a slight curve.

He stood straight. "What's so funny?"

"Nothing. Just waiting on orders, boss."

He glanced around outside, then stared back at the house.

"I hate to ask you this, but are you willing to go back inside
and work on the punching bag? I really want you to practice
putting your weight behind your blows, but I'm not real crazy
about the idea of *my* jewels being your target."

Blows, jewels... God her mind was in all the wrong
places. Heat seared her belly, and her cheeks could melt steel.
She'd only *really* known the man a week. Not nearly long
enough to be thinking about the things she thought about, nor
was she ready to jump into something so fast or so rash with
anyone. A change of scenery might be what she needed. His
broad shoulders and hard chest in that tight black shirt only
made the hot flash worse. There was nothing attractive about
a punching bag.

"Yeah, let's do it, I mean, let's go...uh...let's go inside."
She spun so fast she flung mud with her shoe.

"You okay?"

"Yep. Yep. Fine." Waving a hand in the air, she didn't
bother to look behind her. "Just ready to get started."

Tyler's exercise equipment took up nearly every bit of
space in the spare room. A weight bench sat in the middle of
the area, with a treadmill shoved to one side, and a punching
bag on the other. A television hung from the ceiling in the
corner, and three speakers hung from the remaining corners
of the ceiling. Every evening she heard the clink of the
weights and the bump from his speakers, but she'd never
stepped foot in there. Until now. She'd already taken his
room. Least she could do was leave this space for him.

"Pretend these are your three points." He pulled her attention toward the punching bag and taped three pieces of paper
marked with an X to the bag.

His big frame did nothing to help the tightness of the
room. She turned her attention to the bag, zoning in on what
he told her, and not paying any attention to him, his strong

chest, or the yummy scent of male testosterone he emitted. No attention at all.

"Neck, middle, groin," she said and focused on the subject she was supposed to be focusing on. Self-defense.

"Good. Now. Just like we practiced outside. Forearm, elbow, kick," Tyler instructed.

I've got this.

"Forearm." She stepped her weight into her right leg and hit the bag with her arm. "Elbow." Her pointed bone hit the bag dead center. "And kick." Her sneaker hit just left of the X. When she stood tall again, the bag barely moved.

"Good. That was a good first try, but really put some power behind it."

"Okay." She nodded.

Focus. You can do this.

She went through the sequence again. While the bag moved more than before, it still didn't move enough to warrant her faith that she could cast fear in someone while defending herself. No wonder she proved such an easy target for Duke. Even with her ribs mostly healed, she was weak.

"Oh my. That was terrible." She placed her fingertips to her forehead.

"No it wasn't, but I know you can do better. Here." He stood behind her closing in even more on her little space. "May I help you?"

Oh, snap! "Please."

"Lift your arm."

His fingertips tickled her skin as he raised her arm level with her nose. She let out an involuntary giggle.

"What's wrong?"

His breath warmed her ear, stirring that heat in her belly she'd just gotten under control. "Nothing." She shook her head. "Sorry, you were tickling me."

"Sorry." He lightened his grip. "Now, karate chop the bag."

She refocused her attention to the giant sleeve of leather, and smacked it.

"Harder."

She hit it again.

"One more time."

She struck the bag to the point that it swung a good foot away from her.

"Awesome. Now, go for the elbow."

She took her right arm and swung her elbow toward the middle X. The momentum of the bag stopped.

"Nice try, but really get your whole body into it."

Nice try? It was terrible. She reared back and struck the bag again. The sleeve barely budged. Dropping her arms to her sides, she let out a moan. "What am I doing wrong?"

"It's your feet. Here, let's try again. Start from the beginning, and I'll guide you."

"Okay." Annie stood tall and repositioned.

"Neck."

She struck with her forearm as he held his hands on the back of her shoulders.

"Middle."

She swung her elbow out, and he gripped her hips and rocked her body forward. Hesitating slightly at his touch, she refocused and swung. The bag bobbled around in a circle.

"Now groin." He let go of her hips.

Annie reared back to kick the bag, her heel making direct contact with the X. The bag danced around from the force of her blows.

"I did it, I did it." She spun around to face him, and lost her balance in her excitement from the pivot. She gripped his arms for support, just as he reached for her hips to hold her up right. There she stood, not even five inches from his face, their bodies touching, and his hard chest flush with hers.

"I knew you could."

He stared down at her, his eyes narrowed slightly, almost as if they were smiling and devouring her at the same time. She fell deeper into Tyler's embrace, their lips mere inches apart. The heat from her stomach raced back to her cheeks and down to her toes. She leaned closer, inviting him to take her mouth...

Instead, he let out a little moan, let go, and turned toward the window. Coldness whooshed over her, nearly knocking her over just like her uncoordinated feet.

What a fool she'd been. Of course he wouldn't be interested in her. Too much baggage.

Annie's hands shook from the hot and cold emotions running through her. She crossed her arms over her chest, and half-turned his direction. Air. She needed air. She had to get out of the house. She would chance being outside alone for a few minutes, but first she had to apologize. Undoubtedly, she'd just made things weird. "I'm so—"

"I umm...I just realized we don't have anything for dinner." Tyler cut off her apology as he stared at the view of the creek from the window.

Dinner? He was thinking about food, *now?*

"O...okay?"

"When's the last time you went fishing?" He turned toward her.

"With my dad, about ten years ago."

"How about we go outside and catch us some fish? I think there are some vegetables in the crisper, and maybe a beer or two. Interested?"

Fishing? He seriously wanted to go fishing. He wanted to

be near her after he turned away from her? The real question was could she handle being near him?

"Uh…I don't know." Whatever emotions were happening inside of her, obviously, they weren't the same ones happening to him. She'd started to fall for her caretaker, and all he wanted was a fishing partner.

Figures.

"Please?" He stepped forward. "I'd really like it if you went with me."

His gaze fell to the side, distant and empty for a split second before he brought it back to focus on her. While she fought her own battle not to fall for him, he seemed to be fighting something of his own. His distance on the couch had been unnatural for them, and now his eyes. Something was off. Yet, when she needed a savior, he'd been there for her.

Maybe this was her time to be there for him.

"Yeah, okay."

"I'll get us some poles and meet you out by the dock in ten."

"Sure."

Her chest tightened as he left the room, not giving her a passing glance. What was happening between them?

CHAPTER FIFTEEN

Fishing? Why the hell had he asked Annie to go fishing? Tank needed air, but air away from her. Now, with her next to him in those tight little yoga pants and her equally tight tank top, there was no way he would be able to concentrate on fishing. Much less taking in fresh air. And to make matters worse, he'd almost kissed her. *Again.* He knew better—the minute she found out about his past, she would run the other way. Too many issues.

He watched her pull a worm out of the bucket. "You need help with that?"

"Nope." Annie squished the squiggling, burrowing animal between her fingers and shoved it through the hook. When some of the worm's guts oozed, she didn't even flinch.

What a woman.

"I use to help my dad dig for worms so we could go fishing." She cast her line, her bait bobbing on top of the water. "I wasn't much of a girly-girl growing up."

She'd rolled her pants up to her knees to prevent the ends from getting wet. Her toes slung lazily in the water, while her sleek and slender calves basked in the sunshine. The end of her side braid draped over her shoulder and dared to touch the top of her cleavage. He had to turn his head to keep his wandering eyes from searching lower. She might have been a tomboy growing up, but Beauty was definitely *all* woman now.

God, this was a bad idea.

He turned away from her slightly and cast his line the other direction.

"What about you?" Annie nudged him with her elbow.

He swiveled his gaze back to her. "What about me?"

"Well, I told you I liked to go fishing with my dad. What did you do for fun?"

He stretched his neck from side to side. *Fun.* There wasn't much of that for him. At least, not in the beginning of his childhood. "I...I visited my gramps in the summertime. I liked that."

She reeled her line in and tossed it back out into the water. "What else?"

The few good memories he did have always seemed to be overshadowed by the bad: the abuse, his fears, the years of counseling that followed, all things that tainted his childhood. Having fun was a new concept for him.

He shrugged. "I don't know. I got pretty good at lifting weights."

"That's obvious." She stared at his arms.

Lots of people had noticed his muscles before, but when Beauty did it...pride swelled his chest. He had to stop himself from flexing just so she'd notice him a little more. "I also got good at climbing trees, I guess."

"Really?" Her voice raised a few too many notches.

"Yeah." He pulled his head back and caught her dubious stare. "You don't believe me?"

"Yeah." She nodded. "I believe you. I just find it *hard* to believe. That's all."

"Why's that?"

"Well, you're just so…" She raked her gaze over his shoulders and down to his legs.

His blood pumped harder through his veins from her gaze. "So what?"

"So big. I just imagine people who climb trees a little more—"

"More what?"

"Leaner than you. Maybe a little more agile."

"Ha! Agile?" He smiled and stood. He'd show her agile. "I know a dare when I hear one. Put your fishing pole down."

"What?" She stared up at him.

"Come on." He held his hand out to her. "Put your pole down, get your shoes on, and let's go."

"Go where." She grabbed her shoes and reached for his help to stand.

He engulfed her hand in his and wiggled his eyebrows. The feel of her warm, soft skin had him reluctant to let her go. So he didn't. He held her grasp, and her trust as he pulled her behind him to the biggest tree he could find. "We are going to climb a tree."

"No. I don't climb trees," she protested, pulling back on his grip. The momentary trust broken.

He gripped a low hanging limb and pulled himself up. "Give me your hand." He reached down for her, needing to build her trust again.

"What? Tyler no." She took a step back and crossed her arms, her actions wounding his pride.

"Annie, please." He asked again, softly.

She stared up at him, her sneakers dangling from her fingertips. Al left his spot in the sun and came to sit beside her. "This is silly. Even Alfred thinks so. Isn't that right, boy?"

His dog whacked his tail against the ground in answer.

"See." She nodded to the dog. "I'm not going up there. You've proved your point. You can climb trees. I believe you. Now, can you just get down? Please?"

She was scared to have a good time. He'd give good moments back to her.

"No can do." He shook his head. "Put your shoes on, and give me your hand."

Her shoulders tensed near her ears as she glanced off at the water, and her bare foot tapped against the ground.

"I promise." He held a hand to his heart. "I won't let anything happen to you, and I know you won't regret it."

She cocked her gaze back up at him. "You promise?"

"I do."

Annie blew out a breath. "He promises, Alfred," she said to the pup, as she slipped her shoes on.

Once they were on, she took a few steps closer and reached her hand for his. In one quick motion he gave her a tug and had her sitting next to him. She gripped his bicep, her nails digging into his skin.

"It's okay." He pulled her closer, placing his hands around her shoulders. "I'm not going to let you fall. Would you like to go higher? I can get us up there." He pointed to a thick limb about six feet higher.

She squeezed his arm tighter and glanced up. "No, I'm not ready for that high. I can't climb up there."

"Would you like to get on my back?"

"Your back? No, this is crazy. Let's get down." She scanned the ground and the tree, probably searching for a way to get down.

"Hey." He placed a finger under her chin and lifted her

gaze to meet his. "You trust me don't you?" He'd spent the past week trying to prove to her he was worthy of her confidence. But a woman like her, someone who had been through what she had would need more time. Lots of it. Of course she didn't trust him. *What a stupid question.*

Her eyes began to mist, and he dropped his finger from her chin. He'd pushed her too hard. "I'm sorry. I shouldn't have assumed—"

"More than anyone else." She leaned into him and nudged his shoulder with hers. "I trust you more than anyone else in my life right now, Tyler."

Her words gave him pause. "Good," he managed to say and took her hand. "We can stay right here if that's what you'd like. We can still see more up here than we could down below."

"How about just one more branch?" She eyed the thick limb above their heads.

"You got it." Slowly, he stood and balanced on the log, helping her to stand. She gripped the limb above them as he gave her a boost. "You good?" He asked as she sat on the log.

"Yeah," she said, her voice shaky as she smiled.

He climbed and sat next to her.

She relaxed beside him, allowing her legs to dangle freely, holding on to his side. "Wow. Look around. It's beautiful." She smiled at him, and his heart inflated a little at the genuine happiness etched in her features. "Look." She pointed to the left. "Over there. A family of deer."

He followed her hand. "Yeah, and the good thing is this is private property. As long as they stay on the land, they'll be safe."

Just like her. He would keep her safe.

She turned her head to the right. "Look." She pointed. "You can see the chimney top of my old house."

"Wow." He peered where she pointed. "You can. Do you want to go explore back that way?"

"No." Annie shook her head and stared down at her lap. "Too many memories. I think the house is abandoned. Last I heard the mortgage company hadn't found a buyer. The house wasn't in good shape when we lived in it, so I can't even imagine what it looks like now, after nine years of being abandoned. Still, I had such good memories in that house."

A time when everything in her life had been perfect, no doubt. She could have perfect again. He'd like to give it to her.

"Living way out here isn't for everyone."

"I tried to convince Duke into buying the place. My parents' rundown home wasn't good enough for him. But looking back, I'm glad he didn't. I don't want to share that place with him."

"I'm sorry, Annie."

A silence fell around them, and a nag in his gut told him the happy moment had turned sad.

"This is wonderful," she said. "How did you learn to climb trees?"

He shrugged, thankful for the change of subject, but this wasn't the one he wanted to discuss. "Self-taught, I guess."

"Why? I mean, did you like heights as a child?"

"No." Tank let out a little chuckle and shook his head. "Quite the opposite actually. I hate heights."

"Then why climb trees?"

"Just something I did." He glanced toward the sky. "Sun's about to set. We should get down and figure out dinner. I'll go down first, then help you down." He turned his back toward her, thankful for a reason to change the conversation.

Annie gripped his arm firm, but not with the same intensity as when her fear had kicked in from climbing the tree.

"Tyler." Her voice turned soft and honeyed. "You can talk to me, ya know? I'll listen."

Her words were like a spear to his center. Annie had nothing left to hide about her past. He'd asked her to tell him about her life so he could keep her safe, give her solstice, and here, he couldn't even so much as mention the name of his father without his stomach rolling.

And even though the sound of her voice wrapped him like silk and made him feel safe, he couldn't go there. Not today.

"Not now, okay?" He patted her hand.

"Sure." She nodded.

He shimmied down the branch then helped her down until they were both on the ground. Her loyal companion stood waiting, while their fishing poles sat on the dock, empty of dinner.

"Listen, don't worry about dinner for me, okay?" she said like she had read his mind. "I'm really not that hungry, and my ribs are hurting a little from all the activity." Annie gave him a polite smile and turned toward the house.

Damn it. Why didn't he think about her injuries? Not only did he physically hurt her, he'd made her feel bad. He did everything he swore he would never do.

"Hey, wait." He ran after her. "Annie, I'm so sorry about your ribs. I wasn't thinking."

"No worries, Tyler. It's not your fault. I had a good time this afternoon. You fulfilled your promise. Thank you." She turned again.

Damn it. She was distancing herself, pushing him away because he wouldn't open up to her about his past. They could open up about other things.

Tank chased after her again. "I have some popcorn in the pantry. How about a movie? You can just sit on the couch. I promise I won't make you do anything physical."

"A big guy like you is going to survive on popcorn for dinner?" Annie cocked a thin brow. "I've seen how much you eat. I don't think there is enough popcorn in that pantry to tame the beast that lives inside your stomach." She poked him in the belly.

If she kept poking him like that, it wasn't the beast in his stomach she needed to worry about.

"So, that's a no?" He reached for her hand and pulled her closer.

Damn it, he was doing it again. About to do something he shouldn't. But hell, he was tired of fighting. Her red toes, her tight pants, low cut tank tops, all physical things about her he liked, really liked. But her love of the outdoors, and her desire to stand on her own and take care of herself, he couldn't deny those traits didn't arouse him, too. Having her under his roof had been more than he could handle. And while sometimes he felt like that shy boy sitting on the dock years ago, this wasn't one of those times. He was ready for more...but was she?

"I didn't say no." Annie leaned in closer. "Tyler," she whispered.

Her breath tickled his chin, and her lips parted, leaving just enough of an opening for him.

"Yeah?" He stared at her mouth and bent closer.

He had a sordid past. So did she. They could figure it out.

"You have leaves in your hair," she whispered.

Leaves?

Tank pulled back, surprised. "What?"

"Leaves." Annie reached a hand to his hair and pulled out a fat oak leaf.

He scratched his head. Excess leaves fell to the ground. *Damn.* Was their timing ever going to be right? "I guess I need a shower, huh?"

"Might be a good idea." She smiled.

"I take a shower, you pop the popcorn."

"Deal."

Tank took his shirt off as he headed to the house. He gave her a quick glance over his shoulder before he went inside. Her gaze shot toward the ground when she realized he had spotted her staring at him. Her moves weren't quick enough, and he noticed the redness of her cheeks.

Thank God.

He smacked the top of the doorframe on his way inside. At least his feelings weren't one sided. But a question still remained. What in the hell were they going to do about their growing attraction? The timing was all…off. Or was it? He'd ended up back in Black Widow at the exact time she needed refuge. That couldn't be a coincidence. Maybe he was over-thinking everything.

He let out a loud groan and marched into the bathroom. One thing was certain; he was going to need a long, cold shower. A habit he wasn't crazy about forming.

CHAPTER SIXTEEN

Tank woke with a jerk. He panted as sweat soaked his hairline and a searing pain shot down the side of his neck.

A nightmare.

He closed his eyes again and counted to ten, envisioning Annie as a young girl across the water, his grandpa by his side. Anytime he had a nightmare, he tried to push it away with something happy. Something good. The letters he'd received no doubt triggered the nightmare. He'd have to talk to his mom about them, and soon.

He opened his eyes again and tried to move his arm. Stuck. Annie slept soundly cuddled right next to him on the sofa. At least he hadn't woken her. A grown man having nightmares…that, itself, would be a nightmare to explain.

They'd fallen asleep watching *Batman*. Scrubbed clean of makeup, and her bruises fading, he could see her beautiful features again. He peered down at the face of the girl he remembered walking barefoot in the creek with her father all those years ago, the worry of the past six months with Duke waning from her features.

Her lips, so full and rosy, sat inches from his. Tempted to steal the kiss he longed for, he decided to slip his arm out from under her head and scoot his way off the couch instead. If they ever did kiss, she would be awake for it. He wouldn't take anymore from her than she'd already lost.

He hurried to get dressed for work, leaving her to sleep, his furry companion by her side. Tank slipped his cellphone in his back pocket and left her a note.

Sorry to take the phone. Need to call my mom. Father has a phone.

Quietly, Tank eased out the door as the counselor cruised down the drive on his Heritage Softail.

Tank waved to the leader of the pack.

"Morning." Father pulled up beside him. "Where's Annie? I brought breakfast." The man pulled out a package of donuts from his satchel.

"On the couch, being Sleeping Beauty."

"You're making a pretty thing like that sleep on your couch?" Father turned off the ignition to Harley.

"No. Normally, I sleep on the couch, but we were watching a movie, and then we both fell asleep."

The leader's face split in a wide grin. "Uh-huh, sure. You both just *fell asleep*."

"No, it wasn't like that." Tank shook his head. "She's not…it's not…we're not…" He fumbled with his words.

"Lord, son. Are you blushing?"

"No. I'm not blushing." He shook his head again and stared at his boots.

Shit this man sure has a way of busting my balls.

"Yeah, you are. You're blushing." Father slapped him on the back. "You better get to work before you're late, or before Annie comes out here and sees you looking like a tomato ready to gush over thoughts of her."

He ran a hand over his face. "You're annoying, you know that?"

"Yep." The man rocked on his heels, and placed his hands in his back pockets. "Where's your water hose? I've got to wash Harley." He patted the seat of his bike. "She's getting a little dirty."

"Around back." Tank got his nerves under control and stared back at the man. "Why do you call your hog Harley, anyway?"

"One day, son. I'll tell you...one day. Where's your wax?"

"In the garage." He straddled his own bike. "You might want to see if Annie wants to help you. I think she's going stir crazy."

"Yeah, she's cute. Maybe she'll wear a white shirt while she does it."

Tank gave him a hard stare and grimaced. "Not funny, man."

Father folded in half-hooting with laughter. "Oh yeah, the look on your face is hysterical." He stood back upright. "Son, I'm kidding."

"Whatever." Tank revved his bike. "Behave, old man."

"No fun in that." Father hollered over the noise of the engine. "Remember, Bear has court today at three-thirty. Tree's coming to relieve me here. Are you going to make it to the courthouse? Nate asked about you."

The court date that could put Bear's abuser behind bars. He wouldn't miss it for anything. "I'll be there. See you this afternoon."

He drove his bike down the drive to his mailbox. He'd forgot to check it the past few days. Thankfully, a blonde had begun to occupy most of his thoughts. He pulled the door down on the box, grabbed the pile, and flipped through it. A small, white envelope stuck out from the stack of sales papers.

Another one. Damn it. He could no longer put off talking to his mom.

Tank shoved the pile back in the box and drove the ten miles into town, doing his best to ignore the pressure pounding in his chest.

He drove behind Rake's and parked his bike just as his phone buzzed a jazzy ringtone in his pocket.

Speak of the devil.

"Hey, Momma. I was getting ready to call you. How are you?"

"Hey, Ty, honey. I hadn't heard from you in over a week. I just got this overwhelming feeling I needed to call you. How are things in Black Widow?"

"Good. Busy. Hey, Mom…I need to ask you something."

"Must be why I felt like I needed to call. What's up?"

When his mother found out about his dad, her senses had been on high alert ever since. Tank chalked it up to either mother's intuition or mother's remorse. He wasn't sure which. He just wished she had been so in tune with him *before* his father had done what he did.

"I've been getting letters from the prison. Did you give *him* my new address?"

A sigh came over the phone. "Yes, I did."

He grit his teeth. "What? Why in the hell would you do that?"

"He begged me, Ty. He called me one day and begged for your new address so he could keep writing you. He said the letters he sent to your old house were sent back. He even cried over the phone."

So what? He never cared about all the times he made me cry. The sick bastard relished in his tears.

"You had *no right*, Mom. You should have asked me first."

"I'm sorry, hon, but I think, maybe, you should listen to what he has to say."

"I don't give a..." One of his coworkers walking through the back door glared at him. He lowered his voice. "I don't care what he has to say, and I never will."

"Okay, I understand." His mom's voice grew softer on the other end. "I just hate to see you so eaten up inside about... about everything that happened."

"What would you rather me do, forgive and forget?"

"Forget, no, but forgive, yes."

The heaviness he carried from seeing another envelope engulfed his chest again. "I'm sorry, Mom. I shouldn't have raised my voice, but I don't think I can do either of those things."

"It's okay. Let's change the subject. Tell me about Black Widow."

He sighed and hung his head. Changing the subject. Yes, that was best for both of them.

"I... I uh..." He wiped his hand down his face. "I went to a meeting of that biker group I told you about. I've been doing some work with them."

"That's good, hon. Made any friends."

Friends? He chuckled. No matter how hard he tried, he could never stay mad at his mom. She always talked to him like he was still in junior high. Still her little boy.

"Yeah, you could say I've made some friends. There is the leader of the pack, Father. He's annoying as hell, but overall seems like a nice guy."

"What about a lady friend? Have you made any of those?"

Oh, Lord. Here we go. The *I want grandchildren* speech.

"There is someone, but I'm not real sure yet. I like her. I like her a lot, actually, but it's too soon to know anything."

He knew others fell in love, but the notion seemed foreign to him. However, with Annie he couldn't stop the magnetic pull he seemed to have toward her. Yet the timing, their baggage...it was all so intense.

"Oh, I'm so happy you found someone. I'd like to come visit right after the fourth. I'm on shift work this weekend at the hospital, but I'll have a few days off after that. I'd love to meet your friends."

"Yeah, that'd be nice. I may have to work, though, but maybe..." He glanced around to make sure no one overheard. "Maybe my friend can help keep you company."

"Oh, the *girl-friend*?" Her voice took on a conspiratorial tone.

"Yes, Mom." Tank rolled his eyes.

Leona stepped out of her car and tapped her wrist. He was supposed to be inside, ready to work. He nodded to her.

"Listen, Mom, I've got to run. I'm supposed to be clocking in right now."

"Okay, hon. I'll see you next week. I love you."

"Love you, too." He clicked off his phone, and ran into the garage. He'd never introduced his mom to a girl before. None of them had ever seemed like the right girl...

Until now.

———

ANNIE TURNED on her side and opened her eyes as a cool draft caressed her skin. Her vision blurred, and she rubbed a hand over her face. A popcorn bag came in to focus on the floor.

Popcorn. A movie.

She glanced around the room. They'd fallen asleep during the movie. But where was Tyler now?

Alfred snored softly on the floor beside the couch. She lazily rubbed a hand over the dog's side and glanced around for him. A whooshing sound traveled through the water pipes coming from inside the walls. She stood and stretched, peeking into the hall at the bathroom door. Open. She peered into the kitchen. Empty.

Where is Tyler?

Alfred stood and barked at the front door. "Hang on, bud." She lifted the curtain and glanced out the window. Father stood in the grass, spraying his bike down. A sinking feeling plopped in her stomach. If Father was here, Tyler was gone.

He didn't say goodbye.

She shook her head at the foolish notion as she slipped her shoes on. Tyler was nothing more than a glorified roommate with bodyguard benefits. He didn't have to tell her goodbye every time he left. He didn't even have to talk to her.

Still, an annoying feeling twisted her gut. The same feeling she got last night when he talked about the deer being safe on his land. As long as the creatures stayed on his property, they would be protected. Same with her. As long as she stayed, she would be secure. But she didn't want to play it safe anymore. Not when it came to him, and not when it came to her living there.

She wanted to live her life again.

When she opened the front door, Alfred barreled outside and charged off the steps toward Father, barking; his backside wagged in greeting.

"Morning." The biker gave her a wave as he reached down to pet the pup.

"Good morning. Do you know what time it is?"

"A little after eight. Tank just left about fifteen minutes ago." The man reached into a sudsy soap bucket for a sponge as the dog stuck his head in it.

Fifteen minutes. She'd missed telling him goodbye by fifteen minutes.

That same, nagging feeling from yesterday sank like a hard rock in her gut, and turned into a slight fear. What if he didn't want to tell her goodbye? Perhaps he *did* see her as nothing more than a glorified roommate. Someone to help with the laundry and the dishes.

"You okay?" Father asked. "You look a little confused."

"I'm fine. You need any help with that?" Annie stepped down the porch steps. She needed to busy herself. Worrying about Tyler leaving without saying goodbye was irritating her. Even though she told herself she shouldn't care.

He stared back at her. "Your shirt is white."

She looked down. "Yeah, so?"

"Then, no." Father slapped the sponge on his bike. "I've got it. I wouldn't want your shirt to get ruined."

The man mumbled something under his breath. She couldn't make all of it out, but it sounded like *Tank wouldn't like that.*

"Okay then. I think I'm going to go for a little walk. Stretch my legs a bit."

"Don't go too far. I brought donuts." The biker pointed to a box on the porch. "And *The Morning Show's* coming on in fifteen minutes."

The Morning Show. The older man's favorite. Annie had told him on his first time babysitting that she enjoyed the show. In truth, she couldn't stand two of the four co-hosts, but Father seemed giddy to watch the garbage, so she lied to please him. Now, at least twice a week, she was donned with the horror of watching the gossip reel.

"Sure. I won't." She gave him a little wave.

"Why don't you go get the mail? I saw Tank check the box, flip through it, then put a bunch of it back in. Looked like he hadn't checked it in days."

The mail. She hadn't seen the sales papers strewn all over the countertop lately. Not that she missed it. "I think you're right. I'll do that."

Annie strolled down the drive, Alfred on her heels. The morning sun felt glorious on her skin. Even though the humidity was comparable to walking in a greenhouse, she'd gladly suffer the suffocating air, as long as she didn't have to be trapped inside. Even her fear of being outside seemed to dissipate slightly. Then again, she did have her scary protector trotting beside her. Al's tongue hung out the side of his mouth, and his tail wagged his whole backside.

Yeah, real scary.

She flipped the lid down on the mailbox and reached inside. On top of the pile sat a small envelope addressed to Tyler. The return address read Wade Correctional Facility. She paused and stared at the package, her fingers trembled holding the contents. Why was Tyler getting letters from a prison? In her haste to get away from Duke, she never once thought about Tyler having a criminal record. But hadn't JoJo said they did a background check on him?

Her whole body shook slightly as she gripped the pile of mail tighter. Alfred licked her leg and stared up at her as he flopped his tail against the dirt-covered drive.

She glanced at the dog. Tyler had rescued Al, and he'd never once made her feel unsafe or uncomfortable. Surely, a hardened criminal wouldn't be so kind. She shuffled her feet against the dirt as she made her way back to the house.

Father dumped his bucket of soapy water in the grass. "Annie, you ready for breakfast?" he called to her, then looked up from his task. "Whoa, you look white as a sheet. You sure you're okay?"

She licked her parched lips and pressed the mail against her chest. "Yeah." Annie nodded as her heart pounded faster. "Umm...when you guys let someone into the Blue Guardians, JoJo mentioned background checks. Do you do one on everyone?"

"Of course. Why?"

"So, you did one on Tyler, right?"

The man put his hands in his back pockets. "Of course we did. In fact, I did it myself."

The shaking in her limbs eased a little. "So, nothing came up, right?"

"He's as clean as Harley here." Father reached over and rubbed a hand on the seat of his bike. "Where's this coming from? Did Tank do something, because—"

"Oh, no. Not at all. He's been great, but I just realized in my haste to get away from a bad situation, did I...could I maybe be jumping into another...oh never mind. It's not important."

He shot her a concerned look. "Are you sure, Annie? Because if you're not comfortable here, the Guardians can help find another place—"

"No." She shook her head and cut him off again. "Tyler is great. Come on. It's almost time for *The Morning Show,* and I'm starving."

"Okay. If you're sure." He held his arm out for her to wrap hers around it. "Here, let me carry that mail for you."

"No." Annie pressed the pile tighter to her chest. "I've got it. You grab the donuts." She pointed to the box. "I hope Sandi put an éclair in there."

"She did. Just for you." He held the door open. "Let's turn the T.V. on. Those pretty underwear models are supposed to be doing an interview this morning."

"Oh, you didn't hear. The models canceled. Something about having to do a shoot in the Bahamas and getting trapped there by a hurricane."

"What? Oh, man. That ruins my whole morning."

She snickered as some of the pressure from worrying about Tyler lifted from her shoulders. "Just kidding, old man. Come on."

"Old man?" Father slapped the donut box to his heart. "That hurts. I'm not old, I'm seasoned."

"Like a fine wine," Annie teased.

"Now you're talking. Let's go girlie."

She followed the man into the house, her heart lighter knowing Tyler had a clean record, yet her curiosity weighed heavy with concern. If he was a friend of criminals, what did that say about his own morals? Duke seemed nice at first, too, but he changed.

And yet, here she was falling head over heels for another man that she didn't know much about. Who was Tyler really? And *was* she safe in his care?

CHAPTER SEVENTEEN

Tank pushed through the double glass doors of the courthouse. Father and a few of the other bikers he hadn't learned the names of yet stood in a huddle at the end of the hall. The leader waved his hand toward him, and the group stepped to the side, revealing Bear.

The kid sat on a bench with his mom. Steele sat beside the woman, while a man in a suit stood over her talking. Mary shook her head, focused on what the suit said.

The lawyer.

"Tank." Bear stood and ran toward him, the ever-present teddy clutched in his hand.

"Hey, big guy." He lifted Nathaniel in a hug. "Your cheek looks great dude. Can't even tell you had a battle bruise anymore."

"Yeah. It feels better, too."

Duke walked down the hall with the short cop he'd seen at the diner and stood by the double doors of the courtroom.

Tank's heart rate sped, causing the veins in his neck to pulse. He took in a deep breath as his hands moistened.

Subtly, he set Bear down and wiped them on the side of his pants.

Not today. He wouldn't allow his fears to get the better of him. He was stronger than his anxieties, and he sure as hell wouldn't let that bastard, Duke, see how he bothered him, nor would he let anyone else see his unease.

The Chief of Police stopped mid-conversation and stared, his gaze hard on Tank. He gave his own hard stare in return as the bailiff opened the heavy wooden doors of the court-room, nearly hitting Duke in the ass.

Too bad he missed.

"Case of The State versus Franks. Court will begin in ten minutes." The bailiff pushed the doors open all the way and set the stoppers.

Bear reached up to grab his hand, his grip firm.

"You okay, big guy?"

Nathaniel nodded.

Tank kneeled eye level with Bear. "What's the matter? Are you scared of seeing your dad?"

The kid glanced down at his shirt, and nodded again. "I'm also…" He leaned in to whisper in his ear. "I'm scared of that cop."

"Why are you scared of him?"

Nathaniel shrugged. "He looks mean."

He gave the kid credit for being a good judge of character as he glanced over at Duke again. A woman in a tight-fitting dress, with a stack of papers in her hand and a large political button stuck to her chest, flipped her hair as she talked to the chief. The button read *Duke for Sheriff.* The man smiled and gently touched the small of her back as he turned to whisper in her ear. The woman giggled as she walked away, sashaying her hips and giving the cop a backward glance.

No doubt Duke used the same charm to win over Annie.

Tank stared at him.

That man…with *Annie*.

He knew the facts, but he had a hard time placing the two of them together in his mind. Never again.

Tank glanced back at Bear. "You don't have to be scared anymore, okay? You've got all of us here to protect you. As long as I'm around, I won't let anything or anyone hurt you. Got that, big guy?"

Nathaniel nodded.

"Good." He stood.

Mary walked up to her son. "Nathaniel, I have to go inside now, but Steele has offered to stay out here with you, okay?"

Bear glanced to Steele then back to him. "Can you stay with me instead?"

Tank looked to the mother then to his biker friend.

Steele shrugged while a slight look of dejection marred his face. "Yeah, whatever you want little dude."

"Mary, is that okay with you?" Tank asked.

"Of course." The woman knelt down to kiss her son on the forehead. "Nate, be good for Mr. Tank, okay?"

Mr. Tank.

"Yes, ma'am."

The lawyer walked up to the group. "We should get inside. Judge Mannis doesn't like it when his court starts late."

"Sure." Mary nodded. "Wish us luck."

Father strolled by and leaned in closer to him and Nathaniel. "I know Mannis. We won't need luck. Just solid facts, and we have them." The leader of the pack patted Bear on the back and gave him a nod. "See you guys soon."

The Guardians, along with a few others, walked inside the

courtroom. Duke gave him another hard stare before he went inside himself, small cop hot on his heels.

At precisely four p.m. the doors closed. Bear fidgeted on the bench beside him, while Tank wiped his brow with his bandana and sat back on the seat.

"Why are you sweating?"

So much for getting my nerves under control. "Just something I do when I see cops."

"You don't like them, either?"

He stared down at the kid. "This is the part where I'm supposed to tell you cops are fine, but I'll be honest, while most are, not all cops are good. But it's not cops I have a problem with, it's the uniforms."

"Why?"

He placed his bandana in his pocket, thinking about how to tell such a small child adult problems. "Remember when I told you my dad was a bad guy?"

"Yeah."

"Well, he used to wear a uniform. It was a different uniform, but similar. Ever since then, the outfit makes me nervous."

"Oh." Bear nodded. "You know what makes me nervous?"

"What?" He raised an eyebrow.

"Girls."

"Ha!" Tank laughed. What a change of subject. "I hate to tell you son, but it doesn't get any better as you get older."

"Do girls make you nervous?" Bear eyed him, curious.

"Yeah." He nodded. "Sometimes they do." *One in particular.*

"Do you have a girlfriend?"

His smile faded. "No. Not right now, anyway." He

crossed his arms. "I've got a girl I like, but she's...she's not my girlfriend."

"Why not?"

He shrugged and glanced around. Despite the fact he didn't mention any names, he wanted to make sure their conversation wasn't being heard. "I don't know. It's complicated, I guess."

"What does that mean? Complicated?" Bear twisted his nose up.

"I guess it means things aren't always as easy as we would like them to be."

"Oh." The boy placed his hands under his legs and stared down the hall.

"What about you?" Tank nudged him. "Do *you* have a girlfriend?"

"No." Bear shook his head adamantly.

He leaned closer. "Is there a girl you like?"

"Yeah." The kid sighed. "But she doesn't know I like her."

He smiled at the boy's obvious confusion about the opposite sex. "Is she pretty?"

"Uh-huh." Nate's eyes got big. "Real pretty."

"Oh, I bet she is for a guy as handsome as you to like her." He sat back again. "Do you talk to her?"

"No." Nate shook his head. "Well, sometimes I do." Bear stared at him, his eyes still round and curious. "Can I meet the girl you like?"

"Sure." He nodded. "I'm sure she'd like that."

"When?"

A good question. When could he take his Beauty out of hiding? He placed his arm on the back of the bench. "Soon. I hope real soon."

"Okay." Bear finally seemed content with his answers.

"I'm tired. Can I lay on your lap?"

"Sure." He patted his leg.

The kid settled his head down on his lap and his small frame curled up on the rest of the bench. "Wake me up when my mom comes out, okay?"

"You got it."

Bear clutched his teddy to his stomach and closed his eyes. Within minutes, a slow steady breathing poured from the boy's chest.

He watched as Nate slept. How could a father ever abuse his son? His own heart heavy of emotion, Tank propped his head against the wall, and rested his eyes.

The sound of the courtroom doors startled him, and he snapped his eyes open. The bailiff's shoes clicked on the tile as he walked over and knelt down to Bear's level. "The judge would like to see the boy in his chambers." The court official glanced up at Tank.

"Okay." He shook Nate. "Bear. Bear. You've got to wake up. The judge wants to talk to you." He patted the boy's arm.

Nathaniel sat up and rubbed his eyes. "What?"

"The judge would like to see you in his office," the bailiff said. "If you come with me, I can take you back there." The official stood and held out his hand.

"Can you go with me?" Nathaniel stared up at Tank.

He glanced at the bailiff. The man gave a slight shake of his head.

"Uh, I don't think so big guy. You've got to do this one on your own, but I'll be right here when you're done, okay?"

"Can my bear go?" Nate stared at the bailiff.

"Sure. Your bear can come."

Reluctantly, Nathaniel took the man's hand. He gave Tank another glance as he walked down the hall.

"I'll be right here when you get back," he called out.

Tank's heart hammered in his chest. Why did the judge want to see Bear? Surely, the man wouldn't ask him any questions to upset the boy. Thinking back to his own court proceedings, he couldn't remember much. He'd blocked most of his past out. His counselor said it was a defense mechanism. While he chose not to remember the legalities, he remembered the pain. Nothing could defend him against that.

Tank glanced at the courtroom, but no one came out. What the hell was going on? He stared at his phone and tapped his foot on the tile. His pounding heart not slowing down, he nearly tapped a hole in the floor. Needing to do something different, he stood and paced.

Please, let everything be okay.

Just when he thought he might barrel into the judge's chambers, the door swung open and Nathaniel came running out. "Tank, guess what."

"What big guy?" He lowered to a knee.

"I get to live with Mom. I get to stay with Mary."

Custody. Of course. The judge wanted to get a feel of Nate's emotions, alone, without the prying eyes of adults.

"That's awesome, big guy. Your mom will be so happy."

Five minutes later, the doors to the courtroom opened. Mary ran out with tears in her eyes, all the Guardians close behind her. "It's over baby." She gripped her stepson in a hug.

Father came to stand by him.

"How did it go in there?" he whispered.

"As good as could be expected. The man didn't even try to defend himself. He knew he didn't have a leg to stand on. Four people testified against him. Even our Chief of Police had to get on the witness stand."

"Really? So *he* helped our cause?"

"He wasn't helping anyone but himself. His campaign for

Sherriff is blowing full steam ahead now. He's putting on a good face."

"What was the verdict?"

"Three years in prison. Mary gets temporary custody for the time being."

His jaw dropped. *Three years?* "That's it?"

"Yep." Father rocked on his heels. "First offense."

"So, he still has custody of his son." Tank crossed his arms.

"It appears so." Father nodded.

What the hell kind of justice was that? He shook his head. "That's disappointing."

"I agree, it's less than I expected, but at least this way, he can't hurt them for three more years. We'll do our best to make sure it's never again."

Three years. Bear will be ten when his father comes back in his life. Still, young and impressionable. "I hope the kid can move on."

"That's why we're here. To help." Father slapped him on the back.

The man was right. They *were* there to help, and if he had to check in on Nathaniel and Mary every day—once the man left prison—to make sure they were safe then he would.

"How about we all go out to eat at Sandi's. Hamburger Steak is the special tonight, and I don't know about you guys, but I'm hungry." Father patted his stomach.

"Me, too," Bear squealed.

"Well, great." The leader rubbed the boy on the head. "Mary, I've got you two covered. Rest of you heathens, you're on your own. Come on guys, let's go."

Duke exited the courtroom, the same hard stare from before creased his face. Tank's palms began to sweat. *Annie.*

"Hey, man." He slapped Father on the back. "I think I'm going to sit this one out. You guys go ahead without me."

The leader followed his gaze over to Duke before he leaned in and whispered. "Normally, I would say okay, but not today. You need to come, be seen in town. The way that man's looking at you, it's almost like he suspects something. Don't give him a reason to follow you home. Come have dinner. I'll give Tree a call to pass the message on."

Staring at Duke had his skin crawling. He needed to get home to Annie, wrap his arms around her, and make sure she was safe. He couldn't keep her safe if he couldn't see her. But Father had a point. He needed to be seen around town and act like he had nothing to hide.

"Besides," the counselor cut into his thoughts, "JoJo is coming. And she said you owed her a thank you dinner."

"She told you about that?"

"I have no idea what you're talking about." Father tossed his hands in the air. "And I don't want to know. See you at the cafe in ten." The leader headed for the exit.

Tank turned and saw Duke in the corner flirting with the same button clad woman as before. He fisted his palms at his sides. He'd go to the diner and play his part, but he'd be damned if that man ever laid another hand on Annie. He'd give his life before that happened.

Pulling his shades out of his pocket, he put them on just as the lady slipped Duke a small piece of paper. Probably her number. *Bastard.*

————

SANDI LED their group back to a table big enough to seat eight. Tank spied as Father gave her a slight ass pat when she laid the menus on the table.

Horny old man.

The bell on the front door jingled. JoJo scooted in the restaurant and pulled up a chair next to him.

He glanced at his partner in crime. "Hey, long time no see."

"I didn't want to be seen around you too much," she whispered. "You know? Just in case." She glanced down at her jacket to a slight hole at the elbow.

"What happened to your leather?"

She shushed him and stared around the room just as Duke and his accomplice ambled into the restaurant. Much to their luck, the hostess sat them a couple of tables over at the only empty space left.

Beads of sweat formed around Tank's hairline.

"It got ripped."

"Ripped?"

Her eyes widened as if he needed to catch on to what she tried to say. He gave her his best dumb stare before she cocked her head toward the side of them.

"I think I left a little piece of myself at a *friend's* house," she whispered.

He passed the cops a glance as they took their seats then licked his suddenly dry lips and nodded. "Why didn't you tell me before about your jacket?"

"Like I said, keeping my distance."

"Why are you wearing it? What if he sees you?"

She gave him a hard stare. "I *always* wear my leather. I'm proud of who I am, and what I've been through. I'll be careful. He won't see."

Steele smacked him with his menu. "It's not nice to tell secrets, you two."

Father glared at them over his own menu. "Steele, in this case, it's best we don't know."

JoJo leaned in. "Counselor here is a stickler for following the rules and the law."

"I gathered," Tank muttered.

"Too bad our own force don't seem to think those laws apply to them," Steele mumbled to where only they could here.

"Tank, why are you sweating?" Father asked.

"It's hot in here." He gripped his menu tighter and took in a deep breath.

"Look who it is." Father's gaze skirted to the entrance of the restaurant.

Tank tossed a glance to the right of him. A tall man wearing a button up and khakis walked in beside another tall man wearing a suit. "Who is it?" he asked JoJo.

"Tall and lanky— the chief's father. Tall and fat—Mayor Glass."

"Duke, my boy." The father slapped his son on the back.

The chief stood, shaking the mayor's hand. "Good to see you both."

"I've seen your signs around town these past few days. Your campaign seems off to a fine start."

The mayor spoke loud enough for the whole restaurant to hear. Just what this town needed— the mayor's stamp of approval for Duke. And considering the fact that daddy and the mayor were having dinner together, there was probably some dirty secret scandal behind their friendship.

Crooked politicians.

"Well, thank you, sir," Duke said. "Please, have a seat."

Tank cut his gaze back to the menu and heard the scrapping of chairs.

"Where's that lady friend of yours, Miss Annie? I haven't seen her around the diner lately."

Tank kept his gaze firmly on his menu as he strained to

hear what they were saying over the noise of the restaurant. Even though the mayor had his back to him, he could imagine a man like Glass tucking his napkin into the collar of his shirt.

"Annie is visiting her mother. She'll be back any day now."

He cracked his neck as he listened to the lies.

Stay calm, Wilde. Duke will never lay another hand on her.

"You set a date for that wedding of yours?" the mayor asked.

"Not yet, sir, but it'll be sometime in the fall."

"Before election time of course," Duke's father answered.

Tyler gripped his menu harder. "Did you hear that?" he whispered to Steele and JoJo.

"Yep," the firefighter said.

He cocked his gaze to JoJo.

She nodded. "He hasn't given up," she whispered.

Annie was still in trouble. He tapped his foot under the table, anxious to leave and get home to her. The silverware rattled from his knee bumping the underside of the tabletop.

JoJo placed a calm hand on his arm. He glanced at her embrace and stilled his leg, nodding. As long as Duke was in the restaurant, Annie was safe.

"I've been telling Duke how important it is to have a wife on the campaign trail," the father continued. "A man's campaign is only as good as the woman backing him."

"Ain't that the truth?" the mayor said. "My Georgia, she keeps me straight and helps me remember what's important."

"So, you get Annie back here, son, as soon as possible. The town needs to see her by your side for the speeches in a couple of weeks at the town hall," the father advised.

"Of course," Duke agreed.

Speeches? Tank focused his attention back to his own table. Annie wasn't safe as long as Duke ran his campaign.

Tossing his menu to the side, he laid his palms flat on the table. "I have to get out of here. I need to get home."

Father shook his head. "Watch your back, son."

"Will do." He tapped the tabletop and pushed his chair back before he waved goodbye to the group.

He made it to his bike before Father ran to catch up to him.

"Tank. Wait up." Father stood next to him.

"Yeah?"

"Quick question. You still going on the ride?"

The Fourth of July ride. He'd nearly forgot. He still had a few days to prepare.

"You bet." He reached for his helmet.

"Hey listen." Father held out his hand to stop him. "I don't know if this matters and I didn't want to say anything in front of everyone else, but…" He glanced around and leaned in. "Our friend was asking some odd questions this morning."

"Odd?" He placed his helmet back on his handlebar. "What do you mean?"

"Well, she asked me if we did background checks on our members. Then she specifically started asking about you and your background. She was white as a ghost."

White as a ghost? Why?

"When exactly did this happen?"

"Early this morning. Right after she checked the mail."

The mail? The letter. *Oh shit.*

"She checked *my* mail?"

"Yeah, she wanted something to do. I saw you toss a bunch of the mail back in the box, so I thought we could help out by bringing it inside."

"Fuck," he whispered and shook his head.

Father took a step back. "I'm sorry, man, if we over-stepped. I mean, it was the mail. It seemed innocent enough."

"No." Tank shook his head. "It's not your fault or Annie's."

"I have to ask. Is everything all right?"

"Everything's fine. At least, I hope it will be after I talk to her. I gotta go." He tossed his helmet on and hopped on his bike. "See you for the ride."

"Yeah, man." Father waved at him. "See ya, and make sure you bring your friend."

He'd be lucky if she wanted to have anything to do with him after tonight. His past was dark, and not something a woman like her needed to worry herself with. She needed a new beginning, not his old problems.

CHAPTER EIGHTEEN

D uke gripped his fork tighter. If his father talked about having a wife on the campaign trail one more time, he might slug the man. Worse, he couldn't seem to get a break on finding Annie. His source at her mother's home hadn't seen her. Besides the piece of leather he found, it was like she had vanished without a trace. Her phone hadn't been turned on in over a week, and her car wasn't at any of the impound lots.

Where the hell did she go?

He'd had to start running his campaign on his own, and people were beginning to ask questions. Making up one lie after another, they began to jumble in his mind. She was somewhere, and he would find her. No one just disappeared without a trace.

The group of Guardians that sat at a table across from him all stood and strolled to the cash register. He did his best to glance at each one, spying for a hole in their jacket. More than likely, whoever ripped their leather wouldn't be wearing it, but it was worth investigating nonetheless.

And that big guy, Wilde. What the hell was his deal? He'd

been at the courthouse, staring at him like he had something to hide. He didn't have a jacket, but he sat at the same table they did. Was he part of the group? Whether he was or not, the guy rubbed him the wrong way which made him worth investigating.

The young redheaded waitress tending his table laid the ticket down. His dad reached for the bill. "Here, Dad, let me get that." Duke pulled out his wallet and grabbed the check.

"Well, gentlemen, thank you." The mayor rubbed his fat stomach.

The bill came to seventy dollars, nearly forty from the fat ass alone. He would gladly pay the check. If fatso could help win him more votes, and get his father off his ass, he'd buy the man a steak every damn night.

"I'll be back. Excuse me." He stood and walked to the cash register, stopping a few feet behind the biker group. He scanned each of them as they went to pay.

"What time are we meeting, Saturday?" A burley biker with a mustache asked.

"Ten," the short woman said while she handed the cashier her credit card. When she stretched out her arm, a nice hole stared back at him.

He gripped the ticket book tighter and glanced straight ahead, like he hadn't seen it. The opening in the window had been small. Someone of her size could have easily slipped out.

Finally. A lead.

She signed her receipt, then glanced up and noticed him. Immediately, she placed her arm against her ribs and used her other hand to accept the receipt.

"I gotta go, guys." She shoved her card in her back pocket and spun on her heels.

"Later, JoJo." One of the men called out.

Yes, later JoJo.

He would see more of her soon. Very soon.

After paying the tab, he sauntered back to the table. Duke caught Brayden staring down the waitress' shirt. He'd seen that waitress before. She'd worked here when Annie did.

Maybe she knew something. He stared back at Brayden— his key to picking the waitress' mind.

"Well, gentlemen, dinner was great, but Brayden and I have to get back on duty."

"We do?"

"Yep." Duke slapped a firm grip on the rookie's shoulder. "Ready?"

"Uhh…yeah." The guy had a questionable look on his face.

"Yes, duty always calls." The mayor stood. "If I don't get a chance to talk to you before the big debate speeches, then good luck, Fields. However, I'm sure you won't need it." The man stuck out his hand.

"Thank you, sir." Duke shook then reached around to shake his father's. "Dad, I'll talk to you soon," he said then hurried Brayden out the door.

"Boss, what's up?"

"Not here. Get in the unit." He crossed the street at a clipped pace and unlocked his patrol car. Once the officer got inside, he asked, "Brayden, how would you like to be my right hand man when I make Sherriff?"

"Really? I'd love it, sir."

"Then you've got to prove you're worthy."

"How do I do that?"

"First thing you've got to do, sleep with that redhead in there. Find out anything you can on that boss of hers and that old biker. I saw the old guy get pretty chummy with Sandi. I want to know if they have something going on."

"Okay, but why?"

"Don't worry about that. Also, ask the waitress what she knows about the bikers. All of them. Start by questioning her on the blond guy we saw at the courthouse, Tyler Wilde."

"What makes you think she knows anything about this Wilde guy?"

"Waitresses talk. They wait on a lot of people in this town. Surely, she can tell you something. Find out where he works, too. That's important. Maybe the waitress knows."

The rookie pulled out a notepad from his pocket and started jotting notes. "Sure, but can't I just ask her? Why do I have to sleep with her?"

"Because, it will be more fun for you if you do. Trust me." He slapped the rookie on the shoulder. "Then, I want you to find out the names and addresses of everyone in the Blue Guardians, including that chick, JoJo."

"Sure, but again, I have to ask why?"

He grit his teeth and took in a deep breath, searching himself for patience. This rookie asked too many damn questions. "I've got reason to believe that group isn't as good as they seem." He cuffed the guy on the neck. "Also, you should know, in the future, a good employee just does what's asked of him. No questions. Got it?"

"Yes, sir. Sorry, sir."

"No problem. Someone's got to show you the ropes. Now, let's see how well you can prove yourself. But remember, everything we say is confidential police business. Not a word of this to anyone, got it?"

"Yes, sir, I've got it."

"You're a good man, Brayden. Now, let's get back to the station so you can get to work. The more you find out about this Wilde guy and the Blue Guardians the better."

CHAPTER NINETEEN

Tank turned off his motorcycle and stared at the front door. His gut sank as he unsaddled his bike.

What the hell would he tell her? The truth? The idea seemed too harsh. She would stare at him with pity. As bad goods. He didn't want her sympathy, or anyone's for that matter. He wanted to ignore his past and the person who damaged him.

He inserted his key into the lock and opened the door. Al greeted him with a bark and a wag of his tail. "Hey, buddy." He bent and rubbed a hand down the dog's side. Tree sat at the kitchen table.

"Hey, man. Thanks for staying with her."

The biker stood. "Yep."

"Where's Annie?"

"Bedroom." Tree pointed down the hall. "Since you're here, I'm going to head out."

"Yeah, man." Tank held out his hand. "Thanks."

"No problem." He shook. "Bye, Annie." Tree hollered down the hall.

She walked out of the bedroom. "Bye, Tree. Thanks for staying with me."

"Yes, ma'am." The man saluted her and left.

Glancing up, Tank stared at Annie. The silence between them thick and heavy. He looked past her and saw her overnight bag sat in the middle of his bed. Full. And a white envelope clutched in her hands.

Shit.

He swallowed. Time to face the issue. "Annie—"

"How was the trial?" She asked, avoiding eye contact.

Stalling. She was stalling. He could use this to his advantage.

"Okay. The man got prison time, and the Guardians are going to make sure Bear gets the help he needs."

"That's wonderful." She gave him a tight smile, gripping the letter in her hand. Her fingers shook.

"Annie?" He took a step closer. "Are you okay?"

"Yeah." Her voice cracked and she kept her head down. "I was just waiting…waiting to say goodbye."

All because of a letter? She couldn't leave. He had to explain. "What do you mean goodbye? Where are you going?"

She raised her head, her eyes glossing with tears as she slowly stepped toward him. "I can't stay here anymore, Tyler. I appreciate everything you've done for me, I do, but after seeing this letter, I've realized that maybe I'm jumping into something… Well, I'm not really sure what I've realized. I'm just not sure it's a good idea for me to be here anymore. With you." She handed him the envelope.

He stared at the scribbled writing, the words *Correctional Facility* practically screamed from the top of the letter. His past always seemed to tear him apart when he felt the least bit of joy.

"Annie." His voice cracked, and he cleared his throat. "I can only imagine what you're thinking, but I'm not a criminal."

"I know you aren't, Tyler. In my heart, I knew when I saw this letter, and Father told me about the background check." She turned and paced. "But there is something going on here, something you aren't telling me, and I'm not sure what it is or what to think. I'm not even sure I know how I feel about anything right now. I'm so confused." She ran a hand through her hair. "I think it's best I find somewhere else to go."

Go? Leave? She couldn't. Not with Duke still on a hunt to find her.

"Annie." He moved closer. "Please, sit down and let me explain."

She stared at him long and hard, her green eyes bright against the gloss of her tears. Her chest rose in a deep, long rise as she lowered her gaze and glanced at the floor.

He did this. He made her cry. Without even trying, he'd hurt her. He'd obviously been reading their connection wrong. Their night on the couch, him waking up to her snuggled in his arms, the excitement, the joy, it was all one sided. Still, one sided or not, he cared too much for her to see her put herself in danger.

"Annie, please don't cry. Stay. What I have to say, it's important."

Just when he thought she would say no and turn to leave, she sat down. "Okay." She sighed, her eyes softer as she wiped a tear away.

He breathed a small exhalation of relief, and sat beside her. "It's Duke. I overheard him at the diner. He's telling people you guys are getting married in the fall. He's not giving up, and I believe he's still searching for you. Please, it's not safe for you to leave. Stay here. With me," Tank begged. Something he hadn't done in twenty years. The notion sent a shiver through him, but for her, he would relive the fear.

She stood, and ran a shaking hand through her hair again as she paced. "All the more reason I need to leave. If Duke is still searching that means I'm still putting *you* in danger. I don't know much about you Tyler. That's become more obvious with this letter." She pointed to the envelope. "But I know you are a good person, and…well…I feel *several* emotions toward you. It's all so scary and complicated. I can't stay here knowing I'm putting you in danger."

If her leaving was her way of protecting him, the feelings weren't one sided. But he agreed to protect her, not the other way around.

He couldn't let her go. Not yet.

"Annie." He stood and gripped her shaking hand. "I can't consciously let you leave knowing you will be putting *yourself* in danger. This letter." He wafted the envelope in the air. "This is a part of my past I never want to relive. This means nothing." Ripping the letter in half, he tossed the paper in the air. "Please, believe me." He gripped her hand again. "Stay. Here. With me. Just for a little while longer. Let me protect you."

"I'm sorry, Tyler, but I don't believe you."

He let go of her hand. How could he make her see he cared? He'd given her a safe haven. What more could he do?

"What can I do to make you believe I want you to stay?"

"I'm not talking about staying, I'm talking about the letter." She pointed to the shreds of paper on the ground. "That letter means something, or else you would tell me. I'm tired of secrets, Tyler. I'm tired of hiding. I want to live my life again, like a normal person. I want to go back to work. I'll get a restraining order if I have to, but I don't want to live in fear or in the dark, and if living with you means living in secrets, I can't do it. I'm sorry."

"Annie…" He shook his head, desperate to make her understand.

Secrets. Hiding. He understood her emotions, even felt them at one time, but telling her about him, all of him, he couldn't, and he couldn't hold her hostage. But if he let her leave, and walk out of his life, she'd be taking a piece of him with her. A part he thought his father had taken from him.

"Please, just give me some time." He ran a hand over the back of his head. "And if you really want to start back to work, there is nothing I can do to prevent you. I'll even go with you to file the restraining order, even though I think— and you know—it's a terrible idea. But, before you go back to work, before we go to the police, go on the ride with me. Let's get out of here. Get some fresh air."

"The ride?"

"Saturday. The Blue Guardians are camping out for the Fourth of July. We'll dress you in a black outfit, black helmet, and you can pull your hair up. No one will know it's you as we drive out of town. Please?" He gripped her hand again. "Come with me. I promise, I'll keep you safe."

She squeezed his hand. "I believe you, Tyler. But what happened in your past? Why won't you tell me? You know my secrets. Why won't you share yours with me?"

"Annie…" He shook his head again.

"Does this have something to do with what you started to tell me in the truck?"

The break in. When he'd nearly revealed it all.

"Yes." He nodded. "I'm not ready. Not yet. But I promise, in time, when I'm ready, I'll tell you. Just know, I'm not a criminal and I don't keep in contact with criminals, but I'm broken. Very broken."

She stared at him, her eyes full of concern as another tear threatened to fall. She seemed overflowing with care, and fear, and he could relate to her on so many levels, it frightened him.

"So am I, Tyler."

He caressed her cheek. "No. You'll never be broken to me."

Tank leaned in, moved his hands to her waist, and gently pulled her body closer to his, her breasts pressed firmly against his chest. In a slow, steady motion, he inched closer, his lips nearly on hers, giving her ample time to move away.

Instead, she rose, placing her soft, supple mouth to his.

Fire charged through his center. Her salty tear fell to his lips and mingled with the taste of his desires. Slow, steady, she pushed her moist, warm tongue against his. His grip on her firmed as his body hardened.

Don't mess this up, Wilde.

Fearing his need too intense, he eased the pressure of his mouth on hers. She snaked her arms around his neck and pulled him closer, her hand gripping the back of his shirt.

Emotion ricocheted in his gut like a boomerang. She deserved more than him.

He placed his hands, soft and gentle on her cheeks, and pulled back. Her ragged breaths matched his. Wiping away her moist tears with the pad of his thumb, he focused on slowing his breathing and the throbbing in his body.

"If we don't slow down, there may be no going back for me." He pressed his forehead against hers.

"You're right. We should slow down." Her gaze glowed in the aftermath of their kiss. "But Tyler, after that kiss, do you think it's such a good idea I stay here with you? My feelings for you were one of the main reasons why the letter frightened me so much. We haven't known each other that long, and we both have pasts. What if we're rushing into this?"

"I won't make you stay." He leaned back, so he could see her face. "But I don't want you anywhere else. We can go slow."

She reached for his hand. "Good, because there isn't anywhere else I'd rather be. Sleep with me tonight? Just sleep. You think you can do that?"

Inwardly, he groaned. Was he capable of just sleeping in the same space as her? He'd done it once before, but he didn't want to push his luck. What if he had a nightmare?

Old images flooded his mind, carpet fibers under his bed, his fingers trembling in front of him as he stared at the ground, praying, wishing his dad wouldn't find him. The same nightmare he repeatedly had over and over.

"I don't know if that's such a good idea."

She stepped closer, and pressed against him. "Please."

The firmer she pushed her body to his, the more he tightened to try and block out any sensations. The fear of his past was replaced with the thrill of his future.

"If you keep doing that, then I know I won't be able to just sleep."

She let out a soft giggle that hardened his body all over again.

"Fine, we'll let Alfred sleep in the middle."

At the mention of his name, his dog trotted next to her and stared at him, his tongue lobbing to the side. Sleeping in the same space with Annie had just as much to do with his willpower as it did his nightmares. In the throws of one, he could thrash around and hurt her. He wasn't ready to talk about them. Not yet, but he couldn't sleep with her without warning her.

Her green stare intoxicated him, and her lips pointed up at

him, swollen with his kiss. In her gaze he saw heaven. A heaven he had searched for amidst his own personal hell. Screw his past.

Who needs sleep anyway?

"And let this hairy rascal snuggle with you? To hell with that. Let's go." He pulled her hand and headed for the bedroom, praying he could keep Little Tank in his pants and his nightmares away.

CHAPTER TWENTY

T ank loaded a cooler and two tents in the back of his truck, along with his motorcycle. Annie walked out of the house, her black jeans tight against her skin, her hair up in a loose bun, and her overnight bag thrown over her shoulder. He stared at the beauty as she strolled toward him, and let out a low whistle.

"Flirt," she joked. "I didn't have anything black to wear up top. Clean anyway." She tucked her locket inside her button-down shirt. *Smart.*

"That's okay. I have something better." He hopped out of the back of his truck, reached inside the pickup, and pulled out a helmet and a leather jacket.

"For me?"

"Yes, ma'am. Just for you. I hope it fits. JoJo helped me pick it out."

Beauty dropped her shoulder bag, turned, and held her arms out as he helped her in the leather. "How does it look?" She spun around, modeling the jacket for him.

Damn sexy. He bit back the words. He'd be paying for

this bounty for the next few months, but Annie was worth it. Every penny.

"Uh…good. Here." He raised the helmet up. "Let's see how it fits." He put the fiberglass cover over her head. "Now, you look like a true biker, all decked in black."

She flipped the eye cover up. "Just call me JoJo Junior."

JoJo had turned into a good friend, but not a nickname he wanted for Annie. When he thought of JoJo, his body didn't burn with desire. Irritation maybe, but not lust. He and Annie hadn't kissed since the other night, but his need for her grew with each passing day. While he ached to do more than touch her, he wouldn't rush her. But he sure as hell wouldn't call her *JoJo Junior* in the meantime.

"How about Moonlight? It sort of flows with your hair… it's so blonde, and your jacket is so black. And your tattoo with the moon and stars."

"Oh, I like that." She shimmied her head out of the helmet. "But I have to admit, this jacket is a little hot out here in the July heat."

"I know, but you don't have to wear it long." He reached back into the truck for a black ball cap. "Here, put this on while we head in to town." He flipped up the collar on her leather to further hide her face. "Once we arrive at the meeting spot, you can put on your helmet. I'll take mostly back roads there, so hopefully, we won't run into anyone."

"Because wearing a helmet in a truck might look a little suspicious." She placed the cap over her hair.

"Yeah, and a little stupid." He winked and grabbed her bag from the ground. "Ready?"

"Yeah, I think so."

"Alfred, let's go," he hollered for his dog. The big lab bound in the truck and plopped right in the passenger seat, his head hanging out of the window. "Al, move over buddy. That's Annie's spot."

His dog stared at him.

"Alfred. Move."

"It's okay. Really." She laughed. "This might be better. If I'm in the middle, maybe it'll be harder for people to see me with both side windows being covered by you and Alfred."

Yeah, and easier for us to accidently touch. Or maybe, not-so-accidently.

"You sure?" Tank scratched his head.

"Positive." She shimmied around him and slid in the truck.

He hopped in behind her and placed her bag on the floorboard. He'd cleaned the junk off the floorboards the day before when he fixed the broken taillight. Last thing he wanted was another run-in with Duke.

He pulled back, and his arm grazed her thigh.

Damn it.

"Sorry about that." *Not really.* He gripped his steering wheel and cranked the truck.

She gave him a little shrug. "It's okay. Not like we haven't touched before."

She smiled and his insides quivered.

Rein it in, jackass.

Alfred turned in his seat and bumped Annie with his backside, causing her to lean in closer to him. He got a big whiff of her flowery perfume. The same perfume that seemed to soak into the fibers of his home. *Christ almighty.* Every time he walked in the door, all he could smell was *her.* If he had such a hard time sitting next to her now, what the hell was he going to do in thirty minutes when she straddled the back of his bike all the way to Jasper?

God help me.

"WE'RE HERE." Tank put the truck in Park and hopped out. He cracked his neck and took a big sniff of the muggy, hot air. At least it didn't smell like Annie. All that sweetness made him dizzy with need. Thankfully, he'd have on a helmet in a few minutes to help block the glorious smell.

"Hey." Steele slapped him on the back. "Right on time. We're leaving in about twenty minutes. I'll help you get your stuff loaded."

"Thanks, man."

"Morning, beautiful." The firefighter nodded toward Annie and winked.

Flirt.

"Hey, Steele." She slid out of the truck and held her bike helmet in her hands.

Annie kept a cool smile on her face, but her cheeks didn't blush, nor did she wink back. His heart gave a slight bounce.

"You think I need to go ahead and put this on?" She darted her gaze back to him.

He glanced around the grounds. Besides the group of Guardians, the land seemed pretty deserted. "I think you're okay for now."

"Hey, sweetie." Sandi walked to her and gave her a hug.

"Sandi." Annie's eyes misted right before she tossed her arms around the woman. "I've missed you."

"We've missed you around the diner, that's for sure." The older lady hugged her back. "You have a job whenever it's safe to come back."

"Thank you." Beauty wiped a tear from her eye.

"I tell you what." The diner owner pulled Annie in a side hug. "How about you come sit in the SUV with me. We'll turn on the AC and wait while these guys finish loading their gear."

"That'll be great, thank you."

Sandi pointed to Alfred as his dog jumped out of the truck. "Who's this, and more importantly, why is *this* here?"

"That's Alfred. Father said he could ride with you."

"He did now?" She cocked her head toward the leader. "Mentioning it to me would have been nice, Jack."

"Sorry, babe." Father pecked her on the cheek. "I thought you might want a companion on the way."

"Yeah? You're going to pay for this." She shook a skinny finger at the leader.

"Can't wait." The horny bastard winked and skirted off to help Steele load supplies.

"What am I supposed to do with him when we stop to eat?" Sandi asked.

"Either leave him in the car with the windows down, or let him out," Tank offered.

"He won't run off?" The woman stared at Alfred. The pup licked her hand.

"Naw. He stays close by."

"All right." Sandi let out a little huff. "Come on, babe." The mother figure pulled Annie's hand. "We've got some catching up to do."

Beauty gave him a little wave as her employer pulled her away, Al hot on her heels.

Damn dog. The minute Annie walked into their lives it was like he didn't even exist anymore.

"I think you lost your companion." Steele held Tank's tents in his hands.

"Yeah. I think you're right."

"What the hell are these for?"

"Sleeping quarters." Tank pointed to each. "One for Annie. One for me."

"Yeah. Okay." Steele cocked a sly grin as a smug look took over his face.

"What the hell is *that* look for? There is nothing going on between me and Annie." Not anything this flirt needed to be concerned with at least.

"Nothing, man." Steele shook his head. "No reason. Whatever you say." His friend sauntered off toward Sandi's truck, still shaking his head, his boots shuffling on the gravel beneath.

Nosy bastard.

"Everyone about ready?" Father yelled to the group. "We head out in five minutes."

JoJo pulled up on her black sewing machine and parked beside the leader.

"Nice of you to join us." Father tossed her a glance.

The woman whipped her helmet off. "I'm not late."

"Yeah, well, you damn sure ain't early. Get loaded, let's go." The leader pointed to the SUV.

Tank marched around to the back of his truck. "Morning, JoJo."

"Morning."

"You're new leather looks nice."

"I know." She gave him a self-assured grin.

When she had helped him pick out Annie's, she had selected one for herself as well, and he'd gladly paid for it. Least he could do for her after what all she'd done for him and Annie.

He jumped in the back of his truck, and dropped the ramp to unload his bike. "A simple thank you would suffice."

"Not my style."

"Imagine that."

"Enough chit-chat." Father hollered. "Let's ride."

Tyler unloaded his bike, and Annie ran over to him.

"Hey, leather looks good." JoJo remarked, staring at Beauty's outfit.

"Thanks for helping, JoJo. You did good." Annie stood beside him.

"I know." Little Bit threw her helmet on and revved her engine.

"She's too damn cocky for her own good." Tank shook his head. No way in hell was his sweet and beautiful Annie a JoJo Junior. "Here, let me help you." He grabbed the helmet from her hands and placed it on her head. "Can you hear me?"

Annie nodded.

"Okay, hop on Moonlight, straddle the bike, and hold on to me. When I lean, you lean with me. Got it?"

"Yep."

He adjusted himself on the seat. She gripped his shoulders and tossed her leg over the saddle, then snaked her arms down his waist. Her hold firmed before he even took off.

"Are you scared?"

"A little. I've never been on a bike before."

He patted her hand and spoke over his shoulder. "I'll take good care of you. I promise."

"I know." She placed her helmet on his shoulder and squeezed his waist a little harder. "You know where we're going, right?"

"Yeah. I have directions on my phone if we lose the group, and Sandi is holding up the rear. We should be good."

Father drove to the front of the pack and pointed his finger forward. "Let's ride," he shouted above the noise.

Several of the members hollered in excitement. The whooshing sound of revved engines sang out like a melody as bikes zoomed off one by one to follow behind the pack leader.

"We're going to have fun, Annie."

"I know." She gave him another squeeze.

He'd be sure of it.

CHAPTER TWENTY-ONE

T ank parked outside the honky-tonk Father suggested and turned off his bike. He stared back at Annie over his shoulder. "Pit stop."

"Thank God." She released her grip and took off her helmet. Her blonde hair tumbled loose from her bun. Waves of golden glory blew in the breeze, causing her sweet scent to envelope him again. He let out a little groan.

"Everything okay?" she asked.

"Fine. Just ready for a break."

She ran her fingers through her hair. "Me, too. The vibrations from the road shot straight to my bones and my thighs." Beauty gripped her legs. "I might not be able to walk straight for days."

Thighs, vibrations, not being able to walk straight. Even "bones" was too close to another word. All words and phrases he didn't need to think about. And if she kept swishing her hair and touching her thighs, his break would need to take place in private.

Tank grit his teeth. "You about ready to dismount?" He needed space. Lots of space.

"Yeah."

Annie handed him her helmet, gripped his shoulders again, applying the slightest amount of pressure, and lifted her leg over the saddle. She stood beside him and unzipped her jacket. Sweat dripped down her neck and fell below her shirt collar to places he couldn't see, but damn sure wanted to.

"You about ready to take that jacket off?"

She glanced down. "Yeah. It was a nice barrier against the wind but a little hot." She slid the leather off her arms. Her button down stuck to her stomach, a thin layer of wetness covering her torso.

Damn it. Why couldn't it be white?

Tank placed their helmets on a hook off his saddlebag. "Let's go. I'm starving." He glanced around but didn't see Sandi and Alfred yet. Surely, his pup was okay.

Placing his hand, feather light, on the small of Annie's back, he led her into the restaurant behind the rest of the group. Her gait stiff, he studied her walk, and in the process observed how nice her ass looked in those jeans.

Shit.

A couple of other bikers to the left stopped and stared as he and Annie walked into the bar. Tank gave the men his most menacing stare, using his size to his advantage.

"Hey, man, just appreciating the view," the overweight one yelled and straddled his bike, while his skinny friend cowered away from his gaze.

"Go appreciate another one."

She turned toward the men. "What's going on?"

"Nothing." Nothing he couldn't handle if he had to anyway.

He opened the door for her and ignored the men leaving the parking lot. His eyes adjusted to the lack of light inside the bar, despite the bright sun outside letting him know it was some time around noon. Some loud, country song blared from the speakers in the ceiling, and the smell of grease wafted in the air. His stomach churned.

"Hey, Tank. Come over here. We need another player." Steele pointed to the pool table, he, JoJo, and Tree stood beside.

"Naw, man. I don't play pool." He waved a hand. Poking small balls with a long stick... Not his thing.

"Annie? You up for a game?" Steele offered a pool stick in her direction.

"Yeah, Annie. Let's show these guys how it's done," JoJo hollered.

"I don't know. I haven't played much before." Beauty shook her head.

"Come on." Tree wrapped an arm around Steele's shoulders. "We'll go easy on you."

"Please, Annie." The firefighter gave her a puppy dog stare. "We really need another player."

"Oh, all right." She glanced up at him. "Do you mind?"

"Of course not. Go ahead. We'll order when you get done."

"Okay." Annie gave his arm a squeeze and trotted toward the group.

Despite her sore thighs, her steps and mood seemed lighter than back in Black Widow. The fresh air, fresh faces, all good for her. Could *he* be good for her? The need to try increased with every minute they were together.

Sandi opened the door behind him. "Your pup is sleeping in the car. I left it on because it's hotter than blazes outside. If my car gets stolen, you're buying me a new one." She pointed a finger at him.

She could have just turned the car off and rolled the

windows down. Al was used to the heat, but Tank didn't bother to tell Sandi that. Despite the woman's no-nonsense exterior, she seemed to have a soft spot for some of the same beings he did.

"Will do." He saluted her. "But Alfred will protect your vehicle."

"Yeah, right. That menacing thing? Dog 'bout licked me to death for the first hour, then got tired and slept for the past two. And what the hell do you feed that thing? His farts smell worse than Father's."

Tank snickered. "He likes his table scraps."

"Well, maybe it's time to find him a more balanced diet." Sandi glanced around the bar. "I'm going to watch these women kick ass in pool. Steele is a terrible player. No one's ever bothered to tell him. We all figured he should know by now." She slapped him on the shoulder and sauntered toward the pool tables.

He scanned the place, saw Father pull up a chair at the bar, and ambled toward him. "Mind if I sit with you?"

"Not at all. Bartender, another beer." Father tapped the bar.

The man nodded and pulled another glass down from the rack above his head.

"Hot enough outside for you?" The leader asked.

"Oh, it's all right. It's Texas."

"That's right. It's Texas."

The bartender slid a beer to each of them. Father pulled a ten from his wallet.

Tank held up his glass. "Thanks, man."

"Cheers." The leader tipped his goblet, the glasses clinking then took a long pull. "So." He leaned back in his chair. "Tell me, Tank, what's your story?"

Damn, he sounds like Annie.

"No how was your ride, or how do you like living in Black Widow?"

"We small talked about the weather. I thought that would suffice."

Tank took a sip of his beer, the amber liquid going down cool over his parched throat. "What do you mean, what's my story?"

"I mean, you show up here resolute to join the Guardians. You spot a damsel in distress and take her under your wing, determined to keep her safe. You walked into a home with an abused kid and get the kid to open up to you faster than anyone else. You've done more with this group in the short time you've lived in Black Widow than most of them have in the five years we've been established there."

Tank shrugged and glanced back at Annie. He knew his story would have to come out eventually; he just didn't know if he was ready for today to be the day.

He watched Beauty as she made a pocket hole and turned around to give JoJo a high-five. No doubt JoJo asked her to play because of their last poker game. Beauty sure knew how to pull one over on a person, and Steele and Tree were no exception. Both men stood with their arms crossed. Steele shot his gaze across the bar and gave Tank a cross look as he shook his head.

He gave his friend the same shit grin Steele had given him earlier that morning and, with a heavy sigh, turned to prop his elbows on the bar.

Time to face the music.

He glanced back at Father. "You sound like Annie, you know that?"

"Well, from the questions she asked the other day after checking your mail, something frightened her. You've got secrets. Might feel good to let 'em out."

"Don't pull that counselor talk on me. You may be good at your job, but that doesn't mean I'm ready to lay on your couch and let it all out."

"Fair enough, but I promise, you'll feel better."

Tank shook his head and took another long sip of his beer, nearly draining the glass. He needed some liquid courage to relive his past. He sat the glass down with a thud, and shook his head. "My story isn't good."

"I figured, but why don't you tell it to me anyway?"

"Have you ever been in love?" He glanced back at the leader.

Father blew out a breath. "Yeah, I have."

"You love Sandi?"

The leader glanced across the bar. The cafe owner leaned against the wall, watching the pool game. "We haven't been dating long, but Sandi's a good gal. I enjoy her company."

Tank could read between the lines.

"Well, I've never been in love before, but I think..." He shook his head, and glanced back at Annie.

"Hey, man, that's great." Father slapped him on the back. "It's a great feeling. Does she know?"

"Naw." He shook his head. "She's not going to find out either. She's had a shitty deal lately, and the last thing she needs is my shit added to it." He drained his beer.

"Your shit, huh? Does a parent have anything to do with it?"

Tank thought back to being a seven-year-old boy, hiding under his bed, or stuck at the top of a tree clinging to the branch. He let out a sigh. "Yeah. Yeah, it does."

"Your father. He hit you?"

"Some. Yeah." He pursed his lips and cracked his neck. "But it wasn't really the hitting that bothered me."

Father placed his arms on the bar top and whispered, "He did other things to you?"

He cocked the leader a hard stare, and instead of shame, he was met with compassion. "Yeah. He did."

"Shit, man." Father leaned back in his chair. "I'm sorry. How old were you."

"Seven." He tapped a nail on the counter and focused on his paper coaster. "I was seven."

"How long did it go on?"

"A year."

"Did you tell anyone about it? Your mom?"

"Nope. I didn't tell anyone. My father...he would uh..." He kept his focus on that little coaster, as if the cardboard ring would give him the courage he needed to continue. "He would work security service at the community college at night. He'd come home just as my mother would leave for class."

And that's when everything would go wrong.

"She went year round, hoping to get done faster. She attended school during the day and bartended at night. My parents were never together. Mom would kiss me every morning before she left, and I pretty much wouldn't see her until the next morning. She always left me...with him." Tank motioned for the bartender to pour him another beer.

"Explains why you were sweating in the diner. Duke's uniform, it triggered something."

"Yeah. Security officer and cop uniform. They look simi-lar. You know, my mom, she worked hard her whole life, waitressing or tending bar. Right before my seventh birthday, that's when she decided working so hard for so little wasn't the life she wanted forever. When she started nursing school..."

"That's when the abuse started," Father finished for him.

"Yeah." He stared at the wooden bar top. "He would stand in my doorway still dressed in his uniform… and…and watch me as I got dressed for school, or demand that I didn't get dressed at all." He choked the last word out and swallowed. He wouldn't cry. He swore to himself he'd never let the man hurt him again, and he sure as hell wouldn't let the pain start now.

Not again. Not ever again.

"How did it end?"

"One day, after my mom left, my father, he…" Tank stopped and took in a few deep breaths.

"Take your time."

He was stronger than his pain, stronger than his fears. He closed his eyes, and pushed away the feeling of his body shaking on top of the thin tree branch, the pain of the bark digging into his palms, realizing jumping to his death would be better than coming down to face his father. The sound of pictures rattling on the walls as his dad stomped toward his bedroom. None of that existed anymore.

"He got undressed. I ran and hid under my bed. He started hollering, screaming for me. He screamed so loud, he didn't hear my mom come back home. She'd forgotten one of her books. She walked in, heard the screams and went to investigate. That's when she saw my father with his pants down, dragging me out from under my bed."

"That's when it ended?"

"Yeah." He nodded. "She swept me away to my grandfather's for the summer, and my father went to prison. He got twenty-five years."

"I'm sorry, son."

"Yeah. Well, it wasn't your fault I got an asshole for a father."

The bartender set down the fresh beer.

"Thanks, man." Tank reached for his wallet.

"No. I got it." Father threw a five on the bar.

"Thanks."

The bartender took the bill then pointed to the two of them. "Nice to see a father and son having a beer together."

"Yeah?" Father grinned to the bartender. "Too bad we aren't related."

"Could have fooled me." The man placed the money in the cash register. "It's your eyes."

"Nope." Tyler sat back. "Just friends." He slapped Father on the shoulder.

The man shrugged and walked off.

"Maybe I'm starting to hang out with you too much," the leader suggested. "You know how they say people who spend time together start looking alike."

"Damn, then before too much longer, I may grow a tail." Tank laughed, glad for the short distraction.

Father joined in. "True."

"Hell." He shook his head and held his beer to his mouth. "I wish you were my father. You would've been a hell of a lot better than the one I had." He sipped.

"Yeah, but remember, *because* of what you've been through, you've been able to help others going through some of the same situations. You're a good man, Tank."

Father gave a pointed glance back at Annie, and Tank followed his gaze.

Steele re-racked the balls while JoJo marked a line on the chalkboard that hung on the wall. The *Ladies* had one point; the *Idiots* had none. He stared at the woman he'd been living with the past few weeks. His heart pulled.

"I don't know." Tank swiveled back to the bar. "Like I said, she's great, but she doesn't need my baggage."

"Why don't you let her decide that? I imagine Annie is pretty tired of being told what to do."

"Yeah, you're probably right."

"Usually am." Father took a sip of his beer.

"I gave her a biker name today."

"Yeah?" Father sat back. "What's the name?"

"Moonlight. She's decked in black to keep her hidden, and her hair is blonde. The contrast of the two is like the moon in the night. I only thought it fitting." He left the part about her tattoo out. The meaning seemed too personal for *him* to share on her behalf.

"Hot dog. You're right." The leader swiveled in his chair. "Let's go, Moonlight. Kick some testosterone ass."

Annie raised her pool stick, while the others stared.

"Moonlight." Sandi clapped a hand on Annie's shoulder. "That's my girl".

More catcalls came from their crew in admiration for her new name.

Tank tipped his beer to her, and she passed him a subtle wink that made his shaft harden. Damn she was beautiful.

He turned back to the bar. "Okay, I told you something. A big something. It's your turn."

The biker sat his mug down. "Sure. That's fair. What do you want to know?"

"Why do you call your Harley, Harley? Why not something a little more...original?"

Father nodded his head, his eyes taking on a distant gaze. "You asked about love earlier. I *was* in love."

"You were?"

"Yep. Twice. My first love, Gracie, she died after two years of marriage. Cancer."

"Oh, man. I'm sorry. I didn't know."

"Most don't. I don't talk about her much. I had a few

years of drinking, and jumping from one job to the next. My sister, she suggested I get counseling. After therapy, that's when I decided I wanted to be a counselor. So, much like your mom, I went to school later in life. Got my degree."

"What made you decide to start up the Blue Guardians?"

"For my classes, we'd visit different abuse shelters. I'd see kids, women, even some men suffer from abuse, and I knew that's where I needed to devote my time. So, that's what I did. I put my love for riding and my love for helping others out of bad situations together and drove across country starting up the Blue Guardians."

"Why the name?"

"What do you mean?"

"I mean why Blue Guardians? Why not White Guardians?"

"None of us are pure, son."

Tank smirked, thinking about Father gripping Sandi's ass at the diner. He hadn't known the man long, but pure didn't come to mind as a descriptor. Hairy, old, horny maybe, but not pure.

"But calling our group the Black Guardians seemed a little evil, despite our leather color. Blue symbolizes calm. We're the calm in the storm people face, and we protect them."

"Like a guardian angel."

"Right."

Tank nodded. "Makes sense. I like it, but none of this explains why you named your bike Harley."

"Remember, I said I fell in love twice."

"Yeah."

"About six years after Gracie, I met this beauty. Ever heard of love at first sight?"

"Of course."

"Believe in it?"

He remembered watching Annie across the lake. Her toes in the water, her bare legs in her jean shorts, holding her dad's hand as she walked across the rocks. "Yeah, I think so."

"Good, because I'm here to tell you it exists. I met this woman. Blonde, lean…" He let out a low whistle. "Man, she was the most amazing thing I had ever seen. She worked at a restaurant I had stumbled into one night of my travels. She flirted. I flirted. When I went to ask for her name and number she wouldn't tell me. It was a small town, and I was only passing through. She said there was no need to get too serious. Told me to call her Harley, so I did. I told her to call me Jack."

"But that's your real name."

"Yeah, but she didn't know that." He took another swig of his beer. "I met up with her after work. We had a great time. After, we went our separate ways, but I couldn't get over her, ya know? She just hit me in all the right places."

Yes, he did know. "What happened? You ever see her again?"

"I tried to shake her off. I figured love at first sight was just a myth, but after a few months, and no matter what I did, I couldn't get her off my mind. That's when I knew. I knew there was something there, so I went back to that small town. I went to that diner looking for her." Father frowned down at his beer.

"And then what?"

"I saw her through the window. She had a swollen belly, a ring on her finger, and she doted over some man. Obviously, her husband. I was too late. Just her good time before she decided to settle down and get serious. I turned around and left."

"You never heard from her again?"

"Nope. Never. I figured I had fallen in love twice. That's two times more than most. Makes me a lucky man, Tank."

"And you don't think you and Sandi…"

"Like I said, I enjoy her company. She's a good woman with a good heart."

"But she doesn't have yours?"

"Yeah, something like that. Besides, love..." He shook his head and shrugged. "That ship's sailed for me."

"Man, I'm sorry."

"Don't be. Everything happens for a reason, right?"

"I don't know if I believe that." Tank gripped his mug handle tighter. "I mean, why did my dad do the shit he did, huh?"

What reason was there for a boy to be abused?

"I don't know, Tank. I wish I did, but you can't dwell on the past. Focus on your future. Let your past go. Move on, and talk to Annie. Let *her* decide what she wants."

"You sound like my mom."

"Well, then she's a damn smart lady."

"Jack, get over here," Sandi yelled over the noise of the bar. "Come sit with me and let's get something to eat."

Father saluted him with his beer. "Duty calls, man. Let's eat and get to camp."

"Sure. Be right there."

He watched as Father strolled over and took the woman by the waist, pulling her in for a kiss, admiring how easy they moved together—a trust and respect in their motions, even if it wasn't love.

The board behind Sandi had three tally marks for the *Ladies* and still none for the *Idiots*. Beauty tossed him a smile that caused his knees to go weak. He'd never seen her smile so much since they'd been living together, and he'd do whatever he could within his power to keep her smiling.

Annie leaned over the table and made a corner pocket, winning the game. She and JoJo raised their hands to a high-five, gloating in their victory. Steele stared at the table, steam daring to radiate from his ears. The *Idiots* had obviously been hustled.

Tank took another swig of his beer and stood. He'd better go save the firefighter before the man ignited in his own flames. And he really had to be closer to Annie. A whole room's length apart was too much distance. Whoever said that bullshit line about distance making the heart grow fonder had never been up next to a woman like her.

CHAPTER TWENTY-TWO

Tank pulled onto the campsite behind Father.

"We've reserved ten sites. Basically, all of them from twelve to twenty-one. It's first come first serve, so stake your claim."

"Can we get one near the bathroom? Please?" Annie asked over his shoulder.

"Sure." He glanced around the lake. "Where is it?"

"I don't know." She shifted her weight behind him. "Maybe around there?" Beauty pointed to the right.

Tank accelerated his bike the direction she pointed, around a small bend in the road. Sure enough, the bathroom sat on a hill. "I think campsite twenty-one is the closest. You want there?"

"Yeah, and look." Pointing to the view she said, "this is a beautiful spot."

The sun glared on the water, casting an iridescent glow on the ripples. The site sat nestled closer to the lake than any other, and the bend of trees provided the slightest amount of privacy from everyone else.

"Yeah, you're right. It is." He shut off the bike and kicked the kickstand down.

"However, I think your property is just as peaceful." Sliding her bum off the saddle, she stood with her hands laced around her middle, staring at the water.

Standing still, gazing into the lake, Annie's hair tumbled down her back, her curves nice and snug in her pants. Not too thin. Every area he wanted, just plump enough in the right places.

She spun, and he darted his gaze to the horizon, praying she hadn't caught him staring.

"I want to thank you." Annie stepped closer.

"For what?" He unsaddled his bike and stood beside it.

"For bringing me. For rescuing me. For everything really. Without you, I'd be stuck in the diner, wearing long sleeves, and more makeup than any woman should have to. I haven't felt like myself in years. Everything that's happened with my family, and then Duke, I'd lost myself along the way. I feel like I'm getting *me* back again." She reached up to hug him and snaked her arms around his neck. "And that's because of you. So, thank you."

Her scent invaded his senses, causing his groin to harden just like in the truck that morning. Tank placed his hands around her waist and held her close, his lips dangerously close to her neck. Before he could make his move, the rumble of a motorcycle interrupted their moment. Annie pulled back, and he turned. He'd have to have a talk with Father about his shitty timing.

"Sorry to bother you, but here's your tent." The old man tossed the shelter on the campsite.

"Thanks, but I brought two. No worries though, I'll go get the other one."

"Yeah, about that. Steele wanted me to tell you his was

dry rotted, and he needed to borrow one. He took the smaller one. Left you guys with the bigger one."

Tank glanced to Annie. She bit her lip almost like she tried to hide a smile, and her eyes glistened.

"Well, that's his dumbass fault. I'm sure there's a store close by where he can go buy one."

"Tyler." Beauty stared up at him. "It's just a couple of nights. I'm okay with the arrangement if you are. Are you?"

Was he? Hell no, he was *not* okay with the arrangement. Little Tank threatened to pop out of his pants at the idea. Sleeping with her in the same bed, with Alfred shoving his hairy ass between them was bad enough. He wasn't sure how much of the closer accommodations he could handle for the next forty-eight hours. And what if he awoke her with his nightmares. What then?

She stared at him with those green gems.

He'd had a nightmare the other night on the couch and hadn't woken her. Maybe he would be okay.

"Are you sure?" He had to be positive before he agreed to their new sleeping arrangements. He'd have to tell her about his dark dreams.

Or, perhaps he had to stop freaking out.

They'd already slept together twice now and everything had been fine. Sleep being the key word. But sleeping with her in such a confined space, he doubted he'd be doing any actual sleeping the entire weekend if he didn't get his emotions under control.

"I'm sure." She nodded, and gave him a little slip of a smile.

Damn.

"Sure. Fine. Whatever," he muttered and gave Father a cross stare.

"Great. Oh, and the dummy forgot his sleeping bag, too.

Again, he said he'd take the smaller one." The leader revved his engine and road off before Tank could respond.

Beauty threw her head back and laughed. "I think we've been set-up."

"I'll say."

Damn firefighter. I'll be having a talk with him.

Tank stomped toward his tent just as Alfred ran around the bend, his tail wagging as he jumped on Annie.

"Down, Al. You know better." His voice came out a little too harsh.

"He's okay." She frowned. "Tyler, what's wrong? Are you mad about the sleeping arrangements, because if so, we can go get more supplies, or I could ask JoJo to tent with her?"

"No," he snapped. Taking in a deep breath, he worked on calming his tone. *She has no idea what's going on inside your head.* "I'm fine. It's fine."

Would it be fine? What if he swung his arm dreaming he was fighting his dad and hit her instead?

He wasn't mad. He was terrified. But he sure as hell didn't want her going to sleep in a tent with JoJo. Besides, he'd made Annie a promise. He *would* protect her, even if it meant against himself. He could fight his desires, and his dreams.

"Okay. Here." Annie stepped closer to him, Alfred following. "Let me help you with that."

"No. I've got it." He pulled back the tent from her reach. "Why don't you walk on back to the SUV and get the grill I packed. It's light."

She placed a hand on his arm. "Tyler. What's wrong?"

He pulled his arm back. "I said nothing, all right?" Tank bit back his frustration when he saw the look of dejection in her eyes. "Listen, Annie." He dropped the tent and turned fully to her. "I'm sorry. I am. I've just got a lot on my mind, okay?"

"Does it have something to do with what you and Father talked about at the bar?"

He sighed. *That*, and the feeling Little Tank might explode with need for her. He watched her standing there looking at him with those caring, sea green eyes, and his heart pounded as if it would explode with....what? Lust? Love? He needed to figure it out. Hell, he needed to figure everything out.

"How did you know about our conversation?"

"I didn't. I don't. I just assumed. You guys seemed pretty serious nursing your beers." She patted Alfred on the head. "I'm here when you want to talk. I'll be back in a little while." She turned and headed for the trail. "Come on, Alfred."

He'd upset her, and she was doing the thing he asked her to do. Leaving. But now, seeing her backside walk away from him while he was in anguish wasn't really what he wanted after all.

"Where are you going?"

"To get my bag, and to give you some time. I'll see you in a little while." She trotted around the bend, his companion hot on her tail.

"Damn it." He kicked a rock and stared at the lake.

Why the hell did he bring her? He couldn't sleep in the same tent with her without wanting to sleep *with* her, and he couldn't sleep with her until he told her about his past. Everything.

She deserved that much.

Father had been right. He had to let Annie decide for herself if she wanted to get involved with someone as screwed up as him.

Problem was…what if she didn't? Everything amazing they had now would be ruined.

His heart sank deep into his gut like it had been tied to a bag of rocks.

———

TANK SAT on a log near his erected tent. He'd placed the sleeping bag inside, moved his bike closer to the resting quarters, and set up some kindle for a fire. He pulled his phone out of his pocket and stared at the time. Nearly five. Annie had been gone for over an hour. Was she avoiding him? If so, he couldn't say he blamed her.

Time to make things right.

He stood to walk the trail back to the other campsites when he spotted Alfred running, tail wagging. Following closely behind, Annie turned around the bend in the trees. She had her bag on her shoulder, a plate in her hand, and an easy smile on her face.

Beauty wasn't nearly as upset as him.

The stones of sadness weighing his heart down lightened as she bounced along the trail. This trip proved good for the both of them. Him, getting one step closer to becoming an official Blue Guardian, and her becoming one step closer to her old self. More and more each day she resembled the girl he remembered. The girl across the lake.

He met her on the trail. "What's that?"

"Stuff for s'mores." She held up the plate. "Want one?"

"Sure, but I have to get a lighter to light the fire."

"No worries. I have one in my bag."

He took the sack from her shoulder and walked beside her to their camp. "Annie, listen. I'm sorry about—"

"It's okay, Tyler. You don't have to apologize." She playfully bumped into him and stared at him.

"But I do. I shouldn't have taken that tone with you. I just, well, I was caught off guard by Father, and—"

"Our new sleeping arrangement."

"Yeah. That."

"You know, it's not like we haven't slept in the same bed before. I was kinda surprised when you insisted on packing two tents."

"You were?" What was she saying? Was she ready to take things to another level?

Little Tank throbbed in excitement.

"Yes. It's just sleep, Tyler."

Crash and burn. That was the problem. He couldn't just sleep.

"I know, it's just…" Tank stopped and stared at the trees surrounding the lake. "Here." He guided her over to the log. "Let's sit down." He placed the plate on the ground, and pulled her hand until she nestled beside him on the seat.

"You know the ants are going to get that, right?" She pointed to the plate.

"I'll get you more, I promise, there's just something I need to tell you before—"

"Before we sleep in the same tent."

"Right." He blew out a big breath.

She tucked her small hand in his. "I'm listening. You can trust me, you know that?"

Trust her. He trusted her more than anyone else in the world, and yet he'd barely told her anything.

A piece of stray hair blew around her face, and he reached over to tuck it behind her ear. "I do trust you, Annie." He stared in her shining eyes, full of luster and joy. "You're happy being here aren't you?"

"Yes, I am. Thank you for inviting me."

"Are you happy now? I mean, with me. Are you happy with me?"

She trusted him. That much she'd told him. But trust and happiness were very different. He wanted to be more than her bodyguard. So much more.

"Of course, yes."

"Good. I just hope…I hope it stays that way."

He leaned his forehead to hers. Her intoxicating sweet scent filled him. Sucking in another deep breath inhaling the scent of her mixed with the undercurrent of trees and lake, he bid his time, and enjoyed the moment, the quietness with her. After he told her his past, things would forever change. His heart had never known so much turmoil and peace all at the same time.

"Tyler. Please," she whispered. Her breath tickled his skin. "Tell me. What's going on?"

He squeezed her cheeks and closed his eyes. "I'm falling for you, Annie. I've tried not to. I have, but from the moment I first saw you across the lake walking in the river barefoot holding your dad's hand, you've held a piece of me." Tank let go of her face, and turned his head toward the lake. The calm of the water seemed a far cry from the uncertainty inside of him. "But I'm broken…"

"Shh…" She placed her fingers under his chin and turned his head back toward her. She stared in his eyes and wrapped her hands around the nape of his neck. "Don't say that. Tell me."

He took his hand and squeezed her hold on his neck before he pulled back and stood. "My grandfather…there was a reason why he bypassed my mother for the cabin and gave it to me."

"Okay?" Her lids rose in question.

"Gramps knew I wanted to get involved with the Blue Guardians. No, *had* to get involved with the Guardians."

"Why?"

"When I was a boy. My dad, he did…he did some pretty terrible things to me. He'd hit me, and…torture me in ways no child should have to suffer. He would…he would—"

"Tyler, stop." She stood.

Though thankful he didn't have to repeat his past twice in one day, a burning sensation he hadn't felt in years still torched the back of his eyes. She didn't want to hear what he had to say. She didn't want his horrid past. He stared into her eyes, the tiny blood vessels turning a bright red.

"You don't have to go in to detail. I understand." She reached a hand to his cheek. "That's why you learned to climb trees isn't it. To hide from your father?"

"Yes. And it's why I break out into a sweat when I see someone in a uniform. He was a security guard. To this day, I still suffer from what he did to me. Sometimes I have nightmares of him coming after me. I had one on the couch with you that night we fell asleep watching *Batman*. I woke, terrified. I was so glad you didn't stir. I didn't know how to explain myself."

"Is that why you were so testy earlier? Afraid I'll see one of your nightmares."

"Yeah, partially. And I'm afraid I could hurt you while I have one."

She removed her hand from his cheek and clasped hers together. "Oh. I understand."

Her brows creased. Realization of what he was saying seemed to sink in her features, and he wasn't even done.

"That letter you saw in my mailbox, they're from him," he confessed.

"Your dad?"

"Yes."

"I thought you said he was dead?"

"To me he *is*. I don't want to have anything to do with him ever again, but he sends a letter every week. I don't know what he wants, and I don't care."

"What about your mother? Did he abuse her, too?"

"No." Tank shook his head. "She had no idea. But the minute she found out, she whisked me away to my grandfather's for safety…and my father got twenty-five years."

He stepped back from her and turned toward the water. This was it for them. The end before a beginning. Two fat drops fell down his cheeks. He wiped them away before she could see.

"Annie, I can understand if you want to stay with JoJo, or if you want Sandi to take you back to my place. I'll stay here until you decide where you want to go. Truth is, I'm broken, and I know you don't want to add my past to your pain."

Her gentle, yet sure grip squeezed his shoulder. "Tyler."

He kept his gaze on the lake, trying to push his pain down.

"Tyler, look at me." She stepped in front of him. Tears hung in her eyes. "I would *never* walk away from you because of your pain." She placed a palm on his cheek. "And I'm not scared to sleep in the same space as you. I've suffered some of the worst abuse imaginable, too. I know you would never harm me on purpose. Let me help you like you've helped me. We can take precautions, set up a pillow barricade or something if it will make you feel better."

Pillows. Would that be enough? "I don't know, Annie. I couldn't handle harming you. I care for you too much."

"I know, Tyler, and the truth is…I've fallen for you, too." A tear fell down her cheek.

His heart bounced. He gripped her hand holding his face

and used his other to wipe the tear away with the pad of his thumb. "So, you're not...you don't want to leave? Are you sure?"

"No, silly." A small, beautiful smile framed her face. "If anything, what you've told me makes me want to be with you more."

"Oh, Annie." Tank wrapped her in a sweeping hug and squeezed, her giggles floating in the air. Setting her back on her feet, he said, "I can't believe I'm saying this, but I've never cared for anyone the way I care for you."

"I understand."

He leaned in, ready to take her lips between his, when a few catcalls came from around the bend.

"Hey, love birds, we're making dinner," Father hollered. "Better come eat before it's all gone."

Tank let out a low growl, while Annie let out another giggle.

She raised a hand. "Okay, we're coming."

"Hasn't that old man ever heard of a cellphone?"

"The reception probably isn't very great out here."

"You're probably right."

As he pulled her closer, heat seared his body, trailing a hot pool of blood straight to his groin. She leaned up, and placed a feather-soft kiss on his lips, wrapping her arms around his neck. Safety, security, he had both wrapped in her arms, and she in his. He would make sure his dreams never harmed her. Even if he had to lie on Father's couch and work through his demons out loud, he would.

"Tyler," she whispered against his skin.

Little Tank pulsed faster at her low tone.

"Yeah." He groaned.

"You owe me a s'mores." She pinched his stomach as she pulled back and raced up the trail, Alfred trailing behind her.

THE MOON'S glimmer on the lake replaced that of the sun's. Tank sat on the log, tossing pieces of kindle on the campfire. Footsteps crunched the earth behind him.

"Hold this, will ya?" Annie handed him another plate of s'mores makings. She'd changed her jeans for some drawstring pants, and her hair hung in a loose braid off one shoulder. Her shirt—a size too big—made easy invitation for him to slip a hand up her torso.

Stop it, Wilde. You're thinking with the wrong head.

He took the plate and turned away. They mentioned they cared for each other, but they hadn't gone that far. Not yet. Still, he couldn't help imagine the feel of her soft skin against his.

He stared at the plate. Food. Food was a safe topic.

"How can you be hungry? You ate two burgers at dinner. Not including your burger at lunch."

Annie spread a blanket out beside the fire. "I'm not, but I will always have room for s'mores." She picked up a nearby stick and stuck the tip in the flame.

"What are you doing?"

"Killing any ants. Nothing worse than having an ant share your dessert with you."

There wasn't a graham cracker in the world that could cure his hankering for her dessert right now, nor an ant that could stop him. He didn't want what was on that plate.

"I'll take your word for it." He shifted. Suddenly, the log had become extremely uncomfortable.

She sat on the blanket, her feet curled under her legs, and a slip of her tattoo popped out. She patted the spot beside her.

He bit back a groan and slid down to sit next to her. He

would let her make the moves. No way would he move faster than she was willing. He would not mess this up.

"Would you like me to make you one?" Annie reached for a marshmallow.

"Sure."

She slid two candies over the stick and began to swirl the sugar in the fire. Just when he thought the marshmallow would fall onto the embers below, she pulled it back. "Grab the crackers and chocolate."

He caught one candy with a cracker, and then quickly reached for the other before it fell off the stick.

"Here. I'll help you." She placed the stick on the ground and sandwiched the white goo between the chocolate and graham wafers.

"You look like you've had practice with that."

"Yeah." A sheepish smile touched her lips, the fire casting a soft glow on her face. "Me and my dad." She held up her dessert sandwich. "This was another one of our things. He was all outdoorsy, while my mom was the artsy type. She would sit outside and paint the scenery while he taught me how to fish. Sometimes, we would go camping, and s'mores were a must." She dived into her treat.

Living out in the woods was something she'd done in the past. Perhaps bad cellphone and cable reception weren't deal breakers for her, and being cooped up in his home had more to do with her situation than the location of his cabin. Annie seemed to like and miss the outdoors. Maybe she'd be willing to get back to her roots, in his cabin, with him.

Despite the fact she was living with him now, it wasn't the same. What he wanted was for her to *want* to be there, not *have* to be there. He'd become accustomed to her moose mug in the dish drainer, her laundry mixed with his in the wash, and her tantalizing perfume seeping into his bed sheets.

Don't think about sheets.

He stared down at her delicate ankle and pointed to her tattoo. "So, is this the better times you talked about? Would you and your dad star gaze on your camping trips?"

"Yeah." She nodded. "I figured a tattoo of the stars and moon were better than that of a dessert." She bumped him with her elbow and giggled.

"Yeah." He smiled. "I guess you're right."

"But why a tattoo? You have your locket."

"I know." She nodded. "But, I wanted something more permanent, ya know? Just in case anything ever happened."

"To your locket."

"Yeah." She nodded again. "Like it almost did." A flash of sorrow lit her eyes at the mention of her past. "But, what about you?" she changed the subject.

"What about me?" He bit into his own crackers.

"Did you have something special with your mom?"

"Not really. My grandpa and I, we would get donuts and eat out by the dock. His favorite was a bear claw. In fact, the morning I met you at the diner, I saw one in the case. Maybe I should have taken that as an omen."

"An omen?"

"Yeah." He placed his sandwich on the plate. "In a silly way, maybe it was his way of leading me to you. Pointing me in the right direction. I know, dumb." He wiped his hands on his jeans; crumbs flaked to the blanket.

"Hey." Her pointy elbow nudged his arm. "That's not dumb. When we get back, we'll have a bear claw just for him, okay?"

She understood. Him, his situation, even his crazy way of thinking his Gramps was looking out for him. She got him.

A smile tugged his lips. "I'd like that."

Annie returned his smile, and his limbs went tingly and weak from her acceptance.

She turned her head back to the fire and finished off her dessert, licking her fingers and leaving behind a string of marshmallow that trailed down her face.

"You have a little on your chin."

"I do?" She smiled, and tried to wipe it away. "They're always so messy." She missed the food.

"Here. Let me."

He took the pad of his thumb to wipe the sticky away. Her nature-green eyes stared back at him as her mouth split in a supple part. He caught her gaze and moved his palm up her cheek until the tips of his fingers caressed her hairline. Edible. God, she was edible, just like the marshmallow.

She leaned in closer, her thigh bumping his, and raked her gaze from his eyes to his mouth. The vein in his neck pounded as his body seemed to get back feeling. No longer weak and tingly, his body ached. Ached with need, ached with lust, just ached for her. And the only cure was with a big dose of Beauty.

"Annie," he whispered.

"Yes."

Their mouths daring to touch, he moved his hand to her braid, and played with the plaited strands. "I want to kiss you."

"I *want* you to kiss me," she whispered. She gripped his knee, balancing herself.

"If I kiss you, I don't think I'll be able to stop myself from doing other things."

"Then don't stop."

His yearning raged at her permission. Wrapping his hand in her hair, he pulled her mouth to his. Quick-fire ignited in his veins, her scent the explosion for his desire, and her tongue the kindling for his groin. He wanted her, all of her, right there on the blanket under the stars.

He pulled the band out of her hair and let the golden waves fall over her shoulders. "You're so beautiful." He moved his mouth to her neck, kissing her silky skin, while tracing the rim of her pajama pants with his fingers. "Do you want to go in the tent?" His fingers burned to pull the barrier down that separated him from her.

She shifted slightly, allowing him better access to her pants. He placed his hand just under the band, gripping her hip.

"Ouch." She gasped and sat up straighter.

Tank pulled his hand back and stared at her. "I'm sorry. Did I hurt you? I didn't mean to."

"No." She shook her head and laughed. "It was just a rock under the blanket."

He stared down at the ground. "God, Annie. I'm sorry." He rubbed his head. "You deserve a bed, not the hard ground."

Damn his lust. What the hell was he doing, trying to take her outside? She deserved better. They hadn't even started much of a relationship, and he was already messing it up. "I don't know what I was thinking." He placed a palm down to stand.

"No." She gripped his arm. "I want this. I want it right here under the stars with you." She bit her bottom lip and slid her hand down his arm to grip his. She scooted, pulling him with her. As she lay back on the blanket, her hair, wild and tempting like a sun goddess, framed her face.

"But Annie, I don't...I don't have anything with me." Good Lord, how far away was the nearest convenient store. He didn't expect this to happen. He hadn't come prepared.

"It's okay. Sandi slipped a few in my bag while I was

back at their campsite." She pulled his hand harder, inviting him toward her.

Father.

Undoubtedly, the man said something to Sandi. "Meddling bastards."

"Thank goodness for those meddling bastards. Otherwise, we couldn't do this."

She bit her lip, her body tensed underneath his, and the lusty gaze in her eyes screamed she wanted this as bad as he did. Desire pulsed through him, causing his breath to come out raspy, shaky.

He skimmed up her body and placed his palms flat on both sides of her head, positioning himself over her. "You're sure?" Turning back now would be damn near next to impossible, but he wouldn't pressure her. Her pace. Always.

She nodded a blessed yes and reached for his hips.

This is it.

He stared down at her and stretched for her lips, taking her mouth in his, slow and steady. Her kiss matched his, soft and easy, as a slow moan purred from the back of her throat. His shaft screamed to come loose from its denim prison.

Hell, the condoms.

He rose. "Hold those thoughts. Please, hold those thoughts. Where's your bag?"

"In the tent."

Quicker than he'd ever moved in his entire life, he scrambled inside the tent, and pulled open her bag. Right on top. A fresh *box*. Few his ass, this was an army's load, and in the right size. Annie was right. *Thank goodness for those meddling bastards.*

He grabbed an extra blanket in case any of those meddling bastards decided to come pay a visit while they enjoyed each other and hurried back to Annie, praying she hadn't changed her mind in the twenty seconds it took him to retrieve the items.

She stayed in the same spot, her chest rising in a steady, quickened rhythm, her hair and skin glistening against the firelight.

Tank dropped the blanket and knelt down to the same position, roving his gaze over her feminine figure, devouring her with his eyes before he could with his mouth. Leaning toward her again, she reached for the back of his neck, and probed his mouth with her tongue as she ran her other hand under his shirt, gently clawing his back.

The feel of her fingernails on his skin, and her warm mouth, shot another bolt of energy to his groin. He lowered a hand back to the bottom of her T-shirt, and slowly moved his fingers up her torso. His palm met a handful of warm, luscious breast, his fingertips grazing her nipple. He gave the soft flesh a little tap, and she gasped, her body rocking upwards, her center bumping his shaft.

"Oh, God, Annie. I want you."

"Then take me."

She pushed on his chest, raising herself to a seated position, and placed her hands on the bottom of her shirt. Following her lead, he helped her raise the cotton over her head and tossed it aside. Two supple mounds stared back at him in the glow of the firelight. Her perk nipples begged to be tasted.

Placing a hand behind her neck, he lowered her back to the ground, taking his time licking from one delicious nub to the other. Her body wiggled beneath him, her back arching, and in that moment he thought his heart might stop.

He took more of her breast between his lips as he suckled; his manhood throbbed hard against his zipper.

Don't blow this, Wilde.

Slowly, he counted to fifty as he took his time traveling from one hilltop to the next, while she rubbed her fingers in his hair, his scalp tingling from her touch.

She lowered her hands to his shirt and tugged. "Take this off."

Gladly. He wanted—no scratch that, he *needed*—her body flush with his.

He rose, obliged her command, tossing his shirt to the side. She placed her hands on his chest, her breast pushing together with the movement of her arms.

Oh, sweet Jesus.

He bit his lip…hard, and began counting backwards from fifty.

"You're amazing." The touch of her small hands traveling down his abs tingled his skin.

"No, Beauty." He shook his head. "You are."

Her eyes glistened a take-me-now shine at the sound of his nickname for her, and she didn't waste her time reaching for his zipper. While his body ached for release, he wanted her to have pleasure first. She *deserved* pleasure.

"Not yet." He stopped her hands, and pinned them above her head as her breasts bounced a glorious jiggle from the movement.

Her eyes grew wide, and a ripple of fear overtook him. He immediately eased his grip, worried he'd made the wrong move, too aggressive in his desire. A slow smile parted her lips as she arched her back against his hold. Taking that as his cue, he dove back down and placed his face in her chest, kissing down her ribs to the sacred freckle that had tempted him since their first night together. He continued his trail down to her bellybutton as he toyed with the band of her pants.

"Take them off." She raised her hips, allowing him easy access.

He didn't have to be told twice. In one swift move, he yanked her pants down, her tantalizing V void of underwear.

Mercy.

"No panties?"

"I never sleep in them."

"As far as I'm concerned, you don't even need pajamas... ever again."

"I may take you up on that."

Beauty giggled and his manhood thumped in agony—or ecstasy—the line so fine between the two, he couldn't tell.

Releasing her hands, he nudged his knee between her legs, opening her up for him. Taking his time, he licked the inside of her thigh, gripping her hips. His tongue so close to the sweet dessert he longed to taste. "Annie," he said against her skin. "Are you sure?"

"Yes." She bucked in anticipation.

He moved his mouth up her hipbone as he slid one finger inside her heat. Moistness covered his flesh, and he dared to add another finger to the mix. She jerked and gripped the blanket, her knuckles white as her chest heaved. He rocked his fingers in and out, while placing the pad of his thumb on her nub, rubbing until her center tightened around his hand, and her eyes squeezed tight.

He continued to count, slowly in his mind, to keep himself from finding release inside his own pants. When her body stilled, he removed his fingers and trailed his lips back up to her stomach, to her breasts, and then to her mouth.

"Tyler, oh my God," she panted. "That was, that was..."

"Good," he whispered near her ear.

"No." She shook her head. "Amazing."

"Good." He nipped her ear, reached down for his zipper,

and moaned in relief as his shaft broke free. "It's about to get even better." He shucked his pants and placed another kiss on her lips, her moist mouth feeling much like her insides.

Casing himself in a condom, he nudged her legs open wider and used his tip to toy with the slip of her heat. Beauty raised her hips again in anticipation. Her moistness allowed him to fully insert himself inside of her.

Tank gripped her curves as she reached to join their mouths. His heart raced as she squeezed her thighs against his hips, and wrapped her arms around his back, tightening her hold on him…everywhere.

In that moment, there was no going back for him. His heart, mind, and body soared, buzzed with love for this woman. Their secrets, their pasts, all laid out in front of each other, only to be met with pure acceptance, pure love. She was his. Not by possession, but through desire.

He squeezed one of her hips as he balanced his body weight on his other hand, her tongue and center driving him wild. Beauty met his demands with every thrust, accepting all of him.

Just when he didn't think he could handle anymore, her insides squeezed him harder, taking him for everything he had. She let out a satisfying scream, and he swooped down to steal it with his mouth.

Her body jerked and withered around him as he supported himself on his palms, her soft, golden tresses tickling the end of his fingers.

Their pleasure ended together, and he stared down into her satiated eyes. Eyes so deep he wanted to lose his way in them.

Her breaths came out raspy, and her heart pounded against his chest, their beats syncing. A soft smile touched her full, just-been-kissed lips, and damn it if his ego didn't soar, knowing he made her so breathless. He leaned down, placing a slow, supple kiss on her mouth then stared into her eyes—eyes that cut straight to his soul.

His own heart hinged on his next words. "I love you, Annie."

A tear shed from her eye, and she wrapped her arms around his neck. "I love you, too, Tyler."

"You're safe with me," he whispered.

"And you're safe with me."

"I know."

CHAPTER TWENTY-THREE

Duke parked his truck in an old abandoned parking lot three blocks from the biker chick's apartment complex. Lucky for him, her building was on the outskirts of town, and not too many people rode the streets of Black Widow at midnight. Still, better to be cautious.

He zipped his black jacket, and cursed the stifling humidity. Wearing long sleeves in the middle of summer might cause people to stop and stare if anyone saw him. Duke clung to the trees for cover as he jogged the few blocks to the complex.

Brayden had found the addresses of all the Blue Guardian's in Black Widow, including Jolene Missy Swan—a.k.a. JoJo. Duke nearly jumped in his seat when he saw the name of the apartments. Heritage Park. *Not* a gated community.

His little accomplice had gone above and beyond getting him information. The rookie had flirted with the redheaded waitress so much, he'd learned the gang was on a ride, and the dearly beloved diner owner went with them. Which meant JoJo was gone, too.

Exactly the break he needed.

He found the second building and scanned the outside doors for her apartment number. Upstairs. He took the steps two at a time, careful not to make a noise, and eased into the darkened corner next to her door. With his gloved hand, he turned the knob.

Locked.

Staying in the shadows, he pulled an old grocery store membership card from his wallet. Wedging the thin plastic between the door and the lock, he pushed down on the card, and turned the handle, shoving on the door with his shoulder. One strong thrust, and the barrier flew open.

Cheap ass locks.

Duke checked around the complex to make sure no one watched as he quickly pushed over the threshold and shut the door behind him. Pulling a flashlight out of his jacket pocket, he scanned the apartment. Tidy, minimal. A couch eased against the far wall and a coffee table sat in the middle of the room while a television stand and TV stood on the other wall. A small kitchen, clear of any clutter, only held a few dishes in the sink. All of which seemed to be clean.

He opened a door in the hallway. Linen closet. Minimal towels, minimal sheets. Everything folded to perfection. Across the hall, he opened another door. Small bathroom. Pulling the drawers open, he glanced for anything that looked familiar. Anything Annie used. Her makeup. Her toiletries.

Nothing.

No sign of anyone else living in the apartment except JoJo. Duke opened the last door down the hall. A bedroom.

In total, the hole of a home consisted of four rooms. Everything tidy and put away to precision with no sign of Annie, anywhere.

A nagging feeling overtook his stomach as his jaw

twitched. There had to be more. The reflection of a doorknob bounced off his flashlight. A closet.

He stormed across the room and yanked open the door. Shinning his light over the garments, he flipped through the hangers. Nothing of Annie's. He ran his hand over something smooth and thick in the back of the closet.

Leather.

Duke pulled the jacket out and placed it on her bed. He shined the light up the sleeve and searched for the hole.

There.

Reaching into his back pocket, he pulled out the little plastic bag holding the small piece of fabric that had been left at his house and placed the piece inside the hole. A match. But he'd already known that, having seen the shape of the hole at the diner.

His temples pounded, and he gritted his teeth, irritated about the things he didn't know. His big break seeming like a big flop.

Where the hell are you, Annie?

She wasn't there, and there was no sign she'd been there.

Carefully, he picked up the coat and placed it back in the closet, sure to move the hangers back the way they'd been. Retracing his steps to make sure nothing was out of place, he pocketed his flashlight, exited, and locked the door behind him. At a clipped pace, he ran back to his truck.

Duke jumped in his vehicle, pulled out a flask from under his seat, and stared at the address book on his dashboard. He took a quick swig. What the hell *did* he know?

Annie wasn't at her mothers, and she didn't have much money, or any other family.

She wasn't living with JoJo, but JoJo had been in his house, getting Annie's clothes, so that meant the biker chick probably knew where Annie was. And this woman was a Blue Guardian, a Guardian that was friends with that big blond guy from the diner and the courthouse.

He dug through his notepad and searched for Wilde's address. He lived near Virginia Creek. Annie's old address was near the creek.

Of course. Her old home.

The piece of shit she begged him to consider buying. He slapped his head for not thinking of the shack before.

Fucking stupid.

That's where she was hiding, and he'd bet the big-ass blond guy knew it.

Duke cranked his ignition and set his truck in the direction of Virginia Creek. He'd go and search the old home himself. Hell, once he found her, he'd do one better, and promise to buy it for her. A little wedding present. He'd get his Annie back.

His phone buzzed in his cup holder. The station.

What the hell do they want?

"Yeah, it's Fields."

"Hey, Chief, it's Opal. A couple of the officers had to go home sick tonight. Stomach flu. You think you can come in and cover their shift?"

He turned left to head back toward town versus turning right to head to the creek. Damn his campaign.

"Yeah, Opal. I'll be there in thirty."

He hung up the phone and placed it back in his cup holder. This was better. He couldn't just barge in on Annie in the middle of the night. He needed a plan to win her back, and he still had some time before the town meeting. Before his speech. Plenty of time to come up with a sure-fire way to get his woman back.

His heart leapt with excitement. His little lady had been hiding in plain sight all along.

I'm coming for you, baby.

CHAPTER TWENTY-FOUR

Annie woke to the feel of something tickling her leg. She jerked and opened her eyes. Tyler sat propped on one elbow, his fingers tracing the inside of her thigh.

"Good morning."

She smiled and arched her back in a stretch. "Good morning." The blanket shifted below her collarbone, her breasts ready to pop over the top of the cover.

"You move like that again, and I'll be having you for breakfast." He kissed down her neck, across her collarbone, and placed a finger on the top of the sheet, staring back at her with puppy dog eyes.

"You look like you've seen a treat."

"Oh, I have."

He kissed her skin where the top of the blanket lay; her toes tingled in delight. Last night, she'd *made love* for the first time. Her body burned for Tyler in such a way she would have jumped inside of him completely if given the choice. Now, as his lips graced her skin, the tingling shot from her toes to her core, her insides begging and burning for another round.

He lowered the blanket, trailing more kisses down the top of her breast, seeking the center.

She squirmed in delight then pushed his head away. "Don't you want breakfast first?"

"Nope." He ripped the blanket off her completely. "I want dessert."

She giggled and reached an arm around his neck. Just as she pulled him toward her, Alfred let out a wail of barks.

"What's he howling at?"

Tyler ran a hand over her stomach and down her thigh. "Who cares?" He lowered his head to her center just as a voice boomed from outside.

"Knock, knock."

"Ahh!" She yanked the covers back up.

She could see the shadow of Alfred jumping as the dog wailed at the intruder. Al's tail bumped the side of the tent in delight.

"Steele, damn you, man. What the hell do you want?" Tyler yelled at the tent's door.

The only thing separating her—naked—from Steele was a thin sheet, and a thin zippered doorway. Tyler protectively covered her with his body.

"I see your sleeping arrangements have worked out nicely. You're welcome." The cocky Guardian sounded as if he snickered.

Tyler pressed more of his weight on her. "Again, what the hell do you want?"

"I'm supposed to tell you breakfast is ready. Sandi's making dirty eggs."

"Yeah, thanks. Got it. We'll be there in a minute."

"Take your time, man. Sorry to interrupt your morning

slumber. Come on, Alfred. Let's leave the lovebirds alone."
His and the dog's footsteps grew quieter.

She trailed her fingers through Tyler's hair. "I think we've been found out."

"Well, they did make sure nearly every obstacle was seen to." He leaned into her caress. "I don't mind if you don't."

"No." She wrapped her hands around his neck. "But I'm not in the mood for eggs."

"You're not?"

"No, I think I'd like to give sausage a try."

"I thought you didn't like pork."

"I wasn't talking about a pig."

"Mercy."

While she never wanted to experience the pain Duke put her through again, she'd never imagined something so cruel and dangerous could lead her to a place of total bliss and love. Tyler had her heart and soul, and in him, she found her purpose. A place she never wanted to lose again.

"I love you, Tyler."

"I love you, more."

His eyes glistened as he lowered his lips back to her collarbone and kissed every part of her into sheer oblivion.

So, this was love.

———

ANNIE PLACED her head on Tank's chest, making lazy circles over his stomach with her finger. Never in his life had he felt he could care for someone so strong, so powerfully. She held his soul in her tiny palm.

"I wish we could stay this way forever," she said, mirroring his exact thoughts.

"Me, too." He squeezed her closer to his chest. "But

there's been a stick jabbed in my ass for the past hour. I wouldn't mind a bed."

She let out a giggle that made having a stick up his ass worth it.

"My mom, she's coming to town tomorrow. You'll meet her, won't you?"

"Of course. Does she know about me?"

"A little. I haven't told her much. I didn't know what to tell her, really. I was scared. Scared my feelings were one sided."

"I don't think your feelings have ever been one sided." She reached up and tapped him on the nose.

He squeezed Annie tighter. Not only did his love run deep, but also his desire to protect her from harm. Any harm. Especially Duke. An image of the two of them together caused his stomach to churn. How did she wind up with a guy like *him*?

"Annie, I have to ask you something."

"Sure. What?"

"Why Duke? What about him made you fall for him?"

She sighed and lay back on his chest, using her fingers to make lazy circles again over his stomach. "I guess it was his charm. When we met, I had just moved back to town from finishing college in Austin. I wanted to stay closer to Mom, but figured I might have a better shot of getting a job here. Smaller town, less competition than a big city, also the cost of living is much cheaper in Black Widow. Besides, I had fond memories of Black Widow, despite the pain from my parents' accident. I figured being here might make me feel closer to my dad's spirit somehow."

He wrapped a protective arm around her, drawing her closer, wishing he could pull in her pain, take the load from her.

"I took a job at the diner until I could find something more substantial, and that's where I met Duke. He came in the restaurant and swept me off my feet immediately. It was Christmas time, and he asked what my plans were. When I let him know I didn't have any, he made sure I lacked for nothing that Christmas. We spent every day of his vacation together. We visited my mom, and then he took me to the Bahamas for a few days. Gave me everything I could have ever wanted...I thought." She turned her head and glanced up at him. "For a girl who was low on funds, and had college loans to pay back, he seemed like a dream come true. Little did I know the nightmare that was about to begin."

While his nightmares were at night, he could wake up from them, try and shake them off. Beauty, on the other hand, had walked in one daily just like he did as a child.

His childhood fears lurched in his stomach.

Never again.

For either of us.

"You didn't know Duke from school? Didn't he grow up here?"

"Yeah." She nodded and pushed off his chest to rest on her forearms. "He did, but we are a few years apart, and I rode the bus. I didn't participate in after school activities like he did, so I never really knew him in school. The only really good friend I had here moved away. When I came back, it was like I was new all over again."

"So, you had no idea about his behavior."

"No, and as far as I can tell, no one else really did either. Besides, Sandi. I suppose she saw through his act. Looking back, she dropped hints here and there, but I was so enamored with him, I never noticed. On Valentine's Day, Duke proposed." She raised her gaze to the ceiling. "It all felt like a fairy tale." She shook her head and stared back at him. "I can't believe that was only a little over four months ago. He came from money and influence, and he adored me. What more could a girl ask for? But after I said yes, everything changed."

"Changed how?" He propped on an elbow and rubbed a hand through her hair.

She stared into her hands. "His family started pressuring him to campaign for Sherriff. He started drinking more. A lot more. He stopped taking his medicine altogether. Little by little, his anger escalated...until a couple weeks after proposing he began hitting me. After the first time, he apologized profusely. Sent me flowers three days in a row, and swore he'd never do it again. I figured I could forgive him. I mean, he loved me after all, or so he said. But the more his dad pressured him about revving up his political campaign, the more he drank, and the less he took his medicine."

"Medicine for what?"

She refocused her gaze back on him. "He never would say exactly, but when I looked up the prescription, it was for bipolar disorder. Sometimes there would be another prescription he would take. I think that one was for depression. Problem was, he didn't stick to them for very long. When he did while he was courting me, he seemed to think clearer, act more normal. Maybe it was all a ruse. I don't know." She shrugged her bare shoulder.

Damn him.

"A little over a month ago, I realized there was no escape for me. His money, his resources were all too vast and too wide for me to get out of his grasp. And it all happened so fast it almost gives me whiplash thinking back on it all. From being completely independent to completely dependent on him in the matter of months. It's crazy, but it's true, and I have no idea how I let myself get so wrapped up in it all."

"It's the abuser behavior, Annie." He scooted closer, their bodies flush, hoping to offer a shred of comfort in his touch. "Don't beat yourself up over it. You're safe now."

"I know, but what I really can't believe is I've been hiding under his nose the past couple of weeks, and he hasn't figured it out. It's only a matter of time, though, and I'm tired of hiding."

"I won't let him hurt you." *No way in hell.* Her rubbed her bare shoulder.

"I know, but like I've said before, I'm not going to keep hiding. I'm going to talk to Sandi today. I want back on the schedule, and I want the Guardians to stop babysitting me. It's Independence Day after all. I want mine back."

Her green eyes pleaded with him, and pulled his heart-strings as well as his groin. Everything she did got under his skin.

He wanted her to have what she wanted. Hell, he wanted to give her what she wanted, but what she wanted was dangerous. Duke was still telling everyone he and Annie were getting married. How were they going to resolve that issue…safely?

"Annie, I can't always be with you. What if our work shifts don't coordinate? Besides, I have to work the next four weekends in a row to make up for taking this one off."

"I thought about that, and I'm sure Sandi will work with me as much as she can. But what if we take my money and get an alarm system at the house?"

"An alarm system." He trailed his palm down the center of her back. "That *may* work, but I'd still rather have someone there with you."

"I know you would, but Tyler, I need to live life again."

"Ugh," he groaned. His Beauty was tired of being locked

in the wooden tower. He couldn't blame her. She deserved so much more than what she was getting.

"You're serious, aren't you? You're going back to work, in town, with Duke and everyone else able to see you."

"Yes, I am, and I would like your blessing on this. I need to be me again."

He could give this to her. He *would* give her the leeway. She wasn't his possession, and she could do as she pleased. *He* was the lucky one getting the privilege of her company, and he did enjoy her company. Too much. He'd be damn sure she was kept safe. Every Guardian would know to keep their eyes and ears open when it came to his woman.

"All right, and we'll get an alarm system. But." He placed a quick peck to her forehead. "You're not paying for it."

"I've lived with you rent-free for two weeks. Let me take care of this."

"Nope." He pecked her head again. "I pick the system, and I pay."

"You're stubborn, you know that?"

"Tossing my own words back at me, I see."

"Well, let me repay you somehow."

"You want to repay me?" He raised an eyebrow.

"Of course I do."

He flipped her over and settled his body over hers. "I can think of a way." He nudged her legs open with his hand as he dipped his head to her bellybutton.

"Tyler." She giggled "What are you doing?"

"Partaking in the dessert you made for me." He lowered his lips to her hip, his face hovering above her warmth.

"That doesn't seem like I'm repaying you for anything."

"Your pleasure is plenty payment for me, babe. Now, relax, while I enjoy."

He lapped her pleasure point until her body wiggled, and she panted his name in sheer joy.

Definitely payment enough.

CHAPTER TWENTY-FIVE

Duke drove down the long gravel drive to Annie's old house. He hadn't remembered where the old dump was. She'd shown him once, but he didn't pay attention. According to the map on his phone, only two properties sat this far out of town. The other property belonged to Wilde. When he got done here, he'd have to check the guy's place out for himself. Wilde kicked his police senses up.

He gritted his teeth as he parked his truck, mad he was a day behind schedule.

Fucking stomach flu.

Half the station had supposedly come down with it, making him work a double on the Fourth. The bastards were all probably lying, soaking up some sun on the river. When he finally clocked out of his double shift, all he could manage to do was sleep.

Now, he was two days closer to his speech at the town meeting. Annie *needed* to be by his side and home, in his bed.

He turned off the ignition and stepped out. The hot summer sun beat down between the old tree branches covering the property. He glanced around the house, looking for signs of inhabitance. Definitely remote. If she were here, this would be a great place to hide out. Only problem with his previous thinking was he knew this place was here, and she'd been the one to show him. Why would she hide in a place she had showed him before? Would she be stupid enough to hide out in a place he could find her?

He glanced around the property, but didn't see tire tracks or Annie's car. His hopes began to diminish as his anger boiled. How had the little bitch outsmarted him this far?

Duke stomped up the front steps and jiggled the door handle. Wouldn't budge. He peeked through the windows. No furniture. Slamming through the door would be easy enough, but the point seemed useless.

Stepping off the porch, he scanned the back of the house. Trash cans empty, the kitchen windows uninhibited of curtains. A quick glance through the pane confirmed there was no food on the counter, nothing. She wasn't here.

"Shit.*"*

He kicked the ground, stirring up dead leaves, and stared into the trees. She could have gone on that ride with the Guardians. If so, perhaps the big guy did, too. According to that bimbo redheaded waitress, the diner owner was due back today. Which most likely meant they were all due back today.

He set at a clipped pace through the woods as he reached for his cellphone. One bar.

Fuck.

He dialed Brayden.

"Hey, boss."

"Brayden, can you hear me?"

"Yeah, barely."

"I want you to station your patrol unit on the edge of

town. If you see an old blue pickup pass through, call me. A 1970s model."

"Got a plate number?"

"No, but if you run the plate, it'll belong to a Moss. Got it?"

"Yes, sir."

"Don't fuck up, Rookie. I'm counting on you."

"Yes, sir."

Duke tore through the trees and stumbled upon the creek. He glanced right and left. A cabin sat off to the left, across the water but there was no sign of a bridge anywhere, just a fallen log and some step stones. Several rocks jutted from the ground, making enough of a path for him to get to the other side. Carefully, he hoped across the water, and crawled up the slope of the bank. The other cabin sat quiet and dark with the curtains pulled shut. On the dock, fishing poles lay on the old rafters.

Two.

Garbage cans stood by the back of the house. Full. Too much trash for just one guy. He crept around the side, the front appearing as deserted as the back. No signs of a bike, or a truck, but tire tracks flattened the grass near the garage.

Duke ran around the front of the house and over to the small one and a half car garage. He jiggled the door. Locked. What was in there the guy wanted hidden so badly? Sliding his shopping card through the crack, he bumped the door open.

His clutch tightened on the door handle. Annie's car.

Little bitch *had* been hiding right under his nose. And the big blond was her personal security guard. Explained why the ogre went to a bank he didn't use...and just what had been under the tarp in his truck?

Annie.

Mother fucker.

His phone rang in his back pocket. *Brayden.* "What did you find?"

"Blue truck. I'm trailing it. Computer says it belongs to Moss."

Annie's on her way.

He scanned the garage and the grounds. Tree's everywhere. Plenty of places to hide.

"Boss...you there?"

"Yep. Good job, Brayden."

"Sir, I believe, well, I believe I saw that big blond guy driving, and Annie...I think she was in the truck, sir."

"Rookie, not a fucking word. Do you understand me?"

"Yes, sir."

He clicked off the phone, and locked the garage door. A patch of trees to the right held plenty of brush to hide him and his shadow.

Duke ran for cover. He had to catch a glimpse of her, make sure she stayed with the giant ogre before he made his next move. And if she was staying there, what in the hell *was* his next move? His chest tightened with uncertainty.

He counted to ten and controlled his breathing.

Must have control.

He maneuvered behind a large oak trunk, using the downed branches to cover himself. The rumble of the truck had him squatting lower in the trees. Glancing to the right, a blur of blue whizzed down the driveway as the ancient vehicle barreled to a stop in front of the small garage. Doors slammed, and then...he heard her.

"Do you think that cop saw me?"

Annie.

"I don't think so, babe."

Babe? The ogre calling his woman such an intimate name caused an inferno to burn in his chest.

Little whore.

Quietly, Duke sucked in another deep breath and continued counting. *Breathe.*

"He did follow for a little while, but I was speeding. I'm sure that was why."

He watched them walk together in front of the truck and up the porch steps. A black dog followed behind, sniffing in the area where he'd stood at the garage.

Damn dog. Stay put.

"You're sure it wasn't Duke."

"No, baby. It wasn't Duke." Ogre pulled her in for a hug.

Baby? Hugging?

Duke cracked his neck and grit his teeth. *His* woman was so close, yet, he couldn't touch her. Not yet.

The dog sniffed the handle of the garage door then stuck his nose back in the grass. As much as he didn't want Annie out of his sight, he needed her to go inside before the black beast gave away his hiding spot. He placed a hand on the butt of his gun. Just in case Fido tried to get too close.

"I don't know why I'm worried," she said as she stared into the giant's eyes. "I'm going back to work in a few days."

Returning to work? People would ask her where she went. He'd have to get to her first, tell her what to say, match their stories.

"I'm going to run into him again."

"I know, and I'm still worried about you. What he did to you…"

Wilde dared to snake his hands down her back, lower, nearly gripping her ass.

"Don't be worried. I have to return to life at some point. I have school loans still to pay. Besides, Duke isn't going to do anything to me at the diner. Not in front of his voters."

"He'll never hurt you again. I'll never let him."

Hurt her? He was saving her from herself. Apparently, he still had more work to do.

"I know, baby."

The words, the groping, his Annie with her hands all over another man… Her hands should be on him. *Damn it.*

The branch he used to help balance himself snapped under his grip, the noise low, yet loud enough for the dog to hear.

Black beast let out a bark.

He moved back behind the trunk, deeper into the shadows, his heart pounding in his chest while his grip tightened on the gun.

"Alfred, hush," the ogre yelled.

The dog turned and trotted toward the porch, his tail wagging.

"Do you think something's out there?" Annie turned toward the woods.

"I'm not sure. It could be a deer or something. I'll go check."

Fuck. No.

Duke looked left then right where a fallen log sat. He could hide on the opposite side of it. *If* he could get to it in time.

Wilde took the first step off the porch.

"No. Don't go." Annie pulled the giant back. "Al barks at everything.

As if on cue, the dog ran to the back of the house, barking the whole time. Ducks quacked in the distance.

"See," she said. "He was just barking at the ducks. Come

on. Let's get out of this heat. We have to clean the house. Your mom's coming in tonight, right?"

Meeting the mother? So soon? Annie needed to be taught a lesson or two, especially about cheating, but he didn't think she was delusional. The poor bitch *really* thought she would get to pursue a relationship with this ogre. He'd have to teach her. Train her.

My Annie. What a slow learner you are.

"I can't wait for you to meet her." Wilde sounded excited.

Poor bastard.

"I can't either."

The monster kissed *his* Annie on the lips.

She kissed him *back.*

Little tramp.

"But." The giant took her hand, pulled keys from his pocket with the other, and opened the door. "I had a better idea than cleaning. I promise you'll like it."

Just before entering, Annie jumped into his arms, snaking her legs around the mammoth's waist. The furry beast ran back up the porch steps, following behind them before the guy kicked the door shut with his foot.

Annie, *his Annie*, was inside that house getting ready to fuck another man.

The ogre's hands would touch her in places reserved only for *him*. Giving her pleasure that only *he* should be giving her.

Pleasure the little bitch didn't deserve.

Duke took the broken branch and smashed it against the trunk. He'd teach her a lesson all right, and take care of that guy while he was at it.

CHAPTER TWENTY-SIX

"When is your mother getting here?" Annie asked as she checked the oven.

The scent of the cinnamon cake she made lingered through Tank's cabin and made his stomach rumble. "You mean how much sooner from when you asked me five minutes ago?" She fidgeted with the oven mitt, and he eased over to her. "Mom just texted me. Said she was about five minutes away. Why are you so worried?"

"I don't know." Beauty tossed the mitt on the counter top. "What if she doesn't like me? Or what if we tell her about me, and she thinks I'm just using you. You know, for a free place to live."

He wrapped his arms around her waist. "Are you?"

She pushed against his chest, her small hands flush with his pecks. "No, of course not. Is that what you think?"

Tank firmed his hold and couldn't help but smile as she blustered. She was cute when she was irritated, and that got him a little excited.

"Of course not. Now come here." He squeezed her tighter.

Her soft flesh in his hands got him even more excited. "My mother will love you. I promise. Stop worrying."

He kissed her forehead, and the warmth of her body snuggled next to his got him *really* excited and his mind racing. He couldn't seem to get enough of her. Maybe this could be a good time for their first quickie.

"Hey, you wanna?" Squeezing her backside, he raised his eyebrows, and smiled.

"Tyler Wilde, you *are* wild," she teased as she firmed her grip on his waist.

"So, is that a yes?" He waggled his eyebrows again.

"It's a big yes." She jumped into his arms and snaked her legs around his body, her center pressing next to his.

Mercy.

"You make me crazy, you know that." He plunged his mouth to her neck and turned them toward his room. Just as he was about to whisk her to the bed, a thud sounded on the front porch, then a knock.

Alfred's barks echoed through the house.

Damn.

"So close." He hung his head into the crook of her neck and gave her ass one last squeeze.

"She's he-re," Annie sang as she slithered down his body, her feet flat on the floor. "If only we'd had a couple more minutes." She pinched his stomach.

He tossed his head back and sighed.

I love my mom. I love my mom.

I'm glad she's here. I'm glad she's here.

He repeated the words to himself as he stepped to the front window. Thankfully, Little Tank hadn't had too much time to get out of control.

"Hush, Al."

Alfred reined in the wails and went to stand beside Annie. He pulled back the curtain.

Oh, damn.

"Not my mother."

He sighed, and reached for the lock. He was really going to have to have a talk with this man about his awful, piss-poor timing.

Tank pulled open the door. Father stared back at him from the front porch. "Hey man." He let out a sigh. "What are you doing here?"

"Don't look so happy to see me." Father whisked off his shades. "Holy moly, what is that smell? I smelled it out here on the porch steps before I ever made it to the door."

"Annie made a cinnamon cake. What are you doing here?"

The reason better be damn good.

"You guys were so...private all weekend, Steele didn't get a chance to return your tent or your sleeping bag before you took off. Your head must have been in the clouds." The man leaned in and whispered, "Or other places." Father nudged him with an elbow.

Tank couldn't help but return the dirty old man's smile. Still, his head could be in that *other place* right now if this man hadn't of shown up.

"Yeah, I guess I did forget."

"No worries, my man. I brought them back." He pointed to a pile on the front porch.

"Well, you want to come in? Have some cake?" Might as well invite him in now that Wilde's wild plan was cancelled. "My mom will be here in a minute. You can meet her."

"Sure. That'll be great." Father stepped over the threshold. "Hey, Annie. You got some coffee to go with that cake?"

"Of course." She gave the leader an easy smile and reached for the coffee filters.

"I'm going to put the tent in the garage. You guys get settled." He grabbed the camping supplies and strolled across the yard to the garage. Pulling his keys out of his pocket, he heard the sound of a car engine in the distance. He unlocked the door, tossed his tent inside, and shut it back just as the little red sports car came easily down the drive. How the woman got her long legs in that car, he never understood.

His mom pulled to a stop and got out with a smile. "Tyler, baby."

Always her baby.

"I've missed you."

He sauntered over and wrapped her in a tight hug. "I've missed you, too, Mom. There are some people inside I'd like you to meet. Where's your bag?"

"Trunk." She reached inside the little excuse of a vehicle and popped the latch. "Who's in the house?"

"Annie, the girl I told you about, and Father. The leader of the biker group I've been involved with."

"I'm so glad you're making such a great start here. I'm happy for you." She ruffled his hair.

Tank pulled his head back. "Ma, my hair."

"Ha! Since when are you one to care about your appearance? This Annie gal must be pretty special."

"She is." He nodded. "Very special."

"Oh, my baby's in love." She pulled him in for a side hug and squeezed. "I'm excited to get to meet her."

Annie being the first woman he'd ever introduced to his mom felt right and sure. The connection the two of them shared, undeniable, and a part of him was excited the two women he loved were meeting.

They charged up the steps, and he held the door open.

Annie and Father sat at the kitchen table. The leader had his back toward them, pouring some coffee from the carafe on the table, while Beauty stood and offered him a warm smile.

"Mom, I'd like you to meet Annie."

She walked around the table, and gave his mom a warm hug. "It's so nice to finally meet you, Ms. Wilde."

"You as well, Annie, and it's Clara dear. Tyler thinks very highly of you."

Beauty gave him a little wink. "And I can assure you, I think highly of him as well."

Father stood and turned.

"And mom, this is Father."

The two locked gazes, and all coloring seem to leave his mother's face.

"Ma? You okay?"

"Oh my God." She tossed a hand to her mouth. "Jack?"

"Harley?" Father asked, his eyes big in question.

Jack? Harley?

"Wait?" Tank glanced from his mother to the leader and back again. "How do you know his name is Jack? And you." He glanced at Father. "What do you mean, Harley?"

The leader fell back in his chair.

"Tyler." His mother gripped his arm, her face even whiter. "I need to sit down."

"Yeah. Yeah. Here." He rushed to help her to a chair.

Slowly, she sat beside Father and stared at him like she saw an apparition.

Annie flipped her gaze between him and the two sitting. "I don't understand."

Neither did he, but a dim light started to spark in his mind, slowly shining brighter and brighter through the muck of his knowledge as he started to place the pieces together.

Father's last true love, his one night-stand all those years ago...

Mom?

"That's her." Father turned his head up toward him. "That's the woman I told you about."

"The woman you were in *love* with? *My* mom? This doesn't make any sense. Seriously?"

"Seriously." He nodded, his stare still wide-eyed, as if he couldn't believe the words he was saying.

"Wow."

Tank glanced at his mother. She'd been alone all these years, ever since his dad went to prison. Now, she sat across from a man who, at one time, had loved her. Still did according to the conversation the two of them had over the weekend. Tank glanced at Annie. The one woman on this earth he loved more than anything, and his heart swelled. He wanted love like that, like this, for his mother.

Maybe, her and Jack could finally have their chance.

"Well, congratulations on finding each other again, I guess?" He gave his mother a slight smile, her face still ashen. "Ma, you okay?"

"Tyler." His mother glanced up at him, her voice low, and her eyes still full of disbelief. "There's more, and I think you should sit down."

He didn't like the sound of this.

"I'm good." He crossed his arms. "Just tell me. What's up?"

"Please, Tyler. Sit down."

Her gaze pleaded with him. The same desperate gaze she'd had when she begged him to tell her what all his father had done to him. A weight sunk in his gut like an anchor as he recalled the events, the emotions. Something was wrong.

Very wrong.

"Mom, just tell me." The anticipation of what she was going to say had to be worse than her news.

"Tyler, ple—"

"Mom, just say it."

Annie gripped a hand around his bicep. "Tyler, honey, calm down."

He gave her a gentle smile. Last thing he needed was to scare her. "I'm calm, babe" He pulled her in close and lowered his voice. "Mom, just tell me. What is it you have to say?"

"Well." She curled her hands in her lap and fidgeted with her fingers. "I don't really know how to tell each of you this, but Tyler, I'd...I'd like to..."

He fidgeted, growing impatient. "To what?"

Annie squeezed her grip on his arm again, warning him against his tone. His mother was taking too long. The heaviness in his stomach grew, making him wish he *had* taken a seat.

His mom took in a deep breath. "Jack is...well... He's your real father."

The weight in his stomach dropped to his feet, and his head began to spin. The muscles in his biceps tensed, and he let go of Annie before he squeezed her to death.

Father, his father?

Surely not.

The leader's story echoed in his mind, the words swirling around and together like his brain was on a tilt-a-whirl. How many years ago was that one-night stand?

A swollen belly, a ring on her hand, and she doted over some man. Obviously, her husband.

His mother's good time before she settled down. *Father?*

"My...my father?"

She nodded. "I'm afraid so."

"Oh, shit." Father slumped in his chair. "Are you sure, Harley?"

The mention of his mother's nickname suddenly had his veins burning.

"Yes." She turned to the leader. "I questioned myself for a long time, but now, seeing the two of you together, how can you not see the resemblance?"

Annie focused on the Guardian leader then back at him. "Oh my God, she's right."

The muscles in his jaw twitched. "Just because we look alike doesn't mean he's my father." A lot of people looked alike. It didn't mean they were related.

"Ty, baby, I can't imagine what this is like for you, but it's true. I didn't know how to get a hold of Jack after I found out, otherwise, I would have tried."

Would have tried. She hadn't tried at all.

"Well, you should have tried harder. Both of you should have tried harder." His voice escalated as his head continued to spin. His past, his torture...all of it preventable.

"All that time of being abused by a man I thought was my father," he said, his teeth clenched. "A man who I wanted more than anything to love me, and I prayed over and over he would, and that he would stop hurting me." His heart sped and his lungs felt like they were constricting, squeezing his other organs to his throat. "All that time, and he was nothing more than what? Just some man you could pawn off as pretending to be my dad?" he ground out the last words, his temper bubbling to nearly uncontrollable. Years of anger, pain, and frustration he'd tried to push down, delete from his past, came simmering back to the surface. His fists balled, the skin on his knuckles daring to crack from the pressure.

Annie scooted toward the table, and Alfred whined beside her.

Seeing her move away from him as a slight expression of fear passed over her face brought his anger down. He unclenched his fists and forced himself not to punch the wall, or take his anger out on any object. Despite his rage, he would have better control of himself. For her.

"Tank, that's enough," Father reprimanded.

He glared at the man and controlled his voice. "Just because you may be my actual biological father, doesn't mean you get to act like my dad, old man."

"Tyler, I understand you're upset—"

"Upset?" Tank paced. "Upset doesn't even begin to describe what I'm feeling. I have to leave. I have to get out of here." He grabbed his helmet off the hook by the door.

"Tyler." Annie reached for him.

His heart and head spun with sorrow, with anger, with love. Love for her. His rock.

He grabbed her hand and pulled her in for a tight hug, kissing her hairline. "Not now, babe." He whispered near her ear. "I'm sorry I scared you. I love you, but I need to be alone right now."

She nodded. "I understand, and I love you," she whispered back.

"I know." He released his hold on her and didn't even so much as offer his mother or Father a passing glance.

CHAPTER TWENTY-SEVEN

Annie stared at the two people at the kitchen table.
Tyler's biological parents.

Seeing him in so much pain as his mother told him the news, so broken, and so mad, she would have given anything to trade places with him. He'd suffered enough in his past.

Picturing that shy boy across the river holding his fishing pole almost too scared to glance up at her, she'd often wondered if maybe he didn't like her. Still, she had been drawn to him like a star to a constellation, a place in her heart being shaped just for him since she was a girl.

As a child, she never could have understood him or his pain. Now, as adults, the realization sliced through her core. She had to help him.

"What...what should we do?"

"Let him be," Clara said. "He'll come around, and when he does, he'll have questions."

"Harley." Father stared at the other woman, a state of shock still etched on his face.

"It's Clara. Clara Wilde." The mother folded her delicate hands in her lap as her shoulders slumped. "What's your real name?"

"Wait…you two don't actually *know* each other's names?" She glanced back and forth between the two of them. "How is that possible if you are Tyler's father?"

"Annie, you might want to have a seat. I'll get us all some fresh coffee." Father stood, taking the coffee carafe that sat in the middle of the table with him.

"Well, I have to admit, this isn't exactly how I planned our first meeting going," Clara said. "And please, don't judge me, Annie, until you know the truth."

Father placed a coffee cup down in front of Clara.

"I'm listening," she said as she took a seat across the table.

"Jack and I, we met at a time in my life when I was with someone else. A man I thought was good. A man I thought I wanted to marry, but he was moving a little slower than I wanted. I was in my early twenties. Young and naïve. Jack, here, he came into the restaurant I worked at, and something about him caught my attention." She passed a subtle glance toward Father. "You were different. Charming, ruggedly handsome, dare I say exotic from the men I'd seen. Something about you enticed me."

Father nodded. "Same here, Harley."

Clara stared back at her; the woman's hands trembled on her coffee mug. "I told myself that I was allowed one exciting night in my life. Nothing about Mark excited me like Jack did, but I could tell he wasn't one to settle down. He was only passing through after all." She took a sip of her coffee.

"So, you thought what harm could one night do?" Annie asked.

"Yes, I did." Clara nodded. "That's why I didn't even tell him my name. I figured it was all meaningless anyway, but what happened next, I didn't expect."

"You wound up pregnant." Father took his seat again, crossed his arms, and leaned back in his chair.

"Yes, and I was scared. I wasn't certain who the father was. I suspected you, Jack, but I had no proof. Not without a DNA test." She gave Father a sad glance. "I wished, God how I wished, I knew where you were or even what your name was. I wanted to tell you so bad. I felt such a deeper and stronger connection with you than I ever did with Mark. I couldn't stop thinking about you, but I knew my feelings were one sided. After all, how can you love someone after one night?" Clara clutched her mug tighter, perhaps to help ease the tremble in her hands. "Besides," she continued, "I figured if you cared for me like I had begun to care for you, you would have come back. And since you didn't, I took that as a sign that my baby was with the dad he was supposed to have."

All of Tyler's pain because two people wanted no strings attached.

Annie knew it wasn't her place to judge. But still, she couldn't help but be angry with these two right now. Father was a good man, and while she didn't know Clara personally, the woman was Tyler's mother, and he was wonderful, so this lady had to have redeeming qualities to raise such a magnificent son. However, Annie had a hard time seeing the good in either of them right at the moment.

"So, you married another man and passed Tyler off as his son because you were unsure who the real father was?"

What a bold move.

"Yes. I didn't have much money, and I had no idea how I

would raise a child on my own. I married Mark for the sake of my baby, or so I thought at the time. I'm not happy about what I did, or how I handled things. Especially after, well after…"

"After what that monster did to him," Father finished. He pushed his chair back, the legs screeching on the wood floor. "Damn it."

"I'm sorry, Jack. I didn't know for sure who the father was, and I didn't know how to get a hold of you. It wasn't until Tyler got older that I began to really see the resemblances in you two, but even still, I only met you once. I tried to convince myself I was wrong. That I'd forgotten what you really looked like. I can see now that I didn't."

"I don't blame you, Harley. I'm just as much to blame as you, but you want to know what's the worst about all of this?" He paced and stared back at Clara. "I *did* come back. I came back for you. But I saw you through the window of the restaurant, pregnant and sitting on some man's lap with a ring on your finger. I knew I had missed my chance, so I left. Christ. I left." The man let out a ragged breath.

"I'm so sorry, Jack." Tears spilled from Clara's eyes. "I blame myself for everything. If I hadn't insisted on us keeping our names secret, none of this would have happened. I could have protected my child like a mother is supposed to do. But I swear to you both, I had no idea Mark was the way he was until it was too late. I swear it." Tyler's mother broke down in sobs, the cup falling loose from her hand, and coffee sloshed over the table.

Annie reached for a napkin and busied herself with cleaning, soaking in all the information. Despite what that monster, Mark, did to Tyler, she tried to place herself in Clara's shoes. Poor, baby on the way, uncertain of the real father…who's to say she wouldn't have done the same thing. No one can predict the future. She of all people understood that.

"Oh, Clara." She tossed the towel aside and grabbed the woman's hand. "You couldn't help what your husband did to Tyler. And I know deep down, he doesn't blame you."

"But it's my fault. All of it."

Father grabbed his chair, flipped it around, and straddled it, his chest hitting the back. "Harley, baby, none of this is completely your fault. I should have manned up. Walked in that restaurant and told you how I felt."

"How you felt? What do you mean?"

"I fell in love with you that night, and I haven't got you out of my mind since."

"You did?"

"Yes." He reached for Clara's free hand.

"Oh, Jack. What do we do about our son? What about Tyler?"

"Like you said. We'll give it some time. He'll come back. Annie's here, and he loves her. We'll just wait him out."

Tyler did love her. The feeling in Annie's chest, the warmness of his embrace when he held her, the way his eyes glimmered when he stared at her in the mornings just after waking up, all told her he loved her. And the heaviness that set in her chest thinking about his pain reminded her of how much she loved him.

Clara squeezed her hand again, and cut through her thoughts.

"I'm glad he has you."

"I'm glad I have him. He's been there for me through everything. I'll be here for him." She just wished she knew what to do to help him.

"Thank you," Clara said.

Annie wrapped the woman in a hug and reached for

Father's hand as fresh, solid tears welled in her eyes. She choked back a sob for the man she loved and another one for his two heartbroken parents, their embrace making a circle of love, for Tyler. She had no idea how she would help him, but she would. She had to.

CHAPTER TWENTY-EIGHT

J ust great. Tank pulled up in his driveway. Father's motorcycle was still there. His beloved *Harley*.

His mother, Harley.

His *real* dad, Father.

How much worse could things get?

And Annie. What would she think when he went in and didn't speak? He wasn't mad at her, but he wasn't ready to talk yet either. God, this was all so messed up.

He turned off his bike then pushed the kickstand down. As much as he didn't want to walk inside, it was his house after all. The rest of them needed to leave. Except Beauty. Even though he wasn't ready to speak, he needed her there. Her love provided the only reassurance in the entire cluster-fuck of events.

He stomped up the steps, opened the door, and charged over the threshold. Everyone sat around the dining room table, staring at him.

"Tyler, you're back." His mother stood.

Holding out his hands, palms up, he said, "Stop. I'm not ready to talk to anyone, okay? Just let me be."

Father stood. "I'm going to go. Maybe we can talk tomorrow, okay, Tank?"

"Maybe. I don't know." He shook his head. "Don't count on it."

"Tyler." Annie rounded the table.

"Not now, babe, okay?"

His words stopped her forward motion.

"Just...not now." Turning back to his mother, her anxious eyes made his next words almost impossible to speak. "Mom, I think...for tonight, I think it's best you stay in a hotel." A look of rejection slashed her face, and his heart bled. "I'm... I'm sorry."

"I understand. Of course."

Annie held out her hand for his mom. The action cut him deeper than his mother's hurt expression and swelled his heart equally. The love of his life and his mom cared for each other, but at the same time, he didn't like the idea of sharing Annie. Beauty should be holding him, embracing him, not the person who hurt him.

But then again, she had just tried to go to him, embrace him, love him, and he had rejected her.

Christ, nothing made sense. Not his feelings, not what he had heard, or what he was seeing. Father—his biological dad. How had he not seen the resemblance before now?

"I can't...I can't see you guys right now." He turned and headed to his bedroom. "I'm really sorry," he muttered out before he shut the door.

Plopping down on his bed, he kicked off his riding boots, the weight of his day sitting heavy on his shoulders. Exercise. Sweat. That's what he needed. Needed it now. Standing, he tossed his phone on his dresser and opened the drawer for some workout clothes. The pile of letters stared back at him.

Shit. Could he not catch a break?

He reached inside, grabbed some shorts, and slammed the door shut, the drawer popping back open.

Forget it.

He could not deal with his past right now. He just couldn't.

———

ANNIE WALKED Tyler's parents out of his home and placed her back against the door. How strange to realize all this time, Father and Tyler, actually father and son. How had she missed the resemblance? How had anyone? Granted, Father had the slightest bit of Native American features to him that got lost in the genetics with Tyler, but still. The resemblance was there.

The boom of his stereo vibrated the walls of the cabin as the clanging of his weights slammed the steel holder. She'd never seen him like this, and didn't have a clue as to what to do. Attempting to put herself in his shoes, she thought about what she would need. A friend.

She glanced around the living room. No phone. Annie sauntered around the house, searching for the device and ended up in the bedroom. Right there, on top of his dresser. When she reached for the cell, his top drawer sat slightly open. The entire right side covered in letters. All from the prison. His dad's letters.

No. His stepdad's.

Annie grabbed the phone and scrolled through until she found the number she needed and hit dial.

"Hey, man, what's up?" Steele's voice asked through the receiver.

"Hey, Steele."

"Oh, not a man. Hello, there Moonlight. To what do I owe the pleasure?"

"Tyler needs a friend. There are some things that have happened. I think you need to come over here."

"Is he all right?"

"Physically? Yeah." The metallic slap of weights hit the steel bar again. "At least for now."

"For now?"

She could hear the question in his voice.

"Yeah, okay. Give me twenty minutes."

"Thanks, Steele."

She hung up and clutched a few of the letters in her hands, each one about the same weight as the other. Perhaps the man had written the same thing over and over, hoping for a reply. A reply that never came. Tyler needed to face his past, whether he wanted to or not, and she would be by his side when he did.

———

TANK CRANKED his music louder and did another set of chest presses. He'd alternated between fifteen presses and twenty pushups for seven sets already, focusing on the numbers. If he kept his head occupied with counting, he could ignore the slow ache that burned in the back of his mind, heart, and eyes, and only pay attention to the one burning in his muscles. He pumped out his last set when a loud knock came on the spare room door.

Annie.

God, he'd essentially ignored her since he heard the news. She had to understand.

"It's open." He reached for his stereo remote to turn down the noise.

The door slowly opened, but his beautiful girlfriend wasn't on the other side. Instead, Steele's goofy-ass grin stared back at him.

"Why are you here?"

He shrugged his leather-clad shoulder. "I don't know, man. You tell me. Moonlight thinks you might need a friend. From the hard as stone look on your face, and the amount of weights on that bar, I think I agree."

Tank shook his head. "It's been a shit day. No, that's a lie. My morning was good. Damn good. My afternoon's what's sucked."

"Well, I'm here to make your evening better."

Cocky bastard.

He shook his head again. "No offense man, but I don't even know if that's possible. Annie didn't tell you what all has happened?" He stood and took off a few weights on each side of the chest press bar.

"No. Just said you might need a friend."

"No offense, dude, but even a friend can't fix this shit."

"Might help if you talked about it."

He stopped midway from the chest press to his weight rack. "Christ, now you sound like *him*."

Just when he was trying to clear his mind, not think about his biological *father*, in walks Steele screwing everything up. What was up with these Guardians and their damn timing?

"Him who?"

"Father. Jack. Shit. I don't even know what to call him anymore." Tank racked the weight, turned around, and wailed on his punching bag.

A picture of his stepdad burned in his mind. He'd pounded the leather many-a-nights pretending he pounded the life out of that sick bastard.

"Easy man. What did that bag ever do to you?" Steele

stepped across the room and held the sleeve in place. "Here. Go to town, and when you're done, you can tell me what the hell is going on."

Tank let out a fresh batch of punches, until his biceps and shoulders burned like his mind and chest.

"It's everything." He gave one final blow then wiped the sweat from his eyes with his shirt.

"You ready to talk now?"

"Are you going to leave if I don't?"

"No." Steele crossed his arms.

"Hell, fine." He paced.

Where did he even start? How did he even start?

"You're not talking."

"I'm thinking."

"Thinking's not talking."

He gave his friend a cross stare. "You know how Father always calls his bike Harley?"

"Yeah, stupidest name on Earth. What's that got to do with anything?"

"Well, I asked him why on the trip. Turns out, he met a woman years ago, about twenty-eight to be exact, fell in love with her, slept with her. Turns out, they never told each other their real names."

"So, it was a one-night stand?"

"Yeah, something like that. Except, that one-night stand produced a son." Tank tossed a hand to his chest.

"Shit, dude. So, Father is *your* father?"

"According to my mom, yeah."

"Now that I know that, I can see it in your eyes. You do sort of favor."

Damn it with the eyes.

"That's what that bartender at the restaurant we stopped at along the way to the lake said, too."

"So, what about your dad? Your other dad, does he know?"

"I don't keep in contact with him. I have no idea, and I couldn't give a horse's shit less about what he knows or thinks."

"Well, if you don't keep in contact with your dad that raised you, what's so wrong about having a dad now?"

A dad.

A dad like Father. Something he wished only a few weeks ago he could have had.

"Nothing's wrong with it, it's just that…that I needed a father growing up. Steele, do you know why I want to join the Blue Guardians?"

"I have an idea, but no, not specifically."

"Because my piece of shit father—the man who I *thought* was my father—abused me. For a year of my life, he did unspeakable things. Things that no seven-year-old should *ever* have to go through. If my mother, or even if Jack, had made a better decision, used proper protection, or even as much as told each other their real fucking names, I might have had a better chance. I might have had a dad who gave a shit about me. Not one who tortured me." Tank plowed his punching bag again and let out a growl of frustration as he fought the stinging that burned the back of his eyes.

"I would have given anything to have a father like Jack in my life. *Anything*. And what's so hurtful is…I was *supposed* to. He was *supposed* to be my dad." He slapped his chest before he slammed the bag again until his biceps burned, his muscles feeling as if they would rip apart from the tension. When he couldn't punch again without feeling as if his knuckles would break, he sank down on the weight bench and slumped his shoulders. His breathing fast and hard.

"I'm sorry, man. I am." Steele sat beside him and slapped him on the back. "But you can't change the past. Neither can your mother or Jack. All you can do is move forward. If you hadn't suffered like you did, then we might not have you as a part of our group. And because of your shitty past, you've been an excellent addition to our cause. Think of Annie and Bear."

"Christ." He stood. "Do you Guardians have a handbook that y'all pass out and study?"

"No." Steele raised an eyebrow. "Why?"

"Father said the same shit. My past has shaped who I am today to help others. Blah. Blah. Blah."

"He's a smart man, and he's right. Yesterday, you thought the same thing about him. Don't let his mistake ruin a future relationship between you two."

Father's mistake.

The mistake that produced him, and gave him life. Despite how shitty the beginning turned out to be.

"I don't know." Tank wiped a towel over his cracked and bleeding knuckles. "I need some time."

"Of course you do. Take it. I know Father. He's loyal. He'll be waiting whenever you're ready to talk."

Talk.

That's what everyone wanted to do, while he just wanted it all to go away. But damn it if his friend didn't have a point. Father had been loyal, and nothing but good the little time that he'd known him. Still, he wasn't ready to jump onboard the new daddy train. Not yet.

"Yeah." He slapped his friend on the shoulder. "You're right. Thanks, man."

"I know I am. Now, you've got a pretty little thing out there." Steele pointed toward the direction of the living room. "Who is ringing her hands worried sick about you. It might not seem like it now, but you're pretty lucky. I wouldn't mind having someone like her on my side."

"Don't even think about it." Squeezing his grasp into the man's flesh, he gripped Steele's shoulder harder.

"Jeez, man, ease up." The firefighter wiggled away. "I would never step on your turf. All I'm saying is don't screw it up."

"I don't plan on it."

"Good. I'm out of here. You going to be okay?"

"I'll be fine. Thanks, man."

Steele hugged him and slapped him on the back. "That's what our group does. Help each other. Put some Vaseline on your hands." He pointed to Tank's bleeding knuckles.

"Will do." He led Steele out to the hallway. Annie sat on the couch, a pile of letters beside her on the end table.

Shit. Can this day get any worse?

She stood. "Is everything okay?"

"It will be." He reached for her hand.

"What happened?" She glanced at his knuckles.

"Bag won," Steele said as he opened the front door. "Bye you love birds." Something crinkled under the firefighter's feet as he stepped out. "What the heck? Roses?" The man picked up the arrangement. "If this is Father's way of apologizing, it sure is a girly way to do it."

Annie's grip tightened in Tank's hand. A note stuck to the top of the flowers. "Let me have those." He took the bouquet.

"Tyler." Her face whitened, her lips straight.

"I know." He released her hand and pulled out the card, passing the flowers back to his friend. "Steele, shut the door, will you?"

He stepped back over the threshold and closed the door.

Tank ripped the seal and opened the letter.

My Dearest Annie,
I want you back.
Please forgive me.
Love, Duke.

IT WAS ONLY a matter of time before their relationship, and where Annie lived was made public, but he wasn't ready for Duke to know. Not yet. Reading the note, the word love seemed to jump off the page. No way was that man allowed to love Annie. He never did, and he never would.

"He found me." She placed a hand to her mouth.

"I'll call the Guardians. We can set up twenty-four hour surveillance." Steele reached for his phone.

"No." She held out her hand to stop Steele, and straightened her shoulders. "Don't. I'm not afraid anymore. I'm going back to work this week. It was only a matter of time before I saw him anyway. He'll have to come to terms with the fact that we aren't together anymore."

"He's watching you, Annie. He's watching *us*." The corner of the card dug into Tank's palm. The cop trailing them earlier. Was that how Duke knew she was there?

"Let him watch. He can't control me anymore or us. He won't do anything to ruin his campaign. If I go back to work and tell everyone we're separated, he has no choice but to agree."

She was underestimating the man. *He* had underestimated the man, *again*. Al had barked at the trees. Sure, the dog barked at everything, but he should have checked the woods, secured the area instead of thinking about another way to get her in his bed. Never again. He could not allow his desire for her to muddle his thoughts.

"I'll keep you safe." He pulled her into his chest, his tired muscles quivering. From exhaustion or anxiety, he wasn't sure.

"I know you will."

She had too much faith in him. Placing a gentle kiss on her forehead, he released her. "Let me just walk Steele out."

Outside, Steele asked, "You worried?"

"Yeah." Tank scanned the trees.

"You think Annie is making too light of this?"

He glanced back at his friend. "If you'd seen her the night that monster nearly killed her, then you would know she is. She's scared, but she's trying to be brave."

"You can't out-brave crazy."

"True. So true. Be safe, man."

"You, too." Steele revved his bike and shot down the driveway.

Alfred sat on the front porch, licking his paws. "You're supposed to protect us, man." Tank bent to pet his dog behind the ears. "Why didn't you bark a little while ago when Duke dropped off the flowers, huh?" Annie had been right. Damn dog does bark at everything. But, why not now? A quack sounded in the distance. "Too busy chasing, ducks, huh?" He rubbed Alfred's belly. "Useless pup."

It wasn't his dog's place to protect them. It was his. And he would. A warm realization washed over him as he ran a hand over Al's soft fur.

He'd give his life for Annie.

Without a doubt.

Back inside, Beauty sat back on the couch, the pile of letters in her lap. Time to switch gears from one psycho to another.

"You found them, I see. He closed the door behind him.

"I'm sorry. I wasn't snooping, they were—"

"In my top drawer, and I left the drawer open. I gather you saw them when you went to call Steele."

"Yeah." She bit her bottom lip.

He crossed over to her. "I'll read them, but not now." He got down on his knees and took the letters from her grasp.

"I hope you're okay with me calling Steele. I didn't think you needed to be alone, and I figured you might want to talk to a friend. Someone other than me."

While his reality had been shifted, his life wasn't in danger. Not like hers could be. Her crazy ex was on the hunt for her, and here she sat worried about him. How in the hell did he get so lucky?

"I'll always want to talk to you babe, but you're right. I did need a friend. Thank you." He rubbed his hands on the top of her thighs; the bleeding from his cracked skin ebbed. "But what has me more worried is you. I want to protect you. Tomorrow, we are getting that alarm system installed, okay?"

"Okay."

"Are you still set on going back to work?"

"Yes. I can't let him run my life."

In his head, he knew Beauty was right. In his heart, he wanted to wrap her in his protective embrace forever and never let her go. Yet, he also knew he couldn't smother her with his love. Love didn't abuse, and love didn't bind unwantedly. He had to let her be free, make her own decisions.

But tonight, he *would* keep her close.

"I agree, but we have to be smart. He's dangerous. Tomorrow, the alarm will go in place, but tonight, I'm going to hold you close. I need you, in my arms, safe."

She pressed her forehead to his and closed her eyes. "Make love to me."

He felt her desires. She needed to put both of their

worries aside, if for only just a few moments, and get lost in what they shared.

"I love you, Tyler," she whispered near his ear.

"I love you, more." He tapped her nose and placed a gentle kiss on her lips, preparing her for the soft and slow rhythm he wanted their love making to take.

———

TANK LAY QUIETLY, Annie's naked body curled next to him on the couch, his hand wrapped protectively around her stomach, while Alfred snored on the floor below.

They'd pleased each other, slow and easy, forgetting their sorrows, their worries, getting lost in the bliss of their connection. When she finally found slumber, he stared at her delicate frame wrapped next to him, determined to stay awake, protect her from harm.

The pile of letters on the end table taunted him, reminding him of his pain, his past all over again. He needed to open one, get the agony over with. Just like ripping a Band-Aid off.

Gently, he released Annie and wiggled his arm out from under her and grabbed the letter on top. Postmarked two months ago. He tore the tab and pulled out the slip of paper. His father's small print stared back at him.

Dear Tyler,

This will be my one hundredth letter I've written to you. By now, I've assumed you aren't reading them, but I will keep writing them, and keep sending them. My parole hearing is in six months, and my prayer is to receive an early release.

I understand this might not be what you would want, but please know, I have asked the Lord for my forgiveness, and I will send a letter every week asking you for yours. I've suffered in many ways here in prison, many of the same ways in which I made you suffer. I'm sorry. While I know you may never forget, I pray that you find it in your heart to forgive me.

If you could kindly write a letter back saying you did, I would stop all correspondence with you if that's what you wish.

Love,

Dad

He crumpled the letter in his hand. *Forgiveness.* The bastard wanted forgiveness.

As did his mother and his real father.

How could he find it in his heart to forgive them?

Annie shifted in her sleep and kicked his leg with her foot. He stared down at her ankle, her tattoo staring back at him. A tattoo that represented love. Love was his answer, but even still, he found loving them right now hard to do.

CHAPTER TWENTY-NINE

Tank stared at their new alarm system. The damn thing cost him his whole two weeks' paycheck, but Annie's safety was worth every penny.

"What are you doing?" Beauty laced up her shoes.

"Staring at the new monitor. Isn't this cool? If they ring the doorbell, we can see who's outside before we open the door."

She sauntered by his side. "Yep. Welcome to the twenty-first century big guy." She poked him in the stomach. "You ready?"

"Yep. I'm ready." He grabbed his keys from his pocket. "Motorcycle or truck?"

A slight curve turned up from her lips as she reached for her bike helmet off the hook. "Motorcycle."

"I've turned you into a regular biker chick, haven't I, Beauty?"

"It's Moonlight, remember?" She gave a sultry wink that had him wishing they could stay in bed a bit longer.

"Yeah, I remember." He punched in the code and escorted

her outside before he locked the door. "Are you sure you want to work a double today?"

"I'm sure. Sandi's short-staffed, and besides, you need some alone time with your mom. You did a fabulous job avoiding her yesterday."

His mom had come over and watched the installation of the alarm system. A sharp pain shot through his stomach at the way he had treated her, barely speaking more than five words to her all day. His mood had been sour enough to make buttermilk. Something he needed to apologize for.

"Yeah." He blew out a breath. "I guess you're right. I'm just not ready to forgive yet. I don't know when I will be."

"I understand." Annie grabbed his hand. "But the longer it takes you to move on, the longer it will eat at you. Don't allow people to make you unhappy, Tyler. It's not worth it. Besides, your mom loves you. She didn't expect to end up pregnant with you, and she only tried to make the best of the situation. She wanted her son to have a father."

"What a damn fine one she picked," he muttered.

"We all make mistakes."

Pulling her in for a hug, he said, "How did I get so lucky to land you?"

"Through another's mistakes. Same way I landed you." She pecked him on the chin and squeezed his waist. "Let's go, or we're both going to be late."

He drove the ten miles into town, with Annie clinging to his back, his mind heavy with what he was about to do. He pulled up to the back door of the diner, and turned off his bike. "Sandi's going to be here, right?"

She took off her helmet. "For the thousandth time, yes."

"I don't like this. At all. I hate leaving you."

"I know, but you are literally a block away over at Rakes,

and I will be seen through all the glass windows inside the diner. He won't hurt me. Not here with customers around."

"Not anywhere." He pulled her in for a kiss. A kiss so tempting, his body burned to pull her back on his bike and take her back home.

"What did I do to deserve that?" she asked, her breath ragged, and her lips swollen with his mark.

"I wanted to give you something to remember me by. In case…"

"Are you afraid I'll change my mind about us?"

He shook his head and gripped his bike handles tighter. "I…I hope not. I've just never cared for someone like I do you. You have the power to break me to pieces."

Life without Annie. He didn't want to imagine it.

"You're a big, strong man, Tyler. You'd be fine."

He reached for her waist and pulled her closer. "Not when it comes to you." The denim of her jeans and short sleeve shirt hugged her nice and snug. Her face bare of makeup. She was free. Free of all extra layers covering her beauty. With each other, they'd both found a type of freedom. One he was just beginning to enjoy. "Be careful, Beauty."

"I will. Now go, before you're late. I love you."

"I love you more." He kissed her hand. "I'm not leaving until you are safe inside."

"Fine." She skipped up the backdoor steps. "You're stubborn."

"I'm *your* stubborn."

She gave him a wave as she stepped through the door and shut it behind her.

He reached for the handles of his bike, and glanced around the alley. Only a matter of hours now before Duke realized she was here. He reached for his phone and clicked

Steele's number to make sure all Guardians were on high alert.

His mission was to protect her, and he wouldn't fail.

———

DUKE SAT in his unit and peered through the diner window. Through the glass, he spotted her. Annie.

My Annie.

His heart fluttered at seeing her standing there so close to him. She looked just like the day he'd met her. Little makeup, smiling, happy. Her hair was pulled back in a ponytail, showing the nape of her neck, and his mind raced with the idea of them in bed, him pulling the back of her ponytail as he screwed her from behind.

His dick hardened at the thought. He'd be doing just that tonight if all went as planned. Annie loved him—she'd come back, like the good fiancée he'd trained her to be.

She sauntered out from behind the bar area and went to a table with two elderly gentlemen. Leaning down, she gave one of them a hug. His erection fell as he gripped the flower stems tighter in his hands, and cracked his neck. What the hell was she doing flirting with old men?

Little whore.

As he sat there watching her, a paralyzing fear began to take over. What the hell had she been telling people about her absence? He had to make sure she didn't say the wrong thing. One wrong word, one slip up, could throw his whole story off kilter, and his campaign down the drain.

How dare she show her face without talking to him first?

Calm down. Play it cool. Breathe.

He needed to regain her trust, not push her further into the arms of other men, especially the giant ogre.

Duke stepped out of his unit, and squinted at the harsh summer sun. He reached for the door of the diner, holding it open for a couple of old ladies.

"Why thank you, son," the woman wearing bifocals said.

"You're that boy running for Sherriff aren't you?" the friend asked.

"Why yes, ma'am. Can I count on you ladies for your vote?" He gave them a toothy smile, and held his hand out for Bifocals to cross the threshold.

"You've got my vote, dear." The lady gripped his hand tighter and blushed slightly at his help.

"Whoever is receiving those flowers is sure lucky to have you." The friend smiled, her teeth baring her pink lipstick.

"No, I'm the lucky one." At least he would be after he set Annie straight. But he could and he would. She *would* behave.

He helped the women inside and waved. "Good day, ladies." When he turned to face the bar, Annie stood there, refilling someone's drink glass, the end of her hair just grazing the top of her bra line. His body tensed with crazed lust for his fiancée. This was his chance.

Be Easy. Relaxed.

He sauntered to the bar and laid the flowers down. "Hey there, pretty lady."

Her back stiffened. He glanced around the restaurant to see if anyone noticed. His instincts screamed to pull her behind the building, let her know how much of a fool she'd made him look the last few weeks. His mind warned him to stay in control.

She turned, and gave him a fake smile. "Duke. How are you?" She spoke as if she barely knew him.

"Better now that you're back." He leaned in. She

wouldn't meet his stare. "These are for you." He held the flowers up.

"They're lovely, but I don't want them."

She pressed her lips together, her chest rising and falling in a faster pace. Her expression was dimmer than before he had walked in the door.

He tightened his grip again on the stems. *Control the situation. Get her to listen.* "Annie, honey, I think we need to talk."

The bell above the diner door jingled. Her focus shifted, and her face lit up as her chest heaved a huge sigh.

Of relief?

He swiveled his head toward the door. The same look she gave him months ago when he first started dating her and told her he was whisking her away on a vacation flashed across her face. She hadn't looked at him like that since, and now, she stared longingly at the giant in the same manner.

The stems threatened to break in his hands.

Ogre took one look at him and stomped over to the bar, his steps hard and heavy. One of his biker goons followed on his heels, while a tall, older woman brought up the rear. By the resemblance, must be the ogre's mother.

"Why are you here?" Ogre crossed his arms and asked down to him.

"I'm here to talk to my fiancée." He crossed his own arms and pressed his lips together, waiting. One wrong move and he could have this man arrested.

"Everything's fine, Tyler." Annie rounded the bar and placed a gentle hand on Wilde's arm.

Anger boiled in his chest.

"Why don't you guys grab a seat over at that table right there, and I'll be with you in a minute. Hey, Clara." Annie waved to the woman.

"No, that's okay. I'll wait." The oaf didn't budge.

"Tyler, please. I'm fine." Annie stared at the idiot's friend and mother. "Steele, Clara, you guys go over there. Please." She glanced around the restaurant, obviously worried about causing a scene.

Good girl. His woman still had some sense.

"Sure, Annie," the mother said.

The biker friend slapped the ogre on the back. "Come on, man. We can see everything from two feet away." The shorter one pulled his giant away.

"I think I see steam coming out of his ears," Duke joked.

Annie finally stared at him. "What do you want?" her tone a searing whisper.

"I want to talk to you, in private."

She began to shake her head. "No. Whatever you have to say—"

"Please, Annie." He leaned closer. Duke could practically feel his back burning from the giant's eyes. "I've been on my medicine ever since you left. I'm better now. I promise, and I'll never get off of it again."

"It's too late for that."

Too late? Never.

"I know, Annie, but please, let me apologize…in private. Please."

"Duke…" Her shoulders slumped.

Her resolve was breaking. If he could just get through a little more, get her away from the watchful eye of the giant and his goons, he could win his Annie back.

"Everything okay over here?" Sandi rounded the corner behind the bar and began to refill a tea pitcher.

"We're fine, Sandi, and how about yourself? I see business has been good to you this summer?" He gave the owner a half-smile and glanced around the restaurant.

"Yep...just peachy."

Annie turned to the owner. "Everything's fine, Sandi. Do you mind taking care of Tyler's table for a moment? I'm going to the back with Duke. It appears we have a few things we need to discuss."

"You sure?" The owner raised a questioning eyebrow.

Jesus Christ how much did these people know?

"Yeah, I'll be fine."

"Mo's back there."

Annie nodded in understanding.

What exactly was that fat cook going to be able to do to him?

She turned toward the back. "Come on, Duke." She motioned for him. The ogre stood. "It's okay." Annie held up her hand. "We're just going to the back."

The blond's face sat stone hard as his fingers twitched at his sides. The giant liked control. *Good to know.*

His mother pulled his hand. "Tyler, let her go."

Yes, Tyler. Let her go.

Ogre stared at his mother, then to his friend. "Steele, run outside and block the back exit. I'll call you when it's safe."

"On it." The other biker stood.

"For God's sakes," he hissed. "What do you think I'm going to do, run off with her?"

"I don't put anything past you, *Chief.*"

"Tyler, this isn't necessary," Annie insisted.

"Maybe not." Wilde leaned in and lowered his voice. "But he hurt you once. He won't do it again. I'll be standing right here, watching."

Hurt her once?

What all had his little bitch lied about? He never hurt her. He only taught her lessons. Lessons she had to learn. Lessons he had every right as her fiancé to teach her.

She studied the brute and gave him a soft, subtle smile, her cheeks reddening.

Duke fought the urge to punch the man as he glanced around the restaurant, seeing if anyone noticed the encounter between his woman and her ogre. The little old ladies he'd helped inside, stopped and stared. He gave them a subtle wink and a smile. His actions seemed to please their curiosity.

Annie glanced back at him, the color leaving her cheeks almost instantly. "Come on, Duke. Follow me." She marched to the back, and stopped just inside the back room. She turned to him and her words came out in a rush. "Duke, I'm happy that you—"

"Annie, let's move back here okay?" He cocked his head toward Mo. "There's a little more privacy." What part of privacy was she not understanding? He didn't need another damn audience.

She studied him, her eyes narrowed in concentration before she conceded. "Fine. Mo, I'm stepping into the office with Duke," she called to the fat chef.

The guy raised a butcher knife and waved like he heard her.

What the fuck was that? Some kind of threat?

He rolled his neck and followed as she walked farther into the back of the restaurant, slipping into the back office. She stood by the doorway, and he stepped past her deeper into the space. Her back was positioned to the doorframe. Her work schedule pinned to a board on the half wall behind her. Exactly where he wanted her. He could see her entire two-week schedule just above her head. She worked the night of his speech. That wouldn't do.

"Annie, honey."

Tossing the flowers aside, he reached for her hand. She

pulled it back and crossed her arms. He fought the twitching in his jaw.

"Okay. We won't touch." He placed his hands in his pockets. Time to say what he'd practiced. *Dig deep, work on the tears*. "I'm sorry, baby," he said, keeping his voice low, controlled. "I know what I did was wrong. Can you ever find it in your heart to forgive me?" Frowning, he dropped his chin and rubbed his forehead. "I'm just so sorry." He faked a sniffle, a dab of moisture leaked from his eye.

She blew out a breath. "Yes, Duke, I can."

"Oh, baby." He raised his head, and reached for her hand again. This time, she let him. "That's good news."

Women could never resist tears. Breaking through was going to be easier than he thought. He would win her back. He would.

"But, Duke, we're over. I don't love you, and I never will. I'm not marrying you."

His eye twitched. He rubbed it like he was wiping a tear away, trying to control the tick. Bitch was being difficult. Who the fuck cared about love? He didn't need a marriage of love, but a trophy wife. And she was one of the best looking women in Black Widow. The town already knew them as a couple. Why the hell wouldn't she cooperate?

His pulse pounded as his blood swam through his veins like a raging inferno. He released her hand before his anger caused him to break her fingers. "Annie." *Remain calm.* "I thought you said you forgave me."

"I did, and I do, but I won't spend my life with you."

"How many people have you told this to?" His heart raced. His campaign was in full swing, she being the crutch to him winning his race. She was the only way his father stayed off his ass.

"The Guardians know, but they won't say anything. I

figured I'd let you do that. I know how important your image is to you. You can tell everyone you dumped me. I'm fine with that. I won't run your name in the mud as long as you don't do the same to me."

"Annie, I would never do that to you."

"As much as I would like to think that's because you care about me, I know it's only because I'm a reflection of you."

"That's not true, Annie. I *love* you." If the word was so important to her, then he would tell her what she wanted to hear.

He gripped her hand again, fearful. The apprehensive look in her eyes had changed to pity, and that caused his blood to rage all over again. He was losing her.

He couldn't lose her.

"I think in your own way, you actually might, Duke." She squeezed his hand. "Unfortunately, our versions of love are completely different, but if you do love me, then you will let me go. You need to seek help."

Help? He didn't need help. He needed his fiancée back —willingly.

"If I do, will you reconsider coming back to me?"

Voluntarily, at least.

"Annie? What's going on back here?" Ogre turned the corner and placed his hands on the top of the doorframe, covering the exit.

"I'm coming, babe." She dropped his hand and stepped her back into Wilde's chest. He snaked a possessive arm around her waist.

"I wish you all the best, Duke. I'll see to it you get your ring back. Good luck with everything."

His ring back? He watched as she turned into her new lover, and the man moved his hand to the small of her back, whispering in her ear.

Duke wasn't losing her...he'd already lost her. To a giant, blond, monster. The man cocked a hard stare back at him, and he could see small beads of sweat lining the giant's hairline.

He had to stay calm. Figure something out.

"Annie, wait," he called.

Her and her bodyguard stopped.

"I really am sorry, and I'd like for you to have these." He passed her the roses. "I know flowers aren't much after everything I've put you through, but I do really love you, and I meant what I said. I won't get off my medicine. I hope in time, maybe you'll see that I'm sincere."

"For your sake, I hope you do stay on your prescriptions." She gripped the roses tighter to her chest. "I remember what you were like when we first started dating. I see that same person now, but it's too late for us, Duke. Move on with your life. I have to get back to work." She turned on her heel and walked back toward the dining room with her new beau, and out of his life.

What the hell am I going to do?

His speech was coming up, and his father expected Annie by his side, playing the role of good wife. Half the town would expect it.

The brunette from the courthouse came to mind. Big-bottom Becky or Bethany. *Shit.* He couldn't remember. While she may have been fun to screw, she wasn't what he considered trophy material. Hell, for now, she might have to do. Make Annie jealous.

His phone rang in his pocket. His father. Christ.

"Dad, hey."

"Son, a speech writer will be here Monday at four to help you with your speech. He also wants to meet with Annie, prep her on what to say in an interview. She'll be your wife, so she needs to be trained as well. Is she back from visiting her mother?"

"Dad…" He rubbed his forehead. "Annie and I, we're having some relationship problems. I'll make sure I'm there by four, but I can't guarantee she will be." The phone stood silent. "Dad, did you hear me?"

"What do you mean, you're having *relationship* problems?" His father's voice escalated. "What have I told you all along? You have to have a wife on the campaign trail."

"I've got a replacement in mind."

"A replacement? *A replacement?*" His father's tone grew. "Are you a fucking moron? Have I taught you nothing? You can't replace Annie so close to the election. People will think you are unreliable, untrustworthy. You get her back. I don't care what you have to promise her. You have money, use it."

"Dad—" The line went dead.

Duke shoved his phone in his back pocket and clenched his fist as he stepped out of the office.

Sandi's voice echoed down the hall, and he took a quick step back inside the small room.

"What do you mean, his father?" the older woman said.

"I mean, I'm Tank's father. His mother and I, we have a history. I'm just as shocked as you are. I had no idea."

"Oh my gosh." The woman gasped. "What about Tank. What does he say about it all?"

"Didn't you see the cold stare he shot me? He won't talk to me. Not yet, anyway, and from what Clara said, he's barely talking to her. She leaves on Wednesday, and for her sake, I hope he comes around a bit more."

The leader of the Blue Guardians…the ogre's father? Won't talk to him? Mad at mom. His mind began to spin.

"Give him time, Jack. He will."

"I don't know, Sandi. I'm going to let him make the

moves. I hope he can come around, if not for me, at least for Clara."

"I hope so, too."

Footsteps echoed down the hall, and grew quieter.

Duke peered around the corner. When everything was clear, he stepped quietly out of the office and poked his head out the back door. The brute's friend had disappeared. He slipped out, the heat of the sun searing his head. He'd just received the information he needed. If Annie wouldn't come to him by choice, then he'd make her come by the only other way he knew.

Force.

CHAPTER THIRTY

T ank stood with his back to the kitchen counter, sipping coffee. The top of Annie's thigh peeked at him from under her nightshirt each time she raised her hand to flip the omelet, the shirt daring to go higher.

"What's that smile on your face for?" She plated his eggs for him.

"Just enjoying the view." He sat his coffee cup down and nibbled her neck before grabbing both of their plates.

"Rascal." Annie shooed him away. "I'll refill your coffee."

Tank set the plates down in what had routinely become their spots, and tossed Alfred a piece of bacon.

"I'm excited we both have the day off together. Too bad you have to work the rest of the week though." Beauty frowned.

"I know. The only reason I got a Wednesday off is because I'm working all weekend." He cut into his egg. "Speaking of that. I wanted to talk to you about me being gone. Now that you've talked to Duke, and he knows we're together, I'm not comfortable with leaving you alone yet.

Even with this new alarm system. I think we should have someone here at all times. Until we figure out new living arrangements, or he gets a new girlfriend."

Tank clenched his fist. Poor woman. If he had his way, the bastard would be behind bars so he couldn't hurt another person again.

"What?" Annie pointed to his hand. "Why are you doing that?"

He glanced down and relaxed his fist. "Because, undoubtedly, whoever he picks, the Guardians will have to come in and save her, too."

"Oh." She nodded. "True, and while that will be terrible, I just want you to know, she's not living here." Annie gave him a half-smile.

He reached over and squeezed her thigh. "I only have eyes for you, babe, but I'm serious. I don't like the idea of you being alone. Duke knows you're here. Perhaps we should consider moving? A new town."

"Moving? This is your home, Tyler. Your grandfather's cabin, and the Blue Guardians are here."

"The Blue Guardians are in other cities, too. Father can help me find a new club."

"Father?" She raised an eyebrow. "The man you currently aren't speaking to?"

She had a point.

"Besides, I don't want to move. I like it here, with you, in this cabin in the woods. And that's why you spent all of that money installing the new alarm system. The minute the door even so much as opens, a signal goes straight to your phone. And if the alarm fully sounds, your phone will go bezerk with a warning. *And* if I put in the distress code, then the call center also knows something is wrong. If anyone walks inside this house, you will know, and you can come be my hero, *again.* Also, I have a phone. I could call someone."

He'd bought her a new cell along with the alarm system. At least Duke couldn't track her exact whereabouts. Still, the guy was too dangerous.

"That's all technology that could fail."

She rolled her eyes.

"Annie, this is serious. Even with all of these alerts, what if I can't get to you in time? Or I can't call the Guardians fast enough to alert them for help? Or what if the call center does send someone out, and Duke, as Chief of Police, talks his way out of it before I have a chance to show up? If anything happened to you, I…I don't know how I could handle that."

"Hey." She stood, scooted onto his lap, and snaked her arms around his neck. "I know you are concerned, and I love that you care for me so much, but I really don't believe anything is going to happen to me. Not anymore. Duke is on his medicine. I could tell yesterday when we talked. As long as he stays on that, he'll be fine."

"Yes, as long as he *stays* on it, but you yourself have told me he isn't good about that. What if he gets off of it again? Then what? What other terrible things is he capable of? I can't take the chance when it comes to your safety."

She let out a sigh. "I understand, and I know you're right, but I just can't keep living like a prisoner. I need a life again."

He could see the passion and sorrow in her eyes. She wanted a normal life back. He couldn't blame her. Normalcy was something he wanted to give her, but taking the chance, leaving her alone… it was all so risky.

"Besides." She sat up straighter on his lap. "His campaign is in full swing. He doesn't want to do anything to jeopardize that."

"Why?"

"Why what?" Beauty pulled back and stared in his eyes.

"Why is this campaign so important to him?"

"His dad. His father pushes him to do more, be more. I didn't spend much time with his parents, and he didn't talk about them much, but I gathered different mental illnesses run in the family, each one suffering from their own demons. And each pushing hard trying to prove themselves to the other one."

"Sounds sad."

"Yeah, it does, but they are no longer my concern. You are."

"And you're mine." He pulled her closer, resting one hand on the lovely thigh that had been taunting him in the kitchen. "That's why I don't feel right about leaving you alone. At least until you press charges. He needs to be put away for what he's done."

"That'll really send him over the edge. Besides, who are people going to believe? Him or me?" She let go of him and stood, crossing her arms. "Him. Which is why we didn't have the alarm trip straight to the police station, but to your phone. If he does break in, you were right, he *could* just use his pull and tell the police it was all a misunderstanding. And they would believe him."

"Again, which is why I don't like leaving you alone." He reached for her hand. "Annie, I'm a nervous wreck just thinking about it."

"I understand, Tyler, I do, but I refuse to be trapped forever."

He clenched his jaw. This was a conversation they had over and over, and it seemed to always get them nowhere. Until legal actions took place against Duke, he wouldn't feel comfortable.

Give her time.

Perhaps in another month, he could convince her to seek council. Before anyone else was hurt.

"Then what about gun safety?"

A slight fear crossed her green eyes.

"I know you aren't keen on the idea, but please, if I knew you could handle yourself with a gun, I would feel a little better about leaving you alone."

"Let's bed the conversation for now," she said, and pulled her hand away from his. "Let's enjoy the day, and think about it later tonight. I'm tired of Duke taking up my thoughts. I want to move on."

She was equally as stubborn as she was beautiful.

Still, he could understand her opinion. He remembered what is was like to feel trapped in his fears. No one deserved that feeling.

"Sure." He nodded. She was safe now, and right now was all that mattered. "What would you like to do today?"

"I don't know. Shouldn't we see your mom off this morning?"

"We said our goodbyes last night. She said to give you her love."

"When do you think you'll be ready to really talk to your mom?"

"I don't know. I just… I don't know."

"I understand." She sat back in his lap. "When the time is right, you'll know."

"Thank you." He wrapped his arms around her waist.

"I was thinking we could walk through the woods, to my old home. I think I'm ready to see it now. I'd like to show you."

She wanted to open up more of herself to him. He could definitely handle that.

"I'd like that."

"And I was thinking, maybe we could go to the bank and ask about the price?"

"The price?" He took a sip of his coffee, and she slid off his lap and into her own chair.

"Yeah. I mean, I know the house isn't much, but it comes with some land. Maybe we could fix it up and rent it out or something, or maybe restore it for my mom? I just hate to know it's sitting over there, empty, and my mom, she's just so far away. I'm sorry, I know it's a stupid idea, I just thought—"

"Annie." He reached his hand out to her. "It's not a stupid idea. It's a great idea. I'd love to give it to you, but we just can't get ahead of ourselves, okay? We'll call the bank. Talk to them first. See how much money we would need, and work out a plan to start saving for it. And as for your mom's care, maybe my mother can give us some ideas on how to establish it. She's a nurse after all."

"Really? You mean it?"

"Yes. Of course. Your mom is all the family you have left. We should see about moving her closer regardless if we can get the house or not. We could make sure she is cared for properly if she lived close by, and you could visit her as much as you'd like."

"Oh, Tyler." She jumped back onto his lap. "Thank you so much. I love you." She peppered him with kisses as a tear slipped from her eye and fell on his cheek. Joy. He'd given her joy.

His cellphone danced across the table.

He reached for it. "Annie, baby, I can't breathe. Need air." He joked as he answered his phone. "Hello."

"Tank, it's Steele."

"Hey, man. What's up?"

"It's Bear."

His little buddy. He sat straighter and tightened his grip on Annie.

"Bear? What's wrong?"

Annie pulled back, her expression changing from happiness to concern.

"Nothing's wrong, dude. Mary's sitter is sick and had to cancel on her last minute. She doesn't have anyone to watch Bear today. I can't do it because I'm working, and JoJo went out of town to visit her grandparents or something like that. I haven't tried Father yet, but the kid really wants you. Are you off today? Can you babysit?"

Babysit. His endorphins slowed. He pulled the phone back from his mouth and asked Annie, "Can we babysit Nathaniel today?"

"Sure." Beauty shrugged. "It'll be fun."

"Yeah, man," he said into the receiver. "We've got it handled. I'd rather do it out here though. We can take the little man fishing."

"Yeah, good idea. I'm sure little dude will love that. I'll tell Mary. She'll probably be out there pretty soon with him. It's almost eight-thirty, and she said she has to be at work around nine."

"No problem."

"Thanks, man." He clicked off the phone. "We have about fifteen minutes before we have company."

"I need to run and grab a shower." She wiggled off his lap and stood. She did that on purpose. His excitement grew.

"Woman, you've got it coming to you now."

"I hope so." She raced down the hall, as he chased her into the bathroom and straight to the shower.

T ANK PINCHED Annie's behind as she turned her blow dryer off.

"Behave, you rascal. We're about to have company, and the boy doesn't need to see you act like a horndog."

Horndog? He wasn't a horndog, but a man in love.

"Maybe he does. I gather his dad didn't show his mom much love. Perhaps the kid needs to see what love is."

Beauty turned to face him. He stepped in closer, causing her tight butt to smack the counter top as their bodies touched.

"Love is completely different than lust, big guy." She poked him in the chest. The arch of her back caused her breasts to stick out.

Mercy.

"Maybe so, but right now, all my lines are crossing."

Her chest poked in the air, her cheeks slightly red from the heat of the blow dryer, and her hair all down and wind-blown looking. Tank was about to lose his mind. He reached for her hips as his mouth dove for her neck.

The doorbell rang.

"Ah! Saved by the bell." She shimmied out from underneath him.

"Oh, man."

At least he had their romp in the shower to start his day. He reined his lust under control as he watched Beauty check the monitor to make sure it was Mary and Nathaniel. She unlocked the door, as the alarm announced, *"Door Open."* Alfred bounced by her side.

"Hi there." Annie greeted their guests. "I'm Annie, Tyler's girlfriend."

His heart inflated as she claimed herself as his.

Beauty stuck out her hand and pulled the dog back with another. "This is Alfred. Sorry, he's excited."

"Hi, Annie." Mary shook Annie's hand. "Nice to meet you."

"Down, Alfred," Tank reprimanded as he walked to the door. Nathaniel hugged his teddy close to his mom's side. The boy's eyes grew when he spotted him walking to the door. "Hey, little dude."

"Tank," Bear squealed and ran into his arms.

"Thank you so much for doing this," Mary said. "Are you guys sure you don't mind?"

"Not at all. In fact, we're looking forward to it." Annie released her hold on Al. "I'm sorry I haven't met you before, but it's nice to officially meet you now. I've heard a lot of good things."

Of course Beauty would be looking forward to taking care of Nathaniel. She was one of the kindest and most caring people he knew. The way she worried and looked out for him when he got the blow of who his real dad was, she hadn't been concerned with the danger surrounding her, only him.

"Thank you," Mary said, "but I'm sorry. I haven't heard anything about you."

"All for good reason." He wrapped an arm around Annie's waist and pulled her close. Her safety had been his number one priority from the beginning. Now that Duke knew they were together, it was safe, and for the best others knew now, too. If the town got the message Duke and Annie were over, maybe Duke would, too. Even though a sinking feeling in his gut told him otherwise. "Annie has been under Guardian protection."

"Ah, I see." The mother nodded. "Well, it's wonderful to meet you. And I cannot thank you guys enough. I'm willing to pay you for today."

"We wouldn't even think of it." Annie took the blue backpack Mary passed her. "We'll take good care of him. Is it okay if we take him fishing and walking in the woods? There are trails, and we'll make sure he stays with us."

The boy did a little hop. "Yeah, yeah." He nodded to his mother.

Mary laughed. "Looks like he'd love that. He packed some movies he likes in the bag." She glanced at her watch. "Oh shoot, I have to leave, or I'm going to be late. My numbers are also in the bag if you need to get a hold of me."

Bear beamed a smile and glanced up at him like he was a true-life hero. He couldn't hold back his own grin. "We'll be fine. Don't worry about us," Tank assured.

"Okay." She bent down to kiss her son. "Love you, sweetie. I'll see you this afternoon, okay."

"Okay. Bye, Mom." Nathaniel waved her off, and Annie closed the door. "Jeesh. I thought she'd never leave." The kid rolled his eyes.

Beauty suppressed a giggle.

"Dude, your mom loves you. Be thankful." Tank ruffled Nate's hair, his hand covering the size of the boy's scalp. He should be taking his own advice. "Did you have breakfast?"

"Yeah."

"Okay, well, what do you want to do today? Want to go fishing before it gets too hot?"

"*Yeah!*" Nathaniel bounced on his toes.

"Then let's go fishing." Annie squeezed the little guy by the shoulders. A blush crept up the kid's cheeks.

"Don't go getting any ideas, Bear. She's mine." He ruffled Nathaniel's hair again. "I'll meet you two by the dock." He stepped outside to grab an extra fishing pole out of the garage. This was going to be a fun day. Nathaniel had been put through hell and back. A feeling he knew all too well. He'd be sure they all had a great time. Even if he had to perform clown tricks to make the boy laugh.

Behind the house, Beauty and Nate stood waiting, while Alfred ran into the water, his tail wagging, as he chased the ducks.

Tank's heart gave pause watching the two together, the impression of a ready-made family standing on his dock. He'd never given a family much thought before, but now, seeing the two together had him thinking. Could he be a father one day? Would he be a good one?

A slight breeze blew through the air, causing Annie's hair to fly in the wind. She hardly ever wore it down, but man, when she did, another protective claw secured her place in his heart. She was beautiful as she held Nathaniel's hand and pointed to the birds in the water. "We can feed them later if you want," he heard her say as he walked closer.

"Will he hurt them?" Bear asked.

"Naw." Tank laid the pole down. "Al's just excited. He likes to chase them, but he never hurts them. We've even got a couple of new babies. Anytime he tries to get close, the mother duck will hiss and spread her wings like this." He opened his arms wide, impersonating the momma duck. "Alfred runs off with his tail between his legs."

Beauty laughed. "Big baby."

Al jumped out of the water and ran over to them by the dock before he shook full force. Nasty creek water flew everywhere.

"Oh, Alfred." Annie threw her hands up to protect her face.

"Ha!" Tank hooted, and Bear joined in on the laughs. "I guess that's what he thought about you calling him a big baby."

"I guess so." She wiped her face with her sleeve then bent down to pet his nasty dog. "Bad boy, Al. Bad boy."

"Can we fish now?" Bear bounced in anticipation for his day's adventure to begin.

Coming out to the water with his gramps, he'd been excited all the same. Something about the open air and open land that had him just as eager as Nathaniel was now.

"Of course, sweetie."

Annie hooked a worm through each of their lines, and he taught Bear to cast. Once all lines were in the water, the three of them sat there in silence. Bear's leg twitched over the dock. Tank glanced over Nathaniel's head and gave Annie a slight wink and nodded toward the anxious child. He was bored already. She smiled in return.

As if on cue Nathaniel asked, "So, now what do we do?"

Beauty echoed his laughter, their thoughts in sync with each other. The boy was impatient. Then again, he was only seven.

"We wait," Annie said.

"On what?" Nathaniel gave him a questioning look.

"On the fish to bite," he said.

Bear slumped his shoulders as he held his pole. "This could take forever."

Yep, impatient.

"It could." He passed Annie a slight grin. "Or it might not."

Ten minutes into their babysitting adventure, and he and Annie had already bored the boy. He glanced around the land, thinking what they could all do together when his gaze landed on the tree. *Of course.* What kid didn't love climbing trees?

"I tell you what, kid. You want to do something more active?"

"Yeah."

"Okay, give me your pole." He took Nathaniel's rod and placed it in the rod holder. "We're going to climb a tree."

"No way. Really?"

"Really. Follow me." He brought Bear over to his and Annie's tree. "We're going to climb to that first limb. You think you can handle that?" The branch sat about ten feet off the ground. Plenty to make any child feel like they've climbed something without going too far up where he could do serious damage if he fell.

Lord, please don't let the kid fall.

"I'm going to go first. Watch where I put my feet."

"Okay." Bear nodded.

"Hand here. Foot here." Tank placed his hand and his right foot on the tree truck showing Nate exactly what to do. "Then pull." Going slow, so Bear could follow his movements, he pulled himself up then positioned himself on the branch. He reached down his hand. "Okay, your turn."

Bear did exactly what he'd instructed, pulling himself up with no problem.

"Good job, Nate," Annie hollered from the dock. "You did it."

Just then Bear's line gave a little tug. Beauty jumped up and took hold of the pole. "Looks like you caught a fish," she yelled as she reeled in his line for him.

Nate shimmied down the tree in excitement. "Let me see. Let me see." He ran to the dock as Annie grabbed the line and pulled his fish closer to him. The little perch thrashed and wiggled for its life. "Wow. Cool." His eyes widened and his face lit up as he reached out to touch the fish. "It's slimy." He let go, and wiped his hands down his pants. "What do I do with it?"

"Up to you, man." Tank squatted down beside him, and glanced at the fish. "But I would suggest you throw it back."

"Throw it back?" Bear glanced at him, his little brows creased. "Why?"

"Well, because he's really too little for us to cook and eat. He can grow and get bigger, then we can catch him another day and eat him, or maybe one of the new baby ducks could eat him."

"Or he could just swim and live." Bear's brows smoothed back to normal as he stared at his catch.

"Yes." Annie agreed. "Or he could just swim and live. Is that would you would like?"

"Yeah. Can we put him back?"

"Sure, sweetie." Beauty unhooked the fish and tossed him back in the water.

"Want to try again?" he asked Nathaniel as he reached for the worm bucket.

"No. I don't want to fish."

He stopped mid-reach and faced Nate again. Fishing was about the only entertainment he had for the little guy. Besides an all day movie marathon, and staying inside on such a beautiful day seemed like a crime. "What would you like to do then?"

"I want to climb more trees."

That, he could do.

"Sounds like a great idea. Let's go. I'll race you." He shot to his feet and ran for another tree, Bear running fast behind giggling, while Annie followed.

This *was* going to be a great day after all. While he had never thought much about kids and family, being next to Bear and sharing the boy with his Beauty made him think a family was something they could share in the future. Perhaps, even the near future.

CHAPTER THIRTY-ONE

"You boys ready to come down from there? I've got lunch ready," Annie yelled across the lawn.

He and Bear had climbed trees all morning. The kid's balance was exceptional for being so young. But Tank was glad for Beauty's lunch call. He was hot and hungry.

"What do you say, little guy? Ready to eat?"

"Yep."

He helped Nate shimmy down the tree.

Annie stood at the bottom ready to catch him. The two of them worked as a team. The way it should be.

"I see you scraped your knee on the trunk." She pointed to Nathaniel's leg. "When we get inside, I'll get a Band-Aid for you."

"Thank you, Miss Annie." The boy smiled.

"You are just the cutest thing ever." She bent down to give him a kiss on the top of his head.

Tank landed with a thud right beside the two of them. "I think I have a booboo, too. Can I have a kiss?"

"No." She smiled and shook her head. "But I'll give you a Band-Aid."

"No fair."

Following the two toward the house, Bear placed his little hand in Annie's, swinging it back and forth as they trotted up the back steps. The vision becoming exactly what he hoped his future would hold.

Inside, three place settings held turkey sandwiches and potato chips.

"I love chips." Nathaniel shrieked as he dropped Annie's hand and raced to the kitchen table.

"Me, too, kid. But you aren't eating until you wash your hands. Go." Tank pointed to the bathroom. Bear's head dipped before he ran to wash up.

"Man, you're tough." Beauty poked him in the ribs. "But same for you. Wash up."

Following orders, he headed for the kitchen sink. Bear hurried back to the table and pulled his chair out, the wooden legs scratching the floor.

"Nate, I was thinking after lunch, since it's so hot outside, we could watch *Batman*. Want to?"

"Yeah. That's that symbol on your dandana, right?"

"Bandana, kid, and yes, you're right."

"Why do you like Batman so much?" Annie sat beside Nathaniel.

"It helps him not be scared anymore," Bear said matter of fact.

"What?" Annie gave him a confusing look.

No one but his mother and Bear understood his love for Batman. Now, it was time he told Annie. "That's right, Nate." Turning back to Annie, he explained, "It's a long story, but Batman had something bad happen to him as a kid—"

"Did his dad beat him, too?" Nathaniel picked up a potato chip, examining the size.

Tank gripped the kitchen sink. Poor kid thought beating

was normal. Of course he would. "No, Bear, he didn't. But a bad guy hurt his parents real bad. And Batman made it his mission to keep the city of Gotham safe from bad people."

"I see." Annie nodded in understanding. "I always thought you were a superhero." Her eyes held a twinkle of love.

"What's a mission?" Nate asked, oblivious to the moment he and Annie shared.

"A mission is a purpose, or a goal. Batman's goal, or his desire, what he wanted was to keep the city safe from bad guys. And that's what I want to do. I had something bad happen to me as a kid just like you. I want to keep other kids safe from bad guys."

"So, you're like Batman?"

"I try to be."

"Oh." The kid shrugged. "That's cool."

"Very cool." Annie tapped his leg as he sat.

Perhaps Father and Steele had been right. His bad past really *did* help him help others.

His phone rang in his back pocket. He didn't recognize the number. "Hello?"

"Is this—?"

His phone cut out. He moved his head to the side. "Hello? Hello?" Damn reception.

"Tyler Wilde?"

"Yes, who is this?"

"This is Bra—"

"Who?" He asked again. Moving his head to the side again.

"Bradley Moore from the hospital."

Finally, he could hear. The voice sounded deep, but young. One he definitely couldn't recall ever hearing.

"Okay. Can I help you?"

"Yes." The voice shook. "We have a patient here by the name of Clara Wilde. She's been in a car accident, and—

"What? An accident? Is she okay?"

"She's in surgery now. It's standard for us to call the next of kin."

Next of kin. Surgery.

"What are her injuries? Can you tell me?" Tank pushed his chair out from the table. Searching for his keys.

"No…I umm…I'm not a doctor. I was just informed to call you to tell you in case you wanted to come to the hospital."

"What hospital?"

"Black Widow Medical Center."

His mom hadn't even made it out of town this morning?

"Yes, of course…thanks. I'll be right there." He clicked off the phone.

"Tyler." Annie rushed to his side. "What is it? What's wrong?"

"It's my mom. She's been in an accident. I guess on her way out of town. She's in surgery. At the hospital." *His mother*. He'd been so nasty to her while she was visiting. Would that be the last time he ever got to talk to her again?

"Oh my God. Go. Here." Annie thrust his jacket to him.

"You…you have to come. Both of you." He glanced at Nathaniel, sitting by the kitchen table, a scared look in his eye.

"Honey," Annie whispered. "I don't think that's a good idea. He's seen enough, and the last time he was in a hospital…" She didn't finish her words.

She was right. The last time Nathaniel graced the corridors of a hospital was when he'd been an abuse patient. And, honestly, Tank had no idea what he was about to see. He didn't need a child seeing him break down if something happened to his mother.

"I have to go, but I can't leave you alone."

"Yes, you can. We have the alarm. I'll call Sandi, see if she's willing to come out and help when she's done at the diner."

"But, Duke. Annie, it's not safe."

"I have the alarm, Tyler. I have Al, it's the middle of the day. We'll be fine. I promise."

Torn. His heart was completely torn between his two loves, his mother in the hospital receiving surgery, and Annie, his lover, here at the house, alone. "I'll call Father, see if he can come out."

"Do it on the way. I'll lock up. Go. Now."

"I'll try to be fast. I'll call you as soon as I know something. Set the alarm behind me."

"Of course. Be careful. I love you."

"I love you, too." He kissed her hard on the lips. When he pulled back, Nate still stared at him, a confused look in his eyes.

"Bear." He stepped toward the kid and knelt down, eye level. "I have to go to the hospital. My mom, she's sick. Can you take care of Annie for me while I'm gone? You're the man of the house. You think you can handle it?"

The boy squared his shoulders and nodded.

"Good. No going outside, okay? Not until I get back or Father comes, okay?"

"Yes, sir."

"Good deal."

"Are you scared?" the kid asked.

"Yeah, Bear. I am. A little."

"You have Batman." Nate pointed to the bandana sticking out of his jacket pocket. "He'll help you."

"You're right." Tank placed the bandana over his head. "He will. See you soon."

He kissed Annie one more time. "Lock up," he said before he rushed to his bike and tossed on his helmet.

His mom. Shit, how could this be happening? After their time together, and the way he acted. He had to get to talk to her again. Tell her he loved her.

Hands shaking, he dialed Father's number. Straight to voicemail.

"Hey, man, it's Tank. I need your help. My mom's been in an accident, and I'm headed to the hospital. I want someone at the house with Annie. Please, get to her as soon as you can."

He clicked off his phone and revved his bike.

His mom had to be okay. She just had to.

CHAPTER THIRTY-TWO

D uke gripped the steering wheel of his truck tighter and waited on the call. The call that would set everything in motion for him to get his Annie back.

When he found out Daddy Biker and the ogre weren't speaking, he knew exactly how to lure the giant away. A phony phone call from the hospital about the woman they shared in common. What he hadn't expected was for the giant to put in an alarm system for Duke's dear little fiancée.

Not that an alarm system scared him. He could convince anyone on the police force the trip of the alarm was an accident. But what he didn't know was if a signal went to the giant's phone when the alarm tripped. Not that he couldn't take out his opponent. He had a gun after all. Problem was, he couldn't get his hands dirty.

But as he'd watched the alarm guy install the false sense of security for his dear Annie, he realized there was a card sitting in his back pocket. The rookie card.

Brayden had been such a good boy, doing exactly everything he was told. Including sleeping with the redhead. Problem was, Rookie hadn't stopped to ask how old big-tits was first—a glorious sixteen, just three weeks *shy* of her seventeenth birthday. The legal age of consent in the state of Texas.

Now, if their rendezvous became public, Brayden would face statutory rape charges and up to twenty years in the pen. And everyone knew what inmates did to little cops in prison.

Duke scared the shit out of his little partner so bad the man shook and cried like a baby, begging him not to say anything.

And that's exactly how he got what he needed.

Brayden not only made the phone call luring the ogre to the hospital, he had strict instructions to run the biker off the road, while making it look like an accident—a deadly accident. No one would put a cop behind bars over a pair of faulty breaks.

With the ogre dead, Duke wouldn't have a thing to worry about when it came to getting his woman back.

No alarm system or big ass biker is going to stop me.

And with Rookie's dreams of working his way up the police ranks sitting in the palm of Duke's hand, Brayden was a sure bet. Duke let out a rich, deep belly laugh as tears of joy peppered his eyes. Everything was going to be okay, and the deed would be done without him having to lift a finger.

Now, all he had to do was talk to Annie. Just talk to her, make her see she belonged with him. She would understand. She would come back. She *would*.

The burner phone in his cup holder rang. His heart pounded in his chest and his hands shook in excitement as he reached to grab the phone, only to drop it on the floorboard.

Fuck.

He scrambled for the handset. "Hello."

"It's...it's done. He's face-down in the ditch."

Duke's hands shook. "Did you make it look like an accident?"

"Yes. I need to call an ambulance now."

"Good boy, Brayden. Hide this phone under your seat until I can dispose of it properly."

"Yes...yes, sir." The young man's voice wavered.

What a fucking titty-baby.

"And Brayden."

"Yes, sir."

"Your secrets are safe with me." He smiled as he said the words. "All of them. Welcome to my team, son."

"Yeah...thanks."

Duke hung up the phone and screamed, "Yes!" as he slapped the steering wheel. "Finally. Fuck yeah!"

The little cop had followed through with his end of the plan, conquering the monster. The knowledge of the ogre dead caused his heart to dance.

Bye, bye, lover boy.

He'd be sure to reward the cop heavily. Maybe even slip the guy an envelope of cash. Like his father said, he had cash. He should use it. Money *was* the best way to keep the kid in his back pocket. Who knows what other little *chores* he may have for the Rookie down the road.

Duke cracked his neck and swallowed a swig of his rum, not bothering to mask it with a cola this time. His hands and legs shook. Eager. Happy. This was his chance. His time.

Their time.

No one else could have his Annie. Only him. He needed her by his side, and now with the ogre dead, she would see she belonged with him.

He took another swig and eased his truck down the long drive, parking in front of the small house. Grabbing the flower arrangement off the seat, he opened his truck. All women loved flowers. His Annie was no exception.

Here I come, baby.

CHAPTER THIRTY-THREE

"**I**s Tank going to be okay?" Bear asked, as he shoved his last chip into his mouth.

"I sure hope so."

"Are you worried?"

"Yeah, a little." She rubbed Nathaniel on the shoulder. "But you don't worry about that, okay."

"Can I have some more chips?"

Annie stood and headed toward the kitchen sink. Her sandwich had lost its appeal. "Big guy, I think you've had plenty of chips."

"Please." He pouted his lower lip.

"Fine." She shook her head—he was a cute kid. "But only a few."

She couldn't deny those big round eyes, and they'd both had quite the excitement with Tank and the news about his mother. Maybe a chip would make the boy feel better.

She reached for the bag and poured a few more. His milk glass sat empty, undoubtedly, to wash down all the salt from the chips. "You want some more milk, too?"

"Please. Look." Bear jumped out of his chair and ran to

the sliding door. "There are the baby ducks, and Alfred is running back and forth." He placed his hands on the glass. "Can we go out and see them."

"Yeah, but after lunch. Okay? Besides, I need to make a few phone calls first." She reached for his cup off the table and carried it into the kitchen. "Alfred loves the ducks." Opening the refrigerator, she grabbed the milk carton, and began pouring.

A knock sounded from the door. Her heart pounded. *Stupid.* She couldn't jump at every noise. It was probably only Father coming at Tank's request. Still, she had to be cautious.

"I'll get it." Bear ran to the front.

"No, wait." She turned the corner into the living room, the milk carton still in her hand as Bear flipped the lock and reached for the door handle. "Nate, wait."

Not bothering to listen, he swung the door open wide. The alarm sounded—*"Door Open."*

Nathaniel immediately began to back up as Duke crossed the threshold. Another bouquet of flowers filled his hand, his knuckles white from his grip and a crazed look held steady in his eyes. The same look as the night he nearly killed her.

Her heart hammered as the carton slid from her fingers, milk sloshing over the floor. She darted her gaze to the monitor to see how much time she had left before the panic alarm went off. Thirty seconds. Fear rose inside her chest. Surely, Tank was already alerted the door opened. And in less than thirty seconds, he would know something was terribly wrong and would come. He would send help.

She glanced down at Bear, standing between her and Duke.

"Bear." Her throat felt parched as she tried to keep her voice calm and held her arms out to him. "Come here."

The boy ran to hide behind her. Duke closed the door, standing between her and the alarm. She glanced outside. Alfred trotted up the back porch, and pawed at the door to get in. Once Al noticed Duke through the window, the hair on the pup's neck stood straight up as a low growl emitted from his throat.

"What a vicious dog you have there," Duke mocked.

"He doesn't know you." Annie reached behind her and squeezed Bear tighter to her body before she took a slow step to the left.

"Do you like the dog?" He glanced down and fiddled with the flower stems.

"Yes. Alfred is great." She took another small step to the left while he wasn't looking. If she could get closer to the door, let Al in, maybe her and Bear would have a chance to escape.

The alarm began a faster beep, warning of its soon sound off.

"What's the code, Annie?"

No way would she give him that. But, the panic code. The code that would silence the alarm but still alert Tyler...

"One, nine, eight, nine."

Duke punched in the numbers. "Any significance?"

"The year the best *Batman* movie came out."

"I didn't take you for a superhero kind of girl."

Keep him talking. If Duke was talking, he wasn't beating. She had to stay calm, give him what he wanted.

For Nathaniel.

The boy's limbs shook under her grasp.

"Everyone needs to be rescued from time to time." She shrugged.

"Yes, they do." He smiled a sad smile, and the corner of his eyes turned down in pity. "Which is exactly what I'm here to do. Rescue you." He glanced around her and pointed to Nathaniel. His face took on a stone demeanor. "Why is he here? He isn't supposed to be here."

Bear pulled tighter on the back of her shirt.

"I'm babysitting. Nathaniel's mother had to work and needed some help."

"Yeah, now that she put the dad away in prison, I suppose being a single parent may be hard." He tossed the flowers on the coffee table and took a few steps toward the couch.

Annie took another step closer to the back door, dragging Bear behind her. Wouldn't be long now. Tyler would come back. She had to keep him talking. "Why are you here, Duke?"

"To bring you home of course. I love you. You belong with me." His voice seemed so relaxed, yet his hands shook.

Calm. She had to remain calm.

"Duke, I think you should leave. Tyler will be back soon, and he won't like that you're here." She glanced over at the console table by the front door. Her cellphone lay too far away. If she could get to it. Call for help.

A mischievous grin covered his face, his eyes glowing in sinful glee. "Oh, Annie, I took care of that little problem. Your precious Tyler won't ever be coming home again." His grin rose to a full smile.

Won't be coming home? Her heart pounded and her brain fogged at his words.

"What…what do you mean never coming home again?"

Alfred still pawed furiously at the glass. She glanced around for a weapon, a knife, anything, then remembered her self-defense. *Neck. Middle. Groin.* She ran through the moves in her head, but she'd have to get close to Duke if she wanted to use them.

"Annie, dear, why don't you come sit by me. I'll explain

everything. You can let the boy go play outside with the mutt, but let him out the front door. I don't want to have to shoot the fur bag."

Gun. Of course he had a gun.

She checked his hip. No holster. Where would it be? Could she outrun a gun? Did she have a choice?

"Yes. I think that's a good idea." She encased Bear's trembling hand in her own. He stared up at her, tears brimming his eyes, and she gave him a nod. "You go outside and play, Nathaniel, okay?" Then she pulled him to the front door and opened it.

"Hurry up before that dog comes from around back."

"Sure, Duke." She pushed Bear out the door then raised her hand in a rush to grab her phone. Device in her grip, she screamed, "Run" to Nathaniel as she took his hand.

She ran down the front steps as Alfred bound around the house, the fur on his neck fully erect. The dog growled and charged.

"This way," she hollered, running as fast as the boy could. Looking back, she saw the shape of Duke in her peripheral vision as the dog leapt to attack.

A low growl emitted from Alfred's throat as he made contact with Duke's leg, and she lost the view of them as she rounded the house. She had to get to her old house. Closer to town. Better phone reception. And she prayed she could lose Duke in the woods along the way.

Annie pulled Bear to the embankment just as she heard a gunshot, and Alfred let out an ear-piercing wail.

She stopped. *Alfred!* Her heart ached, but her instincts told her to keep moving, save Nathaniel.

"Come on. We have to keep going." She pointed him toward the rocks and gave a gentle but firm push. "Hop on those all the way to the other side. Go."

A quick glance back to the house made her heart almost stop. Duke hobbled toward them, blood seeping through his jeans from Alfred's attack.

"Go, Nathaniel, go," she screamed. "Get to the trail." She splashed through the water, pulling him alongside her.

A duckling running on the grass let out a horrible yelp right before Duke stepped in the water to follow. Annie rushed to the embankment and pushed the boy up.

He slid twice before he could reach the top. She scrambled to pull her own self up, when her phone slipped from her grip and tumbled into the water below. Her chance to call for help—gone.

"Go." She hollered again as she clawed the damp ground for leverage

A large hand snaked around her ankle, gripping hard, and pulling. Each finger making an impression into her skin.

"Agh," she screamed and lost her grip, sliding down toward the water. "No." She kicked, thrashing out of Duke's grip, and reached for a fallen log to help pull herself up. Her head spun as she stood, her knees and legs shaking as she went to plant her feet.

Neck. Middle. Groin. Neck. Middle. Groin. Neck. Middle. Groin.

"It doesn't have to be this way, Annie." Duke climbed the small hill with his injured leg. "All you have to do is come home to me. Be my wife."

"That'll never happen, Duke. I don't love you."

Her abuser stood tall, favoring his good leg, his eyes narrowed. "The man you *love* is dead, Annie. And if you aren't careful, you will be, too."

"You'll have to fight me first." Sucking in a breath, she charged, hitting his neck with her forearm. Her attack unexpected, he stumbled and lost his balance as he fell to the ground. She skipped the knee to the chest and went straight for the groin. With his legs open, her foot made straight contact to his crotch. Duke rounded in pain, and she took advantage of his distraction, running after Bear and deeper into the woods.

She needed to stop and think, figure out her next move, but her body told her to just keep running. Get to her old home.

She'd gotten them off the trail a few times, before she stopped to assess where they were. Nathaniel bent over in a pant. "I can't...run," he heaved. "I can't run...anymore."

She glanced around the woods. A big tree, with relatively good limbs sat in front of them. "Remember what Tank taught you?" she whispered and patted the tree. "I want you to climb as high as you can, and be very quiet, okay?" Annie picked the boy up and placed him on the lowest branch. He immediately began his ascent. She jumped to grip the limb, but not having the upper body strength, she couldn't pull herself up.

"Annie," Bear whispered, "are you coming?"

"I can't. You go as high as you can and be very quiet. Be the lookout. Help's coming soon."

The boy nodded and continued his climb.

She glanced around the ground and grabbed a fallen tree branch. Placing her back against a tree, and keeping Bear within her vision, she prayed help would arrive.

Duke had entered the panic code. The dispatch center would send someone.

They would.

Soon.

Tyler sprang to her mind.

Her heart ached thinking of him...dead? Tears filled her eyes as her chest heaved, the burning from the exertion and fear overtaking her. She pressed her back deeper into the bark. She could not die like this. Nathaniel deserved better, and if Tyler really was dead, she had to fight for the boy...the way Tyler had for her.

Please God, let someone come.

It was their only hope.

CHAPTER THIRTY-FOUR

Tank ran to the check-in desk at the hospital.

"Can I help you?" an older lady with white hair asked.

"My name is Tyler Wilde. I got a phone call about my mom, Clara Wilde. She's been in a car accident."

The woman gave him a puzzled look. "A car accident? We haven't received any accident victims today."

"You haven't?"

"Tank," Father hollered from the entrance of the hospital. "I got your message."

"Why are you here? Why aren't you with Annie?"

"I sent Sandi. I wanted to be here with you. How's Clara?"

"I don't know." He turned to the receptionist again. "Can you please check again? Clara Wilde. Is she here?"

The lady punched her keyboard. "No sir. No patient by that name."

"I don't understand. There has to be. I got a phone call from the hospital…" He stopped.

Shit. No.

No. No. No.

He turned to Father. "We have to go. Something's not right."

The bastard. He used his own mother against him.

"What's going on? I don't understand?" Father kept pace beside him.

A wailing noise blared from his phone. He looked at the screen; the alarm's app flashed bright red. "Oh God, Annie." He darted for the door as a police cruiser flew by. "It's Duke. He's after her."

"I'm coming with you."

He hopped on his bike and prayed he wasn't too late. If Duke did anything to hurt Annie, or Nathaniel, he'd kill the man with his own hands.

He sped past the police cruiser. In record time, Tank drove down his long drive. A blue pickup sat in his spot. Alfred lay on the ground, howling, as Sandi sat on the ground beside him.

He ran to his dog. "Oh, buddy."

"A bullet pierced his hip. I'm trying to stop the bleeding." She had her diner shirt over Al's leg. "Don't worry about Al. Go. Find Annie. I'll get him to a vet," she ordered just as Father and the police car pulled in.

"What happened?" Father yelled.

"He's been shot," Tank said.

The officer stood outside his unit. "I'll call the station to alert the vet, let them know he's coming," the man said as he reached inside for his radio.

Tank ran through the house. "Annie," he yelled. "Annie?" Milk covered the floor. He hurried to the back door. Something feathered lay motionless on the grass. He charged back through the front door yelling to the cop and Father. "He's after her."

"Who's after her?" the uniform asked.

"Duke, the Chief of Police. That's his truck."

The officer glanced at the vehicle.

"He shot my dog, and he's after Annie. They're in the woods. She has a kid with her."

"Why is Duke after Annie? That's his fiancée."

Tank stormed to the cop. "*Ex*-fiancée because the last time they were together he beat the shit out of her and nearly killed her. Just like he did my dog. Call for backup."

The cop's eyes grew wide in fear. There was no time to argue with this dipshit. He had to find Annie.

He ran for the back of his house and stared at the dead duckling in the grass.

"The uniform's calling for backup." Father ran after him. "Did Alfred do that?" The man pointed to the pile of feathers.

"No." He ran toward the water. "Duke did. They're in the woods."

Annie knew these woods. She could be anywhere, but he had a feeling of where she might have gone. He started for the other side of the water, hoping his instincts were right. She'd go to a place where she used to feel safe. Her old home.

"Tyler, he has a gun. Wait for backup," Father yelled.

"Not on your life, old man." He sloshed through the water. "Annie and Bear are both out there."

"I'm coming, too."

"No," he shouted. "Get more help. Tell the police to circle around the woods. Annie's old home is on the other side. She knows these woods better than anyone. They're in here somewhere."

"Be careful," Father called and turned to run back to the house.

His adrenaline charged full steam as he raced into the

trees, and prayed he was on the right trail. Why had he left her alone? All of this was his fault. All of it.

He went about fifty yards before he stopped to listen. He felt as if he were running in circles. All of the trees began to look the same.

The faint sound of Duke's voice vibrated to his left, and what he hoped was backup to his right. Following the sound toward the monster, he was careful not to make too much noise. If he were lucky, he could charge the man from behind and knock his gun out of his grasp. Hold him steady until backup arrived. *If I'm lucky.*

He shot straight ahead until a little clearing came into sight. The chief stood straight in front of him, his back to him...and a gun in his hand by his side. Ten feet in front of Duke—Annie.

Still alive.

Thank God.

Where's Bear?

He scanned the grounds, but didn't see any sign of the boy. His heart hammered and he focused back on Annie. A log clutched in her grasp ready to be swung, her body in a batter's position. If he charged, the monster could turn and shoot.

The man's hand shook, his finger pulsing over the trigger as he favored one leg. "Annie, just come home. That's all I want you to do. It doesn't have to go this far."

Beauty made eye contact with him, and he held his finger to his mouth. She quickly reverted her gaze back to the monster.

His mind raced, taking in his surroundings. He could charge straight ahead, but the chance he would get shot was too high. Several sticks and brush lie between him and the man. He glanced to his right—a giant tree, with gnarly limbs…and a branch so long it hung almost directly over the monster's head.

If the maniac would just stay where he was…

Tank gripped the tree and pointed up to the branch above Duke's head. Annie's expressions never changed.

That a girl.

He reached for the branches, the bark digging into his hand. Slowly, he climbed, doing his best not to overexert himself. The last thing he needed was to take in a big breath. One so big and loud the monster could hear. He reached for a limb and it snapped. He stopped his momentum.

"Duke," Annie raised her voice a little louder, surely to cover the noise he made in the tree. "Just put the gun down, okay? We can talk about me going home with you."

The distraction worked. Tank slowly continued his ascent, thinking twice about where he placed his hands or his feet.

"Is that what you want, baby? For me to drop the gun?" He raised it up and stared at it, the barrel nonchalantly pointed at Annie.

Tank's heart quickened as he stood to his full height. He focused his gaze straight ahead. Bear stared at him from an equally high limb across the path. Relief the boy was okay ran through him and tossed him off balance a little. Tightening his core, he focused straight ahead and braced his legs as he walked like on a balance beam out to the farthest end of the branch. He motioned for the boy to stay quiet. Nate nodded.

"Fine, Annie," Duke said. "I'll put the gun down. If you drop the stick and come here." He dangled the gun from his middle finger."

"O…Okay, Duke. I'll put the stick down." Hesitantly, Beauty laid her weapon on the ground and took a step closer.

Her move was his cue to act. He sucked in a deep breath,

bent his knees, and leapt off the tree, his stomach flying to his chest as he soared downward. The side of his body crushed into Duke's shoulder. Stars flashed in Tank's eyes as his breath jerked from his lungs, and his ribs seared in pain. He lay on his side, fighting for breath as Duke scrambled to his hands and knees.

Move.

He had to move.

"Tyler, the gun," Annie screamed, her voice quavered through his pain.

He crawled on the leaf-covered ground, reaching for the gun at the same time Duke did. Fighting for control with one hand, Tank reared his other arm back. The impact of his elbow to the man's skull caused his own bones to ache. The firearm hit the ground as Duke's eyes rolled back in his head and his body flopped over, motionless.

Rolling painfully to his side, Tank reached for the weapon and slid it out of Duke's reach.

It was over. It was finally over.

"Oh my God, Tyler." Annie ran to him and fell to her knees, wrapping her arms around him. "He told me you were dead. I thought you were dead." She gripped his face, planting kisses on his cheeks, her hold on him weak and shaky.

"I'm here. More help is coming." He squeezed her tighter, his ribs aching with each new breath he took in. "I am never letting you out of my sight again."

"Your mom?"

"All a ruse. I never should have left you guys alone. I'm so sorry."

"Tank, watch out," Bear screamed from the tree.

He glanced to the side as Duke sat up, gripping another pistol in his hands. Annie let out a shrilling scream as he pushed her on the ground, rolling to cover her with his body. and reached for the other gun.

"Stop," a voice screamed from the side.

Before he could grasp the pistol, a shot echoed in his ears. He ducked his head, squeezing Annie tighter as he waited to feel the impact, the pain.

"Oh my God, Tyler," Beauty cried beneath him.

The world around him went silent, as an eerie pause took over... the pain never setting in.

"It's done. He's dead," the faintly familiar voice said.

Tank glanced at Annie, searching over her body. "Are you okay?"

"Yeah, I'm fine. Are you?"

"Yeah." He rolled off of her and helped her to her feet, wincing at the sharp pain in his side.

Turning to see their savior, a man stood with his gun poised as Duke lay motionless on the ground, a bullet hole straight through his head.

"Brayden, oh thank God." Annie leaned her weight into Tank.

He wrapped a protective arm around her as he stared at the man. He dressed in street clothes, but his face, he remembered seeing the officer at the diner. The short cop.

"Are you guys..." Brayden ran a hand over the back of his neck. "Are you guys okay?" Brayden asked.

The deep tone of the man's voice resonated in Tank's ears. The fake phone call? *He* was the one who made it. And the one who saved them?

None of it made sense.

Cops from every direction swarmed out of the woods, one officer holding back a K9. As they came closer, guns drawn, many of them stopped and stared at their dead Chief on the ground.

Tanks body heat soared seeing so many uniforms. His breathing escalated, and his grip on Annie clammed

They're here to help. Calm down.

"Drop your weapon." One yelled. He wore a star on his chest. The current sheriff.

Brayden threw his gun to the ground.

"Hands up, everyone."

Tank let go of Annie and grimaced as he raised his hands over his head.

"What happened here?" The sheriff stepped closer, both hands still on his gun that rested at his side, while another officer came to secure the visible weapons on the ground.

"Officer Brayden, sir. Chief Fields held a gun at point blank range towered Wilde and Annie. I told him to stop, and he turned his weapon on me. I shot in self-defense," Brayden answered.

"Someone call an EMT, and the coroner. Let's get this mess cleaned up," the sheriff demanded.

Another officer came over and demanded they both stand. The man patted him, Annie, and Brayden down. "All clean, sir."

The sheriff nodded. "You can all lower your hands. You two," the leader said to him and Annie. "When you get back home, I'll need statements. And you." The man pointed to Brayden. "Why are you in street clothes?"

"I wasn't on duty today, sir."

"Then why are you here?"

All questions Tank had and wanted to know answers to.

"I...I..." Brayden stuttered.

"Don't go too far." The sheriff pointed a finger at the short cop. "And where is the kid? The officer at the house said a child was involved." He swiveled his head from side to side.

Loud sobs came from above.

"Bear," Tank hollered and hobbled toward the tree. "I'm coming."

God, the poor boy. Beat by his father, and now he'd seen a man shot to death. Father's counseling skills would have to work miracles.

Tank pushed up the tree, his sweaty palms hindering his grip as his body ached in protest. Still, he reached Bear's branch. "Here, man. Grab on to my back." He helped Nate get a good grip. "Just hold on. I've got you."

Slowly, he brought the boy down, and set him on the ground. Lowering to one knee, he held Nate at arm's length and watched as his lower lip trembled.

"It's all okay. It's all going to be okay." He wrapped the boy in a hug, fresh tears moistening Tank's shoulder.

Bear pulled back and looked at him in his eyes. "I told you that cop was bad."

"I know buddy, I know." He cuffed his hand around the back of Nate's neck and guided his head back into his shoulder. "Just don't look. We're going somewhere safe."

Annie joined their side, and eased her arms around both of them. "We're all going to be safe now."

CHAPTER 35

Six Weeks Later

Tank sat and stared at the clear glass partition as he waited. He'd come to terms with what he had to do. Annie had helped him. She'd sat with him night after night as he read each and every letter, every apology, every plea for forgiveness.

Being in a room with so many officers would usually have him breaking out in a sweat, yet his hands were eerily dry, even though the man of his nightmares would soon walk into the room and sit down to talk to him.

Being in a police station so frequently after his last nightmare, giving statement after statement, he'd learned to conquer his fears. And Beauty had been by his side every step of the way.

The love of his life had forgiven Brayden so easily for his mistakes. The young officer confessed to aiding the monster unaware of the end goal: The address searches, following Tank home from the camping trip, sleeping with the young girl for information, and even using burner phones to make the crank call. But through all that he swears he had no idea Duke planned to kidnap or murder anyone.

Scared of his own future in prison for having relations with an underage girl, he followed through with the monster's plans, but declared he couldn't follow through with intentions to kill.

Despite Brayden's ill choices, if the man hadn't followed his gut, and followed Duke into the woods at a safe distance, Tank might not be alive today. And despite all the man's wrong doings, Annie saw it in her heart to forgive the guy, claiming if he had of ignored his gut, she would have lost the one true love of her life.

Me.

Annie claimed he was more important to her than holding any grudge against someone scared for their own fate, and she'd been right.

The past was in the past. She'd taught him that. He needed to face his demons, so he could move on with his future. With her.

Slowly, the man he'd thought for twenty-seven years as his father walked to the seat across from him. He'd aged exponentially in the past several years. His once large and towering frame seemed gaunt and small. Nothing to be afraid of.

Being here was the right thing. No longer would he let this man and his past control him.

The person sitting across from him picked up the phone, and Tank did the same.

"You came." His father's voice sounded much scratchier than in years past.

"I did."

"Did you read my letters?"

Tank stared at his dad, his eyes filled with dejection and hope all at the same time. His own heart split down the middle. Still, after all these years and all the hate, he still felt something for the man. Endearment? Like? Love? He couldn't pinpoint the emotion, and more importantly, he had no idea how it was even possible. But he did know, no matter what, he would never be like the person that sat across from him. His blood was not in Tank's veins. He was his past.

"I did," Tank said, determined to keep the emotion out of his voice.

"I've got a hearing soon. Early parole."

"I'm not..." He clenched the phone tighter. "I'm not here to make small talk. I'm not here to talk about your parole. I'm here to tell you I read the letters, and I forgive you."

Glazed eyes stared back at him. Eyes filled with a genuine happiness, the lines of the old man's face turning up with his smile. "Thank you, son. Thank you."

He didn't have the heart to tell the man he wasn't his real son.

"But understand, that doesn't mean I can forget. I'll never forget. I wish you no harm, but we can never have a relationship. Do you understand?"

The once happy features turned down as quick as they had come up. "Yes. I understand."

"Good luck with your parole. I hope you find happiness in life."

Tank hung up the phone, the click of the receiver indicating the beginning of the end, as he stared at the man he had called dad for so many years for the last time. While a heavy burden lifted from his chest, he couldn't help but feel sorry for the shell of a person sitting across from him.

Still, it was all over.

He could burn the letters, and leave his past behind where it belonged.

Start new.

Fresh.

With Annie.

His phone rang in his back pocket as his feet hit the pavement of the prison parking lot. Steele. "Hey man. What's up?"

"Dude, where are you?"

"Just had some business to take care of. What's going on?"

"Father is calling a mandatory meeting tonight. He's got some families that need to be on our radar. Seven o'clock."

Tank glanced at his watch. Five. He needed every bit of the two hours to get home, and he had other plans tonight. Plans he'd been working on for weeks.

Shit.

"Man, I'm not in Black Widow. I'm on my way home now, but that'll be pushing it."

"Just get here, and be careful. I'll pass the message along."

"Yeah, yeah, okay."

He tossed his helmet on and saddled his bike. He and Father still weren't on the best of terms yet. That's why the man didn't call him himself. Hopefully, they could resolve their issues, and soon. He was ready to have a family. A mother. A father. A wife.

Five after seven, he pulled through the parking lot of the barn. A few extra cars sat in the grass. The lot was void of any people, everyone already inside.

Shit.

The meeting must've been important to warrant this many Guardians, and he was late.

He threw down his kickstand and tore off his helmet, placing it on the handle of his bike before he pushed through the barn doors.

A giant crowd gathered in the middle. He stopped and

stared, taking in all the guests just as their hands rose in the air and they all screamed a boisterous. "*Surprise.*"

"What the…?"

Annie ran to him and placed her arms around him. "Surprise, baby." She placed a kiss on his lips.

"Surprise for what?" He wrapped an arm around her. He'd take a kiss from Beauty anytime.

Father ambled toward him. "For being the newest member of the Blue Guardians." The man held up a new, black leather jacket with the angel insignia and a spider crawling up the sleeve.

He took the jacket, the weight thick and solid in his hands. The size on the tag read the jacket would be a perfect fit. "But I don't understand. It hasn't been a year yet."

It hadn't even been four months.

"We took a vote. It was unanimous. You've proved you're worthy. Good job, son." Father slapped him on the arm.

His mother stood out in the crowd and blew him a kiss. Bear and Mary stood near her. The boy gave him a thumbs up, and ran his other hand over Al's fur.

He wrapped Father, his father, in a hug. "Thanks…Dad."

The crowd hooted as he embraced his dad. He pulled back to notice the man had a tear in his eye. "You crying, old man?"

"Naw." He wiped his eyes. "My eyes just sweat sometimes, that's all."

"Eye sweats. That's a new one." He laughed and slapped his *real* dad on the back.

"Speech," Steele hollered from the middle of the crowd.

"Yeah, speech," JoJo yelled.

"Speech? Oh man." Tank held up his jacket then glanced at Annie.

Beauty gave him a sly smile and his heart puddled at his

feet. His past, his present, his future, all coming full circle, and every bit of it contained her. She was his reason. He knew what he had to say.

"I came to Black Widow to join the Blue Guardians. I knew I never wanted a kid to suffer like I did as a child. I thought if I could prevent one kid, just one from having to go through what I did, then my time joining this group would be worth it." He shot a glance back at Bear.

"What I didn't expect was to make new friends, find out the identity of my real father, and meet the love of my life." He handed his jacket to Father. "Annie." He took her hand in his and shot down on one knee, his palms clammy from nerves. "This isn't how I planned this, but it's the only thing that would make this day absolutely complete. I love you more than my own life. I think I have since I was a boy and saw you walking barefoot in the river in your short shorts while holding your dad's hand."

Someone did a catcall behind him.

"You would make me the happiest person alive if you would marry me." His heart pounded in his chest as the group behind him stared on. Beauty had his heart and soul completely; the power to crush his future or make it hung on her answer. He couldn't imagine his life without her in it. "Will you do me the honor of being my wife?"

She squeezed his wet hand. "I'm sorry, Tyler, but no…no you wouldn't be the happiest person alive."

He heard a faint gasp behind him as blood pounded and whooshed in his ears. "What…what do you mean?" He stood.

Annie pointed to herself as a faint smile touched her lips. "I mean if I married you, *I* would be the happiest person alive."

She was playing with him. His heart beat a new rhythm, skipping a few beats.

Stepping closer, he asked, "So, is that a yes?" He couldn't let himself get too excited. Not until she officially said the word.

"Yes. It's a *yes*." She did a little jump. "I would *love* to marry you."

"You mean it?" He squeezed her hand back.

"Of course, silly. I love you. *You* are *my* Guardian Angel."

"And *you* are *my* stubborn, beautiful fiancée." He tapped her nose.

"Yes." She nodded her head. "Yes I am."

She flew into his arms, wrapping her legs around his waist as she dipped her head and placed an ardent kiss on his lips, a kiss that sealed the past and provided new hopes of a future with them. Together.

The End

————

If you want to be up to date on my latest news and releases, join my mailing list. As a thank you, you'll get the first chapter in my story Love Comes In The Mourning. Sign up here.

Thank for you reading the first book in the Black and Blue Series. I hope you fell in love with Tank and Annie just as I have. If you enjoyed this story, please keep reading the next book in the series, STEELE.

And if you really, really enjoyed it, please consider leaving a review here. I need all the help I can get!

Many blessings,
Erin Bevan

STEELE

Chapter 1

I have to save her.

I can do it this time. I can save her.

Blake Steele's heart hammered as his head spun. He gripped the chair in front of him, taking in his surroundings. Flames licked the walls, growing higher and higher, scorching the curtains, the drywall, even the hardwood underneath to nothing but a cloud of thick, black smoke. Through the crackling of the noise, the hissing of the fire, and the heat daring to char the hair on his skin, he heard her. Scream. Again and again.

I have to save her. Mi Peaches.

The thought ran over *and over* in his mind as he charged, the smoke so dark and so dense he couldn't see his foot in front of him. He went on instinct, using his hands to guide him forward. Every turn, every hallway he knew; the need for vision was unimportant as his gut and heart led him to her.

"Blake," she cried, her voice growing fainter, followed by a round of thick, hoarse coughs.

Her bedroom.

I have to save her.

He stormed straight ahead, slamming into the door, causing more black smoke to engulf the room as he shot through the entrance. She lay on the ground, a towel over her nose and mouth, her eyes bloodshot and wide, pleading for his help.

Mi Peaches.

Running to her, he wrapped her in his arms. They were going to get out. They would make it *this* time. With her in his arms, he flung himself toward the second story window... just as the ceiling caved in.

Why didn't you save me?

Her words echoed in his mind as they sailed out the window.

Read the rest now!

ACKNOWLEDGMENTS

This book wouldn't have been possible without the help of some very important people.
Thank you: Jack, Carrie, Colleen, Angela, Fran, and my hard working editor, Stacy.

To my husband and beautiful children, thank you for being so awesome.

ABOUT THE AUTHOR

Award winning author, Erin Bevan writes small town Americana romances straight from the heart. Born and raised in rural South Arkansas, she uses her past experiences to enrich her stories while infusing the right amount of heartache and humor to see her readers through until the end. With the perfect blend of sweet to steamy, Erin Bevan has something for every romance reader.

A stay at home mom of three, Erin spends her time juggling her three little people and trying to keep everyone's lives flowing as smoothly as possible. When she isn't using her super powers to wipe sticky goo from her children's faces, she spends as much time as possible bringing small town dreams to life. Some days she even brushes her hair.

Connect with Erin Bevan online.
www.erinbevan.com

BB bookbub.com/authors/erin-bevan

f facebook.com/erinbevanwrites

g goodreads.com/ebev85

○ instagram.com/authorerinbevan

Made in the USA
Middletown, DE
12 February 2020

84576845R00217